TEEN Fiction PURDIE Kathryn
Burning glass /
Purdi

D044024

JAN 1 0 2018

I couldn't say what urged me to show this stranger I was more than the pitiful girl staring back at him, looking no better than the charred bones of the convent. I was. At least as far as he should believe. I pulled my spine erect, elongated my neck, and met his stare with every ember of fire burning within me.

Dare to think of me what you will, I hoped the look I gave him said. *I am Sonya Petrova. And I am not broken.*

He didn't blink from our connection. Not even with the wind in his eyes. As the horses guided the sleigh into the stables, and right before he passed out of sight, I felt a spark of admiration, though his stern face hadn't cracked. It made me stand even taller.

When the stables swallowed him from view, I caught my reflection in a pane of broken glass, flames still smoldering behind me. That admiration, which must have been nothing more than my own foolish pride, vanished like a puff of ashes. My eyes were bloodshot from tears, and the many I had shed today left paths down the sooty planes of my cheeks.

I *was* broken. Through and through.

BURNING GLASS

BURNING GLASS

KATHRYN PURDIE

KATHERINE TEGEN BOOKS
An Imprint of HarperCollins Publishers

Katherine Tegen Books is an imprint of HarperCollins Publishers.

Burning Glass
Copyright © 2016 by Kathryn Purdie
All rights reserved. Printed in the United States of America.
No part of this book may be used or reproduced in any manner
whatsoever without written permission except in the case of brief
quotations embodied in critical articles and reviews. For information
address HarperCollins Children's Books, a division of HarperCollins
Publishers, 195 Broadway, New York, NY 10007.
www.epicreads.com

Library of Congress Control Number: 2015943595
ISBN 978-0-06-241237-9

Typography by Carla Weise
17 18 19 20 21   PC/LSCH   10 9 8 7 6 5 4 3 2 1
❖
First paperback edition, 2017

FOR JASON,
who always said I could
and that I would

BURNING GLASS

# CHAPTER ONE

I CLUTCHED THE CARVED FIGURINE OF THE GODDESS UNTIL A splinter of wood bit my finger. The sting was only a fraction of the pain I felt—pain that wasn't entirely my own. "You shouldn't be letting her bleed."

Sestra Mirna startled, whirling around with wide eyes. When she saw it was only me, her face settled back into its complex array of sags and wrinkles. "Sonya, what are you doing here?" She pressed a bandage to the crook of Yuliya's arm. "Novices aren't allowed near the diseased."

Ignoring her, I crept farther into the convent infirmary.

I breathed through my mouth to avoid the stench of sickness in the air, lifted the hem of my nightgown, and tiptoed around the blood spatter on the floor. Despite the coldness in the rest of my body, the heat from the fireplace stung my eyes, and the tiles near the hearth baked the soles of my feet.

I pulled my shawl closer across my chest and peered around

Sestra Mirna. A notched porcelain bowl rested on Yuliya's bedside table. Blood skimmed its highest measurement line. My friend's eyes were closed and her ginger hair lay plastered against her bone-white face. I swallowed. "There must be another way to treat her. She doesn't have any more blood to lose. Have you seen her legs? She cuts herself." I winced as the figurine's splinter dug deeper past my skin.

"It's her emotional release," Sestra Mirna said, and rubbed her brow with the back of her hand to avoid her stained fingers. She wasn't careful enough. A smear of blood marred the kerchief tying her gray hair away from her face. "You would do well to find one, too." Harsh lines formed between her brows. "Perhaps then you would be able to refrain from sneaking into forbidden wings in the dead of night."

I pinched my lips and curled my toes, fighting to keep my frustration at bay. I wanted self-control without cutting myself like Yuliya, pulling the hair from my head like Dasha, or weeping night and day like Kira. Besides, my frustration wasn't solely my own. I must be allowing Sestra Mirna's emotions to nest inside of me.

"I came to give Yuliya this." I held out the figurine of Feya while keeping my shawl together with one hand against the chill. My time with the Romska had dispelled any religious notions I'd had, but Yuliya was even more devout than the sestras of the convent. I hoped seeing the goddess of prophecy and Auraseers nearby would give her strength to recover from the ague.

As I watched the faint rise and fall of her chest, I bit my

trembling lip. The rattle of her breath was too soft, her pulse too slow.

The truth was, *I* needed Yuliya to be better. I couldn't endure this place without a friend, without someone to make me smile and tell me stories into the long hours of the night.

Sestra Mirna took the figurine, and the lines on her face softened, changing pattern. The frustration inside me also faded, though I grew colder as she reached up to set the goddess on the frost-rimmed windowsill, all the while keeping her hold on Yuliya's bandage. Outside, the snowfall kept its steady torrent.

My stomach rumbled. Sestra Mirna must be famished. When had she last allowed herself a meal or a moment's rest? Little Dasha and Kira, fast asleep in their beds on the other side of the room, had regained some of the color in their skin, and many of our peers had been excused from the sick wing after recovering from the epidemic. But Yuliya kept declining.

When Sestra Mirna began murmuring prayers to the goddess, I took advantage of her eased guard and sat beside Yuliya, my dark-blond braid falling over my shoulder. If my hair were any longer, it would have brushed her bloodied arm.

My gaze traveled to her lifeless hand. Did I dare touch it? Sestra Mirna would make me leave at once if I so much as whimpered with Yuliya's pain. Still, I wished to give my friend my vitality, even if such a thing wasn't possible, even for an Auraseer. All we were good for was divining what others felt. An agonizing way to live and a pitiful existence. Being born with the gift meant becoming the property of the Riaznin Empire and being trained in this convent for one purpose only—to protect the emperor. Most girls involuntarily revealed their ability when they were old enough to learn their letters but too young to control their feelings. Evading the empire until the age of seventeen was unheard of until eight months ago when the bounty hunters had brought me through the convent's doors.

"I've brought you your idol," I whispered to Yuliya. Half-heartedly, I waited for her eyes to open. Once we'd played at trading the color of our irises, her sapphire blue for my hazel. "I'll give you mine," she had said. Yuliya was the only girl at the convent who dared to befriend me. "The girl raised by gypsies," the others would whisper when they thought the stone walls of the corridors wouldn't carry their voices. Little did those Auraseers know, Yuliya and I would sneak into their rooms at night and guess at the dreams they were having.

Our games taught me more about my ability than any of the sestras' fruitless exercises for separating what I felt from what everyone else did. At least Yuliya believed in me. She had a way of making me feel her equal, despite being two years older. Even if she outlived the other Auraseers and became guardian to the emperor herself, I trusted I could always depend on her genuine friendship. That was why she *needed* to live, why I ached to give her some means of healing, instead of a lump of wood depicting a nonexistent and powerless goddess.

"You're trembling." Sestra Mirna's attention returned to me, her wrinkles twisted with the shape of worry.

I shrugged a shoulder. That strange and still-present hunger gnawed inside me. "Yuliya must be cold."

The sestra's wrinkles deepened. "Yuliya has a fever."

"Then you must be cold," I said while she felt my brow.

She was no Auraseer, but her sharp gaze seemed to look through me.

Unease prickled the downy hairs of my arm. "I am cold?" I didn't mean for my voice to sound small or my words to be a question. Because I was more than cold. Deep in the pit of my stomach, an unknown something was forming and clawing its way through the rest of me. Worse than hunger, it made my hands clench with urgency, my jaw lock with an angry need, my eyes mist over with helpless desperation.

"This room is a furnace, child." Sestra Mirna frowned. "And your skin is like ice." Her wrinkles crisscrossed into fear. I felt fear, too, its force thudding my heart against my rib cage.

"Am I ill?" Perhaps she was right; I shouldn't have come to the infirmary. But I'd had the ague last winter at the Romska camp, so I thought myself immune.

She stood and released the pressure from Yuliya's arm. "Hold this," she commanded.

For a brief moment, I hesitated, watching the blood pool from my friend's inner elbow. Then I inhaled, squared my shoulders, and pressed the flat of my palm to Yuliya's bandage.

At once my muscles cramped, my spine rounded, my breath spilled out in a ragged gasp. A weak but determined longing seeded in my chest. A fight to live. Pure and simple.

Sestra Mirna squinted out the window. Warm light danced

across her face. I mistook it for the glow of the candle bouncing its reflection off the glass. Until the sestra's weathered lips parted in horror. "Feya, protect us," she whispered, and made the sign of the goddess by touching two fingers to her forehead, then her heart. "They have come."

Her fear—my fear—perhaps *both* our fear—collided.

"Who?" I angled my position in an effort to see what she could. "What is happening?"

When she didn't answer, my trembling doubled and the yearning in my belly grew teeth. I needed to eat. Now. Something. Anything.

I slackened my hold on Yuliya's arm. Blood trickled between my fingers. It almost looked the color of wine. Staring in fascination, in desire, I raised my hand near my mouth to smell it.

Basil burst into the room. The old man bent over, hands on knees, panting to catch his breath.

I blinked at the blood and wiped it off onto my nightgown.

"Peasants . . . at the gates," he managed to say between rasps. His bald head gleamed with a sheen of sweat. "A mob—no, more like an army—of them."

I took a step to the window, but caught myself as I remembered Yuliya's arm. "What do they want?"

Sestra Mirna's shriveled lips pressed into a flat line. "What they always do when they bring torches and every sharp implement they farm with—our food." She looked back at me, her gaze skimming me over. "Let me guess, you're not only cold now?"

In response, my stomach emitted a vicious growl.

Her eyes narrowed on my mouth. "What is that?" She stepped closer. "Did you taste blood?"

I shrank back. "No." *Did I?*

In an instant, her countenance changed. "Basil, take her away this moment. Lock her in the east wing with the other girls. She is a danger to us with so many emotions on the loose."

I pressed the crook of Yuliya's arm with renewed purpose. "I'm not leaving."

The sestra yanked me to my feet. My shawl fell to the tiles smattered with Yuliya's blood. "You must accept your fate and at least *try* to control your ability." She gripped my shoulder. "You put us all at risk!"

I winced, the hurt registering deep in my chest. "I would never harm Yuliya." I struggled to reach her bleeding arm again, but Sestra Mirna held me fast.

"Do you know what starving peasants are capable of?" Her gaze bored into mine. "Shall I tell you of the three widows from my village who lured strangers across their threshold, only to poison them and eat the flesh off their bones?"

My hunger briefly subsided as my gut roiled with nausea. "My caravan heard that same story spread from town to town. It's a folktale. No one would resort to that."

Her graveness settled over me and rooted my legs to the floor. "You are wrong, Sonya. This is the fourth harsh winter in Riaznin. You survived with the Romska because you traveled south. We survive here in Ormina by the grace and rations of the emperor. The peasants have nothing."

My mouth watered and the animalistic hunger inside me drifted to thoughts of the convent's overflowing pantries and cold storage cellars. "We have more than we need. We should help them."

Sestra Mirna's eyes went flat and transformed the cold in my veins to ice. "Basil, take her *now*." She shoved me at him and threw my shawl after me.

Faint cries pierced the air as the peasants advanced nearer. My knees shook, threatening to give way. "Please, please, I beg you." I looked between Sestra Mirna and Basil. "Just a few loaves of bread. If you could feel—"

"Enough!" She escorted me to the door herself, where Basil took my elbow by a gentler hold.

On the far side of the room, Kira and Dasha awoke in their beds. They felt the mob, too. I knew it. Kira's face was tear-stained as she moved to Dasha's bed, where the younger of the two little girls clutched her hair at the scalp.

"Once she is locked in the east wing," Sestra Mirna said to Basil, "barricade the front door. Are the gates reinforced?"

The old man nodded. "I hope it will be enough. With any luck, the wolves will come before the peasants find a way to break through."

I gaped at him. "You wish the wolves to devour them because they are hungry?" Basil's floppy ears and close-set eyes always made him appear sweet. But even he had no pity. "What a horrible thing to say."

"Not another word!" Sestra Mirna said. New lines of fury

carved paths across her wrinkled face. With her emotion escalating inside me, it was all I could do not to strike out at her. I'd never seen her so unraveled. She wasn't quick to anger, but tending to the sick night and day over the past weeks had pushed her to extremes. "Latch your mind onto someone else's aura and forget the peasants!" Her nostrils flared. "Your unrestrained empathy will be the ruin of us all!"

Before she could see the tears spring to my eyes, she slammed the door. I clenched my hands. It was no matter that she didn't know how she hurt me. My unshed tears weren't for her. They belonged to the freezing swarm of people pressed against the convent's gates.

As Basil haltingly led me to the east wing, I dug my hands through my hair and clawed at my arms, fighting not to lose myself to the aura of the mob. Their relentless desperation pulsed through my body. They weren't just hungry. This famine would destroy them, body and soul. It was a pain worse than death if I didn't feed my children, my village. No, *their* children, *their* village.

I flinched and whimpered as Basil dragged my weight through corridor after corridor. The peasants' single purpose throbbed through my skull until there was no difference between us. Until I was one with them. Until everything became as clear as polished glass.

I formed the only barrier between them and their need.

I was more than the mob. I was the convent gate.

My bones were its welded iron.

I could open my doors. Let them in.

I alone could help them.

With a sidelong glance at Basil, I sized him up, as if seeing him with new eyes. He startled at every shadow, every noise. A mouse could overtake him. He wouldn't stand in my way.

I scanned the dark alcoves for something with which to incapacitate him. A candlestick for a blow to the head. A length of rope or a sturdy chair.

The entrance to the east wing loomed nearer. Six or seven girls near my age huddled together around the light of a candle—Nadia's candle. The senior Auraseer was only nineteen and already a master of controlling her ability. Every measure of her ink-stained skin proved her skill. She marked herself when she needed release, and the sharp cut of her quill made the etches permanent. In the last weeks, when the ague had claimed the lives of her elder Auraseers, Nadia did not weep with the rest of us. Instead, she accused me of bringing the disease from the "filthy gypsy camps." Even if that were true, which it wasn't, it only gave her cause to rejoice. With her elders now dead, she was next in line to serve the emperor, and that pride showed in the stiff elegance of her neck and the precise way she balanced her head upon it.

She lifted her nose at us as we crossed the threshold into the east wing. "Basil, tell these girls they have nothing to fear."

He forced a reassuring smile, even though every one of us had the gift to divine what he was really feeling. "Everything is fine. Go back to your warm beds. This happens every winter.

The peasants have yet to penetrate the gate."

A pinch-faced Auraseer—Lena? Lola? I could never remember her name, nor did I wish to—folded her arms. "The peasants have never come in such numbers." She shivered and the girl beside her placed a hand to her own stomach. They must have sensed the mob, but not like I did. They wouldn't be standing here if they truly understood the peasants' need.

"Yes, well, I have firearms if it comes to it," Basil replied. He drew one of the great doors closed. As it thudded into place, my heart pounded with the peasants' ravenous urgency. I couldn't be locked in here. I couldn't. Not when there were so many mouths to feed.

He set his hand on the latch of the opposite door when the solution to my dilemma presented itself.

Nadia's eyes narrowed, riveted to mine. The careful balance of her head tipped to the side. "Something is very wrong with you," she said slowly, her words laced with accusation.

I retreated behind Basil. My fingers grazed his over the latch.

His wiry brows peaked. "What are you—?"

"Stop her!" Nadia shouted.

I kicked Basil in the pit of his knee so he crumpled to the floor. I fetched the gate keys hanging from his pocket, shoved him into the huddle of girls, then darted into the hallway and flung the door shut behind me. The wooden beam boomed into its iron casings as I pulled it down across both doors, fastening them closed. The Auraseers were locked inside. They couldn't stop me now.

Cries rang out from the other side as the girls rammed their fists against the barricade.

I smiled. They deserved to panic for all the spitefulness they'd doled out on me.

Basil's throaty voice rose above them. "Sonya, don't do this! Don't let them in. For the sake of all you love and hold dear—for Yuliya's sake—*do not let them in!*"

I backed away from the doors. My hands shook. My heart beat wildly in my chest. A morsel of reason—of warning—wormed its way into my mind.

What was I doing? Had I gone too far?

The thought snuffed out like a breath on weak flame when the peasants' tidal wave of emotion called to me. They waited for me. I had to deliver them.

I spun around and tripped over the hem of my nightdress as I raced through the corridor, down the winding flight of stairs, past the dining hall, and into the foyer of the convent. I tamped down all remembrances of how the Auraseers would tease me when the sestras took us to the market. Our abilities needed to be tested in crowded places, they said. Within minutes, I would inevitably be huddled on the ground, rocking back and forth and raving like a madwoman. But not now. Now I welcomed the multitudes. Now I knew with clarity what they felt and how to help them.

"I'm coming," I whispered, my eyes wide and unblinking as I flung the lock and opened the cedar doors. The peasants were outside, waiting in the distance, and held back by the gate.

I needed to grant them entrance, let them share our food and warmth, be even closer to their auras. I needed to be whole again.

Swirls of white danced past me and dusted the marble tiles. I stepped into the calf-deep snow. The cold was nothing new to my bare feet. I already felt the sting of a thousand frostbitten toes. "I'm coming, I'm coming!"

Hitching up my nightdress, I pressed forward, riveted to the peasants' wash of torchlight like a beacon. Could they see me? I hadn't thought to bring a candle. Did they know the end of their suffering was at hand?

I halted as a new sensation took hold of me, more ferocious in its desire—in its hunger—than the mob had yet been. The twist in my gut buckled me to the ground until I rested on hands and knees like an animal. The deep snow cradled my belly with a coldness I strangely felt numb to. I thrashed forward to the gate, certain only in my target of the peasants. I had to reach them.

Their cries broke apart until the night gave way to the silence of snowfall. The quiet was short-lived. Only a stunned, stuttering heartbeat.

What was happening? Three breaths later, I found my answer. I heard it. Far away, as if from the muffled madness of a dream.

The howling of wolves.

CHAPTER TWO

THE HOWLING FELL LIKE MUSIC ON MY EARS. IT LURED ME, MY shoulders rising and falling in rhythm. My lips pulled back to bare my teeth. Hunger—raw, pure, and deadly—encompassed me. My fingers clawed into the snow, ready to shred whatever necessary in order to satiate the greatest need I'd ever felt.

The chorus of wolves built in volume. Urgency flooded my limbs. I tore through the snow, and the gate loomed closer.

The peasants didn't see me. They had their backs to the convent. Their murmured arguments sifted through the air. A few of them darted away, followed quickly by others, running in the opposite direction of the echoing wolves.

"No!" My voice ripped through my throat, garbled and guttural. "Wait!" I lunged forward, then ground my hands in the snow, trying to stand as the emotions of the peasants grew stronger inside me than the wolves' deadly urges. "I'm coming!" I called to the people. "Don't leave!"

No one turned. No one heard me above their own cries and growing frenzy. A single howl sliced through the frigid night, louder and much nearer than the others. The remaining peasants shrieked and launched after those who had left.

"No, please!" I kicked past the snow until, at last, I reached the gate. I shook the iron bars as I fought to gain their attention. "There is enough food for all of you!"

They fled into the forest without glancing back at the convent. Or me. I cried out in frustration and hit the gate again and again. My hands smarted with pain, but I didn't care. All of this had been for nothing.

Crumpling to the ground, I hit the gate once more, then screamed as hunger bit inside me with renewed ferocity. A large wolf raced across the clearing between the convent and the forest. Its jaws gaped open to reveal a flash of deadly teeth. The howls of his companions mounted behind him, and they emerged past the evergreens. The pack ran, streaks of brown and gray against the field of white.

I thrust my arms between the bars and tried in vain to reach the wolves. They would feast on their prey without me. I threw myself to the icy ground and started digging. I could tunnel a path. Join them. I wasn't too late.

I paused. Blinked. I'd forgotten about the keys. I must have dropped them in the snow. I crawled in a circle, sniffing at the ground. No, I couldn't smell them. What was the matter with me? I stood, trying to think clearly and retrace my steps. I didn't move one foot before I buckled over and growled again. My entire body trembled as I fought to gain control of my bloodlust.

Keys, keys, keys . . . I had to stay focused. The wolves' howling softened with their growing distance. My hunger faltered. I clawed at my stomach, trying to trap it there. The wolves would have release when they ate—after they earned it. I would feel the same.

Dull silver winked at me. I flared my nostrils and flung myself at the ring of keys. Just as I touched them, the warm light emitting from a convent window dimmed and darkened a patch of snow. I clutched the keys to my breast and glanced up. Sestra Mirna's unmistakable silhouette framed itself in an upper-story window.

A fragment of logic nudged me to hide. I crouched behind a currant bush and peered past its dead foliage. The sestra didn't move.

"Go away," I growled.

The swish and patter from the wolves' feet lightened as they left the clearing and raced after the peasants. Their howls sounded mournful. Or had I twisted the sound to mirror my own deepening loss? How could I catch up with them now?

"Go away, go away," I said to the silhouette at the window. *The wolves are gone.* I imagined Sestra Mirna could hear my thoughts. *Go back to Yuliya. She might bleed to death if you don't watch over her. She needs you. The convent is safe.*

My heart thundered. The howling grew faint. The silhouette hesitated.

"Please." My breath misted in the air.

Sestra Mirna stepped back into the room. The patch of snow pooled to amber once more in the full light of the window.

I muttered a prayer of thanks to Feya—a mark of my profound relief that I stooped to acknowledge my threadbare belief in the goddess—and raced back to the gate, keys in hand.

The last wolf exited the clearing as I reached the lock. "Wait!" I called as I jammed the largest key into the hole and fought against the rusted and frozen inner workings. "Wait!" I called to the peasants who were already gone.

The key turned, but a locked chain wrapped the barred doors together. Basil's reinforcement. Hands shaking in anticipation, I tested the smaller keys on the padlock. At last I found the right one. I yanked the chains off the bars, and with a great exhale, pulled open the gate. It creaked on its hinges, but only budged a finger's length. I growled with frustration. The deep snow dammed its path. I crouched and beat at the snow. Trampled it down. Flung it aside. Scooped it away by the armful.

"Come back," I told the wolves.

"Come back," I told the dwindling yearning inside me.

"Come . . . come . . ."

I shivered, leaning back against the bars. My legs splayed out in front of me, pink with cold and exposed from knee to ankle. Snowflakes collected in my tangled hair, which had escaped my braid. I couldn't feel my toes or fingertips. My chin wobbled, whether from the unbearable chill or my stunned recollection of myself, I didn't know.

What in the name of Feya, or all the holy gods, had come

over me? I turned slowly and observed the trodden snow beyond the gate where the masses of peasants had stood, where the wolves had tracked behind them.

Nothing more remained of the madness. Their madness. Mine.

"Basil," I gasped, and pressed my hand to my head. Had I really locked him and the Auraseers in the east wing?

Nadia was right. Something was terribly wrong with me. Perhaps my parents should have turned me over to the bounty hunters a decade ago and not given me to the Romska. My chance at freedom wasn't worth this. At the very least, I should have worked harder at my lessons with the sestras. It was unnatural to feel the urges of animals, even for an Auraseer. *This is what happens when an ability goes unrestrained*, Sestra Mirna had once told me. *It becomes wild.*

I was more than wild—I was a walking keg of gunpowder. What if I'd made it to the gate mere moments before I had? What if I'd let the peasants in? Or the wolves?

A whimper stirred the air. I craned my head. Stone towers mirrored each other from both sides of the gate. At the base of the left one, something shifted. A huddle of black. Another whimper came.

"Hello?" I said.

A pale face lifted at my greeting. I stepped closer and pressed my body against the bars. A gnarled-looking man rested there, curled into himself. His face was so thin it seemed strangely oblong. Dark hollows cut beneath his eyes and cheekbones. He tugged a ragged coat closer to his chest. That and his matted fur hat were all he had to keep him warm.

A flicker of emotion burned its way past my frozen ribs and lodged inside my heart. This man was desolate, without hope—nothing like the powerful pulse the mob had radiated, but just as real. I ached with him. At the very least, I could help one person tonight. What harm could one famished man do?

"Excuse me." I curved my numb lips into a semblance of a smile. "If you can reach past the bars and help me clear this snow, I would be happy to repay you with a warm meal and a seat beside our fire."

❦∾✦

I removed the man's snow-laden coat and draped it over a kitchen chair, then drew up another one until its legs butted against the raised hearth. "Sit here."

The man removed his fur cap and twisted it with bony fingers. His nails were jagged and filthy. I felt shameful for staring, so I lifted my gaze to his bare head. His hair stuck up from the wrath of dueling cowlicks and strange partings. Physical signs of insanity. Perhaps that's why he hadn't spoken a word as we worked together to open the gate and made our way inside.

Muffled noises echoed above us. The man jumped as the copper chandelier rattled. The candles weren't lit or else they might have flung hot wax onto his skin.

"Never you mind about them." I nodded at the ceiling. Above us, the Auraseers remained trapped in the east wing. Their anger tried to smother me, but I ground my teeth and pushed it back, only letting it prick at my skin. My own shame felt more insufferable. I couldn't face them yet, nor bear their reprimands for my loss of self-control. Could I help it that I took pleasure in confining them, when that's all they had done for months—confined me with their ostracizing? Nadia and her ring of friends could wait it out up there a little longer.

Taking hold of the man by his shoulder, I gently guided him to the chair by the fire. Sestra Mirna once told me the sense of touch heightened an Auraseer's awareness. I would use that to lose myself to the man's numbed emotions and drown out the fury of the barricaded Auraseers.

He sat stiffly on the chair. His energy was so focused on his physical needs that it served as a blissful escape from reality. I kept my leg brushed against his knee as I ladled him a bowl of stew. The sestras always kept something bubbling in the iron pot, adding water, herbs, and chopped roots throughout the day. After passing him the bowl, I added another log to the coals. In moments, the dry wood crackled with flames.

"That's better." I broke our contact to draw up another chair beside him. That brief separation was enough to make my gut twist with guilt. I had prevented a catastrophe tonight by not letting the peasants inside the convent, but I had also failed them. How many would still suffer from their hardships because of me, and for how long?

I quickly ladled a second bowl for myself—no matter that I'd already had second helpings for supper—I had to do something to quell the ghosts of hunger inside me.

I sat down and scooted closer so my knees touched the man's. My stomach rumbled in time with his, and I sighed in relief at his simplicity. We ate to the chorus of the rattling chandelier and the *drip, drip, drip* of the ice melting from my nightgown. I wriggled my toes as I tried to draw feeling back into them and wrapped my makeshift shawl—a kitchen towel— more snugly across my shoulders.

"Are you from Ormina?" I asked at length, uncomfortable with our silence. "Of course you're from Ormina. You couldn't have walked from anywhere else, not in this snow."

The man's eyes reflected the undulating flames. He didn't bat his lashes to acknowledge I'd spoken. Instead, he tapped his spoon against his empty bowl.

"Would you like more?"

Tap, tap.

"Yes?"

His hand snaked out to the pot.

"No!"

A horrible sizzling hissed out as his fingertips met the hot iron. He wailed, his mouth falling open to reveal a row of chipped teeth. I leapt to my feet, rushed to the buckets of ice thawing into water, and yanked the kitchen towel from my shoulders, letting it sponge up the moisture.

"Here." I knelt at his feet and wrapped the wet cloth around his hand. He rocked back and forth, biting his lip. "I made a mistake situating you so close to the fire," I said. "Shall I scoot you back, or do you promise to be more careful?" I cringed at my tone. I sounded far too similar to Sestra Mirna. "Do you promise?"

He swallowed and gave a rough bob of his head. I couldn't be sure if it was a nod of acquiescence or simply an incoherent movement.

"All right, then." I settled myself at his feet with my shoulder pressed against his leg.

It was warmer here, nearer the white coals of the fire. I denied myself the urge to hold my hands to the flames. That would only encourage the man to do something rash. I made do with basking in what little warmth penetrated the wet threads of my nightgown.

The log split in half, and the flames danced taller. Fire was a fascinating element. The way it teased you, swaying one moment, snapping at you the next. I could watch it for hours. I might do that tonight. Perhaps by morning my gown would be dry and the Auraseers wouldn't be at my throat for a night locked in a wing they would have spent their sleep in, anyway.

A trembling hand reached past me and snatched at the flames. I grabbed the man's arm. "Not that again. You mustn't . . ."

Whatever I intended to say died on the tip of my tongue. The orange, pulsating light was so beautiful. It curled like fingers beckoning me. I would never be warm until I lived inside that light. Until it blossomed within me and took root in my veins. My blood could be fire. I could be made of light. I was meant to be light. I would be warm forever.

I let go of the man's arm. Why had I been holding it? Heart pounding, I crept closer to the flames. The heat kissed my cheeks. I closed my eyes and let it burn my lids. It wasn't enough. I had to touch that warmth.

My hand crawled into the outlying ashes, near the coals. A long shard of wood lay forgotten, away from the heart of the fire. Only its tip was charred. It must have splintered off from the log. Feeling sorry for it, I picked it up and set its end into the most inviting lick of flame. The wood popped as the flame spread. I pulled it toward me. Beautiful.

So beautiful I would share.

I twisted around to face the man and smiled. My eyes blurred with tears. He would be so happy when I—

He abruptly stood, kicking the chair out from beneath him. He thrashed about the kitchen. I stared dumbly after him, unsure what was the matter. Had he burned himself again?

My gaze dropped to his smoking trouser leg, and fear spiked through my chest. I must have come too close with the flame. The flame still burning on the shard in my hand. The flame closing in on my fingers.

I gasped and hurtled the shard into the fireplace as sparks flew around me. The man screamed. I spun around, crying with his pain. His leg no longer smoked. It was on fire. It ate at the cloth like perfect kindling. I sprang to my feet, limping in agony as I advanced on the man and sidestepped him as I racked my brain for what to do. Terror—his and mine—froze my logic.

At last I remembered the buckets of ice water. *Stupid girl.*

How could I have forgotten?

I raced to them and lifted the closest one, then whirled back to the man as water sloshed at my feet. I was too late. He fled the kitchen. The flames overtook him as they clawed up his tunic.

My heart seized. I chased after him, my movements clumsy as I lugged the heavy bucket. "Stop! Come back!" His panic had enough hold over me to amplify my own.

He didn't slow his pace. His shrieking bounced off the corridor walls. I stumbled behind him, leaving a trail of water. Soon all I'd have left would be ice.

He veered right, headed for the dining hall. At least there I could corner him. "Feya, please," I prayed. "I'll offer you my soul if he doesn't die."

I hadn't intentionally burned him. It was an accident. *Wasn't it?*

He flew past an archway into the dining hall, his body nearly engulfed by flames. I rushed into the room and followed him to the large windows at the far wall.

"Stop! I can help." I tossed the contents of my bucket at him. A feeble amount of water splashed his face. The ice clunked at his feet.

He threw himself backward. The flames on his clothes—untouched by the water—caught the window draperies. My stomach plummeted with dread.

"Don't move!" I shouted as he did the opposite and

smothered himself with another curtain. He only succeeded in spreading the fire.

I jumped back as the flames raged higher. They fed off the curtains like they'd been soaked in oil. The man crumpled to the ground, moaning and twisting and rapidly losing his battle to live. The curtains fanned in the flames, and the fire next caught a rug.

Growing frantic to find a quick exit and help the man, I hefted a wooden bench and charged the window. Glass shattered all around me. I barreled past it and tumbled outside. The bench crashed in the snow, and I along with it. Coldness sliced through my nightgown. I welcomed it, needed it. The man needed it, too. I would save him, then do something about the fire. What, I didn't know.

I lumbered through the snow, back to the broken window. Before I could enter, the curtain rod fell and landed at an angle to create a flaming barrier. There was space to leap over it, but not from where I stood at the foundations of the convent.

"Jump!" I shouted, hoping my voice carried to the man above the roar of the fire. "Please! Save yourself!"

I couldn't hear him moving. I crept closer, coughing on the smoke, and struggled to see past the flames burning spots in my vision. "Jum—"

A dark figure crashed through the jagged hole. Shards of glass fell over me like glittering snow. I threw my arms up to protect my face. Nothing could protect me from what came next—the bony, flaming leg of the man as it connected with my skull and knocked me backward. My spine hit the wooden bench. My head whiplashed back, taking a second blow. The snow crunched as I ricocheted into it.

The last thing I saw were writhing flames devouring the dining hall.

CHAPTER THREE

I OPENED MY EYES TO DAYLIGHT. TO A DEAD MAN LYING BESIDE me. To fire-eaten stone walls. Scattered, smoking wooden beams.

Half of the convent was in ruins.

I gasped in horror. Head throbbing, I sat up slowly. My heart trembled a stuttering rhythm that reflected my confounding awareness. Growing more panicked, I scanned the convent and tried to orient myself from the outside.

Which half was destroyed? *Which half?*

I located the library chimney—the library below the infirmary. My lungs expanded, allowing a breath. The half with Yuliya had survived. The half with Sestra Mirna, Kira, Dasha. But the bell tower was gone. The half with the east wing. With every other Auraseer and sestra. The half with gentle Basil.

The half I'd locked inside.

My hand clapped to my mouth to stifle a ragged sob. Only four had escaped. *Four.* The rest of the Auraseers were dead.

I knew it. I felt it. The pulse of their auras was absent. The remaining flickers of energy buzzing along my nerves could only belong to the ill and the sestra who watched over them.

So much life had been snuffed out while I slept without dreaming. While a stranger died beside me. So much death and destruction.

All because of me.

A soft keening arose from my throat. It grew louder as I curled my legs to my chest and rocked back on my heels. I hid my face in the folds of my skirt. Why hadn't I unlocked the door to the east wing? Why hadn't I let everyone out?

The pain inside me was unbearable. It crushed me to the core. It made me rip up clumps of half-frozen grass. Slam my fists on my breastbone. Wail like a lost child. I didn't know it was possible for one person to feel so much sorrow and regret. Such rage. No borrowed auras were necessary to complete my misery.

I saw myself as if outside my body. I watched the smile on my face when I barred the door to the east wing, how I'd casually sipped my soup with a man I didn't know while my sister Auraseers pounded the floor above me, begging for release.

I'd wanted to help the peasants. I thought I had so much empathy, but a compassionate person could never have done such a terrible thing.

The shame, the shock, rooted me to the spot. I sat balled with my legs bent up, the nightdress over my knees wet with tears. The rest of me was strangely dry. It had been from the moment I'd awakened. The heat from the burning convent, which had ended the lives of so many, had saved me from freezing to death while unconscious. The irony did little to bring me comfort. Neither did the man lying beside me on the thawed ground. He died after all the risk I had taken. His skin was black and blistered. His face was burned beyond recognition. The remnants of his half-eaten clothes were seared to his body. I'd never seen anything so horrific. Still, I couldn't make myself leave his side. Some part of me waited for his eyes to open, as if that could also awaken me from this nightmare.

But no matter how long I remained, his emotions didn't stir. No one's did but my own.

I'd often wished for solitude, to be alone with my thoughts and not bear the weight of someone else's feelings.

I would never wish for anything again.

Hour after hour passed. I'd awakened sometime in the late afternoon. Now the sun bled through the skeletal branches of a tree in the west garden of the convent, casting long shadows that crept toward me with the fading light. I stood on shaking legs. I needed to go inside. Face Sestra Mirna. Resign myself to a life of penance. A lifetime wouldn't be enough.

I crossed my arms over my chest to trap in any remaining warmth from my body and made my way around the convent, climbing over fallen, charred pieces of who knew what. Perhaps the bed I would have shared with Yuliya if she weren't in the infirmary.

If there were something to be grateful about, it was that she had survived.

The debris from the fire still smoldered with heat. As it scorched my toes and became too cumbersome to climb over, I widened my circle around the convent and searched for a safe place to enter. I lifted my hem above my ankles and trudged through the snow. My nightdress was smudged with black from ash and smoke, and my hair was singed at the ends. I could only imagine how disheveled the rest of my appearance was. Sestra Mirna would suspect the worst. And she would be right.

My head hung low, my gaze trapped on the ground, when the sound of sleigh bells made me glance up. The sleigh wasn't yet visible on the snow-drifted road, and the gate to the convent was still ajar from last night. I hadn't troubled myself to close it. Between then and now, enough snow had melted beneath it so the gate fell wide open on its uneven hinges.

My muscles tensed as I waited for any emotion to take hold, to warn me of who might be coming—or at the very least reveal the energy of their aura, which might clue me in to their motive. We shouldn't have visitors now. Couriers for food and supplies were the only people who came here, and we'd received a large delivery five days ago.

The sleigh bells jangled louder. Around the bend, gliding through the snow, came a brightly painted troika. The three-horse sleigh made my lips part with surprise . . . until my jaw locked as a rush of protectiveness flooded through me. I had to think of those still alive in the convent. A troika meant whoever had come here needed to do so urgently. And that someone—a man, if I'd judged correctly from this distance—was a noble. Only the highborn in Riaznin had a legal right to be the sole passenger of a troika. It was a luxury reserved for the wealthy. But why was no driver seated on the center horse? No noble would stoop to drive a sleigh on his own.

My heart quickened, but I couldn't be certain if it was my own apprehension—I didn't trust anyone but Yuliya—or if the emotion came from the visitor.

The man raised his arms to whip the horses, but just as he did so, his hands fell and his head lifted as he took in the view of the burned convent. The three horses slowed to a trot, and I saw the man in greater detail. He was clean-shaven like the men from Estengarde, though his features looked more Riaznian. Dark eyebrows were set low near his eyes, and a long and well-defined nose centered his face. His prominent feature was a handsomely sculpted mouth, even if his upper lip was too thin. It was a mouth that didn't look suited to smiling.

As the troika drew closer, he looked younger, no older than Nadia. His dusty-brown hair fell in well-groomed waves that reached his cheekbones. He was definitely noble born; a commoner wouldn't trouble himself with frequent haircuts. The man brushed a lock from his eye and stared at the convent in amazement. I felt the awe of the horrible sight, the awe within him, the awe still lingering in me. As if sensing my connection to him, his gaze shifted to where I stood in the snowy field. His eyes never left me, not while the horses continued down the road, not while they trotted through the gates and kicked up snow from their hooves. I had a keen idea of what I looked like, but did my appearance reveal all I had done?

I couldn't say what urged me to show this stranger I was more than the pitiful girl staring back at him, looking no better than the charred bones of the convent. I was. At least as far as he should believe. I pulled my spine erect, elongated my neck, and met his stare with every ember of fire burning within me.

Dare to think of me what you will, I hoped the look I gave him said. *I am Sonya Petrova. And I am not broken.*

He didn't blink from our connection. Not even with the wind in his eyes. As the horses guided the sleigh into the stables, and right before he passed out of sight, I felt a spark of admiration, though his stern face hadn't cracked. It made me stand even taller.

When the stables swallowed him from view, I caught my reflection in a pane of broken glass, flames still smoldering behind me. That admiration, which must have been nothing more than my own foolish pride, vanished like a puff of ashes. My eyes were bloodshot from tears, and the many I had shed today left paths down the sooty planes of my cheeks.

I *was* broken. Through and through.

❦

I padded on numb toes across the stone floor leading to the infirmary. I hoped to visit Yuliya undetected before I endured the wrath of Sestra Mirna.

Candlelight shone from the library, the predominant room

on the ground floor that had survived the fire. Voices came from within. Sestra Mirna's and a young man's, surely the stranger from the troika.

"Poisoned?" she said when I was just shy of the library's open entrance. My interest was piqued, and I pressed myself to the corridor wall to keep listening.

"Four days ago," the man replied in the rich timbre and style that spoke to an aristocratic upbringing. "She drank from a cup intended for the emperor."

"And Izolda did not sense the danger?"

The name of the emperor's Auraseer made my chest constrict. Something must have happened to her. Had she been poisoned? I'd never met the woman, but she had served the crown for fifteen years. Half of the girls at the convent wished to take her place; the other half lived in fear of it.

The weight of their deaths pressed down upon my shoulders. I would never live without that guilt.

"She did not," the man said.

"I see."

I did, as well. After all her service to the emperor, Izolda had fallen to the fate of every sovereign Auraseer before her: execution for failing in her duty.

But if Izolda had not been poisoned, who had?

"Then you can be here for only one reason." Sestra Mirna's voice was clipped. If her emotions were anything like mine, bitter anger had taken root. What kind of life was granted any Auraseer of Riaznin if it meant an end like Izolda's after pursuing the only occupation allotted to her? Even in the convent, Auraseers were threatened with death. The law mandated we face the noose if we ever refused to serve the emperor. The sestras shared decades-old stories of the women who had hung from the convent bell tower for rejecting their duty. "But I'm afraid I cannot comply in light of our tragedy."

"These past few days have borne tragedies for us all. It does not change the law."

"I have lost over twenty girls!"

A *boom* sounded within the library, like the man had slammed his hand against a table. I flinched as the anger stewing inside me tripled with his emotion. "And I've lost my mother!"

An amazed gasp tumbled out of me. He must mean the dowager empress. *She* was the one who had been poisoned— poisoned when she drank from Emperor Valko's cup. Izolda would only be sentenced to death for failing to protect someone in the royal family. The man in the library must be the emperor's younger brother, Anton Ozerov. But why had the prince come on a servant's errand?

"So I must ask you, unfortunate though the situation may be." Prince Anton's tone was measured as he fought to collect himself. "Who is the eldest at this convent?"

My lips parted as the full implication of the prince's visit— of the fire I had caused—dawned on me with stark and terrible clarity. I burst into the room, my heart hammering so hard I could scarcely breathe.

"You cannot take Yuliya!" I said without the preamble of a curtsy or any ridiculous nicety afforded to a man of his rank. He was one thing only: a viper sent to take away my friend.

Anton whirled to meet my icy gaze. His eyes sparked with recognition from the moment we'd shared outside. He still wore his cloak, flecked with snow. The fact that he hadn't removed it meant his visit was intended to be as brief as possible. He planned to take an Auraseer tonight.

"Yuliya, is it?" His brows lifted, and I cursed myself for giving him his answer.

"Sonya?" Sestra Mirna gasped. She moved past him to me, her eyes so wide the whites showed above her irises. "Praise the gods, you're alive!" She embraced me, something she had never done before. My arms hung stiffly at my sides, not because I wasn't touched by her sentiment, but because it gnawed away at me with shame. How would she react when she knew what I'd done? As she held me closer with trembling arms, I glanced past her to Anton, who observed us with interest. My hands balled into fists. He would not take Yuliya. Somehow I'd help her escape. We would find the Romska, be free.

"How did you ever survive, child?" Sestra Mirna pulled back and cupped my face. "When Basil locked everyone in the east wing, I assumed . . ." Her words drifted away as she waited for my explanation.

"I . . ." My thoughts warred between saving Yuliya—my priority—and justifying myself. "I was never locked in the east wing. Basil . . . he . . ." My throat grew thick with emotion. My

35

gaze flitted to the library's empty fireplace. Would no one in this convent dare to kindle a fire again?

"Yes? Where is he?" Sestra Mirna swallowed. The foreboding she felt, belying the hope in her voice, pounded through my body like a death toll.

"Basil died in the fire," I said softly, slowly, unable to look away from her, though I wanted to. "A—a peasant man died, as well."

The walls of the library seemed to shrink in as the sestra contemplated me, piecing together what I did say with what I didn't. The ash-choked air grew thinner, my legs weaker. She took two steps back, shock and horror and profound disappointment etched across her wrinkled face. Only then did I notice her nursing apron and kerchief. They were stained with more blood . . . too much blood.

I forced a ragged breath. Turned my attention to the prince. And drew back my shoulders to feign strength. "Yuliya is unwell. She cannot serve the emperor." *She is only unwell, she is only unwell.*

"Yuliya is dead," the sestra said flatly.

The air siphoned from my lungs. I gripped a chair for support and waited for the prince, the sestra—anyone—to contradict the words she'd just spoken. My tongue was a foreign object in my mouth. I couldn't make it form words. All I could do was point an accusing finger at the abundance of red on Sestra Mirna's apron. She did this. She bled Yuliya to death.

"The blood-letting worked," she said, her voice still

emotionless. "Yuliya's fever broke. Then when the convent started burning and the flames barricaded me from assisting those in the east wing, Yuliya could no longer endure the suffering she felt from so many. She took a knife to her leg and"—she briefly looked down before returning her detached gaze—"she hit a large artery. The blood came too fast. She was gone within minutes."

Every word she spoke came like a blow to my gut. I had done this, not she. I had locked the Auraseers away. Let the peasant man in. Allowed his insanity to overtake me. Allowed it to start a fire that burned everything, harmed everyone. Killed them. Killed my best friend.

I needed to sit. No, I had to stand. Pace. Leave. See Yuliya for myself. But my legs were made of lead. My heart was heavier. Because how could a person with any feeling do what I had done?

"Pardon me, but . . ."

Distractedly, my eyes wandered to Prince Anton, who had just spoken. He darted his gaze between the sestra and me, clearly uncomfortable with what he'd just witnessed between us. I could only imagine his discomfort if he knew what the sestra did—that I was guilty. He merely understood another Auraseer had died. What was she to him among so many who'd perished at this convent?

"That is to say," the prince continued, "I'm very sorry for your losses. However—"

"You do not care about us or our losses," I snapped, ignoring the prickling sense of fresh sorrow within me. It couldn't possibly be coming from him. "You think only of your own." I referred to the death of his mother, another monarch who surely didn't mind that the Auraseers of her empire were herded like cattle and given a life akin to slavery.

Anton's distinguished brows slid together until they almost touched, and his brown eyes hardened into stone. "You have my sympathy," he said. "Whether you choose to believe me or not isn't my concern. I will not express it again."

I clenched my teeth. *Let him be angry.* Anger was useful. I could latch on to it, let it blind me to far more painful emotions— to the image of Yuliya's face, pasty and drained of life. To the terror she must have felt in her last living moments.

Anton broadened his chest and didn't flinch from my stare. "I am required back at the palace in haste. The *law*"— an intense sentiment ignited in him at that word, so fleeting, however, I couldn't name it—"also requires I bring the eldest Auraseer of Riaznin."

"Sonya," Sestra Mirna said.

"Yes?" I looked to her, but her eyes were fixed on the prince.

"The others are dead," she said. "Yuliya is dead. Sonya is the eldest."

CHAPTER FOUR

A HORRIBLE CONCOCTION OF AMAZEMENT AND DREAD churned in my stomach. Judging by the slack-jawed look on Anton's face, his emotions were the same and compounded those within me. Our eyes met with mutual displeasure.

"Is there no one else?" Anton asked Sestra Mirna in a low voice, as if somehow I wouldn't be able to hear him.

"The remaining two are but children."

Anton frowned, his gaze raking over me. "She cannot be much older."

Dimly, I registered being affronted at that. *He* couldn't be much older than me. But what did it matter how old I was if no other Auraseer could outrank me in age? As Anton said, the law was the law and . . . I could no longer think. Nausea took a sudden hold of me, and I tightened my grip on the chair. This couldn't be happening.

Sestra Mirna clasped her hands together at the front of her

bloody apron. "Sonya will be ready within the hour to accompany you to Torchev."

"Within the *hour*?" I blinked at both of them. "I cannot possibly . . . Yuliya has her burial rites. She cannot be laid to rest for three days." My heart ached with immeasurable grief. My eyes burned, too dry from incessant weeping to release my trapped tears. They wouldn't make me leave now, not without saying a proper good-bye to someone who had died because of me. This day had been cruel enough.

I felt Anton weighing my words over, as if they were a measure of barley cupped in his hands. His booted toe tapped the stones in deliberation.

"She was my only friend here," I said, grasping for his sympathy. Was a prince of Riaznin capable of any—even a fragment?

Tap, tap, tap. His boot kept its cadence. Perhaps he asked himself the same question. Could he give a no-account girl like me compassion?

My heart drummed. "Give me three days." In three days I could do many things. Accept Yuliya was dead. Somehow part with her. Find a way to escape before the emperor required me.

Anton's boot stilled. I held my breath.

"We must leave this night." His gaze lowered to my nose, anywhere but my eyes. My chest fell, collapsing like my bones were brittle clay. "My brother is insistent. Your circumstance will not move him."

"But death has touched *him*, too. Your own mother—"

"Do not speak of my mother!" His finger whipped to point

at me, as threatening as if he'd held forth a blade. "She was buried while I traveled here for *you*. I could not take part in her last rites. I could not even bear the weight of the stone to seal closed her coffin. This errand for another Auraseer"—his hand waved dismissively at me—"for the means to protect the emperor and his *mighty throne*"—those words pelted like acid—"came at the expense of everything else. So believe me when I tell you, Valko does not have ears to hear your plea."

It took all my resolve not to step back, not to hide or throw up some defensive measure against him. Instead, I allowed his visceral anger to absorb through my skin. Until it fired along my nerves and entered my bloodstream. Until I became its source and could spit it out myself.

"If you cannot stand up to your own brother, you are no better than him! You are worse than that, you are his puppet!"

His eyes flashed. "And will *you* stand up to him? Your head would be on the chopping block before you unpacked your trunks."

Trunks? As in more than one? I bit out a harsh laugh. "Only a prince would assume I had that many belongings." Something tickled my face, and I swiped a hand under my nose and at the corners of my eyes.

Anton threw back his dusk-blue cape so it billowed in folds behind one of his broad shoulders. He turned to Sestra Mirna, whom I'd forgotten was here for how statuesquely she stood. "If this girl is the example of how Auraseers are raised at this convent, then this place has wasted far too much of Riaznin's wealth."

The sestra shot me a withering glance. "Sonya has only been with us eight months."

I rubbed under my eyes again. Was I crying? I never shed tears when I was angry. And I couldn't cry when I had wished to a moment ago.

"The emperor will not find that excuse tolerable," Anton replied.

"Yes, you have made the emperor's stance on this convent quite clear." Sestra Mirna straightened her back. "Let us not waste any more words. Sonya will leave—"

"When we have buried Yuliya," I finished for her, "and paid our respects to the fallen Auraseers."

She frowned at me, her gaze drifting to my hair. "What are you doing, child?"

I pulled my hand away from my head to discover a clump of hair caught between my fingers. "Dasha," I murmured, spinning around to the open doorway.

The little girl stood barefoot in her nightdress, her hands working away at what little hair remained on her scalp. Beside her, Kira whimpered, nose running and face streaming with tears. I touched my wet cheek. How much had they heard?

"Are you leaving us, too?" Kira asked me.

My heated emotions took a sudden halt. Looking at the two remaining Auraseers—the only two, besides me, who'd managed to survive—my heart split apart like the last leaf from an ice-frosted tree. What if I did run away? Anton would be forced to take Kira to Torchev. How could I allow a child to be sent in my place to protect Emperor Valko when a seasoned Auraseer had been executed for failing to do just that? It would be a death sentence. And after Kira, Dasha would be required.

Building within myself a shaky fortress of resolve, I crossed to the doorway, knelt by the girls, and took their hands in mine. If I made a show of convincing confidence, they would glean it from my aura. "You must be brave," I said. "Sestra Mirna will depend upon you." My words felt insensitive as they spilled from my mouth. Dasha and Kira were more fragile, more vulnerable, than they had ever been. But I needed them to find the courage to live here in such an abandoned state. "I will go to the emperor myself and see to it you are comfortable here."

Kira nodded, accepting her fate, though her tears never ceased to flow. I swallowed my heart, clawing up my throat, and looked to Dasha. "And when I come to visit"—something the emperor would surely never allow—"your hair will be so long, it will sweep the convent halls."

Dasha grinned a little at that, and I did my best to mirror her flickering hope. Then, biting my lip, I rose to my feet and revolted to face the prince. His piercing gaze was inscrutable, his emotions locked behind some new barrier he'd thrown up against me.

"I will go with you to Torchev," I said. "Tonight. So long as you promise to have these walls rebuilt and send a guard immediately upon our return to protect the convent." At least

CHAPTER FIVE

SESTRA MIRNA STOOD IN THE SNOW BEFORE THE BLACKENED rubble of the convent. Dasha and Kira clung to her skirt. The three of them watched me on the edge of the road, preparing to say one last good-bye as I waited for the troika to pull out from the stables.

Breathe, Sonya. Just breathe.

I pictured Yuliya in the infirmary when I had tried my best to give her a deserving farewell. Sestra Mirna hadn't yet had the chance to clean her body, so I stripped away my friend's crimson-soaked sheets and removed the bandage from the crook of her arm. My hands trembled when I sponged away the dried blood from the gash in her leg and worked the tangles out of her matted ginger hair.

"I'm so sorry," I told her again and again.

Tending to her was a torment. Every time I touched her

blood, the echoes of her last agonizing moments of life rushed into my awareness.

Terror. Helplessness. Sheer anxiety. Pity. Sorrow. Despondency. Her suffering stole my breath, made my body seize with pain, my teeth grind together so I wouldn't cry out.

Then a strange euphoria flooded into me. A blissful abandon, even though her physical suffering intensified. And past it came the most amazing feeling of all—calm courage. She was brave in the face of dying.

Setting my rag aside, I swallowed, closed my eyes, and took her cold hand in mine. This time I let myself cry. I fell to my knees and bent my head over Yuliya's stiff hand.

"Stop that at once!" Sestra Mirna ripped my hand from Yuliya's.

My eyes flew open, and I gasped out a sob from the separation of auras. My wet lashes blurred my vision, but I didn't need to see to feel the sestra's fury.

"Leave her be!" she said.

I absorbed her disdain until it transformed into my own shame. Still, I tried to defend myself. "I'm not harming her."

"Unnatural child!" She flung the accusation in a harsh whisper. Beneath it, I felt her visceral fear of me. "No one should be able to sense the auras of the dead. Your gift is unbridled. You are abnormal."

"Forgive me," was all I could say against the sting of her dagger-sharp words. "Please forgive me."

The sestra's shoulders fell. Her fear turned to remorse. It

paved its way across her weathered face and into the marrow of my bones. "What more could I have done for you?" She sighed, touching my wet cheek. "How was it possible to teach you anything?"

I shook my head. I had no answer for her. And her brief tenderness did nothing to comfort me. It only racked me with more humiliation. "This wasn't your fault, Sestra Mirna."

She dropped her hand. What "this" meant, we both knew— the deaths of twenty-three Auraseers, those whom the sestras deemed holy, blessed by the goddess Feya, even if the empire saw us as nothing more than a race of slaves.

Just as I saw tears glisten in her eyes, Sestra Mirna turned away from me and lifted her chin. "You must listen to me now, once more. It is imperative you strive to perform your duty to your utmost ability. If not, Sonya, you will have the blood of more Auraseers on your hands."

Her warning grounded me with resolve, as well as a resounding chord of foreboding. She spoke of Dasha and Kira. We both understood what would become of the little girls she kept under her wing if I failed the emperor. If he executed me as he had Izolda.

"I promise," I said.

And now as I waited for the troika, I said it again, though Sestra Mirna couldn't hear me from where she stood at the edge of the road with Dasha and Kira, the snow swirling about their faces. Dasha lifted her little hand in a wave and gave me a delicate smile. That she, the youngest of the three, should try to comfort me in this moment nearly broke me—she whom *I* was abandoning, whose life *I* was leaving in shambles.

I wiggled my fingers back at her and forced myself to return her smile. My vow was as much for Dasha and Kira as it was for Yuliya. I would be the best Auraseer I could be. And if that meant guarding the emperor with my gift—guarding the dynasty of rulers whose law brought me the life I had known, a life torn from my family and sent into hiding with the Romska, measures that had all been for nothing—then I would do it.

I'd taken Yuliya's wooden statue of the goddess Feya from the infirmary windowsill and tucked it into the pillow slip that now served as my traveling bag. The idol would be a constant reminder of my promise.

As Anton guided the troika from the stables, my knees wobbled. Did I feel the fatigue of the three horses, whose rest from their initial journey hadn't been sufficient, or was the weariness my own? Did it mark the resignation I would feel until my dying breath? I touched the black ribbon I had tied around my wrist, my emblem of mourning.

The twilight deepened. A gust of frosty air blasted through the thin gray dress I wore. It was nothing more than a laundered gown meant for the sick when they breached their next level of wellness. It was a dress meant for Yuliya. I should have left it behind for her to be buried in, but Sestra Mirna insisted I wear it into Torchev. It was the best the convent could offer. All the other clothes and trinkets in my possession had, of course, been burned.

My gaze drifted to the remnants of the east wing, where I hadn't dared to go and say good-bye, where the bones of the dead Auraseers surely lay huddled together in some terrible dying embrace. Nadia was somewhere in there. She should have been taking this journey to Torchev, not I. As I scanned the fallen east wing one last time, I searched myself for some fragment of gratification that the once-senior Auraseer was gone, but all I found was my own self-loathing.

The troika pulled alongside me. Anton glanced over the blankets wrapped around my shoulders in lieu of a coat. The frigid air cast a pink tinge across his aristocratic nose and sculpted cheekbones. I shivered for him. "Don't you have any furs?" he asked.

"I never wear furs." I closed my heart off from the note of concern in his voice. I would not allow myself to think the prince capable of any small kindness. I would go with him, I would serve his brother, but he would not now, nor ever, be my friend. He represented the empire, whether or not he wore its crown.

"Why?" he asked after a brief hesitation, as if he'd lost the battle of resisting his curiosity, even if it meant engaging me in further conversation. I knew he cared as little for me as I did for him.

"I feel the aura of the beast who gave its life for its hide," I answered plainly. "I feel the pain of its death. I would rather be cold than suffer that."

He had no response, only a slight lift of his brows, which

brought me some satisfaction. Perhaps my confession was disturbing enough to render him silent for the rest of our journey.

As I moved to enter the sleigh, he held out a gloved hand. I slighted him and gripped the carved side myself. I succeeded in hefting in my own weight, but not in the proud way I'd imagined. The sleigh's platform was too high, and I ended up half dragging, half crawling my way to sit on the bench seat beside him. He didn't bother to catch me up by my elbow or assist me again. There was warmth enough in my skin to flush my cheeks with embarrassment.

"Is it customary," he asked, "for Auraseers to sense feeling from the dead?" He adjusted his gloves and transferred the reins between hands. His manner was casual. Too casual. More like affected.

Flecks of white ghosted through the air between us. The snow had started falling again. "It is for me . . . when I touch something. Sestra Mirna said my gift was unnatural." I pressed my lips together. I was speaking too much. He didn't need to know these things. I wouldn't report to him at the palace . . . would I?

I glanced back at the sestra and the two little girls as they shivered and still waited for us to depart. "We should leave." I tightened the blankets around me. "Wolves roam these woods at night."

Something behind Anton's gaze sent a confusing fluctuation of warmth and cold through my body. Was he even listening to me? My thoughts strayed to my appearance. My face must be streaked with ashy grime. Perhaps my quick scrub with the bar of lye soap in the infirmary hadn't been sufficient. I itched to touch my skin to be sure, but that would only reveal my awareness of how unprepared I was to meet the emperor—and my new fate.

He cleared his throat and averted his eyes from mine just slightly, until they settled on the bridge of my nose, like he'd done inside the convent. Then, making a clicking sound with his tongue, he snapped the reins and the horses jolted forward. My heart lurched in my chest. This was it. I was leaving behind everything I had known. Again. I'd never lived in a place long enough to call it my home. Even my years with the Romska were always spent in motion, changing from caravan to caravan to keep me concealed. Now all that hiding was for nothing. The imperial palace would be my final place of residence. But how could it ever be my home?

I worried at my lip and twisted around to look once more at the aged woman who had tried to teach me, to tame me, to prepare me for this destiny if it ever chanced to become mine. I reached with my heart across the widening distance to Sestra Mirna and tried to feel out any sorrow from her at my leaving. The horses' pace quickened. The sestra set her hands on the small shoulders of Dasha and Kira and guided them inside the ruined convent before I was even out of view. My breath hitched. I caged a sob in my throat. My sorrow for leaving Ormina was one-sided. Closing my eyes, I reminded myself it was better this way, better I leave now before I could harm three people I realized too late I loved.

I sat on my hands to keep them warm and steeled my resolve, pushing away the needling thought that the city of the emperor held ten thousand more people than this little village near the sea. Ten thousand more who would come closer to touching my instability. The only remedy was to be cold to them. Distant. Compassionless. Because any love I ever gave in this world only ended up destroying the very ones I cared about the most.

In the end it was I, not Anton, who broke the silence I'd made such a solemn pact with myself to keep. A three-day journey is an insufferable thing to bear with only the thoughts in one's head. Especially if one is an Auraseer and can sense the boy she is alone with has a similar urge to speak. Or at least she hopes he does, because that urge multiplying inside her would be so much easier to justify as coming from *him* than would be the admission it could be originating from herself and her intense need to speak to someone, even a lofty prince, in order to distract herself from her anxiety over her future, which was as overwhelming as the harrowing guilt and sorrow for the dead she left behind. Conversing with Anton was the most viable option for escaping the darkness in my head, the darkness of who I was.

"Is it customary for princes to drive their own sleighs?"

I'd spent the better part of the last hour deciding how to phrase my question and felt rather clever in my choice of words, which were close to matching his from earlier. Would he

notice? Think me impertinent? Or perhaps just think me ridiculous for trying to banter on something he'd said half the night
ago? Because, truth be told, the first morning of our three-day
journey had yet to dawn. We were still in the vast woods outside
Ormina, and here I was already speaking to him. My will was
about as iron as battered tin.

Enough moonlight shone through the canopy of evergreens
that I caught the sharp glance he gave me. Had I startled him
by breaking the silence or merely annoyed him? "It is for me,"
he said, also using the words I'd answered him with before we
left the convent.

"When my caravan traveled near Dubrov," I said, "we
were forced off the road for a good quarter hour while a baron
passed us with an entourage of twenty guards and servants on
their journey to his summer home. *Twenty.* For a *baron*, not a
prince—not the sole heir to the throne of Riaznin." It was a
well-known fact the emperor had yet to marry or bear children.
He was only a year older than his brother. Their closeness in
age spurred a deep rivalry between them. Or so the rumors
whispered. "And yet you came here alone."

Anton stared ahead, adjusting his position to move farther
away from me. It was a subtle distance, only a fraction, but I
felt the icy air take hold of the increased space from his body,
which had been offering me much-needed heat. I locked my
jaw to keep my teeth from chattering. If a fur-lined coat were to
materialize before me, I might trade its warmth for my ideals,
after all. "A caravan?" he asked, avoiding the entire point I'd

been laboring to make. "Do you mean to tell me you're Romska-born? Your coloring is all wrong."

My fingers moved to touch the end of my blond braid. The Riaznian Romska were known for their deep-olive skin, dark eyes, and darker hair. "I never claimed to be a blooded Romska, only that I kept company with them."

"Because you are an Auraseer?"

"Yes."

"Because you sought to evade the empire?"

"Yes."

"Because your parents thought giving you up to the nomadic tribes was a better trade than the loss of your freedom?"

I shivered, not from the stinging cold but the wonder that the prince had me pegged. "Yes."

He nodded and roughly exhaled in a muzzled sort of laugh. His breath frosted the air. "As if anyone in Riaznin could acquire freedom so easily."

His rudeness amazed me. I sat stunned, gaping at him until a dip in the road jostled my mouth into working order again. "You call what I went through easy?"

"I did not say it was easy. Ease has nothing to do with the fact you couldn't have attained freedom no matter what you went through."

"You don't know *anything* about me!" I snapped. He didn't have me pegged, he had me simplified. To him, I was merely another commoner who dreamed of a life the empire's shadow couldn't touch. No doubt he thought himself big enough to be the one to cast the shadow.

"I am speaking of *true* freedom," he said.

"Yes, which you've been kind enough to define as a thing I will never have—a reality of which I'm well aware and have had seventeen years to digest, thank you very much."

His eyebrows arched. "For someone trained in the nuances of emotion, you are quick to anger."

"Trained?" I laughed, my blood flaming. "Don't you see how *untrained*, how unqualified I am? My time spent *without* true freedom while evading *your* empire has cost me the years I could have honed my ability for the servitude that has now been thrust upon me! And if I am angry, it is only because I feel what you, yourself, have not restrained."

"I am not angry."

My fingers curled in frustration and clawed the seat. I felt a flash of blinding pain from the animal that was slaughtered for the leather beneath me and the meat it must have provided at the emperor's table. But that pain was swiftly eclipsed by my fury that Anton was right. He wasn't angry. "You must be," I said, despite the fact his face wore only the markings of piqued curiosity, and nothing I sensed within him could contradict it. That realization didn't diffuse my anger in the least. If anything, it heightened it.

"Do you never take responsibility for your own emotions?" he asked.

"They far too often belong to someone else." My teeth were on edge. Why couldn't he be angry? He'd had anger enough to spare at the convent. Why now make me out for the fool I was?

"Is it so difficult for you to discern the difference?"

I bit the inside of my cheeks to prevent myself from speaking. He would not bait me again. This conversation had proved disastrous. I'd set out to seek the answer to the mystery behind his driving a troika alone, and he'd divulged nothing, yet succeeded in stripping me bare of too many secrets—my upbringing, my history of escaping the law, and the humiliating truth that I was the most ill-qualified Auraseer in creation to meet the task lying before me.

Anton shook his head for a stretch of silence. "Valko will make mincemeat of you."

Nostrils flared, I shifted away as far as possible until my hip pressed the cold side of the sleigh. I didn't need him to remind me of my bleak prospects. "I'm going to sleep now," I announced, as if I could lull my frazzled nerves so easily.

"Very well." He flicked his wrists and sent a light whip along the reins to keep the horses apace. "Dream while you can, Sonya. All too soon you will awaken to a life even I cannot forestall."

I scowled. What did he mean by that? Laying my cheek against the sleigh, I fidgeted and tried to get comfortable. Was he saying he would grant me another life if it were in his power? I pictured his boot tapping the stones of the convent while his gaze swept over me. He knew I would be no good as sovereign Auraseer. So of course he would choose another, if possible, and let me go if it meant better serving his brother—his dynasty. I stewed over that until the steady clip-clop of the horses slowed my breath and made my thoughts scatter and drift and my anger ebb away.

On the cusp of sleep, I heard my name, again and again, echoing across the expanse of my mind. There was something about the way he'd said it. Perhaps because it was the first time my name had fallen from his lips. Or perhaps it was the whisper of the feeling I had when he spoke it—*Sonya*—and the inkling that the prince had, after all, found a small measure of pity for someone else. Pity for a girl like me.

The irony was, I no longer wanted his compassion. I wanted release, from *being* me, from being everything I was, or had done, or would do, which was just cause to be pitied all the same.

CHAPTER SIX

A TICKLE OF SNOW ON MY NOSE AWAKENED ME. THE SHARP
winter light bled through my eyelids, and when I peeked them
open, I found I was alone in the sleigh. The horses' heads
lowered as they chomped on hay scattered across the frozen
ground. I pulled myself into a sitting position. My body ached
from hours spent tucked up at an odd angle.

Where was Anton?

A cottage to my right shaded me. Beyond it was a stable—
too small for the troika. In the distance, a little village sprawled
over the glistening snow. Wisps of smoke curled from every
chimney. I imagined a comfortable inn. A warm meal. A soft
bed. Why hadn't we gone any farther? Why stop here?

I stood—Anton was mistaken if he expected me to remain
in the sleigh for who knew how long—and a blanket fell off of
me. I stared at it, bunched at my feet. It was wool and mossy
green, embroidered at the ends with bright flowers. It wasn't

one of the thin blankets I had wrapped around my shoulders, those I brought with me from the convent. I had the sneaking suspicion it was the blanket Anton had been sitting on as he drove the troika last night, though I hadn't taken great pains to notice it in the darkness.

He must have laid it on me after I'd fallen asleep.

Some compulsion came over me to touch the shining threads of embroidery. As soon as did, I gasped. A flood of powerful emotions washed through me. One of the flowers I'd brushed was a deeper shade of red than the others. Its darkness bloomed beyond its careful stitching. My stomach tightened. It must be blood. At the corner of the blanket, "K.O." was mono-grammed in silver lettering.

Katerina Ozerova. The dowager empress. Anton's mother.

His murdered mother.

I recoiled. I didn't want to touch the blanket again, but I couldn't leave it on the floor of the sleigh. It somehow felt a disgrace to the deceased woman. Careful not to graze the blood-dried flower, I folded the blanket and returned it to Anton's half of the seat.

After stepping down from the sleigh, I skirted quietly around the cottage. Some instinct warned me to be covert. Thankfully the snow wasn't packed here like it was in Ormina. My footfall whispered along as if I walked in nothing more than dusting sugar. Approaching the corner of the house, I peered along its far outer wall.

Several feet away, Anton stood outside an open door, which

blocked whomever he spoke to at its threshold. A small and callused hand extended to the prince and gave him a satchel. Another hand followed, belonging to a third person—a man's, judging by the size, and a noble's, by the amethyst ring that sparkled from his smallest finger. He passed Anton a folded piece of paper. The prince gave a determined nod and concealed the paper in the inner breast pocket of his cape.

I leaned forward and reached for the pull of emotion that might tell me what Anton and the others were feeling, but my hand slipped on the icy slats of the house. I made a small peep, fearing I might stumble over. Anton's head jerked in my direction, and I thrust myself behind the wall.

My heart raced. My chest rose and fell with heavy breaths. Had he seen me? I twisted my hands together. What did it matter if he had seen me? Why would I have assumed that I was intruding or that anything he was doing might be secretive?

Only one answer made sense: the guarded feeling came from *him*. Which confirmed he didn't want me to witness the exchange. I thought over what I'd seen. Even with only their hands to judge them by, I concluded that one person—a woman—lived in this humble place, while another—a noble—did not. Were they having a forbidden tryst? If so, why did Anton bother to protect them from someone like me? Then again, I wasn't just someone anymore. I was the sovereign Auraseer, the sixth sense of the emperor.

Anton's footsteps drew nearer. They were rough, heavy. He didn't pretend at being cautious anymore. Neither would I.

Commanding a show of confidence, I strolled around the corner and feigned a look of surprise. "There you are." I smiled, which was a mistake. If he hadn't suspected me before, he would now.

His eyes narrowed, and he gave me a curt nod of greeting. I'd probably offended him again by not dipping into a curtsy. I would need to learn the habit. The emperor would surely be less patient than his brother.

"Have we stopped to rest here?" I asked, acting as if I couldn't see the satchel in his hands. There must be food wrapped inside, which meant we weren't staying. "The emperor can't expect you to make this journey round-trip without pausing to sleep. At the very least, the horses could use some time to regain their strength."

Anton's fine aristocratic eyes were dulled by shadowy half-circles. When was the last time he'd slept?

"If there were time to rest, I would have let you bury your friends," he replied, his voice neither cold nor warm. A rush of sorrow stole my breath as I thought of Yuliya lying in her infirmary bed, stiff and silent, awaiting her plot in the ground.

The prince's gaze moved past me without meeting my eyes and fastened on the troika. "There's a little food here if you're hungry." He handed me the satchel and walked around me to the sleigh.

I followed him. "That's very kind of whoever lives here." I bit my lip. "Do you know them?"

His shoulders broadened as he inhaled a large breath. "I

thought it wiser to stop here and pass the village entirely. I"—he cleared his throat—"might be recognized, and that would only slow us down."

He stepped into the sleigh. The length of his breeched legs made the maneuver seem easy. This time I didn't shun him when he offered his hand. He pulled me up with a strength that made me feel light and hollow like a nesting doll. But that delicate feeling vanished when the toe of my boot caught the lip of the sleigh. I yelped as my nose collided with the prince's chest. Apparently there was no hope of me entering a troika gracefully.

"Excuse me," I mumbled, my cheeks burning as I peeled away.

A bit of color also flushed his neck. He'd likely never been accosted in such a manner. Once more, his eyes fell to my nose, rather than holding my gaze. I began to wonder if I had some unknown deformity.

"You're bleeding," he observed.

I touched my nose, and a trickle of warmth slipped down to my mouth. "Oh."

"Here." He reached into his breast pocket and retrieved a handkerchief. As he passed it, something fluttered to the ground. The folded piece of paper.

Blood forgotten, I ducked to fetch it just as he did. The paper fell open. Rows of cramped handwriting filled every space. The only words I made out before Anton snatched the paper away were *midnight* and *Morva's Eve*.

He stood abruptly. His cape rustled as he tucked the letter back inside. I remained kneeling and stared at the scratched floor of the sleigh while I chastised myself for my boldness. How would I excuse myself? After a moment, I settled for, "I'm sorry I caused you to drop that." Awkwardly rising to my feet, I pressed the handkerchief to my nose to prevent the blood from dribbling down my chin.

The flush on Anton's neck darkened to an angrier shade. Fire blazed along my nerves, but I tamped it down. It didn't belong to me. I had nothing to be incensed about.

His jaw muscle taut, he sat on the bench of the sleigh and took up the reins. As he was about to snap his wrists and rouse the horses, his brow twitched. He glanced down at the mossy-green blanket beneath him, as if just remembering he'd last put it somewhere else.

I sat beside him. "Was that your mother's?"

His eyes jerked to mine, smoldering like coals.

"Did she have it on her when she died?" I pinched my lips closed as soon as I'd asked the question. The answer was yes. The peaking fury rolling off of him confirmed it. Perhaps now wasn't the time to bring up what I'd felt when I touched the embroidered threads. I'd meant to say something to curb his frustration, but I'd only made it worse.

His brows drew together in a flat, unflinching line. "Do you wish to discuss the death of your friend?"

I shook my head and instinctively reached for the black ribbon on my wrist.

"Then do not speak to me—*ever again*—about my mother."

"I was only—"

"Ever. Again."

I swallowed and nodded. My hands flexed as I fought to contain *his* rage that made my legs shake, my heart pound, my pulse flood my ears.

He blinked, checking himself. My breath came easier. He must be fighting to dam his emotions.

"You should eat something, then rest," he said, and looked down at the handkerchief I held to my nose. Did he realize the difficulty I'd have in eating right now? "I hope to make it as far as Isker by nightfall. It would be better for us both if you went back to sleep."

"I'm not tired."

"I don't care."

I crossed my arms over my chest. "Perhaps if we cannot talk of your mother, we can discuss what will happen at midnight on Morva's Eve." Feya help me, I couldn't restrain myself. How was it possible when I felt exactly what *he* felt about me? His contempt for my impetuousness kept making that selfsame trait multiply like a magician's trick.

His eyes flashed, ready to strike me with lightning. He parted his lips, then clamped them shut again as he deliberated how to answer—how to deal with me.

My body trembled all over, completely at a loss of control. Half of me inwardly begged him to calm himself—calm *me*;

the other half welcomed his rage and how far he could push my limits.

A mad twist of a grin pulled at his lips. "Is this me, Sonya?" He gestured to my coiled tight arms, my clenched fists. "Are you nothing more than my reflection?"

I didn't know how to answer him. The iron taste of blood wetted my mouth. I pinched my nose harder. "Of course I'm more than your reflection."

He leaned forward. "Then I beg you, find that space within yourself and hold on to it, or you will not survive the emperor. If there is one thing I will share with you about my mother, it is that she always said *I* was the mild-mannered child." He raised his brows and gave me a knowing look. "Think on that."

Without another word, he whipped the three horses. The troika slid away into the countryside, gliding through the powdered snow. I bumped along in my seat, but felt like I'd been tossed aside in a snowdrift for how stunned my mind was, how nimbly Anton had put me in my place.

I yearned to dig in my heels at every mile we advanced toward Torchev. The emperor of Riaznin grew nearer to me, and with him the intense foreboding that I was sure to meet my death. The only thing that kept me from flinging myself off the sleigh and making a run for it were the images of Dasha's and Kira's faces and the idol in the pillow slip at my feet. I kept my leg pressed against it. My promise to Yuliya gave me strength. And what brought me more was the remembrance of my friend's calm courage in the moment of her death. I would not let Anton frighten me with his words. I would find that quiet space within myself, and I would cling to it.

Emperor Valko would not be the end of me.

Anton, for all his determination, could not stay awake to drive the troika through the second night. The third time he nodded off and tugged the reins askew, I demanded to drive the sleigh myself. The idea was abhorrent to him, even when I explained my experience with horses. The livelihood of the Romska caravans depended on their horse trade, and with my ability to sense auras, I had an uncanny skill for taming a wild horse. If I could ride bareback, surely steering a sleigh couldn't be so difficult.

None of that mattered to the prince. Perhaps he thought I would drive the troika along a cliff and kick him into oblivion. The idea *had* crossed my mind.

At last he resolved to spend the remainder of the night at a small inn between villages. Removing his cape, he pulled a woolen cap over his royal head and wrapped his mother's blanket around his shoulders, taking care to conceal its finely embroidered edges. He handed the innkeeper three coins and asked for one room to share with his wife. I blanched at that and the small bed the innkeeper revealed when he opened our door.

I needn't have worried. As soon as the innkeeper left, Anton gruffly muttered, "Get some sleep," and nodded to the bed while he rolled up his mother's blanket for use as a pillow on the floor. I watched him a moment, deliberating on whether or not I could take the bed when he was more sleep deprived and of nobler blood. But when I saw him settle onto the floor planks to barricade the door, I flopped down on the bed and stretched out, giving an exaggerated sigh of pleasure. He hadn't given me the bed out of kindness. He didn't trust me. I hoped the floor worked knots into his back.

✳❧✺❧✳

Something jostled me at the shoulder and wakened me when the room was gray and hazy in the light before sun. "What is it, Yuliya?" I asked, my arm thrown over my face in the position I always slept in.

"We need to be going," came the deep rumbling voice of the prince of Riaznin.

The loss of my friend crashed down over me, fresh and acute. My heart squeezed from the weight of it. I didn't move my arm. I didn't want Anton to see the tears clouding my eyes. "I just need a moment," I whispered.

His warm hand, still on my shoulder, lifted away. His footsteps receded until he stood by the doorway. I took measured breaths as I fought to exhale all my grief. Either that or trap it back inside. Now wasn't the time to lose myself. Once I reached the palace, I would have my own room, my own place to mourn in solitude.

Anton didn't say a word, not even when my emotions got the better of me and a quiet sob escaped my labored breathing. He kept his back to me and his head bowed during the several minutes it took me to collect myself. His finger twisted around a loose thread of embroidery on his mother's blanket.

At length I sat up, matted down my tangled braid, and crossed to the door. Anton's chest expanded as if he was about to say something, but I couldn't bear to listen. He'd told me I needed to control my emotions if I wanted to succeed as sovereign Auraseer. I couldn't endure another lecture. I opened the door and left the room.

We walked silently to the stables. I sat in the troika while he hitched up the three horses. The sun emerged above the rolling, snowy horizon as we set off on the last leg of our journey. Because we had traveled through a good portion of the nights, we would arrive earlier than I'd anticipated.

"We'll reach Torchev by the afternoon," Anton said.

Those were the last words he uttered until the massive walls of Riaznin's capital towered over us, and the troika, with its three tired horses and two heart-heavy passengers, crossed into the city of the emperor.

 CHAPTER SEVEN

As I beheld the great city, my eyes widened like a child's. I hadn't felt such wonder since the first time the Romska had performed their strange and mysterious dance around a campfire when I was a little girl. *How is it I have come to live among these people?* I'd asked myself then. *How will I be one of them?*

The same questions overwhelmed me now as we passed a sleigh with a nobleman wearing a tall fox-fur hat and a silver embroidered cloak. A lady sat beside him, pearls dangling from her headdress and connected in deep scalloped rows beneath her chin. Beyond the couple, the magnificent palace glimmered in the late-afternoon sun. My belly ached for something more substantial to eat than the hard cheese and bread Anton had given me from his satchel. Perhaps it was my hunger that made the palace appear like an enormous confection.

The tall arched windows had a candied effect, their edges rimmed with multicolored tiles and brightly painted stonework.

An intricate network of engravings trimmed the various curving walls like icing on spiced cookies, and topping each tower were what looked like giant dollops of gold-plated cream.

Everything I'd ever seen in the vast countryside of Riaznin looked dim and dull in comparison. Several moments passed before I could tear my gaze away. Only then did I glimpse my closer surroundings and what lay beyond the beauty of the quaint shops, their carved wooden awnings, and the streets lined with cheerfully painted houses. Worse, I began to sense it. The ravenous craving of the barefoot boy dodging into a shabby alleyway. The resentment kindling within a sunken-cheeked man as he tossed the contents of his chamber pot outside and turned his glare on the palace. The weariness of a pregnant woman as she strung her dingy laundry on a line. The apprehension of the nobleman who had passed us in his sleigh, the way his eyes leveled on the road and angled away from the steely looks of the peasants.

The people seemed to multiply before us as we traveled deeper into the city. They packed the streets until anywhere I looked, in any given direction, there were hundreds of them. Some extended their palms to beg for coins. Others held up their wares for purchase—lacquer art, bone carvings, furs pieced together from small animals. Beyond the people I saw, I felt thousands more, their pulsating desires and despairs.

But could I really feel them—all of them? Or did I only fear what would happen if I did?

Anton looked askance at me. "Are you all right?"

I'd shrunk down in my seat and gripped the edge with white knuckles. My body trembled. "There are too many."

"Aren't you accustomed to gathered people? The Romska must have taken you into cities."

I shook my head, my nerves tingling with panic. "No, they kept me from them. Even the villages. They passed me to other caravans or hid me in the woods until they returned from their day's work." My experience proved the same at the convent. Unbidden, a memory seized me—being gagged to silence my screams as the sestras dragged me away in a fit of madness, yet another failed attempt of training my ability by testing me in a crowded marketplace.

"Why?" Anton frowned. Behind him, a mass of bodies wove past one another, their movement a constant, confusing swirl of colors. "What happens when you're surrounded by so many?"

A burly man approached the troika and rattled off something about a fair price. He held a slab of meat near my face. I whimpered, smashing against Anton before the bloody flesh could touch me, before I felt the death of the elk or deer or whatever it was.

A baby cried. The sound cut through the shouts of the bartering and bustle all around me. I whimpered harder and dug my fingers through my hair, my body burrowing into Anton's. My movement knocked the reins from his hands, but he caught them up again. Our troika trudged along, slowed by the throngs of people.

"I can't do this," I mumbled through chattering teeth. I

wasn't cold—I couldn't be—not with the warmth of pressed bodies and the thick, cloying air of the streets. But somewhere out there, someone was. Maybe many were.

A young woman, close to my age, leered at Anton from the opposite side of the sleigh. "It's the prince!" She placed a hand on her chest. When he wouldn't look at her, her gaze drifted to me, her thin brows lifting with question. Her aura darkened mine with a stain of jealousy. Something crashed in the square, followed by shouts and pounding fists.

Up ahead, past a large fountain, a market stall had careened over and blocked the road. Two men threw punches at each other. More joined them, yelling and taking sides. Their fury scraped beneath my skin and itched for release.

"Stop that," Anton said to me, voice strained, lips tight.

I realized my fingernails dug into his leg above his knee. I jerked back my shaking hand. "I'm sorry."

The eyes of the thin-browed girl popped wider. "She must be the new Auraseer." The girl pointed at me. Her dark jealousy broke apart into a shower of awe. It prickled a buzz of energy across my skin. "The prince has brought the new Auraseer!"

One by one, the heads in the square turned to me. Even the fistfight broke apart.

Their wonder combined with the pinprick energy of the girl, until together it felt like a thousand knives nicking at my skin. Each cut sliced deeper.

Tears slid down my cheeks. Too many expectations. Too many people to disappoint. Too many teeming emotions begging to be defined. I felt like a glass figurine skittering to the edge of a mantel in an earthquake. Any more of this and I would fall, break into a million pieces. "Make them stop," I pleaded as I hung on to Anton, my words jumbled and scarcely audible. "I can't . . . I can't do this." With the road blocked, who knew how long we might be trapped here?

Tendrils of his anxious concern reached me. I felt them in the warmth of his skin past his shirtsleeve. But the auras of the people swiftly crowded them out. "Don't look at them." He flicked the reins in an effort to budge the horses along.

I squeezed my eyes closed, but the multitude swarmed inside me, bees in a hive far too small. "That doesn't help." My control was slipping away, just as it had on the night the mob of peasants amassed at the convent's gate.

"Think of something—anything else."

I pictured the Ilvinov Ocean. I would stare at it from the bell tower of the convent. I pretended the murmurs in Torchev were the roaring of the currents, the rise and fall of white-capped waves. *Auraseer,* the water called to me. *Just a girl. Too young a girl.* The depths churned with feelings, dark and curious, bitter and dangerous. Rising into an enormous swell, the water slapped down, pushing me under. Tossing me. Thrashing me. I couldn't breathe.

"Sonya, open your eyes." Anton's hand slid across my lower back and held me like an anchor. "Look at me now."

My nose pressed into his cape. My body seized like a madwoman's. I peered up at him.

"Think of me." He set his jaw, striving to radiate a show of powerful calmness. It wasn't authentic. He was worried. I sensed it from our close contact. He didn't believe I could endure this. *I* didn't believe I could.

"You're not enough," I said.

"I *am* enough. Stay with me." His strong grip nudged me closer, and his fingers spread, fitting between the bones of my rib cage. "Look at me. Focus only on me."

My head throbbed. I couldn't concentrate. Behind Anton, flocks of strangers stared and pointed. The road grew more crowded as the steady influx of people were bottlenecked in. Anton shook me, drawing me back to him. "What do you see when you look at me?"

"Well . . . *you*," I replied in exasperation.

"What about me? What color are my eyes?"

My vision dotted with stars. I wasn't breathing properly. "Brown."

"What kind of brown?"

I wanted into curl into a ball and make myself disappear, hide from the city dwellers of Torchev, from their brazen curiosity, their shameless amazement, their confounding presumptions of me. Instead, I clung to the intense challenge of Anton's gaze. In the broad daylight, with no moon to soften the edges of him, with no trees to cast him under their mottling shade, I saw the prince with new clarity. "Butter," I said.

"Butter?"

"Butter," I repeated.

"Butter is not brown."

"It is when it simmers in a pot and smells dark and nutty."

One of his eyebrows lifted in submission. "Very well. And what of my nose?"

"This is foolish." I sneaked a glance behind him at the people.

"You think my nose is foolish?"

"No!" I whirled back to him. "No, of course not."

"I was told I have my grandfather's nose."

"Did your grandfather have a small mole on the bridge, nearly touching his right eye?"

"He did not."

"Then you have been lied to, Prince Anton."

The corner of his mouth twitched. "Tell me about my hair."

My heart pounded. How many people were watching us? How many knew I could see into them? "I've never met a boy so vain."

"My hair, Sonya," he said, keeping me on task.

I swallowed. "I like it windblown. No doubt you will have it slicked to perfection once we reach the palace."

"Speaking of reaching the palace, at the snail's pace we're traveling, I don't believe I'll have enough body parts left for you to discuss." Something glinted in his eye. "You're right. There are far too many people."

"Yes . . ." What was he thinking? "That's what I've been trying to tell you." If only my ability allowed me to read his thoughts. I used to pretend I had a gift for that type of divining with some of the Romska caravans—it helped me earn my keep and complemented the trade of their fortune-tellers—but the truth was, I was as blind to mind reading then as I was now. But what did it matter? I found myself fascinated with the mystery of Anton, with the perfect shape of his mouth, with the thinness of his upper lip, which had once made him look so stern. Somehow, despite the masses surrounding us, my sights and senses had been entirely trapped on him. I released a marveled breath. How had he done it? How had I?

"Do you promise you will stay in the troika while I do something?" he asked.

My nerves flashed with anxiety. "Are you leaving me?"

"No, Sonya." His hand squeezed my side, then carefully drew away. "I'm going to get us to the palace even faster. Would you like that?"

I nodded, though I felt unsure. My thoughts were tangled.

"Then stay thinking on me a moment longer."

He waited, his gaze intent until I nodded again.

He brought us to a full stop before the fountain of the square, then rose and jumped out of the sleigh. I watched him in earnest as he began to unharness one of the horses with practiced hands. My emotions were better grounded, but I was frayed and exhausted. I might lose power over myself if I wasn't careful.

"Feliks!" Anton called out. A young man with a trimmed beard and red cap emerged from the crowd. "Watch these horses and troika and bring them back to the palace when you're able."

Feliks nodded without question or exchange of money. His piercing blue eyes slid to me as he assisted the prince. Once the single horse was unharnessed, Feliks took the bridle of one of the others and whispered something to Anton. "Later," was the prince's muttered reply.

In any other circumstance, I would pause to puzzle over Feliks, how Anton knew him, how he knew he would be there, and why he trusted him with two expensive horses and a troika that belonged to the crown. But with too many emotions battling for ground within me, my questions surrounding the man quickly fled my thoughts.

That is, until Anton passed him the folded slip of paper from his pocket—the letter I'd tried to read. Anton tried to be covert about the switch, but I caught a flash of white in Feliks's palm after he shook the prince's hand in farewell. I remembered another man then. The man hidden by the cottage door where Anton had stopped on our journey to Torchev. The man with the amethyst ring. The man who had given Anton the letter he'd just passed to Feliks.

"Sonya." The prince rounded the sleigh and held out his hand. "Are you ready?"

A flare of panic lit inside me. I looked at the people crowded behind him. If I stepped outside the troika and any nearer to them, I would only sense their auras that much more strongly.

"It's all right," Anton assured me.

I took a deep breath and reached for the pillow slip that held my sole belonging.

"Feliks will bring that," he said.

I shot a wary glance at the prince's acquaintance. "I can't . . . I have something too valuable."

Considering my earnest plea, Anton nodded. He grabbed his satchel from the floor of the sleigh and emptied out the food. "Put it inside."

Quickly, I wrapped the pillow slip's excess linen around the figurine of Feya within. Once I placed it in Anton's satchel, he tucked his mother's blanket on top, then closed the flap and slung the satchel over his shoulder. He reached for me. I stood and the prince placed both hands on my waist and helped me down to the street. A sense of calm descended upon me at his touch. I latched on to it. Now wasn't the time to quell my curiosity over his friend or his ally—whoever Feliks was—not when the collective feelings of several hundred people fought to stake their claim inside me.

"Make way!" Anton said, using the full force of his rich timbre. The people did as he commanded. As they murmured among themselves, I fastened my gaze on the prince's booted heels and struggled to block out the whispered rumors, the quiet hostility of the people, and their astonishment over the new sovereign Auraseer.

Anton lifted me on the horse's bare back, and then, using the edge of the sleigh as a springboard, he hoisted himself up to sit behind me.

He folded his hands over mine, already woven through the mare's white mane, and guided the horse to the nearest alley at the perimeter of the square. His commanding voice once again parted the crowd. Passing through the alley was a more difficult squeeze. Our knees bumped along the outer walls of the neighboring shops, but at length we made it through to a backstreet. Here the people were in more manageable numbers. I seized on to the hope that we would soon be free of this area altogether.

Anton brought the mare to a halt. "All northbound roads converge to the palace."

I nodded, unsure why he was telling me this. We were on a northbound road.

"Now"—the prince eased his grip on my hands—"I'd say it's time you showed me your skill with horses."

My heart leapt with anticipation. Despite the auras of the curious onlookers that clamored for my attention, I inhaled deeply and centered myself against the warmth of the mare. It seemed years since I had ridden, though it couldn't have been much more than the eight months I'd spent at the convent. The sestras couldn't justify the expense of sheltering and feeding horses, for we had no need to travel long distances and the other Auraseers couldn't sense an animal's energy. My gifts were unnatural. But at the moment I didn't care. I felt so at home astride a horse. If there were any beasts worthy of human companionship, they were these magnificent animals. Their auras seemed designed to complement ours.

I bent forward and murmured words of comfort to the mare. Beneath my fingers, her weariness was as palpable as my own. But even more pronounced was the strength of her determination. She seemed to sense we were close to our journey's end and didn't intend to give up until we reached our destination. Her fortitude came like muscle to my bones. "What is her name?" I asked Anton.

"Raina." He shifted closer to me.

I softened my hold on the mare's mane and focused on her energy, not allowing myself to glance at the backstreet city dwellers. I had to keep the fragile control over myself that Anton had constructed for me. "You've been trotting for days, Raina. Would you like to go for a run?"

She whinnied, and I sat back against Anton's chest. "Let's run, then." I clucked my tongue and gave Raina's girth a sudden squeeze with my calves.

She reared. Anton's arms tightened around me, but I felt no fright in the mare's reaction. I couldn't say the same for the few onlookers surrounding us. Surely just as Raina must have intended, they jumped back and cleared us a path. At once, the mare took advantage and lunged forward.

A wide smile spread across my face. We ducked under a hanging sign and raced down the twisting street. At the speed we were traveling, the emotions of the people were nothing but a blur that couldn't threaten me, a thought I could toss to the wind. Steam rose off Raina. Her muscles worked in precision, while, at the same time, with abandon. I felt Anton relax behind me. He even lifted one hand from mine to rest on my waist. I found the pressure there pleasing.

I angled forward and kept my legs secure around the horse's

body. My dress was hitched up and exposed an indecent portion of my legs, regardless of my gray stockings. Throwing my shame aside, I kicked Raina's flanks until we rode even faster. Without the weight of the sleigh or being harnessed to two other horses, she easily maneuvered around the occasional sledge cart and lessening congestion. The streets branched and intersected, but Raina kept choosing the northbound route with little nudging from me. She knew where her home was. We galloped onward. Snow flew off the cobblestones in our wake.

I imagined we traveled south to Illola or east to the borders of Shengli.

I imagined I was free.

The illusion broke when we ground to a halt outside the massive palace gates. The bars were made of pure gold and fashioned into flowering vines. Together, they created a mighty barrier between the city and the home of the emperor.

A soldier, recognizing the prince, turned the heavy lock and let us pass. We cantered up a gravel road lined with manicured, snow-capped hedgerows. At least a hundred guards stood stationed outside and stared ahead, trained not to look at anyone. They wore the colors of Riaznin, red and gold, and strapped onto each man's back was a musket, while a sheathed saber hung from his belt. My thoughts strayed to the men. My awareness expanded as I sought to know if behind their identical facades, they had identical feelings.

"Don't think about them," Anton said, realizing what I was

doing when my head craned to study a guard we were passing. "We're almost there."

My eyes lifted to the palace. Up close, it looked less like a confection, more like the ominous structure it really was. A pretty cage to belie what it held within.

Something winked from the leaded glass of a window three stories off the ground, almost like the sun had bounced off a mirror or a large jewel. Anton's body straightened behind me as he looked up. Then his arms stiffened. "I have to go," he said, and abruptly dismounted the horse. Keeping his head low, he quickly pulled the satchel off his shoulder and passed it over to me after withdrawing his mother's blanket. He tucked it under his arm and departed.

"Anton?" I stared after him.

He paused, no more than ten feet from me, and half turned without meeting my gaze. "Remember what I told you, Sonya. Find a space within yourself and cling to it. Don't lose yourself here." His eyes shifted to the upper window. "Not to him."

Before I could form a reply, Anton strode away, his dusk-blue cape billowing in a brilliant arc behind him. Gone was the almost friend from the last hour, the steadying hand, the assuring voice. I saw the boy assume the role of prince in the way his boots clipped the stones, in the proud set of his chin and the narrowed slit of his eyes. He entered the palace without sparing me another glance.

My chest fell. He had done his duty to his brother. He had

brought back the eldest Auraseer intact. What sheer relief he must feel to be done with me.

The stable master came and helped me off the horse. The palace doors opened and out streamed a flock of maids and attendants. Their pulsing auras revealed their surprise at the unusual delivery of the new sovereign Auraseer. I steeled myself as I let them guide me up the curving steps of the great porch, all the while mourning the sudden absence of Anton. I could no longer hide behind the folds of his cape or let the color of his eyes be my distraction.

My feet crossed the threshold into a spacious lobby where amber-inlaid floors gleamed back at me. I gazed beyond them to four sets of marble staircases, each twirling flight topped with golden rails. A magnificent painted ceiling loomed overhead. The seven gods of Riaznin sat on seven mighty steeds. At their center, beaming with seven rays, was a red sun, the symbol of Torchev—of the emperor.

I breathed in, breathed out, and sought with desperation that place Anton had urged me to find. A place of solitude within my heart. A place no other person could abuse or dominate.

I prayed such a place existed.

CHAPTER EIGHT

I WAS LED TO A BEDROOM ON THE THIRD FLOOR OF THE PALACE—
a great honor. The third floor was reserved for the royal family,
meaning the only two left: Emperor Valko and Anton.

I refused to let myself feel important for sharing such close
proximity to the emperor. As his protector, of course I needed
to be nearby. If anything, it felt like a punishment rather than
a blessing. I was not ready for this responsibility. Though when
I saw what "close to the emperor" really meant—rooms at the
opposite end of the longest corridor I'd ever seen—some relief
opened my balled hands. They fisted again when I thought
twice about my removed situation. Was I near enough to send
warning of assassination or robbery or whatever the emperor
deemed worthy of my intervention?

A luxurious rug rolled out from the gilded door of the
emperor's rooms like the red tongue of a dragon. I counted the
repeating flowers woven into the design. Too many, stretching

too far away. No wonder Izolda had been executed. She was well past her middle ages. Perhaps she couldn't run down this corridor fast enough. I wasn't sure I could do any better.

My attendants guided me inside my rooms and set my satchel on a table. I braced myself for excess, for the opulence that marked every corner and every bit of trimming in the palace. My antechamber didn't disappoint my expectation, though I couldn't say it pleased me. My idea of comfort would have been a bed of earth under a leafy tree, soft grass for my carpet, a ceiling painted with living stars. My time with the Romska had taught me true beauty, and it was not in the room before me.

The velvet couches had a stylish shape, but looked stiff and uninviting. In fact, nothing appeared welcoming. Every item seemed designed for one purpose—to impress. The walls were papered in a rich pattern, so red it made my head ache, and the varnish of the desk and tea table shone so highly polished that I was afraid to touch them and cause some poor servant the extra chore of rubbing away my fingerprints.

A furnace towered from floor to ceiling in the corner of the room, its surface covered in beautifully painted tiles. I was glad to have warmth in the winter, but I couldn't help wondering at the expense of such artistry when a simple wood-burning stove would do. The people of Riaznin were burdened beyond the breaking point from taxation. I hoped the majority of their money didn't go into prettying up the emperor's home—*my* home.

My attendants bustled around me. "Is she truly the eldest Auraseer?" one maidservant whispered to another as they stoked the fire behind the grate of my furnace. Both girls looked to be my age. They were surely used to a sovereign Auraseer outranking them by years, not to mention in clout. I lifted my chin and did my best to appear unaffected by the disbelief radiating from them in waves. They couldn't see my hand behind my back, where I wrapped a loose thread from my sleeve around my finger, making it throb with trapped blood. That sensation kept me tethered when this roomful of intrusive auras threatened to tunnel into my mind, make me lose all my wits, and expose me for the undeserving fool I felt I was.

Two men brought in a copper tub and carried it past the carved door at the rear of the antechamber, which led to, I presumed, my bedchamber. Following the tub came an onslaught of male servants carrying buckets of steaming water. Their eyes strayed to me and some slid down the length of my body. Worse was the way their energy made my skin tingle and my mouth water. I swallowed hard and tore the string from my sleeve as I rushed to wrap my arms around my torso. Heat flamed my cheeks. Was I expected to bathe with everyone here? I was used to doing so with Romska girls and fledgling Auraseers, but not while a host of curious men surrounded me—some boys younger than myself. Who knew what strange customs awaited me and my new status?

I nearly wept with relief when a wiry, black-haired woman clapped her hands and shooed out the men after a little boy hefted in the last bucket. He tripped over his shoes as he scurried out the door and gave me one final look of wonder. The door shut, and I was left with six blessedly female companions. The wiry woman motioned to the others, and they swarmed around me. In moments they had me undressed, naked, save for the black ribbon around my wrist, and shivering under their collective scrutiny.

Too young. Too thin. Too dirty. My imagination supplied their thoughts, and from what I sensed in their auras, I wasn't too off the mark.

The wiry woman pursed her lips. "I am Lenka, head maid of the sovereign Auraseer. I served Izolda before you." Her jaw ticked and a pang of sorrow constricted my chest. Perhaps they had been friends. The sensitive moment passed. Lenka's gaze hardened. I laced my fingers together and strove to appear relaxed with no clothes on.

"You must eat more," Lenka said sharply, her eyes lingering on my belly.

I blinked. *I must eat more?* I'd never seen a thinner woman in my life. She was all bones and harsh angles. Even her teeth brought structure to her cheeks in a horselike kind of way. "Yes, about that," I said, swallowing any tart retorts off my tongue. "I don't eat meat."

My maids exchanged blank stares.

"Pardon?" Lenka asked.

I curled one bare foot over the other. "I don't eat meat, not even fish. So if you could see that my food—"

"We are your personal attendants"—Lenka looked down her nose at me—"not the kitchen staff."

Her irritation, injured pride, and disregard combined like hot needles jabbing all over my skin. I needed to shake them off and protect myself before I lashed back at her with her own venom. I didn't wish to make enemies here. I had to think of Dasha and Kira. I had to succeed. Twisting the black ribbon at my wrist, I asked, "Am I to have a bath now?" I looked about the women, but no one held a dressing robe.

Lenka's nostrils flared. She gave a stiff nod, then clapped. I wasn't sure if it was a call for me or the other maids to follow, but together we complied.

I gasped as we entered my bedchamber. In a flash, the grandeur of my antechamber was gone. Here everything was a monochrome of browns, from the scuffed floor to the planked wood walls. The space was large and empty, except for the copper tub—a temporary furnishing—and a strange box of a bed in the far right corner.

As the women busied about the tub, testing the water and pouring in salts and oils, again, I looked for a robe. I suspected the absence of one was a form of Lenka's cruelty. I'd only spent a few minutes with her and already she didn't like me. She took no pains to conceal it from her aura. Her aversion shouldn't have come as a surprise. Even among the tolerant Romska, only one boy, Tosya, had taken the trouble to form a long-lasting friendship with me—the strange girl passed from caravan to caravan every few months in case my ability drew too much attention to their encampments and brought them danger. The Romska had a difficult enough time dodging the law without the worry of harboring an Auraseer, someone who always carried a bounty on her head. Most kept their distance, but not Tosya.

I eagerly awaited every spring when I would join his caravan. He was three years older and two heads taller, and his aura was open and easy. More than that, it was *easing*. My time with him promised to be full of laughter and adventure. My mad spells diminished when we were together. Maybe he recognized that, and that's why he endured a little scamp like me. He was a gifted songwriter and even taught me how to read. In the most important ways, Tosya was like a brother, realer than the brother the Romska claimed I once had.

I found a stack of towels behind the tub and wrapped one around myself, since the water was still too scalding to step into. As soon as I'd done so, my attention turned to the peculiar bed in the corner of the room.

It reminded me of a covered carriage without wheels. While the maids laid out silver combs on a tray and added spiced herbs to the bath, my curiosity overcame me. I sneaked over to the bed, climbed the stepping stool, and opened a little door. Four walls and a low roof enclosed the mattress. My chest burned for air just looking at the cramped space. How would I be able to sleep—breathe? Why did Izolda have such a bed?

I poked my head inside, craned my neck around, and stopped short when I spied the inner ceiling. Claw marks raked the wood. They peeled back the paint and dug veritable trenches. Some contained traces of dried blood. My stomach folded with dread. Even the celebrated sovereign Auraseer had her secrets, her own twisted form of emotional release.

"Come." Lenka clapped at me. "You don't have time to rest."

I slid out of the box as if escaping the nest of a viper. "Must I have this bed?"

Lenka's thin lips curved. "You will want it soon enough."

I crossed the room to the tub and stepped into the burning water. My heart beat out of cadence. I didn't dare ask what Lenka meant. Her dark forewarning said enough.

The maids scrubbed me over. They lifted my limbs, dug behind my ears, and washed my hair three times. Had I been so filthy? The scent of juniper and spices wafted from the steam. Despite the thoroughness of my cleaning, the bath was rushed. Just as the water cooled to a desirable warmth, I was prodded out and into a crisp linen shift. Next came a corset, which I wouldn't let near me (I'd had an encounter with whalebones before, and it was no pleasant thing to feel the death of that beast), and a honey-colored gown of silk, embroidered at the neck and hemline with shimmering white threads. The gown was supposed to be topped by the golden robe of the sovereign Auraseer, but I refused to wear it because it was lined in fur. Lenka's cheekbones carved into sharper lines as she sucked in her breath with frustration. I promised to wear my token robe in the spring, when I would surely have a fur-less alternative.

My maids next presented my headdress, trimmed with pearls

that would dangle down the sides of my face. Unfortunately for
Lenka, I declined it, as well, seeing as it was also trimmed in fur
where it crowned my head. Several minutes passed before my
head maid gave up persuading me to conform. I held my ground.
I may be required to sleep in a torture chamber of a bed, but I
didn't need to spend my waking moments feeling death brush
my skin. At least I tolerated the foundational dress without any
suffering. Some silkworms were boiled alive after spinning their
cocoons, but the ones that contributed to my gown must have
been allowed to mature into moths and emerge free.

"Let the emperor deal with you!" Lenka threw up her
hands. "Only let it be known I did everything in my power to
prepare you."

Unease troubled my blood at her words. She reminded me
of Sestra Mirna in that moment, another woman who had tried
to prepare me for my destiny and failed, thanks to my own
stubbornness. *But this is different.* This was a simple matter.
Emperor Valko might be a tyrant, but surely my *clothes* wouldn't
infringe on how he ruled his empire or how well I could serve
him. "I'll be certain to tell His Imperial Majesty tomorrow that
you had no hand in my shame," I bit out, Lenka's irritation
finally becoming my own.

She put her hands on her bony, jutting hips. "Did you think
we were dressing you for a private supper in your rooms?"

My ribs seemed to close in and smash my lungs and heart.
"I'm to meet the emperor tonight?" My voice rose in a pitch near
hysterics.

She looked up at the ceiling in exasperation. "Some seer you are."

I was too frazzled to be offended. Besides, she was right. Couldn't I have divined from all the urgency and everyone's rushed, ill tempers that the ritual I'd been led through wasn't customary? Had I been so desperate to put off meeting the emperor that I deliberately ignored the obvious?

The six women stood in a semicircle around me. My shoulders felt heavy with fatigue—their fatigue, as well as my own. They had spent their strength wrestling me clean and dressed. Bridling a wild stallion must be easier.

"I'll wear my hair down," I announced, summoning my dignity and any remaining vigor I could borrow. If only my ability allowed me to keep their auras in my clutches when we parted. I would need all the fortification I could for this evening. Why in Feya's name had I ever opened the convent gates? Why hadn't I listened to Sestra Mirna, to Basil, to all my better instincts, weak though they were?

"The ladies at court wear their hair up," Lenka replied.

"I am not a lady at court. I am Sovereign Auraseer. And if I cannot wear a headdress, I will let my own hair be my adornment." I sounded as proud as any queen, but in truth, I was only anxious not to incur the emperor's wrath at my lack of proper attire.

Lenka studied me. A sense of calm and rightness washed through my chest. She straightened her back. "Very well. You are young, so I suppose loose hair will not be inappropriate.

In fact, the emperor might find the virginal effect it lends you pleasing."

Two of the prettier maids exchanged glances, like they knew something about Emperor Valko we did not. A flood of warmth came to my belly, but I didn't know if it belonged to the two maids or if it was my own apprehension for this evening.

Lenka clapped. "Step closer to the furnace, and we will dry your hair."

She didn't chide me again as the ladies lifted my hair in sections and fanned it near the hot tiles. Once dried, they brushed it with burdock and nettle oil and let it fall in shining waves to the middle of my back. Perhaps Lenka had been testing me all along, waiting to see how far she could push me until I pushed back. Until I proved I might have a spark of Izolda—of greatness—in me.

I only hope it doesn't cost me my head. I glanced back at the box bed and suppressed a shiver. *Or my sanity.*

Guided by Lenka as we left my rooms, I passed a gold-framed mirror. I was a different creature than the one who had entered. My head maid was right—I looked pure and undefiled with my hair down, almost like I wore the veil of a bride. But within myself, I felt a murderess's guilt. If only Lenka knew what I had done. I drew in a deep breath. I wished this unraveling inside me was merely the flutterings of an anxious girl on her wedding day, that the long corridor before me was the aisle of a church leading me to an altar and a groom, not the ruler of Riaznin.

Maybe, if I was very fortunate, Emperor Valko wouldn't be as every rumor suggested. Maybe he would share some traits with his brother.

I pressed a hand to my stomach and reminded myself Anton wasn't as gallant or caring as he'd led me to believe. It had been a show designed to bring me to the palace in haste, as he'd been commissioned to do. No doubt he shared many traits with the emperor, and none of them would bring me any comfort.

CHAPTER NINE

WE DIDN'T APPROACH THE EMPEROR'S ROOMS AS I'D EXPECTED.
Lenka led me down two twirling flights of stairs until we
reached the main level of the palace. She needn't have guided
me any farther. All I had to do was step into the river of people
flowing westward past the amber lobby. Lenka accompanied
me anyway, and for that I was grateful. I wasn't prepared to be
among so many people, so many crowded emotions. I kept my
arm pressed to my maid's, despite her annoyance at my closeness, and fought to leech her energy and forget everyone else's.
We marched together down the marble-pillared corridor. My
belly was a pit of worry. My heart thrummed so hard, I feared
it might bruise my chest. I tucked my chin and latched my gaze
on the parquet floor. I hoped the emperor wouldn't notice me.

It was a stupid idea to wear my hair down. Now I felt even
younger, even smaller in comparison to my enormous duty. I
was supposed to be a protectress. I should *allow* myself to rub

shoulders with the nobles, to glean from them what I could and discern any potential threats, not hang on my maid's apron strings. I took a step away from Lenka as I attempted to *be* the sovereign Auraseer, but immediately my body started shaking. I felt threats *everywhere*.

The auras of the nobles were different from those of the city dwellers, not because of the aristocrats' distinguished societal positions, but because they felt more practiced at veiling the hostility they bore for one another. Life at court made them artists of deception. Still, what I sensed from them was enough to tighten my throat and send a fit of tremors through my body. Clutching my neck, I bumped back into Lenka and cowered from the highborn sweeping past me. How could I be certain their ill will wasn't directed at the emperor?

For their part, the nobles were oblivious to me. Without my token robes, they didn't recognize me as the sovereign Auraseer. Heads held high, they walked onward and in through the doors of the great hall.

Lenka shrugged me away and made me stand up straight. "Pull yourself together, child! Remember your training."

I wanted to weep. What training? While the other Auraseers at the convent had sat in the study hall and wrote essays on the subtle distinctions between hunger, avarice, and desire, I'd scribbled notes to Yuliya or used too much of my inkwell to play mind-numbing games of X's and O's.

I bit my lip to control my wobbling chin. No, I wouldn't think of the convent. I wouldn't remember the last time I saw its burned ruins or inhaled the thick and cloying stench of the dead.

I bent over in a sudden fit of nausea. As I closed my eyes, I saw Yuliya's lifeless face, the gash in her leg, her bloody sheets. My nose stung, a warning I might cry. I should. I hadn't shed enough tears over everyone who had died because of me.

"Stop this at once!" Lenka jostled my arm. Her voice was nothing more than a hiss. Shame, more than concern, permeated her aura. I must be a public disgrace.

I rushed into the shadows behind one of the great hall's doors. Here I was farther away from the nobles, though not outdistanced from the tumultuous memories in my head. "I'm tired from my journey. Please . . . I can't do this tonight. I can't go in there."

Lenka's horselike mouth pursed and shriveled up with wrinkles to match Sestra Mirna's. "Don't you dare speak of shirking from your responsibility! This isn't the convent. You cannot say you are sick and hide away in your room. You *will* attend the emperor, as you will every time he requires you. When you are through tonight, you can take to your box bed. Its design *does* serve a purpose."

Dread turned my stomach to stone, and I wiped the moisture from under my nose. "Very well, then." Lenka was right. I couldn't hide. I had Dasha and Kira to think of. "Just let me collect myself."

"There is no time for that." She prodded me out of the shadows. Her face looked skeletal in the half-light. "Go in there and keep your wits about you!" With one final shove, she launched me into the great hall and promptly abandoned me.

My heart pounded like a volley of musket fire. I struggled to stand up straight and took several long breaths. The serpentine press of the nobles' auras slithered closer. Competing with them was the memory of the convent in flames.

Think of something else. Think of anything else.

My childhood home. No, that wasn't a vivid enough recollection.

The scent of my mother's hair. Rosemary and . . . I couldn't remember.

Think of me. I blinked, recalling Anton's words from this afternoon. "Think of me," he had said when I was on the verge of completely losing all control among the commoners in the square. Anton had done what I couldn't do on my own. He'd distracted me. More than that, he'd brought me back to myself.

I lifted my gaze to the massive domed ceiling in the great hall. *Think of Anton.*

The ceiling was painted a robin's-egg blue and embellished with swirling golds, indigos, and reds—intricate and interwoven like living embroidery. I saw what wasn't there: the prince's buttery-brown eyes in the wintry light of Torchev.

As I focused on his image, the buzz of the nobles' auras softened inside me as if a conductor had hushed his orchestra. I took an astonished breath. *This is working.*

I kept my sight on the ceiling, wishing I could run my fingers over the places where it shimmered in the light of the chandeliers. Remembering Anton's touch, a warm sensation spread across my back where he had placed his steadying hand.

Exhaling, I lowered my gaze and walked deeper into the great hall. Two long tables ran the length of the room, their surfaces draped in midnight-blue cloth and bedecked with evergreen boughs and glowing candles.

I pictured Anton in profile as he snapped the reins of the sleigh, the way his head tipped back in admiration to watch the sun glint off the snow-capped hills on our journey or when the light shone a spectrum of color along the crystalline branches of a frozen weeping willow.

I advanced three more steps. Porcelain plates, crystal goblets, and gold utensils beckoned the nobles to sit on high-backed, velvet chairs. A string quartet added to the enchantment. The courtiers practically waltzed to their designated seats, the ladies in their jeweled headdresses and tiaras, the men in their polished boots and gold-buttoned kaftans.

I remembered how Anton had dismounted from the white mare once we reached the palace, how his cape had billowed as he turned away and left me in a veritable lion's den.

The prince's spell over me broke. In its place came a torrent of dizziness as the nobles' auras pried their way inside my body. In came their pangs of gluttonous hunger as they eyed the first course of the feast. Their tingles of dark passion. Their scraping hatred past the strain to smile. I caught the furtive glance a noblewoman cast to a man who wasn't the one she laid her gloved hand on. Behind her, two men whispered, eyes narrowed, as one inhaled snuff powder from his knuckle. At the nearest table, a gray-haired woman traced a finger down her age-spotted neck while she stared at the milky skin of the lady seated across from her.

The room began to tilt. My faintness grew stronger. So much for trying to use Anton as my anchor. Legs shaking, I glanced around me. I needed to sit down, though I didn't know where.

The quartet went silent. The nobles who had been sitting, stood. The ladies lowered their fans. The men angled their bearded faces to the doors behind a third table—this one on a dais at the head of the room. Two liveried servants advanced onto the raised platform in unison and reached for the ivory handles of the doors. On impulse, I stepped behind a tall nobleman and hid like a child who had broken her mother's favorite teacup.

The silence stretched for an unbearable length. My head prickled from holding my breath. The clip of shoes—the emperor's?—and another one or two pairs echoed into the curve of the dome above me. I searched inside myself for any new feeling, for a spark of something austere or dramatic or even cruel. Nothing so exciting happened. In fact, I couldn't place why moments ago I'd been on the verge of fainting.

I released my pent-up breath with all the grace of a wilting flower. I stared at my slippers, peeking out from the hem of my dress. I tapped the toes together, because that was at least mildly stimulating. The inlaid wood of the parquet floor was cut in the same swirling designs as the ceiling above. Why had it ever mesmerized me with thoughts of Anton?

My eyelids grew heavy. I had an itch at the back of my neck. When could I sit down? I was past the point of exhaustion. I peered around the man blocking me to see what was taking so long.

I caught my first glimpse of Emperor Valko.

He was young. I knew that he would be, but didn't expect him to appear so close in age to myself. The emperor was older than Anton, but he seemed to be two years his junior. I wondered how that aspect played into their relationship. Once my surprise at the emperor's youthful appearance had subsided, I let myself study his face.

Cool gray eyes. Brows so straight they could have been drawn above a rule stick. A pronounced, wide mouth, running a parallel line below. A handsome nose, if a little short. In fact, his face altogether had a slightly compacted look from his forehead to his chin. But somehow it worked in his favor, making him more alluring, more feline, setting him apart from everyone else in the room—in the empire. Proof, as the nobles claimed, that his bloodline was indeed blessed by the gods.

He stood as he conversed with other men on the dais. Councilors, I presumed. One was a general, by his uniform. The Romska had a humorous song about a general's fussy regimentals, from his gold epaulets to his red pompons and plumes. The emperor nodded and said something in a low voice to the general, not deigning to look the man in the eye. The honor of being addressed by his monarch, however slight, was enough to make the man puff out his chest. As the general gave a reply, the emperor leisurely held up a silencing hand. At once, the general's mouth snapped shut and he prostrated himself in a bow.

When the general and councilors turned away to discuss something more, the emperor's nostrils flared with a stifled yawn. He never once turned his gaze to the waiting assembly. As the councilors continued their hushed conversation, the emperor picked his thumbnail on the back of his ornate chair. He was bored, I realized. I *had* sensed him a moment ago. My sudden disinterest belonged to *him*.

I breathed in deeply. Honing in on his aura from across the room—singling it out from so many, even before I had seen him—brought me a great measure of satisfaction. I might not lose my head, after all.

Feeling more at ease, I let my gaze drift away. Apart from the councilors, another man stood on the dais. *Anton*. A little zing shot through my palms and the soles of my feet when I discovered he was already staring at me.

His hair was slicked back, the windblown look from our journey gone. He wore a green silk kaftan. Its hem skimmed his thigh in the new fashion and was belted low at the waist with a brown strap of leather that matched his dark boots. I took in his furrowed brows and pressed lips. I didn't need to decipher his aura to know he was displeased. His eyes fell to my hair, to my gown, and a feeling of nakedness came over me, worse when Lenka and my maids had assessed my body. Perhaps

I should have worn the fur-lined robe and headdress. Clearly without them, I gave offense. And *with* them, I'd have had all the more layers to hide beneath.

I glanced away from the prince and lifted my chin, taking a keen interest in a sconce on the wall, surely the most ordinary thing in the room. For all my rapt attention, it could have been a wreath of diamonds.

At length, the emperor and his councilors decided their untimely conversation was over. Valko seated himself, followed by the court nobles doing the same. Together, they were a wave of rustling taffeta and scraping chairs.

My heartbeat quickened. I clutched the skirt of my dress. I didn't want to call notice to myself by standing alone, but every seat seemed occupied—every seat except the last chair at the emperor's table. Was it reserved for the sovereign Auraseer?

It must be. It would be an ideal position for protecting him.

I took three steps in that direction when Anton shook his head. The motion was subtle, but clearly spelled *no*. I halted. The look on his face said I nearly escaped the social blunder of the century.

Emperor Valko was unaware. He took a sip of wine and idly traced the stem of his crystal goblet. I still had time to find my place.

I scanned the room. The people were a riot of pearls and feathers and winter pastels. For the life of me, I couldn't find a vacant chair.

Anton's eyes widened a fraction, and he tipped his head to

my left. I frowned. He tipped it again. I glanced to that side of the room. Still no chair. He picked up his fork, and while polishing it on his napkin, pointed its prongs to my left. I shrugged my shoulders. He gave the fork a pronounced wiggle.

Where? I mouthed.

There! His lips pursed the silent word.

The emperor's gaze lifted and narrowed on his brother, two seats away. Then his imperial eyes found me. I cursed the seven gods and stumbled a curtsy, ducking my head as I rushed to my left, where I demanded a chair to materialize.

A heavyset woman shifted and leaned to her plate, and the magical chair appeared. I promptly sat upon it and spent several long moments arranging my napkin just so on my lap, all the while praying that the burning in my cheeks looked like a healthy flush and not bright splotches of embarrassment. At last, I stole a glance at the dais.

Emperor Valko was still watching me.

Anton had taken up the fine art of buttering a roll. The emperor's gaze flicked between us, but the prince didn't acknowledge me again.

Valko whispered to the councilor on his right. The man skimmed the crowd. His eyes riveted to mine. The man nodded, then whispered to Anton, seated on *his* right. This was like some infuriating child's game where I was the target of the prank. Anton set down his knife and muttered a reply, never again looking in my direction. The councilor passed the message to Valko, who arched his brows. His gaze returned to me, and he leaned back in his chair. What had happened was simple enough to determine—the emperor had confirmed I was his Auraseer.

He stared without blinking, with the steady eyes of a man intimidated by nothing. In contrast, I seemed to have collected a dozen lashes on my eyeballs for how they twitched and glanced about. I strained to focus on anything but him—when I saw only him. The flush of heat stubbornly clung to my cheeks.

A servant brought me a bowl of creamed beet soup. I took up my spoon straightaway, grateful for the distraction. But even with my vision centered on the murky purple liquid, I felt the weight of Valko's stare. His aura spun around mine, curious, mildly annoyed, and, above all else, no longer bored. How lovely for him. *I*, on the other hand, was left with my own mess of emotions and, worse, trapped in one of those rare moments I couldn't borrow, blend into, or be blinded by another person's energy.

I drew into myself and avoided the fleshy elbows of the noblewoman beside me. I kept swallowing my soup without troubling to cool it. I waited for Anton to look at me. I waited for Valko to stop. When my bowl was empty, I set down my spoon and clasped my hands below the table as I fought not to wring them.

Valko lifted two fingers and whispered something to the servant who came to his side. The servant took a silver platter of meat from the emperor's table, stepped off the dais, and wove around the first table to the second—to me.

My stomach spasmed. My mouth clamped shut. At last, the flush left my cheeks. My blood drained away with a sickening prickle. All heads in the room revolved to watch that silver platter approach me. With a flick of his fingers, the emperor had done what I'd sought to avoid all evening—draw attention to myself. And in the worst way possible. In a way that couldn't please him. Because I would not eat that meat.

The servant stopped before me, and his heels clicked together. I wanted to crawl under the table, rip open the floor, burrow a hole through the frozen earth until I found the Romska camps. I could hide in the woods with Tosya, who always made me feel safe. "His Imperial Majesty, the Lord Emperor and Grand Duke of all Riaznin, favors you, Sovereign Auraseer," the servant said.

The room perked up with interest once my title was revealed. A flurry of whispers emerged from the nobles like a flock of hidden birds. Just as quickly, everyone hushed as they waited to see what I would do. A distracting swell of energy lanced the edges of my awareness. I didn't entertain it. I forced myself to glance at the meat. Instinctively, my nose wrinkled. Roast swan. The head still intact. The beak open and stuffed with stewed figs. The bird's eyes were seared shut. It looked like it was crying.

My lips parted as I struggled to form words to respectfully decline the offering. I managed a small squeak. The candle nearest me flickered and dripped a bead of wax. The guests' curiosity closed in around me. Valko's gaze never wandered.

The room was silent. Not even the clink of a knife against porcelain disturbed the quiet.

The servant's brow gleamed with sweat. He darted a nervous glance over his shoulder to the emperor. The portly lady beside me lifted her napkin to her mouth and whispered, "You rise, take the meat, and then you bow, child."

I swallowed. My tongue felt like paper. "Thank you," I said to the servant, disregarding the woman, "but—"

He dished me a serving, cutting off my protest. My hands went clammy. Perhaps if I did as my neighbor suggested, everyone would go back to their meals and not bother to see if I took a bite.

I stood slowly and lowered in a curtsy. My unbound hair fell in front of my shoulders. How foolish of me to think it would be enough to satisfy the emperor.

He gave me a minuscule nod, but his mouth remained a straight line.

I sat back down. Wished for the nobles to return to their private conversations. Hoped Valko would be bored again.

Vapors of emotion crowded the air. Anger and envy and curiosity threaded around me like the laces of a corset, squeezing out my breath. I turned a pleading look to Anton. Mercifully, his gaze was upon me, but his hands were also white-fisted on the table. I tried to sift out his aura, interpret something from him and find a way out of this. Couldn't he whisper something to his brother to explain my peculiarities—what eating this meat would do to me?

He did not. As his hands curled tighter, he gave me a nod, almost like a command.

My shoulders fell as disappointment spooled through my body. He wasn't my ally. Once and for all, I needed to beat that into my head. I couldn't look to him for my rescue, like some fool of a maiden in a children's story.

I slid a morsel of meat onto my golden fork. My hand trembled. I opened my mouth, and the swan flesh touched my tongue. A burst of pain flowered above my heart. Vertigo gripped me. My emotions were a tumble. They flashed from soaring abandon to earth-rending sorrow and wrath. And for all that, I held my muscles rigid, forced my teeth to thrash the meat, to swallow it, to become one with the misery of death.

Satisfied, the nobles looked away and resumed their chatter.

Valko grinned. His face was blurry through my watering eyes.

I didn't let the tears fall until he grew bored of me. Until he turned to the general at his side, who said something that made him toss back his head with raucous laughter. My brows drew together. Was the emperor mocking me?

His merry mood heightened as the evening wore on, long after I'd swallowed the last excruciating morsel of meat. I'd never witnessed someone shift so quickly from one mood to the next. As more dishes were passed and more spirits drunk, as entertainers and jesters collided and stumbled over one another in rehearsed madness, the emperor clapped and laughed louder. Veins bulged at his forehead and neck.

Some part of his lightheartedness rang falsely. I kept swiping my tears, amazed and furious that his aura—which I'd first absorbed so easily—was now distant and strange. I couldn't relate to his humor. His mother had just died and been buried. Why wasn't he despondent, when that emotion was so largely what I felt? Could all this suffering be my own?

The swan flesh lingered like poison in my bloodstream and only made my mourning intensify. How could I laugh like the emperor when I knew a convent's worth of Auraseers had burned to death behind doors I'd locked? Did I really think if Valko forced a smile, I would as well?

Then I realized—perhaps the emperor's sentiment wasn't humor. Perhaps it was a mask. A mask for his own mourning. And perhaps a small part of his deception was meant to disguise his bafflement over me. A mere girl was now sovereign Auraseer, a position more important than all the ranks of guards standing in perfect formation outside the windows of this room.

A bit of peace descended on me, a bit of power. I clung to it. I didn't spare Valko or Anton another glance. And later, after the emperor had retired for the night and as I crossed the great hall at the beckoning of a nobleman who wanted to meet me, the prince stepped in my path to finally acknowledge my existence. His brows were hitched together as if in pain. All I thought of was the way he'd left me at the palace porch, how he hadn't intervened on my behalf when the emperor's meat was brought before me.

"Sonya . . . ," Anton began, not quite knowing what to say.

I startled with exaggerated surprise, as if I'd just noticed him. "Oh, forgive me, Your Imperial Highness! I had no idea you were here, nor indeed that you were still living."

His eyes narrowed in offense, then he released a heavy sigh. "You should understand that—"

I walked around him, cutting him off. I didn't care to listen to all the reasons why I was too lowly to be publicly acquainted with him.

I marched out of the great hall, and I didn't look back.

CHAPTER TEN

THAT NIGHT, AFTER MY MAIDS LEFT, I STOOD AT THE THRESH-
old between my antechamber and bedchamber and debated on
which room I should sleep in. The box bed seemed to stare like
a dark creature waiting to devour me whole. I could always lie
down on one of my couches. But then all the gilding and orna-
mentation of my antechamber might suffocate me just as surely
as the cramped interior of my bed. At length, I gathered my
blankets and pillows and arranged them on the floor beneath
my window. Perhaps the winter clouds would relent and permit
me a glimpse of the hidden starlight.

Removing Yuliya's figurine of Feya from the travel satchel,
I set it on the windowsill and said a prayer, not out of faith, but
because it would please my friend. The swan's death still trickled remnants of sorrow through my body. I supposed I should
be grateful. That agony had done more to ground me among
the nobles' auras than any thoughts of Anton or musings over

the emperor. This was why the Auraseers at the convent chose a painful form of emotional release, why the ceiling of the box bed was gouged with Izolda's claw marks. Nothing cut to the core of things like physical suffering.

I smoothed the ends of the black ribbon tied around my wrist. Yuliya's burial rites would be tomorrow. Hers and everyone else's. I would miss them. My heart beat a mournful rhythm.

I glanced at the blood spatter on the base of the wooden Feya. I had been careful not to touch it thus far. But now I wouldn't resist its call. Still on my knees from prayer, I reached up and closed my fingers around my friend's dried blood.

Blinding pain tore through me. I cried out and doubled over onto the cool planks of my bedroom floor. Gasping for breath, I stared at the knots in the grain as racking sensations worked their way through my body. Once I recovered, I sat up, gritted my teeth, and touched the statue again.

I shook and whimpered and forced myself to hold it longer. When Yuliya's pain began to ebb to euphoria, I let go. Perspiration wetted my brow as I gripped the idol a third time.

On and on I repeated this, only allowing myself to feel the darkest parts of my friend's death. If I touched her blood enough times, perhaps I'd feel a small measure of the pain every Auraseer and sestra endured as they died.

I never saw the starlight. Hours later, I lay splayed on my side, my breath faint, my heart slowed. My limbs tingled and mimicked Yuliya's blood loss. Tears pooled from my eyes as I reached once more for Feya. She rested toppled over, an arm's length from me. I stretched out, fingers trembling, almost touching her. Blackness crowded my vision. I caught the edge of the statue with my fingertip, but then my hand fell and the goddess rolled away. My eyes fluttered shut.

I didn't dream of Yuliya or the burning convent. I dreamed I had failed the emperor. As I was marched to the chopping block, Kira stood on the palace porch dressed in the too-large robes of the sovereign Auraseer. When the ax arced down for my head, my last glimpse of the world was Anton's dusk-blue cape, billowing as he turned away.

⁂

A gentle rapping on my door awakened me. The clouds were soft with gray morning light and thick with the promise of snow. I rubbed my head, as if that could scatter the lingering anxiety from my dream.

The rapping came again. I leaned up on my elbows. "Come in."

The door opened a handbreadth. In popped the heart-shaped face of a girl maybe a year or two older than me. "I've brought your breakfast, Sovereign Auraseer."

I sat up completely. My nightgown was a mess of wrinkles from all my writhing last night. "My name is Sonya." I couldn't bear the custom of everyone addressing me by my title. The girl curtsied in assent. I studied her, the way her eyes drooped in the corners, not with fatigue, but in a way that spoke kindness.

I took an immediate liking to her.

She opened the door wider, and her bowed lips curved in a timid smile, but I knew better. Vitality surged through my limbs, my back. The kink in my spine from a night spent on the floor was forgotten, as was my sorrow. This girl was brimming with *life*. I drank it in like I'd just crossed the desert sands of Abdara.

"I'm Pia," she said, stepping into the room. "Your serving maid," she added, and then rolled her eyes. "But I'm sure you already knew that."

I released a small laugh. I couldn't help it. Her happiness bubbled through me. "I can only feel your aura, not your station."

She giggled back. "I meant my uniform." She gestured to it like the evidence it must be to anyone with a noble upbringing— to anyone who had ever been *served* before. But to my eyes, all that differentiated Pia's clothes from my personal maids' was that the skirt beneath her apron was blue, not dark gray, and her hair kerchief was tied back in a different fashion.

"I'm afraid I don't know much about palace life," I admitted, "let alone which maid does what or the colors she wears. Lenka nearly bit off my head last night when I requested something particular about my food."

"Well, I can help you with that." Pia rocked back on her heels. "And never mind Lenka. She's all salt and sour milk. I gave up trying to make her smile ages ago." She slid back a loose pin holding her kerchief in place.

I watched everything Pia did with fascination. Something about her reminded me of Yuliya, but I couldn't place it. Perhaps it was simply my hope of having a friend at the palace. One friend had been enough at the convent. One had been enough with the Romska.

Pia smoothed her apron, growing a little self-conscious under my stare. "There's tea in your sitting room and a sweet bun." She bobbed her head over her shoulder to nudge me toward it. "Lenka will come in a quarter hour."

I stood and untwisted myself from my blanket.

"Did you really sleep down there?" She raised her brows.

I frowned at the box bed and gave her a dark look. "Wouldn't you?"

She snorted, then walked over and picked up my blankets and pillow. "Well, let's at least hide the trail. Lenka thinks it's a great honor to sleep in that bed." Pia stuffed her load past the bed's small door. "We don't want her forcing you into a corset today out of vengeance."

"You know about that?" I followed her into my antechamber where a samovar of tea and the promised bun were waiting on a lacquered tray inlaid with mother-of-pearl.

"Rumor spreads fast here. It isn't every day we get a new Auraseer, or a girl who would dare present herself to the emperor without pinching in her waist and pushing up her curves." She chuckled. "I couldn't wait to meet you."

I felt color stain my cheeks. I appreciated Pia's open attitude toward me, but I doubted anyone else in the palace found my eccentricities so endearing. I sat on the couch and nibbled at my bun as she went to pour my tea. "What else have you heard?"

Pia tipped back the samovar when my cup was half full and glanced at the door leading to the hallway, as if Lenka might walk in at any moment. She bit the corner of her lip. "Is it true Prince Anton brought you here on a white stallion?"

"Yes," I said carefully, "though it was a mare."

She sighed and sank beside me on the couch, obliterating what small level of formality remained between us. "Was it very romantic?"

"What do you mean?"

"I was told you rode *together* on the horse." Her eyes searched mine. "He's handsome, don't you think? And his story is *so tragic*."

"Tragic?" I lifted my cup. Did she mean the loss of his mother?

"You know . . . how he was raised thinking he would rule Riaznin one day."

I choked on my tea. "Oh?"

Pia's brow creased. "You really don't know?"

I shook my head and clutched my throat so I wouldn't cough again. "Isn't Valko the older brother?"

She scooted in closer. "Yes, but the boys grew up separately. There was always someone trying to assassinate or usurp Emperor Izia. So to protect his dynasty, he sent the princes to live far apart from each other—and from Torchev. Valko was only six when he left the palace, and Anton just five."

"Why not keep them together?"

She shrugged as if it was simple. "To make sure there was

still an heir in case one of them was killed."

I gaped at her. "But why did Anton think he would be emperor?" For some reason my heart pounded faster. "Both boys lived."

"No, they didn't. Not according to the tale Anton was told—that all Riaznin was told. For years, the people of the empire believed Valko's carriage was overtaken on the road to his hidden manor. He was discovered, and he was murdered." Pia's eyes were as round as my tea saucer.

I searched her aura for any lurking humor and found none. "That's impossible."

Enraptured by the horror of it, she touched my arm. Her energy heightened and pulsed through my veins. "Another boy was murdered in his place."

"Wait . . . I *do* know this story. The changeling prince?" The Romska had a song about it. Tosya used to sing it to me. I'd assumed the tragedy happened long ago, when Riaznin was young. I hadn't even been sure it was true.

Pia nodded. "They say the murder was staged to protect Izia's eldest child, so that no further attempts would be made on his life."

I was beginning to understand. "Meanwhile Anton thought he was the heir."

"Until his father passed away, and Valko claimed the throne. Then Anton realized the full weight of what his father had done."

I set my cup down and leaned back, processing the incredible story. By his actions, Emperor Izia had made it clear Anton's life was less valued than Valko's. Any would-be assassins would have sought out Anton as a child, while the true heir remained safe.

I thought of every moment I'd shared with Anton, remembered his underlying bitterness whenever he spoke of his brother, his despair over the death of the dowager empress. Their time together must have been precious and brief. How often had she been able to visit him in his seclusion?

Pia settled back beside me. "Thus the tragic prince."

I fidgeted with my nightgown and folded a length of the skirt into pleats. "How can anyone be sure Valko isn't the imposter?"

"No one can be. That's why his life is so endangered, why he was almost assassinated, though his poor mother died in his place. It's why *you're* so important. Whenever he is in the nobles' favor, they insist he is Izia's eldest son. He looks so much like his father, the same distinguished brow, the same confidence. But when he is difficult—which is often," she added under her breath, "the debate continues over the changeling prince."

The door opened from the hallway. Lenka entered but halted when she saw my servant and me reclining side by side on the couch. Pia sprang to her feet and tidied her kerchief.

"What is the meaning of this?" Lenka frowned at Pia. "Haven't you finished your breakfast?" she added, turning on me.

I shrugged, already bristling from her irritable aura.

"Well, it's too late now," Lenka said. "I'm to prepare you at once to attend the emperor."

I exchanged a glance with Pia. My mind was still awhirl from all she had told me.

"You can take that tray back to the kitchen," my head maid said to Pia, who gave me a sorry look that I could not finish my meal. "Go on." Lenka clapped at her.

I was about to roll my eyes, when Pia did it for me. My mouth sealed shut as I suppressed a laugh. Did she have to leave so soon?

Once she walked out the door, her liveliness drained out of my body. I slumped and felt the ache in my spine and the loss of Yuliya. My gut twisted at the prospect of having to spend more time in the emperor's presence.

While Lenka laid out my dress, undergarments, stockings, and slippers, my gaze wandered over the fine furnishings of my antechamber and the barrenness of my bedchamber beyond. Izolda had left a strange mark in her wake. She was almost as mysterious as the tale of the changeling prince. Had Izolda, as an Auraseer, ever determined what the nobles could not—if Valko was Valko, the authentic heir to the empire? Had she ever sensed any deceit in him that could prove otherwise?

The bigger question was, could I?

I spent the day in the emperor's shadow, and the next day and the next, until weeks passed and I feared I would vanish into smoke for how little I was spoken to, how easily I was forgotten. It was almost as if Valko was going out of his way to prove his disinterest after my clumsy acceptance of his shared meat.

The nobles followed the emperor's lead where I was concerned. The novelty of the new sovereign Auraseer was fleeting. I was reduced to the new female trailing the emperor to meeting after meeting, meal after meal, sitting in a corner and struggling not to fall asleep. Valko's apathy leaked into me like a disease, and the fatigue of it all made my footsteps heavy. I did not even have the mystery of him to stimulate me anymore. If he was anyone other than the eldest son of Emperor Izia, he hid the clues with a master's precision.

In the wake of the dowager empress's death, I searched for any valid threats from the nobles, not just the dark grumblings I felt when the men lost too many rubles in a game of quadrille, or when the young wives of the dukes tossed the emperor secret glances, only to have Valko stare back at them impassively. The duchesses' eyes would slit like cats' or droop like puppies', their auras half tempting me to gnash my teeth or heave a sigh. None of it was enough to make me think anyone was capable of causing Valko harm. If they were, surely I'd feel it on impulse. I'd scream or do something more than feel the drudgery of my existence. Nothing seemed capable of moving me. Valko's energy, indifferent though it was, held the power to rein mine. And late at night, when I couldn't sleep or bear the torture of touching Feya's statue, I found other ways to sustain my misery.

I took to walking the palace corridors after midnight, as I

had done in the convent when Yuliya was sick and I had no one to keep me company. During my days here in Torchev, at least the emperor's apathy could keep me distracted from my guilt over the deaths at the convent. But at night, in my solitude, I was left to the full throes of my remorse. If I was honest with myself, perhaps my exhaustion and gloom was just as unbreakable as the emperor's. Maybe his energy combined with mine to form an iron fence no other auras in the palace could penetrate. At least it stopped me from wanting to curl up in a ball every time I dined with the assembly of nobles in the great hall. As for the dreaded prospect of being forced to eat meat again, that excruciating experience had yet to repeat itself.

My quarter hour at breakfast with Pia helped me wake up every morning, helped me finally fall asleep, knowing I would see her the following day. She was sunlight. Clean air. Unbridled joy. I soon discovered why: she was in love.

Her eyes followed a palace guard with flaxen hair—a guard often assigned to me. Sometimes he was stationed outside my rooms when it was time to escort me to the emperor. Whenever he so much as smiled at Pia, she glided across my floor as if skating across a frozen pond, her giddiness making me twirl along with her. The day I made her confess her feelings for him out loud, she laughed. "I was wondering when you'd guess! I thought you'd sense it in me the first day we met."

"I knew you were elated." I smiled. "I just didn't know his name was Yuri."

A pretty flush rose to her cheeks, and she held up a

bandaged finger. "Whenever he speaks to me, I end up burning my hands in the kitchens."

"Does he come to you there?"

"Oh, no, he would never! Cook would rake him over the coals. I just get so muddle-headed, recalling every word of our conversations, every look he ever gives me."

I threw a pillow at her. "You're hopeless."

She giggled and clutched the pillow to her breast. "At least I admit to my madness. You won't even talk to me about Anton."

I rolled my eyes. She was still fixated on the idea that there was something between the prince and me, when the truth was, we weren't even on speaking terms. Whenever I rounded a corner and happened upon him—even if he was at the far end of a spacious room—he stiffened and found some excuse to leave promptly. It didn't matter. I'd have done the same if he hadn't beaten me to it. I ignored the way my stomach tightened with anxiety upon our fleeting encounters. The sensation couldn't possibly be coming from him. How could I make him nervous when he scarcely even noticed me?

The worst was when Valko required his brother's presence. I'd learned Anton held the office of viceroy over Perkov. The southwest province bordered the Bayacs, the mountain range separating Riaznin from Estengarde. Although Anton was viceroy, the title was stripped of any ruling power. He served as more of a councilor for that small but important area. I'd guessed Valko had bequeathed him the position as a public show of goodwill, for I never sensed any true sentiment within the emperor for Anton.

Sometimes the brothers had to meet and discuss the border wars, disturbances with the peasants, or concerns over the long famine and what could be done to help the people. I would sit with them, coiled tight like a spring ready to burst from faulty clockwork. The tension was palpable, though I could never determine its origin—if the discord I felt was between them or between me and Anton. Every time our shoulders brushed, he'd flinch. My body would flush with heat until Anton cleared his throat, breathed deeply, and scooted his chair another inch away. Twice his hand wandered to the left pocket of his kaftan, as if he guarded something valuable from me.

I remembered the letter from our journey, the letter regarding Morva's Eve that he had passed to the piercingly blue-eyed man named Feliks in the city. The occasion was a few weeks away in early spring on the night before the festival celebrating the goddess of fertility.

What were Anton and Feliks planning? Would the nobleman with the amethyst ring join them, or was he only the first messenger of the letter? Did the emperor know about it? Based on Anton's covertness and how he'd tried to hide the letter from me, I doubted he wanted his brother involved. But wasn't it my duty to relay any suspicious behavior to the emperor?

My gaze drifted to Anton. We were obliged to suffer through another long council meeting, but his aura was nothing like bored. His intentness and fervent energy awoke me from my tedium. He had his arm stretched over a map on the table, his brows drawn together in earnest as he named the villages near the Bayac Mountains that had experienced the most hardship from famine and the Black Death that took Emperor Izia's life years ago—the villages that had also lost many of their able men to the border wars. Anton proposed we send a portion of Torchev's excess regiments to reinforce the lines against Estengarde and start up a ministry of agriculture to consult with the peasants over which crops could be cultivated in harsher conditions, how to combat the pests that surfaced in abundance once the snows melted, and the best way to rotate plots of soil so the earth could renew its nutrients.

As I listened to Anton, I wondered . . . could I betray him to his brother? He seemed to care far more for Riaznin than Valko, who had spent most of the meeting tracing and retracing the Jinshan River designating the border between his empire and Shengli, our eastern neighbor, rich in jade and emeralds. As the emperor's eyes lingered on that river, his melancholy of the last few weeks lifted. Now his aura made my stomach groan with a sensation close to hunger.

Anton moved next to the topic of serfdom and leaned his knuckled hands on the table. A lock of hair fell over his eye, reminding me of his tousled look on our journey. I had slept in the same room as this man. And when I'd dozed off in the troika, he'd laid his mother's blanket over me.

Would it be treason if I *didn't* betray him?

I examined the prince as I had done that day in the troika, when he helped me overcome the auras of the commoners in the city square. My gaze followed the slope of his nose in profile. The faint crinkles around his eyes, proof he sometimes smiled. The small mole alongside the upper bridge of his nose, his only imperfection, my favorite part of his face. Somehow that little flaw made him appear younger, more like the boy he was underneath the political roles his life had thrust upon him.

An ember sparked in my belly and curled warmth throughout me, from toes to fingertips to ears. The sun cut through the clouds outside, illuminating the prince in a rainbow of color from the stained-glass window. Dust floated around him like gold.

"Riaznin has enslaved a portion of our peasants as serfs for over five centuries," Anton said. "In the last fifty years, that number has multiplied to a quarter of our population. Not only is serfdom inhumane, it is a danger to us. There is talk of revolt." Anton seemed to lose his trail of thought when he caught me gazing at him, my brows lifted, my spine straight as an arrow. The warmth inside me expanded with a tumble of escalating emotion, too rapid-fire to decipher. A little frown tugged at his lips, and he cleared his throat, hazarding a glance at Valko.

I looked at the emperor and froze to find his eyes soft on mine, his finger removed from the river of Shengli. I swallowed.

"What is your name again?" he asked. Across the table, his councilors turned their heads to me, as if just noticing I was in the room.

My hands slid under my thighs. "Sonya Petrova."

"Do you like it here, Sonya?"

I blinked. The sunlight was in my eyes. "Sometimes."

He laughed, his boredom breaking up like a glacier sliding off a mountain.

In response, a smile flickered to my mouth before I could push his sudden mirth away. "I worry for those I left behind at the convent," I said, taking advantage of this, our first conversation together. "The peasants in the surrounding villages are unhappy, too. Perhaps . . ." I looked briefly to Anton. "Perhaps you could discuss that, as well."

Valko laughed again. His grin lingered like I'd said the most amusing thing. "Yes, yes. By all means, let's discuss it." He scooted forward and put his elbows on the table.

I pressed my lips together, torn between emotions. Was he making fun of me? Or had I just awakened him from a deep slumber? Did he truly care about Ormina?

"There's nothing to discuss," Anton said. He folded the map into hard creases.

"What do you mean?" Anger lodged in my breast. I shifted out of the sunlight to see him better. "You promised—"

"The convent has been fortified and food rations sent weeks ago to tide the peasants over until spring." His voice was low and clipped, his jaw muscle tight. He sat down and scooped together his papers, stuffing them into a portfolio. As he bent down to set it on the floor, he muttered for my ears only, "I told you I would see it done." His meaning was clear—*Not now, Sonya.*

Valko's gaze flickered between us. "I have no memory of

this. Was it arranged without my consent?"

Anton busied himself with a loose button on his kaftan. "I didn't see any reason to trouble you."

"Ormina is not part of your province," Valko said.

"You sent me to bring back an Auraseer," Anton snapped, and released a heavy breath. "While I was there, I could not help but see the state of things. As you are tasked with much, I was only trying to alleviate you by helping with a simple matter I could manage myself."

"*My* Auraseers are not a simple matter."

"They are not yours." Anton clenched his teeth. "At least they should not be." A breadth of three fingers separated our legs. The space bubbled with energy.

At the prince's heated declaration, the room fell silent. The councilors' eyes collectively shifted from Anton to Valko. A shadowy swirl of tension mounted inside me. My muscles went stiff with it. My hands trembled beneath my legs. The tension twisted into something deeper, uglier. The sun through the stained-glass window, which had made Anton appear so gilded and beautiful, had an equally mesmerizing, though much darker, effect upon Valko, as his face caught in a patch of unsettling crimson.

All the warnings Anton had given me about his brother came back with full force. The prince had drawn out the emperor as a volatile, heartless creature, though I'd yet to sense those things in him. The subtle Valko of the past few weeks had been tiresome, but at least stable and safe. I could stay alive as sovereign Auraseer with such an emperor. But not with this beast rising within him.

What had Anton unleashed? What had I?

I bit down on my tongue and shrank back. My body shook with the emperor's fury.

"And why, pray tell," Valko began calmly, "should they not be my Auraseers?"

Anton's gaze traveled to my shoulder, not quite arriving at my eyes. "I only meant to say they should be a given a choice to serve you. Most would do it gladly." He spoke carefully, clearly realizing he was now treading on thin ice.

"A choice?" Valko laughed. "Why would any woman—any *girl*"—he flitted a hand at me—"want for more than the life she is given at my side? Why must a *choice* come into play for such a privilege?"

The prince looked down and folded his hands on the table. Pressure crackled inside me like dry lightning as he fought not to speak.

"Sonya," Valko addressed me with the same falsely collected tone. His gray eyes shone like a wolf's. "If you had a choice, would you serve me?"

My heart thumped out of rhythm. How should I answer? His temper, roiling inside me, begged me to lash out at him, to declare I would be far away, to the south with the Romska for the winter, or perhaps with a mother I had scarcely known. A father. A brother. My muscles tensed with fury over everything I'd been denied.

I drew a sharp breath, ready to attack Valko with my account of how unfairly Auraseers were treated, and then I checked myself. Kira's and Dasha's innocent faces seemed to watch me from afar. I didn't want to be the weight that broke the branch. In the past and under the influence of others' auras, I had made rash decisions that caused great harm. I'd vowed to restrain myself for Kira's and Dasha's sakes. If Valko's anger fell on me, would it be enough to sentence me to death? I didn't want to test him, to find out if he could be that cruel. Unshed tears clouded my vision as I strained to muzzle myself, to not say anything that would condemn me, but the emperor's aura tangled me with rage.

"Leave her out of this," Anton said.

Valko's mouth stretched wide into a satisfied grin. He'd found some kind of proof in Anton then—what, I didn't understand.

"Perhaps, brother," Valko said, "you wish they were *your* Auraseers." Anton shook his head, but Valko pressed on. "Perhaps you think *you* should be emperor."

I cringed. This was it. The moment Anton had warned me about. The moment Valko would snap. I gripped the seat of my chair and braced myself for the blow.

"Is that what this is?" Valko stood in a rush. His chair skidded back and toppled over. He flung his hand out to point at the table, as if Anton's map and documents still lay upon it. "Was this a great show of your competence? Were you seeking to impress my councilors? Show them what you would do if you had my power? I am sorry if you were coddled to believe you were entitled to a different life, but *I am the emperor by birthright!*" Spittle flew from his mouth as he shouted. "The eldest son of Emperor Izia. *I* alone was born to rule!" He jabbed a finger to his chest. "And *I lived!*"

Nobody in the room dared move or speak. Anton's nostrils flared. His gaze was fastened to the table.

"Are you scheming to take my place?" Valko prodded him. "Was it you who killed our mother, hoping to kill me?"

That was enough for Anton. He sprang to his feet to meet his brother's accusation.

"Stop!" I jumped up between them, unable to control my emotions with both of them so enraged. "Prince Anton did not harm the empress."

Valko's teeth were bared. He was determined to make Anton confess to a crime he didn't commit. I feared he would somehow find false evidence and have him executed.

"You must believe me!" I said, and pushed the emperor back when he tried to seize his brother. His anger fluctuated with amazement. He surely wasn't accustomed to anyone touching him so freely. "I can prove it."

He huffed. "Impossible."

"On the journey from Ormina to Torchev, Anton brought with him a blanket belonging to the dowager empress. Mossy green with embroidered flowers. Do you know the one?"

Valko nodded. "She had it on her when she choked to death from poison." His gaze hardened and moved past me to Anton, as if this were damnable proof of his involvement.

"There was blood on the threads," I said, "and through them, I felt her dying aura."

Valko's brow hitched. "What do you mean?"

"I am gifted—or cursed, however you may see it—with an enhanced ability to feel the last energy of someone's soul if I touch them—their flesh, their hair, their blood."

His eyes narrowed. "The meat I offered you from my table?"

"Yes." I felt him descending back within the realm of stability. I needed to keep him there. "Also the fur on my robes and headdress, which is why I never wear them."

"Their deaths pain you?" he asked, a note of sympathy in his voice that, for a moment, rendered me silent.

"Yes," I replied softly.

"You felt my mother's pain?"

"Yes."

His gaze lowered to the floor. Behind me, Anton placed his hand on my arm. Something sad and lovely graced my heart at his touch, but I resisted it. I couldn't lose focus. I gently batted him away without turning my gaze from the emperor. "Were you with your mother when she died?" I asked him.

"He was," Anton answered. "And so was I."

I inhaled with understanding. "Then her last feelings were for both of you. And they were neither bitter nor accusatory.

They were not shocked with betrayal nor filled with the malice of vengeance." My voice wavered with emotion. "They were filled with the most beautiful and tender love I have ever experienced."

The wind whistled outside, rattling the intricate panes of the window. The stained glass formed the picture of a coat of arms, and on it, a blossomed rose inside a red sun, the symbol of the Ozerov dynasty, their family. My breath came easier. The emperor's and Anton's heads were bowed. For now, the storm between them had blown over.

Councilor Ilyin—the eldest, with a streaked white beard, but sharp and youthful eyes—broke the silence. "Forgive me, Sovereign Auraseer, but the fact that Empress Katarina loved her sons cannot absolve them from involvement in her death. She would have not known who poisoned her cup."

I shot him a penetrating glance. Did he mean to stir up Valko's suspicion? To what end? For all I knew, this old man had laced the cup with poison himself. Why, any of them could have. I was only beginning to understand the hidden agendas at the palace and my role here.

I searched Councilor Ilyin's aura by studying myself, my body, for what I absorbed of any of his intensified physical reactions. A headache flowered at my temple and I had a pain in my hip. As for my emotions, they only revealed the old man's fatigue and dwindling patience. Nothing hinted he might be guilty of murder.

"The prince is innocent," I said resolutely. I hoped to

frighten the councilor, to halt him in whatever game he might be playing. He was likely a better artist at concealing his aura than any noble at court.

"How do you know?" Councilor Ilyin asked, as if condescending to a child.

I stepped closer to Anton. "I spent two days with this man fresh after the death of his mother. I had every opportunity to see into the depths of him, just as I see into you now. Prince Anton did not kill the empress, nor seek to harm the emperor. Neither does he wish to take his brother's crown."

The words tumbled out of my mouth, fierce and unyielding, whether I knew the truth of my latest claim or not. I wasn't sure why I insisted on defending Anton, only that I felt in my bones that he needed to live. I wouldn't have anyone endangering him.

"Young though I may be," I said, "I am the emperor's Auraseer, and you must learn to trust my word."

In my periphery, I felt Anton's gaze, solemn and amazed.

Councilor Ilyin's aged lips pursed, but he didn't badger me any further. The emperor, the prince, and I awkwardly took our seats, while everyone did a masterful job of pretending nothing had gone awry. The meeting continued, moving on to the issue of immigrants from Abdara and the question of yet again raising the taxes on imported goods. The cord of tension was still taut between the two brothers, but at least more flexible.

I spent the rest of the meeting under the weight of the emperor's stare. I wondered how he saw me now—in painted light, golden dust motes floating above my head, as I had seen his brother, or as a new threat to his throne and a new ally to Anton? From the way my skin flushed with fire and ice and how my heart beat quickly then seized up in my chest, I feared I wasn't merely one simple thing any longer. I wasn't a girl to be forgotten, a girl dismissed to a corner.

I'd captured the keen interest of the emperor, for better or for worse. And only time would tell if I'd made a mistake by coming out of hiding.

CHAPTER ELEVEN

"THEY THINK I'M AN IMBECILE." PIA SHOVED THE LAST FORK-
ful of apple sharlotka in her mouth. We both sat on the floor of
my antechamber so we wouldn't spill any dusting sugar on my
velvet couches. Instead, it sprinkled from our plates into the
weave of my nightgown and Pia's apron. She'd surprised me
with the late-night treat just as I was on the brink of my nightly
penance with the statue of Feya.

"I'm sure that isn't true." I licked a morsel of cooked apple
off my finger.

"It is! You don't understand. Even Yuri's mother can read.
Her husband taught her."

Pia had spent the last half hour rehashing her ill-fated visit
to meet Yuri's parents earlier this afternoon when she had a
rare day off of work. Apparently Yuri's father was a tutor in
Torchev for a nobleman's three daughters. The eldest was Pia's
age and also smitten with Yuri. Her father promised to pay

for Yuri's commission to become a second-ranking colonel in the infantry, a rise in station that would make him eligible for the nobleman's daughter's hand. This offer was exceptional to Yuri's humble parents, but Yuri remained adamant in his plans to court Pia, who was convinced his parents saw her as only a lowly kitchen maid.

She sighed and scraped her fork against her empty dish. "I should have brought the whole cake."

Taking her plate away, I squeezed her hands. "If they could feel a *tenth* of who you really are, they would have no reservations about you marrying their son."

"Yes, well, do me a favor and sneeze on them. Maybe some of your ability will transfer and they'll see me as more than an illiterate tart."

"Tart?" I laughed and tilted my head. Then I quickly sobered. "Do you mean . . . ? Have you and Yuri—?"

"No!" she said, quickly glancing away. Her aura warmed, and the heat rose to my cheeks the same time hers stained red.

I studied her, while I failed to suppress a grin. "You're lying."

"I'm not!" She pulled back so our hands were no longer touching. Her energy waned at the broken connection, but from the strong urge I had to tuck my knees to my chest and burrow into myself, I sensed she was concealing something.

"I can feel what you're feeling, you know." I wiggled my fingers in the air like I was working dark magic.

She managed to simultaneously giggle and groan with exasperation. "It's impossible to be your friend!" Her dimples deepened, and she gave me a playful shove in the shoulder. "I can't hide anything from you."

"Friends don't hide things," I replied, as if this was the root of all wisdom. "Or at least they go about hiding them together. Friends *share* secrets."

She groaned again and buried her face in her hands. Some of her hair tumbled loose from her kerchief.

I nudged her leg as I felt some of her humor give way to trepidation. "It's all right, I won't tell anyone."

She looked up, rubbing her still-flushed cheeks. "Very well. But you must never let Yuri know."

I frowned. "You mean it wasn't him?"

She shook her head in bewilderment. "I have no idea how I even caught Valko's eye."

My jaw unhinged. "Valko?" Had I heard her right? "His Imperial Majesty Valko? The lord emperor of all Riaznin Valko?"

Pia's eyebrows peaked in a way that said *guilty*. "It was months ago. I doubt he even remembers my name." She wrinkled her nose. "I *hope* he doesn't." Retrieving her plate, she collected the leftover dusting sugar onto her finger and sighed. "I really should have brought more cake."

I considered her. The tingling in my palms revealed her anxiety, but my heart didn't pang with unrequited love. "So . . . you don't care for him?"

With all the solemnness Yuliya used to give in prayer, Pia said, "I love Yuri."

"And you *never* cared for Valko?" I couldn't place why I needed to know this. Perhaps the role of being the emperor's guardian made me feel this rush of protectiveness for him. Is that what I was feeling? Protective?

She shrugged. "I'm required to esteem him as any servant must dutifully regard her monarch—surely the same way *you* regard him."

I picked at a minuscule tear in my nightgown. How *did* I regard the emperor? He was arrogant, that was a certainty. Indifferent to others. He also had a reserve of dark passion; I saw it in the council meeting earlier today. Of course he sought out someone bright like Pia, the same way I did. "Then why did you give yourself to Valko?" It was all I could do not to reach out and feel the pulse of my friend's wrist to determine if her quickening heartbeat was overpowering mine, or if my own primal curiosity was to blame for the heat prickling through my body, making my toes curl and flex.

"Give myself?" Pia burst out laughing. "Oh, Sonya! It was a *kiss*."

A strange sense of relief washed over me and eased the tension from my muscles. "You mean . . . that's all that happened between you?"

She nodded. "And only once, I promise!" Biting her lip, she leaned forward as if this were her darkest confession. "You know Yuri holds my heart, but I'll admit even he has never kissed me with such rapture. You don't understand how breathless the emperor can make you feel, how flattering it is to have his sole and private attention, how his gentle esteem causes you to imagine yourself the equal of his high rank and importance. I don't know what I would have done if Lenka hadn't walked in on us!"

I snorted. "No wonder Lenka has it out for you. If you'd told Valko 'no,' you would have saved yourself the wrath of the most contemptible woman in this palace. Besides, even an emperor can't have everything he desires."

Pia arched a brow as she considered me. "Would *you* have told him no?"

My pulse fluctuated again. Perhaps the sweetness of the cake had reached my bloodstream. "Of course."

"Hmph."

A soft knocking came at my door. Three raps, quick in succession. I startled. Pia's eyes popped wide. Had Lenka returned? She'd already dressed me for the night and brushed out my hair. Besides, she always just walked in. My antechamber didn't have a lock.

The rapping came again, a little louder and faster. I stood while Pia scrambled to collect the dishes onto her tray. Lenka would be furious that Pia had come to pay me a visit, even though it wasn't against any rules I could think of. But when I placed my hand on the door latch, my insides flooded with an energy distinctly *not* belonging to my head maid.

Once Pia was standing, tray in hand, I cracked open the door and set my eye to the gap.

My breath caught, for it was Anton who stood outside, his

face lost in the shadows between two pools of light from the corridor sconces. His kaftan was gone, though he still wore his boots, reaching above his knees, his loose shirt haphazardly tucked into his breeches. His hair was mussed as if he'd spent the last hour running his hands through it. I'd never seen him so distressed, so *human*.

"May I come in?" he asked. His voice, naturally rich and low in timbre, always rumbled with volume, making it scarcely possible for him to whisper.

I hesitated, my hand floating to the ribbons at my nightgown's scooped neckline. Wasn't it improper to let a man into my rooms when I was alone? Especially a man I was still angry with for going out of his way to ignore me. But then I wasn't alone. I glanced back at Pia. A huge smile broke across her face. *Anton?* she mouthed. I fought an eye roll.

"Please, Sonya," the prince said. When I returned my attention to him, he glanced toward the emperor's rooms. "Let me in. I must speak with you."

The pained look on his face twisted the fibers of my heart and made me relent. I groaned with frustration for allowing myself to pity him, but that didn't stop me from stepping back to grant him entrance. He strode past me and shut the door behind him. Then he noticed Pia. "Oh, I beg your pardon." He gave her an awkward little bow of acknowledgment. I bit down a grin that he should excuse himself or be flustered by a maid.

"I was just leaving," she replied, and dipped into a curtsy. Anton opened the door for her and as she exited, she waggled her eyebrows at me in the brief moment before he shut the door again.

This time I did roll my eyes.

Anton proceeded to pace about my antechamber. He rubbed at his jaw and mouth. He raked his hands through his disheveled hair. I stood barefoot in the center of the room, my nightgown fluttering as his movements stirred the air. His gaze was cast on the floor, on anything but me.

"What is it?" I asked. Now that Pia's radiant aura was gone, Anton's swept into mine. My nerves tangled together. I didn't know if I should sit or stand. I had the growing urge to hide away in my bedchamber, but I couldn't make myself leave. Why was the prince so distraught?

He wandered to my tiled furnace and absently kicked at the grate. His breaths came quickly. His fingers clenched into tight fists. My emotions expanded then contracted in a dizzying cycle I couldn't interpret.

"Anton?"

He whirled on me, eyes on my gown, not my face. "How could you be so foolish?"

I flinched. "What have I done?"

He laughed forlornly and pinched the bridge of his nose. "You can never defend me to Valko like that, do you understand?" He turned back to the grate and kicked it harder.

My lips parted in astonishment. My mind churned sluggishly to comprehend his anger. "I only spoke what I knew to be true. Would you have me be false?"

"I would have you take care for your life!" His voice rose, and mine rose with it, grafting onto his heated emotions.

"You should take care with yours! The emperor accused you of murder today—of treason. Even princes hang for such a crime."

"I did not kill my mother."

"I believe you! I also want your brother to believe. I want peace between you." A heaviness, like a full winter's snowfall, fell over me. Anton finally met my gaze, the anger snuffed out of him. Something about his helpless expression and the depth of his sorrow made me forgive him for ever disregarding me. Why would he come here like this, be so upset, if he wasn't concerned with my well-being?

"Sonya, don't you see?" he said. "I will never have peace with my brother. And you cannot make it so."

The fire snapped behind the grate. Embers flickered in the air. I wrapped my arms around myself, but not because I was cold. I felt hurt. No matter how much I felt the prince's concern at the moment, I couldn't shake the feeling that I had displeased him. I tried not to let it affect me, but that was becoming impossible. Today, as he spoke in the council chamber, I saw a measure of his greatness, his devotion to the welfare of Riaznin. He would make a fine emperor, though it was treasonous to think it. Was it wrong that part of me wanted to be just as great, just as noble in the cause of helping the empire, in helping anyone—even him? So despite my bitterness at his barging into my rooms to tell me I'd disappointed him yet again, his words stung.

"Why did you come here, Anton? Why did you say I must take care for my life?"

His eyes, having found mine, didn't leave. They glowed warm and soft, illuminated by the candles. He shifted closer, and my heart pounded—in warning, in yearning, in the pangs of his frustration with me. He stopped only inches away. I swayed a little on my feet, caught between wanting to step back and wanting to move forward into the swirl of energy surrounding him.

"My brother craves power," he said. "Above all, power over me."

I struggled to grasp the meaning behind his words. His scent drifted nearer, dark and masculine, yet also fragile like dried pine needles, like a bed of kindling. All he awaited was a match.

"What does that have to do with me?" I asked, my arms still wrapped around my chest, my fingers curled around my elbows.

Anton's brows gathered together, rife with the pained look he wore a moment ago. My stomach tightened and warmed, as if I'd tasted something bittersweet and wanted more of it. Pulled by invisible threads, my gaze dropped to his lips. The warmth within me blossomed. A rush of blood trailed up to my neck and face. My balance faltered again. My eyes flitted to his, brown and deep and full of endless mystery.

Did this overpowering feeling come from him? Or was this me, enamored beyond reason with a prince whom I never ceased to annoy and disappoint? I searched his gaze. Did he still see me as a burden, the Auraseer he so reluctantly fetched from the convent?

The tendons in his neck remained taut as he swallowed. "Valko has asked that you attend him tonight in his rooms."

My nerves flashed with ice. My hands trembled. My heart pounded in alarm. "Why?" I asked. My thoughts rushed to the conversation I'd just shared with Pia—how the emperor's charm had been irresistible to her. How she didn't want to stop kissing him.

"My brother craves power," Anton said again. His next words came softly, the whisper that had eluded him earlier. His eyes looked lost, helpless. "You should not have defended me, Sonya."

I couldn't breathe, couldn't comprehend any of this. "And he gave *you* this errand to summon me?"

He shook his head miserably, in denial of the truth. "Yes."

I stumbled back and turned away, my legs stiff and stunned. "What does he expect from me?" I had to be the youngest Auraseer the palace had seen in a century—perhaps ever. Had Valko found more carnal uses for my position? A wave of nausea washed through my gut. Anton hadn't answered my question. "Tell him I am ill," I commanded.

"That won't satisfy him."

I spun around, my nightgown swishing at my ankles. "I did not come here for this!" I shook with rage. "He owns enough of me." A sob broke through my words.

"Then don't let him take more." Anton's jaw locked.

"How?" My palms pressed to my temples with desperation. "How can I deny the *emperor*?"

Kira's and Dasha's faces haunted me again, as they always

did when I wanted to run away and never return. I couldn't fail in my duty, however sordid it was becoming.

"Did you do what I asked of you?" Anton said. "Did you find a place within yourself, belonging to no one else?"

I shrugged as panic choked me. "It's not that simple."

He gripped me by the shoulders. "There is strength in you, Sonya. I saw it when you came to your friend's defense at the convent, when you refused your furs, when you hesitated to eat the emperor's meat in a room full of gluttonous nobles. Valko's passions are strong, but you can break through any hold he places on you." Anton lifted his brows, bending closer as he tried to reassure me. "Romska boys must have tried to kiss you. What did you do then?"

My hands flew up in exasperation. "I kissed them back!"

Something dark passed over his features. A spark of jealousy? He blinked it away before I could test the pulse of his aura, before I could hold it inside me to see how it made me feel. "Listen to me," he said, forcing himself into a tenuous state of calm that had no strength to soothe my nerves. "I believe in you. You can appear meek, but also draw a line as to what your relationship will be."

I released a heavy breath. "You warned me of your brother. Do you have enough faith in him to respect me if I show restraint?"

"If I cannot have faith in him regarding that, then I've given up on him completely."

He didn't directly answer my question, but I could see he

wanted to say yes, that he longed to find some portion of confidence in Valko. It didn't matter what his reply would have been, however. It didn't change the fact I had no choice but to yield to the emperor's request.

"I will go," I said numbly, though there was something Anton wasn't telling me about the threat of this evening. I suspected it had to do with the danger I'd find myself in if Valko were to form a strong attachment to me. I resolved to ensure that wouldn't happen.

Anton sighed with resignation, his hands still on my shoulders. "Remember what I said. Meekness, yet firmness of character. Keep your visit brief and stay grounded. Think on something else—anything but him."

With hollow eyes I stared at the prince and wished he could come with me. He'd distracted me from the throngs of people in the city square. He stood a chance of distracting me from his brother.

"When you leave his rooms," he continued, "knock three times on my door so I know you are safe. I won't come here and impose on you again."

I nodded like a girl being sent to the gallows.

Anton angled to retrieve something from his pocket—an antiquated key. "Take this." He set the key in my palm and folded my fingers around it. A fierce desire to protect him flooded through me. Or was it *his* yearning to protect me? I longed to take comfort in the sensation, but how could I when

Anton had been unable to prevent this private meeting with the emperor in the first place?

"These rooms once belonged to my great-aunts," he went on. "The chambers are interconnected, a secret long forgotten. The room beside yours is a ballet practice room, no longer in use. If Valko persists after tonight, you may wish to evade him by simply being absent. In the future, he may not use me as his guarantee to bring you to him. He may come for you himself."

I felt the weight of the key, the press of Anton's hands wrapped around mine. At his touch, his fervor and anxiety heightened inside me. "I've never seen another door," I replied.

"It's behind your bed. I doubt even the servants know about it."

Had Izolda? I glanced back at the open entrance to my bedchamber.

"I must go now," he said. "And you must hurry. Valko's impatience will not work in your favor." The prince squeezed my hand, then sucked in a sharp breath as he moved away to leave.

"Wait." I stepped closer. Anton twisted to face me. I held the key to my breast. "You said to knock three times."

"Yes."

I shifted on my feet. "I do not know where your room is."

A candle near him sputtered. Its light danced in his eyes. "Two doors down from you," he answered quietly, "nearer the emperor's rooms."

I nodded, my fingertips tingling as they pressed into the

teeth of the key. All this while he'd been so close. It felt close, anyway, even though the space between our doors was large enough to fit at least a secret ballet room. Being a neighbor to Anton brought me a measure of comfort as my panic threatened to double me over.

"I'll stay awake until you knock," he said. "I'll knock back three times so you know I've heard you." He swallowed and lowered his gaze before meeting mine again. A rush of complicated feelings invaded me, entwining me with warmth and intensity. "May Feya protect you, Sonya."

His words lingered about my ears, but never entered. What I heard instead was *forgive me*.

CHAPTER TWELVE

I WALKED DOWN THE LONG CORRIDOR, MY NIGHT SLIPPERS
sinking into the red carpet running the length of the hallway.
My gaze lingered on Anton's door as I passed by. I forced my
legs onward without breaking the rhythm of my stride. The
sooner I got this over with, the better.

Valko's gilded door loomed in front of me with a relief carving of a seven-pointed sun. The supreme god, Zorog, stood in
the beams of light, wearing a great crown and holding another
in his outstretched arms. Seven painted rubies adorned the second crown, meant for the emperor chosen by the gods to rule
Riaznin through his noble bloodline. Valko wore such a crown.

I drew in a steadying breath. He was just a man—no, just a
boy—with mortal feelings. Feelings that didn't need to ensnare
me.

I rapped on the door, then clutched the panels of my
robe together. I couldn't come to him wearing just my

nightdress—that would only seem an invitation—but Lenka kept my gowns in some unknown wardrobe elsewhere in the palace. The lone article of clothing she left in my room to tempt me with was my Auraseer robe. Before I'd draped it around me, I ripped out the fur lining, despite the death it marred me with and the silent screams of empathy I felt for the beasts. It was a price I'd pay again for the added layer of protection the robe gave me against the emperor.

"Enter," Valko called from within.

I turned the latch with trembling hands and slipped inside.

My lips parted in awe. The luxury of the great hall was nothing compared to the emperor's private chambers. His three rooms were open to one another, separated only by overhead domes and tiled columns supporting them beneath.

The room to the right held a golden bath set into the floor. The water was deep enough to stand in and so wide the emperor could float on his back. Exotic plants surrounded the bath, giving the illusion of a natural pool.

A massive four-poster bed dominated the room to the left. Sheer, veil-like curtains hung from the silk canopy, so light and fine they billowed when I shut the door.

In the middle room of Valko's chambers and recessed two steps was an informal receiving area. A low circular table, lacquered in ebony, centered the space. Around it were an assortment of jewel-toned pillows in all shapes and sizes. There had to be more than fifty of them—some large for sitting on, others for leaning against, and some so small and ornate they could serve no practical purpose at all.

The seating furnishings surprised me. I'd expected Valko's rooms to have fine Riaznian couches and divans. But for an emperor to lower himself to the floor in the tradition of the desert Abdarans loosened a knot of my anxiety. If I could forgive the lavishness of the largest pillow he sat upon, crimson velvet with golden tassels, I could almost imagine he was Tosya, lounging around a campfire, prodding me to tell him which Romska girls' hearts had beaten faster after he sang them a new song. At the very least, Valko's smile seemed as genuine as my friend's.

The emperor's head was bare of its crown, his hair soft and loose about his face. He wore a long, embellished robe, slackly bound together with a black sash. The ties were open on his nightshirt. The neckline parted in a V, revealing a hint of his broad chest muscles beneath. A flux of heat stole through me, and I forced my gaze to his eyes.

"Do you let everyone inside your rooms so easily?" I asked, then after an awkward beat added, "Your Imperial Majesty." It was the first time I'd ever initiated conversation with him. I hoped I didn't sound disrespectful. I was only trying to grasp control of the evening before it had a chance to turn awry. Valko might have been smiling warmly at me, but his aura had me on edge. Beneath the surface of his emotions, he seemed concerned about something. My throat ran dry with it.

He grinned like I'd challenged him. I realized too late I'd forgotten to curtsy. "No one comes here without my sanction," he replied with assurance. "Besides, I have nothing to fear. I have *you*." He rose to his feet and approached me.

I knew we would be alone, but I'd never imagined how different it would feel. In the daytime, during our busy routine, we were always in the company of at least one other person.

I retreated and pressed my back to the door. "Don't you have any guards to attend you?" I kept my voice light and hoped he wouldn't see the fear so evident in my body language. "I may be able to warn you of danger, but I've never wielded a saber or fired a musket."

Reaching the entryway, he crossed to where I hovered.

I held my breath and tucked my hands behind me.

"Relax, Sonya." His smile reached his eyes and made them crinkle at the corners. "A retinue of Imperial Guard keeps barracks in the rooms beside mine. If there were any commotion, they would come. At least they would at any other time. I've dismissed them tonight," he whispered conspiratorially. "My walls are thin so they may serve me better, but I wish to have a private conversation with you."

"Very well." I swallowed.

He tilted his head. "Do I make you uncomfortable?"

Anton's words came to mind—*meekness, yet firmness of character.* "Yes," I admitted. "I was taught never to find myself alone with a man behind closed doors, especially after midnight." Never mind I'd never been taught such a thing, and I'd just met in seclusion with his brother.

"Hmm." Valko's eyes narrowed a fraction. "Am I a mere man?"

"No." I dropped my gaze, wishing to appear humble. "You are my lord emperor, sanctioned by the gods, blessed above common, vulgar men who would seek to tarnish someone's virtue without thought." Was that too heavy-handed? All I could think of was drawing a definite line between what I would and wouldn't do. I looked up at him and raised the pitch of my voice so I sounded young and innocent. "I know I can trust you."

He searched my eyes for a heart-stopping moment, then he erupted with laughter. I hadn't sensed the shift in him fast enough to anticipate it. "Whatever did Anton tell you about my summons tonight?"

I stared at him dumbfounded, not wanting to betray anything his brother had said.

"Come, Sonya." He whirled around and descended the stairs to his crimson pillow. "I only wish for you to give me a report on the last few weeks. I should have had you do so sooner, what with the attempt on my life just before you arrived in Torchev. But you must forgive me, I've been in a rather dreary state since my mother died." At those words, his humor wilted. He cleared his throat and spent a few moments arranging the smaller cushions around him, keeping his face averted from mine.

I followed him as far as the lip of the stairs, then I hesitated. A heaviness came across my chest and limbs, and I wrapped my arms around myself as I observed the emperor closely. His sorrow was authentic. Just as real and weighty as mine at the loss I had suffered.

He sat on his pillow and stared at his empty hands, then

glanced up at me with a smile, as genuine as before, though it seemed to pain him. He extended an arm to the cushion at his right. "Come."

My pulse hammered as I descended the stairs, stepped around the pillows, and lowered myself at his side. I kept waiting for some evidence to reveal him as the man who had charmed Pia or as the schemer Anton had warned me about. I found nothing. Regardless, I hung on every thought, every feeling, assuredly my own. I couldn't let Valko's aura compromise me. His energy was collected enough now, but there was no telling when it might shift. I hadn't forgotten how abruptly his mood altered during this afternoon's council meeting. Even more worrisome was the idea his aura could change so subtly it slipped my detection altogether.

"I apologize for the late hour," he said, and lit a match to a cluster of fir cones beneath a golden samovar on the table. Smoke curled out from beneath it with a soothing aroma. "My days are ruled by tedious affairs, and so I find myself sleepless at night. Perhaps it is my own stubbornness for not wishing to yet face the morning—that or clinging to the fragments of time belonging to no one but myself."

"It's all right," I replied, and relaxed a little more to find we had something in common. "I was awake. I also have difficulty sleeping."

"Truly?" He blew on the lit cones, and their smell of incense came stronger. "But then of course you do, with all those auras rattling around inside you."

I managed a grin to placate him, for I sensed he was trying to understand me. He didn't. No one really could. No one knew the awful extent of my crimes. "It's more than that," I said before I pressed my lips together. I didn't wish to admit to the way Yuliya haunted my thoughts or how I had left Kira and Dasha with Sestra Mirna to bury the dead.

Valko waited for me to say more, but when I didn't, he replied, "I'm sorry if your transition here has been a difficult one"—he set his hand on my arm—"and if that's why you are wakeful in the night."

Under the gentle pressure of his fingers, I was filled with the same stalwart calm and steady reassurance I experienced at Anton's touch. The emperor's aura felt . . . *sympathetic*. It reverberated with the same aching sorrow and regret as mine did, even though he didn't know my dark history.

"I'm well versed in rough transitions," he went on, and drew in a long breath. "When I was a child and en route to the secret manor that would become my home, an innocent boy was murdered to ensure I was raised in safety." He ran a hand through his hair and released a heavy exhale. "I'm sure you know the story."

I nodded as I remembered what Pia had told me about Valko and the changeling prince.

The emperor withdrew his hand from my arm and picked at his thumbnail. "It's difficult to explain the exquisite form of torture it was to grow up in a beautiful countryside manor, knowing I would one day be emperor, when I had someone else's death to thank for that. And the pain didn't lessen after

I ascended the throne—another harsh transition. The choices I've made have caused even more death and suffering. That is the inevitable part of ruling Riaznin—some must be hurt so the majority survive." He folded his hands together and glanced up at me with a sad smile. "But it doesn't mean I've found it any easier to sleep at night."

His gaze lingered upon me, not in a passionate sort of way, but in the way of a friend. "I'm glad I have found someone who understands," he said.

For a moment, he felt his age—a boy, not much older than myself, the weight of the empire resting on his still broadening shoulders.

Perhaps Anton had misjudged Valko. He couldn't know him well; they had been raised apart. Perhaps what the emperor needed most was a trusted companion, since he never had the closeness of a sibling.

"I understand you more than you know," I replied. "I also attained my position due to the death of others." As the words fell from my lips, my eyes widened with astonishment. I couldn't believe what I'd just confessed. My hand flew to the black ribbon on my wrist. Was it the emperor's forthcomingness that loosened my tongue or the realization that I may have found someone who could relate to a measure of the pain I'd endured?

"Izolda's failure to protect my mother wasn't your fault," Valko said.

"She's not whom I'm referring to. There was a tragedy at the convent—a fire," I rushed on, despite my better instincts to stop speaking. "And I—I started it. It was an accident, but that doesn't excuse my hand in it. So many Auraseers—women and young girls—would still be alive if I had been a better person." *Better trained, less stubborn, more humble.* I buried my hands in the folds of my robe. "You would have a polished sovereign Auraseer at your side instead of an unrefined girl."

A wave of shame spread up my neck to my ears. I wanted to hide, but I couldn't tear my gaze from Valko. I scrutinized every feature of his face for an appalled reaction—a disgusted curl of his lip or admonishing slit of his eyes. I searched within myself for any physical manifestation of his reproachful aura—an angry clench of my muscles or humiliating twist of my gut. No such things were present. The shame was my own. It began to fade, however, as I mirrored the steady beat of Valko's heart and the expanding of his chest as his lungs made room for a deep and consoling breath.

He watched me for several moments. What was he thinking? "Do you know what my father's parting words were when he sent me away?" he asked at length.

I frowned and shook my head.

Valko lowered his voice to affect Emperor Izia's menacing tone. *"Come back an emperor or don't come back at all."* He gave a rueful laugh. "I'm sure my father meant to forge within me a desire to return to Torchev with greatness and preparedness for the crown of our dynasty. But as a child, all I felt was the sheer threat that there was no room for failure in my life."

"How terrible," I murmured, though my anxiety bled

through my pity for him. Was he telling me this to distance himself from the horror of my confession?

"Thank the gods I also had a mother," he continued, softly grinning with fondness. "She left me with more hopeful words: *Live your life without looking too far behind you or too far ahead.*" He sighed. "I can't say I've done either parent justice. Like you, I let the past torment me and the future cast a foreboding shadow. Sometimes I fear I will never live up to my destiny. But I believe my mother was right." He shifted nearer, his eyes trapped upon mine with all the fervor of what he was trying to convey. "Though the blood of innocents has been spilled to bring you and me this life, wouldn't we be committing a worse crime to those who died by being ungrateful for our positions? Shouldn't we seize the present, live for *now*?"

He placed his hand on my shoulder and gave a reassuring squeeze. Comfort settled over me like a warm blanket. "What happened at the convent was a terrible tragedy, but I'm not sorry you are here, Sonya. Nor would I wish for another to take your place."

I stared at him in amazement. The slivers of blue in his gray eyes caught the light and lent him a depth and beauty I'd never noticed before. My throat tightened against a rise of tears. I opened my mouth and shut it again, struggling to form words. What could I say in response to his inconceivable mercy and sympathy? *Thank you* was far too trite. In truth, I didn't dare express my appreciation at all. I would surely crumple into a mess of sobs.

"I am not my brother," Valko said. "He would judge a whole person by one error. I know better. People are more than their mistakes." His hand moved from my shoulder to my face. Conviction flowed through me as his thumb brushed against my jaw. "It's what you choose to do in the aftermath that counts. Only the strong can move forward." He stared at me a long moment, and then gently withdrew his hand.

Sitting up taller, I swallowed hard against my emotions and searched for a safe subject to embark upon, something that wouldn't make me feel undeserving of Valko's kindness or remind me that Anton could never know the truth of my dark past. "I, um, haven't ascertained any serious threats from the nobles," I began, launching awkwardly into my report of duty. "I did wonder for a moment about Councilor Ilyin this afternoon—he seemed relentless about your mother's poisoning. But I believe he's harmless—irritable above all else." I twisted my fingers in my lap, not sure what else to add. Was I to give a day-by-day account of all the noble lords? "Do you wish to know more?"

He grinned like I wasn't fooling him with my show of unaffectedness. "Not really. I trust you would tell me if any true malice had been detected." He shifted closer so his knees bent toward me. "When did you first discover you were an Auraseer?"

I blinked twice. "Pardon?"

He laughed, and with the brightening of his mood came a feeling of weightlessness. "Forgive me if I have no further desire to discuss the thinly veiled malice of the people at court.

I know that's why I summoned you here tonight, but . . . well, suddenly I'm more curious about you." Valko shifted onto his side to make himself more comfortable on his cushion.

I studied his aura for sincerity. His curiosity must have been authentic, for I found myself leaning back into my own pillow. "I was five years old when my gift manifested beyond doubt," I said. "I awoke in the night to alert my parents of a thief who had yet to cross our fields or break into our home."

Valko lifted his brows. "Fascinating."

I gave a little shrug, though my heart panged with loss. The story was factual, but I couldn't remember it firsthand. I couldn't even remember my parents' faces or the image of my home beyond a vague memory of skipping across flagstones in our yard. The Romska were the ones to relay the story. They told it to me as I'd once told them.

"Such a gift." The emperor shook his head. "I've often wondered why the gods chose not to grant it to the heirs of the Riaznian throne." Scores of candles on the table, tall stands, and ledges around the room cast his face in full light and made no space for shadow.

"Perhaps the gods knew that too much greatness would not be a blessing," I ventured.

"Do you call your gift a curse?"

"Often."

He laughed again and tossed his head back, giving his whole self to the mirth. It warmed me and brought a smile to my lips. Since arriving in Torchev, I'd only felt this easy with Pia.

"I like you, Sonya Petrova," he said. "I hope we share many long years together."

My heart beat stronger. "As do I. I'm determined to even outlive Izolda."

Valko pulled a face. "Just promise you won't go bug-eyed, mumble incessantly, and smell of rye vinegar."

My smile broadened. "As long as I'm permitted to sprout whiskers on my chin, I won't complain."

He burst out with more laughter. Heat flooded my cheeks, not from embarrassment, but in flattery that he liked my joke. A twinge of guilt pricked me that it came at the expense of my executed predecessor, but that was the wonderful thing about Valko—even something inappropriate felt amusing with him, the way it did when Yuliya and I had made fun of Nadia while she was sleeping.

His gaze followed my hand to where my fingers idly brushed a frayed thread of my robe. He scooted closer and took up the panel to examine the tattered seam.

"I tore out the fur lining," I confided, seeing the question form on his mouth.

"And for this, you touched death?"

I nodded, slightly flustered. "I didn't want you to see me in only my nightdress. At least by wearing my robe, I could show you respect." Not exactly the truth, but it seemed to satisfy him. I sank deeper into my cushions, the smoke beneath the samovar lulling my body backward. I never imagined I could feel so tranquil in the emperor's presence.

Valko's rested his chin on his hand. "I shall commission new robes for you, Sonya. I want Estengarde to herald you in your full regality, and that doesn't require fur."

My limbs tingled with warmth. "Thank you. Are we going to Estengarde?" Traveling with the emperor through the mountain pass would have seemed a daunting affair an hour ago, especially since it meant arriving in a country Riaznin had an on-and-off-again alliance with. But now the prospect infected me with wanderlust.

"No," he replied, "Estengarde is coming here. At least, an emissary will make the journey after he reads my missive." Valko tapped a sealed letter on the table. "Anton thinks he's so clever with his yawning talk of rations and reinforcements, but I have a far better solution."

A giddy eagerness bubbled inside me. "What is it?"

"Marriage, Sonya. I'm going to propose to Madame Delphine Valois, the king's favored niece."

"That's wonderful!" I replied, his enthusiasm contagious. I adored weddings.

"Soon the snows will melt, and the emissary can cross the mountains to Torchev so we can discuss the dowry, the politics, and all the arrangements. Delphine and I will marry in the spring."

I sighed. I adored springtime.

Valko's smile sobered. His hand moved to stroke a lock of my hair, which had fallen across his pillow. "You're very beautiful, Sonya."

My breath hitched. Caution danced around the edges of my mind.

"I hope I can say that without offending you," he added.

His calm assuredness eased every nerve in my body. Any whisper of caution flitted away. "Of course." I curled onto my side so I was nearer to him. I felt safe enough to fall asleep on these pillows. Some yearning within me made me inch even closer. He didn't shy from the dark parts of me; he gravitated to them. He accepted all of me. The moments slid by as I let myself gaze at him. His eyes were twin pools of gray-blue water. They invited me. I could almost feel their cooling rush.

Another nudge forward, and our faces were almost touching. His breath was sweet, like currant tea. I pitied him that he must give over another portion of his life to his country by forming the alliance with Estengarde, especially since his heart didn't seem to be in it.

He tentatively reached up to trace the skin beneath my lower lip. His face, bathed in warm candlelight, appeared so handsome, so open. It tore at my heart. If I kissed him, just once, it might be a kindness, a gift from one friend to another before he married.

The fragrance wafting from the fir cones made my lashes flutter. My aura pulsed with Valko's in perfect synchronicity. I shared his aching desire, the urge to indulge in what we secretly wanted when so much of our feelings were restricted by our lives.

That longing within me—within him—built into a desperate need. It strung taut along my every muscle and pleaded for release. Unable to contain it a moment longer, I leaned into the emperor and closed the small distance to his mouth.

He shut his eyes and parted his lips. Our mouths pressed together. A gasp of pleasure escaped me. He kissed me with more fervor. I coiled my arms around him and worked my fingers up his neck. His hands slid inside the folds of my robe to encircle the waist of my nightgown. His aura flared to life in a shower of dark and wondrous feeling. My entire body shivered with it. I kissed him deeper, abandoning all thought, all restraint, making room for only this powerful craving within both of us. It was exhilarating to surrender to inhibition, to not be tormented by self-reproach and shame and propriety for the first time since the convent fire. I could lose myself completely to Valko. Escape the guilty remembrance of who I was. Or better yet, *accept* myself. For perhaps this uninhibited version of me *was* me—someone I'd suppressed for far too long.

Three knocks sounded in my mind. I cast them away, but they persisted, echoing back a pattern. *Three knocks and a beat of silence. Three knocks and a beat of silence.*

It was a signal. A signal I must give someone.

Why?

Valko's kiss didn't break. I didn't want it to. Something in me might shatter. I feared for that to happen. I wouldn't think of the destruction I always left in my wake when I unleashed the full throes of wildness within me. I refused to fight my true nature any longer.

Three knocks.

I cupped the back of Valko's head and drew our bodies closer.

Rap, rap, rap.

He shifted abruptly and pulled me on top of him. The recklessness I succumbed to felt like freedom. From a life of hiding. From the empire itself.

Rap, rap, rap.

But Valko *was* the empire. He dictated the laws, laws that governed Auraseers, which made it legal to own us. Laws that caused my parents to give me up and made me lose everything I'd known so I might *gain* something better, some piece of myself no one else would be able to master.

A rushing hiss sounded and mingled with the shrill call of a whistle. My eyes flew open to see the samovar venting steam.

At once my nerves fired. My mind cleared. I pulled away from Valko, lips burning, gut twisting. Three knocks. Anton's door. I felt sick inside.

I couldn't lose myself to Valko, even now as the prospect of escaping my own dark reality dangled within reach and formed a temptation so fierce it stole my breath and made my body tremble with need. How could I lose myself when doing so had created my darkness to begin with? My unrestrained empathy for the peasants had led me to destroy a convent of Auraseers.

"Thank you, My Lord Emperor," I said, carefully peeling myself away as I rose to my feet. His hair was on end, making him appear boyish. I ached to comfort that lonely boy. "I wish you happiness in your forthcoming marriage."

He sat upright. "Don't leave, Sonya." His gaze adeptly searched the room and fell on the samovar. "Have a cup of tea with me."

I shook my head and backed away. "I must rise early. I need my sleep to better serve you. I do not take my duty lightly."

"Just one cup."

"Good night." I curtsied and rushed from the room, even after I heard him call, "Wait!"

I ran down the corridor and closed the panels of my robe. Tears pricked my eyes. I slowed, reaching my door, then tracked back to Anton's. I pressed my forehead to the wood, my palms to the carvings. How long had he been waiting? How long had Valko held me in his embrace?

I knocked three times, then startled when the door immediately opened. Anton still hadn't removed his boots, though his shirt was untucked and his hair more disheveled.

Not expecting to see him, I mumbled, "You were supposed to knock back." It was better than saying, *I'm a weak fool with a weak heart, and a completely backward Auraseer.*

He studied me, his mouth hard and unyielding as his gaze traveled over my tangled hair and wrinkled robe. "Are you all right? What happened?"

"Nothing." I smiled, but a tear betrayed me and streaked down my face.

His brows drew together. "Did he hurt you?"

"No." I wiped my nose. "No, of course not." Anton waited, knowing there was more. I touched my lips with a trembling hand. "We kissed is all. I don't know how it happened."

He released a portion of a sigh. I was so distraught I couldn't sense if it held relief or disappointment.

"I'm sorry." Another tear fell. Why was I crying? Why did I seek so desperately to please the prince? What did it matter what he thought of me? I would only ever let him down and bring shame to myself. I could never measure up to him.

He tilted his head. "I daresay my brother wanted more than a kiss."

"Yes." I brushed under my eyes, but the tears were relentless. I didn't confess I was the one to kiss Valko in the first place.

"But you stopped his advances, didn't you?"

I breathed in and out and nodded.

A hint of a reassuring smile graced his mouth. "Then I believe you fared remarkably. You have no need to be sorry."

I stared at Anton, unsure if I'd heard him correctly.

He touched my arm. Warmth flowered in my belly. "Rest well, Sonya." His hand lingered a moment before he drew it away. He shut the door before I could also wish him good night.

I stumbled back to my room in a daze, so unraveled that I climbed inside the horrid box bed, too exhausted to sleep on the floor. I set my hand in Izolda's clawed trenches, ready to make them deeper, when Anton's words echoed in my mind: *You fared remarkably.*

I withdrew my hand and let sleep overtake me.

CHAPTER THIRTEEN

PIA DIDN'T COME WITH MY TEA TRAY THE FOLLOWING MORN-
ing. When I inquired after her, Lenka told me she was being
punished for having been tardy to the kitchens. Cook was making her clean out the second fireplace. Though I missed my
friend's company and felt sorry for the menial task she'd been
assigned, I was more relieved I wouldn't have to give her an
account just yet of what had transpired between me and the
prince last night, not to mention the emperor.

I wasn't summoned for duty until dinner that evening.
Valko was entertaining diplomats from Shengli and Abdara in
the great hall. I tried to expand my awareness to the foreigners,
to deduce any malevolent emotions they might be harboring,
but all my energy kept straying to Valko.

He sat with his councilors at his raised table on the dais, his
gaze often returning to me. I fiddled with the hem of my sleeve
as I analyzed every measure of his aura. Did this heightened

feeling within me mean he was just as nervous as I was to be in the same room together? Or was this eagerness? I touched my neck and swallowed. Perhaps all these internal fluctuations were simply my own embarrassment for forgetting myself last night. How difficult had I made it for the emperor to now treat me as merely his sovereign Auraseer?

I cast my eyes to the empty chair at the left end of the emperor's table. Anton never showed up to the dinner. Had the prince thought twice about the kiss I gave his brother? Was he angry with me, too?

After the last course of the meal, when the guests stood to mingle, Valko remained seated in his chair. He motioned for me to come forward. My heart thudded as I ascended the dais. I curtsied, then knelt at his feet so I wouldn't stand taller than him. "My Lord Emperor," I said, remembering Kira and Dasha. I hoped I hadn't lost his favor.

He twisted a ring on his finger. "What is the sentiment of the diplomats tonight?"

I glanced at the two men—the Shenglin in his silk robes with the insignia of the emerald dragon and the Abdaran in his turban and curl-toed shoes—and chastised myself for not having paid better attention to their auras. Now as close as I was to Valko and with my natural affinity toward him, I couldn't sense a thing from the diplomats. "They're, um . . . doing well. They're satisfied with the fine meal you gave them and seem eager to watch the bear dancers."

Valko nodded, thankfully accepting the pitiful report I

fabricated on the spot. "I'd like to keep them comfortable for as long as possible. They won't be happy when they discover I'm arranging a marriage alliance with Estengarde."

"Of course, Your Imperial Majesty. I'll let you know when that happens."

His gaze swept over my face, and his eyes warmed in the candlelight. "Did you sleep well last night, Sonya?"

"Yes." I didn't mean to whisper, but my breath caged in my chest.

His lips curved. "I'm glad to hear it."

A silence descended upon us and overflowed with heated energy. The kiss we had shared occupied all my thoughts. I remembered the taste of currant tea on his mouth, the sweet aroma of the smoking fir cones beneath his samovar. I had a sudden yearning to be alone with him.

"Will you sit beside me while the dancers perform?" Valko asked. "I want—"

"Yes," my whispered answer tumbled out of me.

His grin deepened, and he finished his sentence. "I want you to keep me apprised of the diplomats' auras."

"Yes," I said again, feeling my cheeks warm.

I remained with him until the dancers came. Some wore bearskins and others were dressed like hunters. When the music began, I settled into my position at the emperor's feet. As the dance intensified—when the eyes of the courtiers and diplomats were on the hunters as they prodded the bears with spears, as they leapt over the animals to the beat of the drums and frenzied strings—Valko's hand met the nape of my neck. He softly traced the scooped edge of my gown and the ridge of my spine. I exhaled against a swirl of light-headedness and curled my fingers in my lap.

Too soon the dance ended, and the emperor's touch withdrew. He stood and clapped while the hunters bowed over their slaughtered prey. Without sharing any more words with me, Valko left the dais for the company of the diplomats. For a long while I sat at the foot of his empty chair, still shivering with a flurry of emotion as I struggled to understand my own feelings. Did they belong to me, or was my racing heartbeat still latched on to the emperor's aura, to his newfound attraction to the sovereign Auraseer? He never did ask me again about the diplomats. It was just as well. I wouldn't have been able to answer him.

I didn't retire to my rooms after the festivities ended. I took an apple off a banquet table and wandered outside to the palace stables. The air was cool enough to frost my breath, but not turn my bones to ice. The season trembled in that tentative place between winter and spring.

I walked past stall after stall, admiring the horses, until I stopped at the gate of a beautiful white mare with a star-shaped patch of auburn on her brow. "Hello, Raina," I said, holding out the apple.

She nickered and walked forward, chomping away at my offering. I stroked her mane with my free hand. "I've missed you," I said, and brushed my nose against her coat. Her aura was peaceful. I closed my eyes and tried to trap in her smell, her graceful strength.

My thoughts, which had been so tangled up with Valko, turned to Anton. I felt the remembrance of his hands on my waist when we rode this very horse from the city square to the palace. I heard the prince's voice, soothing me, asking me to think of him so I wouldn't be overwhelmed by the masses. *You fared remarkably,* he had told me last night.

Raina ate the last of the apple. I wrapped both of my arms around her neck and tucked closer into her warmth. I wanted to stay here all night in the safety of her uncomplicated affection.

A rumble of low voices made my body jolt. Raina jerked back. She heaved a loud breath and stomped her hoof. "It's all right, girl," I whispered, and smoothed her coat with my hand. As the mare settled down, I perked up my ears.

"Feliks is making all the arrangements for him to come," said the deep voice of a man. Accompanying him was the clip-clop of at least one other horse. "How was your visit with Nicolai? Is he still committed?"

A second, slightly higher male voice answered, "He thinks he can persuade Duke Krayev."

As they spoke, I tiptoed to the exit of the stables. The voices were nearer now, though they still spoke in a hush. I reached out for their auras, but there was a delay. I'd attached myself too strongly to Raina.

A burst of laughter rang out from a different direction. I peered out of the stables. In the moonlight, a group of guards advanced toward the servants' entrance to the palace.

"Go and join them when they enter," the first man said in an attempt to whisper, though the low pitch of his voice rumbled with too much resonance to be quiet. I couldn't make out either of their faces from where they stood in the stables' shadow. "I'll take care of the horses."

As the shorter man handed over his reins, I retreated back inside and crawled under the gate of the nearest stall. "Shhh." I patted a brown stallion.

Into the stables, leading two horses, came Anton. A gasp escaped my mouth, but he didn't hear me. Crouching back against the hay, I kept to a dark corner of the stall. It wasn't until several minutes later, after the prince had untacked the horses and left, that I came to my senses.

What was the matter with me? Why had I felt compelled to hide? Had Anton's impulse to be secretive persuaded me, or was I trying to protect him? I sensed whatever he was doing was something he didn't wish his brother to know about. I was Sovereign Auraseer. The prince knew my duty was to the emperor.

I thought back on the conversation I'd just overheard. Anton mentioned someone named Feliks, a name I now remembered as belonging to a man with piercing blue eyes, the same man Anton had given over the care of the troika to in the city square. But who was Nicolai, and what did Anton mean when he'd asked if that man was still committed?

Did any of this have to do with the letter Anton had been given from another mysterious man, the man with the amethyst ring? *Midnight* and *Morva's Eve* were the only words I'd seen on that letter. Morva's Eve was still weeks away. What was Anton planning?

I waited until the servants' door to the palace thumped shut as the prince entered, then I hitched up my gown and ran around to the main entrance. When the guards stationed on the porch lifted their brows at me, I said, "Just taking a stroll in the gardens." *A late-night stroll with no coat in the cold.* Sheepishly grinning at them, I rushed inside, past the amber lobby, and up one of the four twirling staircases as I tried to beat Anton to the third floor.

I succeeded. He entered one minute after I did. There was just enough time for me to catch my breath and pull a stray bit of hay from my hair. My heart, however, pounded like I'd run the length of Torchev. I put my hand on the latch of my door, so it seemed like I was on the verge of going inside my rooms. I wanted this meeting to appear coincidental. I needed a natural way to bump into the prince. We'd had another fresh start for becoming friends last night. Perhaps he would come to trust me and confide his secrets.

Anton came nearer down the corridor, then froze when he noticed me there. The prince's nose was pink from the cold, and he had his hand on the clasp of his cape, as if making ready to unfasten it. My chest panged with a flicker of hope.

I let go of my door latch and broke into a wide smile. "Good evening, Anton." All my nerve ends tingled from his close proximity. I flexed my fingers.

He slowly approached me, still fidgeting with his clasp like he didn't know what to do with his hands. Just as I felt the promise of being able to sort out his feelings, part of him folded into himself with that same secrecy from the stables.

I furrowed my brows. How was he able to conceal his emotions like that from me—*me*, who should be able to read anyone? Then again, I could scarcely interpret my own aura, let alone how anyone else's might be distinguished from it. As for what little I *could* sense from Anton, he felt nervous, as if anticipating my rebuke for some reason I couldn't determine. Or was this *my* nervousness, *my* anticipation?

"How are you?" I asked. "I expected to see you at dinner tonight."

He parted his lips. A door creaked open. I whirled around to see two guards emerge from the room beside the emperor's. When I turned back to the prince, a change had come over his face. His features took on a stonelike but intensely focused appearance. My chest expanded with his as he inhaled a long and steadying breath. With it, his aura shut tight and entombed all of himself. My head prickled with a sensation between calmness and numbness as the excess oxygen flowed through my body.

Anton picked up his pace and walked past me without uttering a word.

I blinked in stunned amazement. What had just happened? Had he used a breathing trick to distract me? He must've known if he calmed his emotions, I could not read them. I watched him as he nodded at the guards, who strode by in the opposite direction. Maintaining his distanced aura and intense focus, Anton entered his room and never again glanced my way.

I slumped back against the wall, overcome with hurt and rejection. I was used to Anton pretending not to see me from across a long room, but I thought after last night something had changed between us, that he might actually care about me. I never imagined he'd resort to some form of meditation to keep me—and the prying person I innately was—well away. But of course he did. I could count on one hand those in my life who had wanted me in their association.

I closed my eyes and rubbed an ache in my brow. What a fool I must have just appeared, beaming at the prince like he were a long-lost friend I hadn't seen in months, like he were Tosya, journeying here from the Romska camps just to wish me a midnight hello.

I kicked open my door and slammed it closed behind me. I paced back and forth in my antechamber and balled my hands into fists. How many times would I put myself through this—through believing Anton would ever see me as more than someone he was duty-bound to help, when the fleeting moments arose? He would never go out of his way to greet me or give me a smile. He didn't need me, nor would he ever confide in me. We would never be true friends.

I slowed my steps, and my hand spread across my breastbone. Was that all I wanted from him, to be friends?

Was that all I wanted from Valko?

At least with the emperor I felt wanted and valued and good enough, like he desired my friendship as well.

With a groan of frustration, I ran my fingers through my hair. From across my open bedchamber, the wooden figurine of Feya stared back at me from her perch on the windowsill. I didn't want to think anymore. I didn't want to attempt to interpret what I was feeling. I swallowed hard, strode into the room, and gripped the base of the goddess with the spatter of Yuliya's blood.

The next morning was the second in a row that Pia hadn't brought me my breakfast tray. Lenka wasn't sure what my friend had done this time, only that it must be another punishment "for slacking in her duty."

Since the emperor didn't require me until the council meeting this afternoon, I hurried to the library, fetched three books of fairy tales—including my favorite story of the Armless Maiden—and made my way to the kitchens. The tiles were littered with chicken feathers, and the wooden table slabs dripped with pig's blood. Pia was nowhere to be seen. I stepped carefully through the room and flinched when the butcher chopped into a leg of raw meat and red flecks splashed the air.

"Have you seen Pia?" I asked a little boy plucking a chicken. The bird's wrung neck hung limply from its body. I kept my distance.

The boy looked up at me. His eyes widened to see the sovereign Auraseer. "Milking the cows," he replied, and blew a feather off his sticky mouth as he shot a glance at Cook. "Pia got caught filching a pie last night," he whispered.

I bit down on a smile. *Filching a pie?* Oh, Pia.

Walking outside, I found her just where the boy said I would. She sat on a low stool, all of her dark hair tied back in her kerchief as she hunched beside a large dairy cow and squeezed milk from her udders into a half-full tin pail.

"Excuse me." I set my chin above the fence that separated me from the palace barnyard. "Have you seen the elusive pie thief?"

Pia squinted up at me. The morning sun made her eyes as warm as honey.

"She's a little taller than I am," I went on, "much more pretty, and in love with a boy named Yuri."

Pia burst into a giggle, and then sighed, shaking her head. "It isn't funny, Sonya. I stole the pie to share with you, but Cook caught me." My shoulders fell as her aura did. She set her brow against the cow's girth. "I've been demoted to dairymaid for a week. I'll die if Yuri's parents find out. It's humiliating enough that *he* knows."

I leaned into the fence. "What happened yesterday morning? Why were you late to work?"

She squeezed out three more sprays of milk. "I overslept." With a little grin, she added, "Yuri had the night off, so we went walking by the river."

I nodded, careful to keep my mouth shut as to why the emperor had sent Yuri and the other guards away. I didn't want

Pia to know I had kissed Valko. So much for what I'd told her two nights ago: *Friends share secrets.*

"Yuri said we can marry in two years if he saves enough money," Pia continued, but her smile faded. "His parents won't support us. They still hope he'll change his mind and marry the nobleman's daughter."

"But he won't, will he?" I asked, trusting I knew the answer as well as she did.

Pia dropped the cow's udders and turned around on her stool to face me. Her lip quivered. "Two years is a lifetime, Sonya."

I felt the aching of her heart, the coldness in her hands from milking cows on a frigid morning, the despair weighing her down at being held back from what she wanted most.

She sniffed and swiped a finger under her eye. "I'm sorry. What a thoughtless friend I am." Sitting up straighter, Pia managed a smile. "I want to hear all about Anton's visit to your rooms. That's why I was bringing the pie."

I tucked the library books to my chest. "First of all, I don't wish to talk about the prince."

"But—"

"He isn't interested in me, Pia." She frowned, but I continued, "Secondly, you don't have to steal a pie to come visit me. I hope you know our friendship doesn't require food. And thirdly, I hope you *do* pay a visit—whenever you can—because I have a proposition for you." She arched a brow, and I lifted my stack of books on top of the fence. "I'm going to teach you how to read."

Her eyes rounded, and the most beautiful smile I'd ever seen stretched across her face.

My gut twisted, marring the moment with guilt. "And before you go thinking I'm sweeter than frosted beignets, I should warn you, I have an ulterior motive."

"What is it?" Her eyes narrowed mischievously. "My help with convincing the prince of Riaznin of your secret, burning affection for him?"

"No." I gave what I hoped was the most definitive of eye rolls. "Your help as I practice my ability. If you haven't noticed, I'm seriously lacking in training and would like to keep my head attached to my neck."

"Your neck is rather ravishing. I'm sure the prince would agree."

"*Pia.*"

She giggled. "I'll come tonight."

❦

After we'd made all the arrangements for regular study, I wandered past the barnyard toward the stables. With the sun higher in the sky and no clouds in sight, the air was beginning to warm. The snow crunched beneath my feet, having melted to a reasonable depth. Perhaps spring *would* come. Riaznin's winters were so long and harsh, a change in seasons often seemed impossible. For the moment, though, I believed in the best, and I had Pia to thank. The prospect of us helping each other made my worries over Valko and Anton shrink to a surmountable size, a much healthier way of dealing with my insecurities than the torture session I'd had with the figurine of Feya last night.

As I walked inside the stables, my gaze fell to my feet while I kicked up straw. Raina was still penned up in her stall. When she saw me, she came to my open hand, even though I didn't bear an apple. I petted her mane. "Don't you ever get a chance to run?"

"Not very often, poor mare," someone answered. I whirled around to find the emperor. He stood a pace behind me, as if he'd followed me inside.

I stared at him, dumbfounded. "What are you doing here?" He raised his brows, and I winced at my words and curtsied. "Forgive me, Your Imperial Majesty. You just surprised me."

"I thought my aura might have alerted you." He came to my side and reached up to stroke Raina himself.

I touched my cheeks, which were surely flushed, and shook my head. "At times, your aura is too similar to my own. It makes it hard to tell the difference."

His lips curved. The emperor wasn't dressed in a fine kaftan, just a gray wool coat to keep out the chill. "Then I'm not the only one who needed a little respite this morning?"

I smiled back at him. "No, you are not."

We smoothed the mare down together in companionable silence. Then my heart leapt, my only warning before Valko removed his hand from the horse to touch my braid. His fingers gently traveled down it to the center of my back.

"I prefer your hair loose," he said.

I inhaled a trembling breath. "Do you?"

"Mm-hmm. The way you wore it the first time I saw you." He pulled out the string tying the ends of my hair together. "The way you wore it when you kissed me."

Hands shaking, I stroked Raina's mane again.

The emperor slowly unwove my braid. His touch was feather soft, but it made my blood flame with entrancing heat. "Why did you leave the other night?" he asked.

I removed my hand from the mare and clutched the gate rail. "I cannot compromise my duty to you."

"I don't believe that's true." He fanned my hair across my back. "I'm never more safe than I am when you are with me. Why did you leave, Sonya?" he asked again, combing his fingers through the waves of my hair.

My eyelids fluttered as his aura grew bolder, as mine grew bolder with it. I kept my grip anchored to the gate rail. My chest rose and fell as I struggled to keep my lungs filled with air. "I can't . . . abandon myself. Bad things happen when I let go like that." Hazily, my gaze lingered on the black ribbon around my wrist.

Valko swept my hair to the side and brought his lips to my ear. The warmth scuttled a chill across my shoulders. "Maybe bad things happen because you don't let go often enough." He lowered his mouth to my neck and pressed a long and warm kiss there. Just as my knees began to give way, just as I was on the verge of surrendering myself to the dark recklessness inside me, the emperor spun to leave. "If you like the mare, she's yours," he said lightly.

I wobbled on my feet, shocked from his sudden departure and his stunning gift. "But . . ." I fought to think through my muddled senses. "I cannot ride her anywhere."

He grinned and tossed me a final look. A spark of cunning lit his eyes, like he was well aware of the dizzying effect he had over me. "No," he replied. "But you'll have the pleasure of knowing she belongs to you."

CHAPTER FOURTEEN

As the weeks passed, I became more vigilant about my role as sovereign Auraseer. I practiced reporting my daily findings to Pia in case Valko might ask me, but often all I came up with were things like "Cook is upset with the emperor, maybe for his request of venison a third night when the hunters have yet to bring back any deer" or "The hunters are irritated, probably because they must journey farther and to higher country to fetch the emperor his favorite-of-the-moment meat."

Nothing earthshaking. Nothing seriously threatening. I didn't want to admit to Pia that what I noticed most were the shimmering threads of blue in Valko's gray eyes, or the way I felt important when he sought out my gaze from among a room of first-ranking nobles.

I kept the key to the hidden door Anton had given me under a loose floor plank in my bedchamber. I waited for the night I should use it, the night I needed to disappear if Valko's attentions became unwelcome. The difficulty was determining if they were.

His apathy had vanished, and in its place grew something bold and vibrant. The emperor's new emotions were a more powerful distraction from my crimes at the convent than anything had yet proven to be. They also made the palace brimming with nobles and servants tolerable. Valko's aura was the most powerful of them all. If mine wasn't already harmonized to it, I found myself searching out its melody, the way it sang inside me with desire and abandon, and then I matched myself to its orchestration—for as long as I dared. Only then could I go night after night without touching the statue of Feya or resisting clawing my own trenches in the box bed.

If council meetings grew too long and dreary, the emperor would summon me to sit closer to him. Under the cover of the satin tablecloth, his hand would find mine and trace abstract patterns along my palm. My breath would seize, my heart hammer as it struggled against opening to him. It seemed every time he touched me, his aura came with the force of a raging storm. He'd let go before I could separate my feelings from his, before I made up my mind if his small acts of tenderness were unwanted—even long after his aura was absent and I returned to my bedchamber to stare at the knot marking the loose plank.

I wandered the palace corridors at night contemplating the same questions. *Can I lose myself? Do I ever dare lose myself again?*

When the answer was no, when the image of Yuliya's dead

face plagued me, I found myself outside Anton's door, searching for the song of his aura, the mystery of its subtler strains. I imagined him breathing deeply as he cleared his mind and body of emotion, like he had done when he'd prevented me from sensing his feelings upon our last encounter.

But when the answer was yes, when I *did* wish to lose myself, I paced nearer the emperor's door. Would he open it? Could he sense the percussive beat of my heart, how thin my resistance to him was growing?

Valko wasn't beastly like the Romska and peasants made him out to be. It was true he craved power, but he accepted what came with it—the tedious dinners with the nobles, the long hours grappling with his councilors over this law or that, the pamphlets that circulated the city, mocking him, drawing him as a snub-nosed baby wearing a crown too large for his head.

Though he was young, he seemed capable of his role as emperor. He understood the charm needed behind politics. How to sway disgruntled noblemen back into his graces. How to flatter the dukes' wives with a secret smile they'd been craving. Soon it seemed there had never been an assassination attempt or an ill-fated dowager empress's death. The whispers that Valko might be an imposter abated for a time, with the changing of the seasons. The emperor's charisma could be thanked for the lifted mood in the palace. Life at court was a complicated game, and Valko knew how to play it. But that didn't mean he was manipulative in all regards.

Often, when the weight of his crown became too heavy, when the nobles would inevitably return to their grumbling, he would find me at the stables grooming Raina. Sometimes the emperor wouldn't touch me at all. Sometimes he would sit on the stool in the corner and share his pent-up frustrations. Must he entertain the nobles so frequently? Did Councilor Ilyin suspect he was merely "the changeling prince"? If Valko had grown up with his father, would Emperor Izia have taught him how to better manage everyone's expectations?

One day Valko fell silent after airing all his grievances. I ran the brush once more across Raina's mane and glanced at the emperor. He leaned back against the planked wall, idly running a hay strand between his fingers as he watched me intently. When our eyes met, he smiled.

"You understand me, don't you, Sonya?"

I set the brush down. "It is my duty to try."

"No, not like that. I mean you understand how I'm feeling."

"I feel everything you feel, My Lord Emperor." Such as I did this very moment, when a bud of sweet awe and curiosity bloomed inside me, outgrowing the dizzying passion I usually felt within the reaches of Valko's aura.

His grinned deepened. "That isn't what I meant, either." Sitting upright, he detached himself from the wooden slats of the stall. "You understand me because you feel how I feel, even when I'm not here to influence you."

I swallowed. Was he speaking of his attraction to me? Did he want me to admit mine?

His gray eyes sharpened, not in an unsettling way, but in the way eyes do when someone has made a great discovery. "You must wonder how your life would be different, Sonya, if your parents had raised you, too," he said gently. "That is how you understand me . . . because we are alike."

I blinked at him, my breath halted at how well he knew me. The sweetness inside me grew until it flowered across every last shadow of winter. I smiled at the emperor, forgetting the very reason I had been separated from my parents. "Yes, we are, Your Majesty."

That night brought another reading lesson with Pia and another pitiful attempt at learning to regulate my ability and rein in my undisciplined mind. After we practiced her letters, she thumbed through illustrations of fairy stories while I struggled to name them based on her inward reactions. But I mistook her quickened pulse of fear for her breathless sense of heartbreak. That made me wrongly guess the story of the Snow Child who melted upon first discovering love was instead the tale of the Bone-Legged Woman who devoured wandering children.

No wonder I couldn't decipher my own feelings.

After Pia left, I paced the long corridor outside my rooms and lingered a little longer near Valko's bedroom door. I even brought my knuckles up, but in the end couldn't make myself rap against the wood—not when the eyes of the supreme god, Zorog, stared back at me from the relief carving. He knew what I had done in Ormina, the blood of innocents I carried inside me like a stain. He knew it hadn't been necessary to lock the Auraseers and sestras in the east wing. I'd wanted to. That's why Valko believed the two of us were alike. Maybe that's why I lost control and gave in to the auras of the peasants. Maybe I knew what might happen if they stormed the convent.

Had the darkest part of me *wanted* the Auraseers to die?

My shoulders curled over my chest. I felt hollow inside. A needling pain gnawed at my stomach, where it had been growing stronger day by day.

Pulling my hand from Valko's door, I spun away to return to my chambers. I sought my penance with Feya and only slowed my steps to meet her as I passed Anton's room and felt his shuttered energy within. Just as I didn't knock on Valko's door, I didn't knock on his brother's. The emperor would have answered, would have spoken to me, but never the prince.

One rainy day on the cusp of spring, I stared at the stained-glass window in the council chamber and watched the water flow around the leaded joints of the panes. I determined to keep my face blank and not sigh at the sensation of Valko's smallest finger circling my knee beneath the table. The emperor was more keen on me than he'd been in a few days—his emotions a heady rush swirling inside me. They begged for me to throw myself at him, despite our audience of stern men. Thankfully, Anton wasn't here to see me so delightfully frazzled. No doubt any fragment of his regard for me would vanish. I'd fall even farther from his high standard.

"What do you think of my proposal, Sonya?" Valko asked. The rain drizzled down the panes of the Ozerov coat of arms. I dammed back my thoughts of the prince.

"Proposal, My Lord?" Did the emperor speak of his marriage offer to Madame Delphine Valois? I often forgot he was marrying at all. I didn't want to think of him kissing another woman the way he'd kissed me. Still, I knew he was impatient for the Esten emissary to arrive with news of Delphine's acceptance or denial.

Valko's fingernail slid over my knee and sent a pleasured chill up my spine. I fisted my hands to ward off a flush to my cheeks. I couldn't allow him to get to me like this, not when he would soon have a bride. "My expansion into Shengli," he clarified with a smile. His gaze pierced mine and searched for what I was feeling, thinking.

"Oh, yes, of course." I collected my thoughts, surprised that he had asked for my opinion on the matter. He'd *never* asked for my opinion in this setting. No one had. But I did have my own feelings regarding the continuing border wars with Estengarde and the ones resurfacing with Shengli after decades of peace. And now, with the strength of the emperor's forthcoming marriage alliance, he wanted to lay siege against Shengli and annex it into our empire. As there was no daunting mountain range between us, Shengli was easier to invade than Estengarde and had more plentiful resources of gems and timber. But the Shenglin army, a lethal force of mastered discipline and skill, posed its own formidable barrier between us.

Valko's councilors had spent an hour debating the wisdom of his latest scheme for bringing more wealth into Riaznin—or, as they put it, "spreading our culture to the east to protect ourselves from threat"—and now they awaited my answer with bored tolerance etched across their faces. Within them, however, I felt their resentment of me. As I studied the councilors and felt their anger twist my stomach, but not jab it with hot knives, I determined they were not dangerous. And after many long weeks of silence in council meetings, I decided to speak up.

"I think it is a false notion that acquiring *more* will bring about prosperity," I began. "I've seen happiness abound in humble circumstances where people don't live in domination under one another." I alluded to the Romska, but the emperor didn't know that part of my history. "Riaznin is capable of greatness without plundering it from another country, especially one with an unbroken history of being able to defend itself against our empire—indeed, it has often sought to conquer *us*. Why should we take the risk? I believe we have the competence to bolster ourselves from within."

The rain softened on the windowpanes. No one said a word for several moments. I swallowed the ticking of my heart and absorbed the auras in the room. Some were caught on bitter humor—jeers they didn't vocalize in the off chance the emperor might be pleased with my remark. For the smile on his face, he might have been. But the edges of his curved lips tightened, and his spidery fingers froze on my leg. A different energy—deep and familiar and flowing with admiration—made me turn in my chair.

Anton stood quietly, just inside the entrance of the room, his eyes trapped on mine.

Valko followed my gaze and stiffened upon finding his brother. The prince looked away from me too late. He cleared his throat and bowed to Valko. "I have a letter for you, Your Imperial Majesty."

"Not now." Valko whirled back to his councilors. "That is all for today," he told them. "You are dismissed." They stood, gathering papers, and shot him curious glances. I moved to stand. "Not you, Sonya." He examined a fresh stain of ink on his cuff.

I bit my lip and eased back down, unable to resist another look at Anton. As the councilors swept past him to exit the room, the prince twisted the letter and watched the emperor and me, his mouth contorting with a frown. A feeling of deep displeasure strung taut between the two brothers. Every muscle in my body cramped.

Valko rose after everyone left—everyone but Anton. He gripped the prince's arm, ushered him out the door, shut it hard, and closed me in with him. Taking a steadying breath, the emperor rolled out a kink from his neck. Pain knotted on my own. With false calmness, he returned to me, hands clasped behind his back. "Stand up," he said.

I did as he commanded, my knees wobbling while storm clouds brewed in my gut. Valko was furious, but for the moment he kept it at bay. Feya willing, he wouldn't unleash it.

"How long have you been at court, Sonya?"

"Three months."

"And how long have I been emperor? No"—he held up a finger—"how long have I been educated to rule Riaznin?"

My voice quavered. "Your whole life, My Lord."

With a deep inhale, he nodded. "My whole life. And before I was born, Sonya, did the gods foresee my destiny as ruler? Did they bring it to pass—bring *me* into being—so I could wear this crown, in this very hour of need, for my empire?"

The storm clouds grew darker, more ominous. "You asked for my opinion, My Lord."

The lightning struck. His face went crimson. A vein pulsed at his temple. "I had supposed the opinion of *my* Auraseer, *my* gifted protector, would support me!" I shrank back, fearing he would strike my face. "Do you have any idea how long I've planned this? And yet on a moment's whim, you prattle off some thoughtless remark to shame me in front of my councilors!" He swept his kaftan back and placed his hands on his hips. "Do you have nothing to say?"

My body shook as I resisted the urge to hit him. I scrambled to throw up battlements against his fury before it consumed me, before I lost my own temper. He wanted an apology, but I couldn't give him one, despite Kira, despite Dasha, despite the price of my own life. Some madness held me resolute. Deep in my bones, I knew the opinion I'd uttered was my right to give—and at his request. What I'd felt in Anton's aura confirmed the justice of it. The emperor would not strip me of that moment when I, for once, felt important and worthy of goodness.

Valko's shoulders rounded. The storm clouds broke apart. "Don't you care for me at all, Sonya?"

My balled hands opened at my sides. Did I? How deep did my affection run? How much of it was my regard for him, and not his attraction to me?

How sincerely did he care for me? He was planning to be married. Still, how often had I craved another summons to his rooms—or for him to knock on my door? There must be a reason I hadn't used the key to the secret ballet room. Was the reason my own true feelings?

Valko stared at me, hard and unyielding. Before I could answer him, he swept closer and crushed his mouth on mine. His body pressed against me with none of the patient tenderness he'd exercised for weeks.

His abrupt passion came like a battering ram against my indecision. I held my body rigid, determined to first understand what I felt for him while he kissed me more roughly, while he yanked his hands through my hair and shoved me back against the table's sharp edge. When I released a cry of pain, the door to the council chambers burst open.

"I'm sorry to intrude, but you'll want to read this letter immediately."

Anton.

Releasing a breath of irritation, Valko drew away and settled his forehead against mine. He blocked my view of his brother. "Give me the news quickly," he said without turning.

Anton spoke in monotone and betrayed none of the furious emotions trapped inside him. "The Estens received your missive," he answered Valko.

I squirmed in vain and tried to pull out of the emperor's arms so I could see the prince, so I could study his features to see if they matched his hostile aura. Had Anton been listening outside the door? Why was he so upset? He'd made it clear he didn't care one whit about me.

"What's more," the prince continued, "the emissary is already traveling to meet you. His messenger rode ahead. The emissary will arrive in two days' time."

Valko exhaled with supreme satisfaction. His impassioned anger transformed into something bright, like the sun had overcome the storm against. The fact that the rain still pattered incessantly outside the windows didn't faze him. He kissed me again, long and deep, not minding the audience of his brother— or perhaps making a greater display *because* Anton was there.

Embarrassed with the prince in the room and still trembling from the rage I had felt at the emperor's rebuke, I willed my body to turn to stone. Inside me, however, was a cacophony of feeling, loud and forceful, midnight-dark and seductive. I longed to fall into the violent path of its rhythm.

Valko didn't seem to notice my struggle. He pulled away from my lips with a gratified smile and smoothed the hair from my face. "What did I tell you?" he said, kissing my nose. "The gods foresaw my destiny. Under my rule, the empire will stretch from sea to sea." He patted my arm. "Go and lie down, Sonya.

You will need your rest. And I will need you to be more watch-ful than ever once the emissary arrives."

Afraid to speak or even breathe in case I broke the thin wall holding the racketing chaos within me, I only gave Valko a small nod.

Placated, he turned away, and in doing so revealed an unob-structed view of Anton. Our gazes locked. The prince's brown eyes held misery, a wound gaping open, as if it had been grow-ing larger every day. My chest ached with it. I didn't understand how I had hurt him, how that was even possible when he'd spent weeks closing himself off to me.

"Come, Anton." Valko motioned for his brother as he approached the door. "We have much to do."

With one last pained look in my direction, the prince left me standing in the council chambers alone, my back bruised where it was still pressed against the table Valko had pinned me to, my hands clenched on its edge. The only sound was the rainfall, washing away every aura but my own.

It was enough to bear.

Later that night, I lifted the knotted plank of wood in my bedchamber, and I picked up the key.

# CHAPTER FIFTEEN

I THRUST MY WEIGHT AGAINST THE BOX BED. FOR SUCH A SOLID piece of furniture, it glided away easier than expected. Slick casters and a perfectly smooth floor made the job simple. As Anton had promised, the hidden door revealed itself—smaller than most doors, its height coming to my shoulders. Faded red paint with yellow daffodils peeled away from it in sections. It was a door meant for little girls. Sisters. Anton's great-aunts. The Ozerov family who had rebuilt this palace.

I ducked my head, opening the door inward, then entered the decaying ballet practice room. It was plain and empty with pinewood floors and varnished oak paneling. The only embellishments were a tarnished, wall-sized mirror and a ballet barre fastened onto it. I held up my candle and inspected my dim reflection in the mirror and the dust that coated everything in the room. Izolda must not have known about this place. Perhaps no one but Anton did.

The strangeness of my bedchamber made better sense, seeing its almost-twin here. Perhaps my room had once been a private performance hall for the royal family, and my antechamber the receiving area. I pictured the girls, like ghosts from the past, flitting through the door to their practice room to change costumes and powder their noses.

This room, unlike my own, didn't have a door off the main corridor. There was another door, however, on the other side of the room—the same size as the red door, only painted lavender with white daisies.

I bit my lip and turned the key over in my hand. Anton had told me there was a ballet room, and that my bedchamber connected to it. I didn't realize there were adjoining rooms beyond the ballet studio. Did the rooms link all the way from my room to the prince's? Surely this lavender door couldn't be his; it was too close. How many hidden chambers separated us?

I had come this far wanting a safe place to hide from Valko. His attentions were growing more suffocating, more irresistible by the day. I didn't trust myself. I had to do something beyond shying away from his advances. They needed to be thwarted altogether. Over the past hour, I had devised a solution. I needed to share it with Anton. After his reaction today in the council chamber, I hoped he would be willing to help me.

With a rush of determination, I hefted the box bed and pulled it flush to the wall with the red door. That way Lenka wouldn't find me if she entered my rooms. I stood, swiveled around, and swept across the ballet studio, next trying my key in the lavender door.

Once I entered, a child's playthings confronted me, all sleeping beneath a thick layer of dust. A rocking horse. Clay pennywhistles and marionettes. Nesting dolls with their gradually smaller companions, all lined up in a row. Riaznian fairy tales displayed in flaking murals upon the walls. The Armless Maiden growing her limbs back to rescue her son from a well. Father Frost admonishing the Impolite Child.

Again, no door existed to the outer corridor, only another door to yet another room.

Heart pounding, I approached the door, painted evergreen with ice-capped mountains and a setting sun. This door was taller than the last two. I opened it, pushed away the chest of drawers blocking the entrance, and found myself in a beautiful bedchamber, also green—almost living. Tapestries of lush forests, streams, and flowering grass covered the walls.

This room had not been as neglected as the others. The furnishings and window glass had been dusted and polished at least once within the last three months. An inviting bed with creamy satin blankets took residence against the corridor wall. This wall, unlike the ones in the previous rooms, had an outer door, though a heavy beam was nailed across it. I scanned the rest of my surroundings. Draped over a cedar chest beside the bed was the mossy-green and embroidered blanket that Anton had brought on our journey to Torchev—the blanket belonging to his mother, the dowager empress. This room must have been her bedchamber.

Surely Valko knew about these hidden places, then. So why had Anton given me a key leading to supposed rooms of safety if his brother was aware of their existence? But then, this bedchamber was boarded up—most likely at Valko's orders—and the door to the nursery had been hidden by the empress's chest of drawers. No, Anton wouldn't have directed me here if he wasn't certain the rooms were secure.

I inhaled a deep breath and revolved to stare at the last intersecting door, painted midnight blue with silver stars.

Anton. This had to be his room. And if it was anything like the ones I had passed through—each lovely in its own way, but not excessive like the emperor's—then it suited the prince perfectly. Knowing Anton, he had chosen such a room himself, despite the grander ones on the third floor that remained unoccupied.

As I tiptoed toward the midnight-blue door, I felt the faint pulsing of his aura. Was he sleeping?

I set down my candle on a small table and put my key in the lock. With a quiet click, I opened the door.

The air, cool with moisture, penetrated my nightgown. A copper tub—the tub brought to my room when *I* needed bathing—rested before me. A cloudy film of soap had settled upon the water's surface. Nearby, a wrung washcloth lay draped over a stepping stool.

"Sonya?"

My hair spilled over my shoulder as I startled to face Anton. He stood up from his desk chair. My heart thrummed, for he was wearing only his breeches, his chest still wet, his hair curled at his neck and temples. I clutched the folds of my nightgown and forced myself to breathe, to think clearly. I had surprised *him* by entering, not the other way around. Though I had never imagined surprising him like this.

Try as I might, I couldn't look away from him. I couldn't be the modest girl who lowered her lashes. A beautiful need coursed through my veins. It was difficult to remember Anton wasn't past his nineteenth year, especially when I saw him this way. Though his aura felt vulnerable, every inch of his body declared his strength and maturity.

With a shaky inhale, I rolled back my shoulders and steeled myself to the reason I came here. I didn't wait for Anton to put on his nightshirt, though he hurriedly grabbed it from a chest at the foot of his bed. "Is Valko truly your brother?" I asked without preamble.

He frowned as he tugged his shirt on. The linen clung to the wet and defined muscles of his chest. I flexed my hands. "What do you mean?" he asked. "Did the emperor come to your rooms tonight?"

"I didn't stay to find out. Is he your brother?" I asked again.

The candle on Anton's writing desk underlit his face, catching on his cheekbones and the hollows around his eyes. "Yes, he is."

Unconvinced, I drew closer. A book with a pale-blue binding lay open on the desk. He shut it and turned it over so I couldn't see the title, then set it atop an unfinished letter. A quill rested beside it. Anton must have been writing when I entered his room. Secrecy shrouded his aura and prickled the hairs on my arm. My chest filled as he began his trick of deep breathing and intense focus to block me. "Are you certain?" I asked, forcing myself to exhale of my own accord. "I was young when my parents sent me away. I can't even remember their faces. How can you be sure Valko is the same boy from your childhood?"

Anton moved away from his desk and folded his arms. "My mother was sure."

"How could she be? Did Valko have a distinguishing feature—a scar or a birthmark?"

The prince's hand drifted to his forearm. His thumb brushed a spot hidden by his sleeve. Something in my belly fluttered. I wasn't sure why. "He doesn't have a birthmark." Anton watched for my reaction carefully. "As for my mother, she alternated visiting both of us when my father could spare her, though she never told me my brother survived."

Releasing a breath of frustration, I paced away from him. The light of his candle cast a weak glow over the varnished woods and deep blues of the room. The window curtains were drawn shut.

"What is this about?" Anton approached me.

I shook my head as helplessness crowded my thoughts.

"Sometimes I wish Valko were the imposter. Then you could rule in his stead."

Anton halted, his brow stern. "I have no desire to be emperor."

"I don't believe that." I moved closer so I could see his eyes in the darkness, feel his aura with more clarity. His intense focus wavered the nearer I advanced. He swallowed and squared his shoulders. "You were raised to assume this position," I said, "just as he was. I've heard you speak in the council chamber. I see how much you love your country, how much you can offer it."

"That does not give me the right, under the empirical order, to govern Riaznin." Anton shifted away, his jaw muscle flexed. "No one man should have that right."

I searched him, trying to weave through his complicated emotions. Trying to understand my own. I'd come here in hopes of finding a way to hinder Valko. I didn't trust myself to not reciprocate his desire for me. One day I might surrender to every dark quality I possessed. I might lose myself completely, live unrestrained, and to everyone's detriment.

Anton was different from me, different from Valko. The prince was careful to keep himself guarded and his impulses in check. He wouldn't sway me or let me sway him. He could be trusted with the empire.

"What if . . ." I went back to the midnight-blue door and shut it, fearing someone could be listening. What I was about to ask was dangerous. "What if you claimed Valko was the imposter? Are there enough people to support you?"

Anton's gaze hardened and flickered to the letter on his desk.

"The dowager empress is no longer here to validate her son," I added as respectfully as possible—I didn't want to disgrace Anton's mother—but my muscles went rigid as soon as the words fell from my lips. I'd set off something drastic in him.

Anton walked toward me slowly, his severity making my pulse race. "Sonya, take care." His low voice quavered. "Your words are treasonous. If Valko were to learn of this, he would have your head."

I lifted my chin. "He would not have the authority to take it if you wore his crown."

He gripped my arms below the shoulders. "Think of what you're saying! You're his sworn protector. If we succeed in framing him as an imposter, he will be executed!" The prince's gaze bored into mine. "Is that something you could live with?"

My throat went dry. I couldn't speak. My jumbled plan hadn't carried me as far as the emperor's death. Of course I didn't want that to happen.

"Are you sure these are your feelings?" Anton continued. "Valko's councilors are nearby; they've been in his rooms for hours discussing the celebration for the emissary. I can only imagine you weren't invited to the meeting due to your opposition this afternoon. But you may not be alone in your opinions. Perhaps some of the councilors are also unhappy at the idea of an alliance with Estengarde."

I blinked. I hadn't considered the councilors' malevolence

today in that respect, only as it might be directed toward me. As sovereign Auraseer, it was my job to anticipate any harm that might befall the emperor, but I'd been relying too hard on the idea that I'd feel any danger to him instinctively, like I had as a child when I'd sensed a robber approaching my parents' house.

But what if the threats in the palace were far more deceptive than I'd imagined? Could Anton be right? Could my impulses tonight belong to another? No one, including myself, had yet deduced who'd tried and failed to poison the emperor and succeeded in killing the dowager empress. Maybe it was one of the councilors, now only a few walls away. But at our meeting this afternoon, their resentfulness had only made me feel uneasy, not truly imperiled.

Were they more practiced at concealing their auras? Anton had a method for doing so. Did they? The councilors must be used to sovereign Auraseers hovering nearby. Perhaps if the villain who poisoned the empress was among them, he was more than unhappy at the prospect of an Esten alliance. Perhaps he'd been unhappy about *many* things—and for some time.

I placed a hand on my stomach and lowered my eyes, sifting through myself for what was mine, what was Anton's, and what could be someone else's. As always, it was never so simple. The feelings holding me together usually felt my own. Most novice Auraseers didn't master these nuanced differences until they were ten years my senior, and the girls at the convent had begun their studies years earlier than me.

"This isn't the answer," Anton said, breaking up my thoughts. "We'll find a different way to divert Valko's attentions from you. With the news of the emissary's arrival, he's already caught up in his plans for marrying another."

I shook my head. My hands clenched with stubbornness. "I fear for more than myself, Anton. Some of these feelings of impending danger have to be my own! I refuse to believe I've attended so many council meetings without forming my own opinions and convictions."

"I do not doubt you have, but—"

"Did you hear your brother today?" I raised my voice, cutting him off. "He means to invade Shengli! Our people are already weak from famine. We've lost too many to the border wars. We don't stand a chance against the Shenglin army. Valko will strip our people of their last shreds of morale and dignity—indeed, their very lives—in order to expand the empire! And he will never be satiated."

In the same respect, I knew Valko would never be satiated by a marriage. He would grow restless, and when he grew restless his eyes drifted to me.

The prince fell quiet. Was he finally ready to truly consider what I was saying? I looked up at him beseechingly. "The people would follow you, Anton. I know they would. You have the potential for greatness and would never stoop to cruel measures in the name of Riaznin's glory. The empire would flourish under your reign."

His grip on my arms softened. His gaze turned heavy, pleading. "Do not tempt me, Sonya."

My lips parted in surprise. He spoke as if I had power over him, not the other way around.

His smell of musk and pine encircled me, and my knees went weak. *Do not tempt me, Sonya* echoed through my mind. Was it possible Anton's words held double meaning? Could he truly . . . did he really long for me the way I longed for him? I gazed into the warm cast of the prince's brown eyes.

My breath caught in stunning revelation.

I wanted Anton.

I cared for him more than I'd ever dared to admit.

We stared at each other, our chests rising and falling in cadence. My heart drummed faster and faster. My arms tingled beneath the sleeves of my nightgown, under the gentle pressure of his touch. I forgot what we were arguing about. All I understood was my deep pull to him, to his strength and goodness—the very traits I lacked and the reason I'd denied my feelings so long. Who was I to think the prince, the same boy who sought to abolish serfdom and fostered self-reliance among his province, could ever fall for someone dark and turbulent like me?

The prince's conflicted eyes wandered over my face. In that moment, I desired something more than for him to be emperor. I desired his hands to slide around my back. His touch to surround me. I shivered with the aching need to be closer to him.

My gaze dropped to his mouth. The wet air from his bath collected in a sheen of moisture above his lip. "I've learned to accept what can never be mine," he said.

Our bare toes touched as I moved nearer. "Then unlearn it."

The base of his throat ticked where his pulse beat rapidly. A new emotion scuttled across my mind. A strange curiosity. Somehow I knew it belonged to him. His hand traveled down my left arm. He turned my hand over and brushed the sensitive skin of my inner wrist. I drew in my breath as he pushed back the hem of my sleeve to my elbow.

He stared at my arm for several moments, his disappointment flooding me.

"What's the matter?" I didn't understand what had upset him, but it made my chest tighten, my heart compress with pain.

He dropped my arm and gave a mirthless laugh, rubbing the space between his eyes. "It's nothing. I'm only tired." He walked to the midnight-blue door. I'd left the key in the lock. "We should say good night."

I held on to my arm, which had triggered his sudden mood change. "Won't you think on what I've told you?"

"No." His mouth formed a straight line. "And I ask you never to bring up the matter again."

My eyes flew wide with hurt. What had come over Anton? A moment ago he was all warmth and tenderness. I even thought he might kiss me. What had I done to cause offense?

Would I never be good enough for him? Or did he have no desire to touch me because Valko had already staked his claim?

I locked my jaw and concealed my wounds with something stronger—my stubbornness. "Is this how it will always be?" I folded my arms. "Will things grow easier between us, or will you spend all your days avoiding me, treating me like I carry the plague?"

His brow hitched in pain; I'd pierced his armor with that. "I wish things could be different, Sonya. You must believe that."

I bit my lip. "Why can't they be? At least *here*? Without the emperor watching, surely we can be friends." Anton must have known that giving me the key would propel me to open door after door until I found his room. He must have wanted me to.

"I suppose so," he answered quietly, then glanced at his feet. He swiftly covered any vulnerability by forcing a light smile. "Though, in the future, I hope you learn to knock. Thank the gods you didn't barge in a few minutes earlier."

Heat burned to the tip of my ears as a stark image formed in my mind. I had to look away; I'd seen too much of him.

"You *do* need to leave," Anton said, a little gentler this time. "The servants will be coming to clean up after my bath."

I nodded and finally relented. And because my gaze was downcast when I walked to the door, it fell upon his desk. The top of the unfinished letter peeked out from beneath the book with the pale-blue binding. It was addressed to a Count Nicolai Rostav.

That name had a familiar ring. Was that the Nicolai that Anton had spoken of when I overheard him outside the stables? The prince had asked his companion if Nicolai was still committed. To what, I wondered.

"Come, Sonya." Anton's aura grew thick with a compulsion for secrecy again, as if he didn't want me lingering near the letter. "You can't be discovered here."

His hand rested on top of the door. I nodded again. Now wasn't the time to barrage him with questions. As I walked away from the desk and then under his arm, I felt a surge of yearning. His free hand moved to cover mine, and I gasped as the need between us flowed stronger. I darted my gaze up at him.

"Your key," he said, his voice nearly breathless.

I felt the cool press of metal slide into my palm. "Thank you." A flush of embarrassed heat rose up my neck. Until he mentioned the key, I'd had another lilting sensation that the prince might kiss me again. But perhaps all this racing emotion was my own. Still, Anton hadn't removed his hand.

His eyes were heavy at the corners. "You can sleep in the room beside mine if it makes you feel safer." My face burned warmer at the thought of spending the night so near him. Clearing his throat, he added, "Only be sure to return to your bedchamber before dawn so you won't be found missing."

His hand lifted away. I swayed a little on my feet, then walked out from under his arm. I'd only crossed two steps into the room of tapestries before I whirled around.

"I didn't wish to kiss him," I said abruptly.

"Pardon?" The prince's brow arched.

"Today, in the council chamber, I didn't wish to kiss your brother." For some inexplicable reason, it felt imperative I tell Anton.

A long moment passed before he replied, "I know."

I nodded, sensing he understood what I couldn't say—that many times I *did* wish to kiss the emperor. When Valko teased me with kisses he never gave. When he threaded the want of them around my heart until my emotions were a mess of confusion. When I was lonely and tired from battling the demons of my past. When the auras of the palace made me sleepless at night.

For the most part I resisted him, and when I felt the pain in my back from where he had bruised me against the table, I was glad of my resistance. But despite all my resolve—despite the veil of the emperor's true motives with me, growing thinner every day—his aura was nesting inside of mine with barbs of iron. The truth was, I still craved his attention and acceptance of me.

"Good night," Anton said. I stole a breath and nodded back my farewell. I didn't wish to leave him. Struggling against my feelings for the prince was just as painful, just as real, as what I felt for the emperor. But I wanted Anton's affection for a much different reason. If the prince could care for me, perhaps I still held a measure of goodness. Perhaps I could one day be forgiven for all I had done. Maybe then he could trust me and confide his secrets.

As Anton's hand moved to shut the door, his loose sleeve fell back. There, on his inner forearm, was a mark, perhaps a smudge of ink. My own arm prickled in the same spot where he had earlier examined me.

The door closed, and I was left standing in the darkness of the tapestry room, lost in the mystery of him and my own conflicted heart.

CHAPTER SIXTEEN

THE NEXT TWO DAYS WERE A PALACE FRENZY, AS ELABORATE preparations were made to herald the emissary. Valko was in constant motion, his eyes slightly crazed like a man withdrawing from opiates. He hurried from room to room with a list of impossible tasks and expectations while his entourage of councilors and myself trailed behind. Everyone was frantic. Their nervous energy escalated inside me. I scratched my arms and fidgeted, wanting nothing more than to crawl out of my skin and go screaming down the corridors.

Perhaps I was learning to hide my drawbacks as an Auraseer, because no one paid me—or my twitching—any heed. They were too self-absorbed with their enormous responsibilities. Even the emperor had no eyes for me as he shouted his orders. I ventured to hope Anton was right: this marriage might make Valko forget about me. If only the marriage was guaranteed. The emissary's letter said he was coming to *discuss* the match with Madame Valois, but nothing more. Thus Valko's all-consuming mania to please him.

The emperor wanted everything perfect in order to meet the high standard of Estengarde, a country that thought itself more refined than us, even if Riaznin was four times larger and had a culture more tested by time.

When Valko decreed that every nobleman was to shave his beard to conform to the smooth-skinned Esten fashion, I could have swept their dropped jaws from the floor. And it didn't escape my notice that Anton—who had been clean-shaven until the decree—began to sprout a shadow of stubble on his chin.

On the night the emissary was due to arrive, there was to be a grand ball. In order to spare more time for dancing and give the emissary a chance to freshen up from his journey, the emperor requested that his nobles feast in their own lodgings beforehand.

At last the day of the ball came, but the nobles' elation only made me tremble harder with panic and dread. The thought of being present in a large room, packed from wall to wall with agitated people, would test my meager skills to their limits.

That morning, when Pia appeared with her tray, she was full of talk about a private banquet the emperor had ordered for the emissary in his guest rooms. Valko would not meet the Esten—a man named Floquart de Bonpré—until that evening, but he wanted him well fed with the finest Riaznian delicacies.

Luckily I'd risen early because of the energy buzzing about

the palace and slid the box bed back to hide the red, flowered door. I'd spent the last two nights sleeping in the tapestry room, but hadn't disturbed Anton again. I didn't dare. His closed-off aura was more pronounced than ever. I wondered how long he could maintain his practice of deep meditation, what letters he might be writing, what the book with the pale-blue binding contained, and above all else, what he might be up to tonight. He could not have known all those months ago that Morva's Eve would fall on the day the emperor would hold such a festivity—a festivity that not only promised to test my ability, but also make me miserable with starvation.

"What do you mean you've brought me no breakfast?" I asked Pia. My stomach was a tight ball of nerves. Some people abstained from food when they were anxious; I, on the other hand, became ravenous. If Pia were to produce a meat pie from her apron pocket, I might have swallowed it whole, deathly aura and all.

Her mouth quirked at me. "No lady eats before a ball. I've brought you a special tea steeped in herbs to ensure you're well dehydrated before the dancing begins."

I frowned. "Why would I want that?"

"To dance?"

"No, to shrivel up like a dried fig!"

She laughed. "Oh, Sonya, please don't tell me you've never been to a ball."

I folded my arms. "Yes, as a matter of fact, we held them regularly at the convent. Each Auraseer took a twirl with a sestra." I'd never been so sardonic with Pia, but I couldn't help it. No food? My body leeched of water? No wonder women had fainting spells.

My maid laughed harder, her hands clutching her sides. I realized too late I'd made a joke at the expense of all the people I'd left dead in Ormina. With lowered eyes, I cast a glance at the statue of the goddess Feya on my windowsill.

"There will be hundreds of ladies in attendance tonight," she said. "How many chamber pots do you think we have in the palace? How many maids to unlace all those corsets?"

I sat back stiffly. "I will not be wearing a corset."

"No." Pia considered me. "But you *will* be required to attend the emperor at a celebration that is sure to last until the middle of the night." She reached across the table and set my tea in front of me. "Trust me on this. You'll thank me later."

Reluctantly, I took a sip of the bitter drink and grimaced. Pia gave a satisfied smile. She leaned back and pulled an embroidered pillow to her chest, wrapping her arms around it. With a dreamy sigh, she said, "Yuri will be standing guard in the ballroom tonight, looking fine in his brushed regimentals. What I'd give to wear silk and dance in his arms." She played with the fringe of the pillow, lost in her own imaginings.

Forgetting the rumbling in my stomach, I touched her arm. "At least you'll be able to see him." Even without a public feast, surely the emperor would provide his guests with refreshments and require his serving maids in attendance. "That's something, right?" I knew Pia's moments with Yuri were fleeting, stolen from their busy days if they were lucky enough to cross paths.

"I suppose." She picked at a stray thread.

My heart went out to her and the rare melancholy in her aura. Since Pia and I had begun our reading sessions together, she'd returned to her bright and contented self. And her cheerfulness intensified as she mastered every consonant and vowel in the alphabet. I'd never been more proud. Tosya would have shared in my delight to watch my friend learn so adeptly, as he had taken it upon himself to be my reading teacher among the Romska. Pia even stumbled through an entire page of the Armless Maiden story without my assistance.

"Imagine Yuri's surprise," I said, "when you're able to read him a love sonnet—or better yet, write one yourself."

A twinge of a grin teased her mouth, but didn't remain. I sighed, wishing I could trade places with Pia. Then we'd both be happier. She could be at the center of a ball she longed to go to, and I could hide away on its outskirts.

Trying once again to lift her spirits, I presented an alternative solution. "With so many guests and so much commotion, I doubt anyone will notice one maid and one guard slip away for a few minutes. There must be some abandoned corridor where you two can share a private dance."

Those words did the trick. Pia turned to me, eyes sparkling. Her lips curved with a radiant smile. "You're brilliant, Sonya!" She kissed my cheek. "You deserve an extra hour of my 'highly sought-after training.'" Her dimples caved. "You might even be able to win our game." She referred to her favorite method of strengthening my ability. Now that she was gaining confidence as a reader, she had advanced from studying illustrations to silently reading snippets from tragic histories, while I tried once more to guess at the content by discerning her emotional and physical responses. "Let's hope Vladimir the Terrible doesn't drown in a pool of his own vomit the next time we study," she said.

I held up my hands. "That was your fault. It's never a good idea to gorge oneself on pastries before tucking into a nice story."

Pia gave a light shrug. "An unfortunate hazard of my occupation. Besides, they were *hazelnut* pastries. Irresistible!" She rose from the couch and smoothed her apron. "I should get going before Lenka catches us enjoying ourselves." She rolled her eyes. "And now that you and I have reminisced over the finer points of retching, make sure to drink up your tea."

I groaned, which made her giggle. Pia glided to the doorway on pointed toes. "I'll wink at you from across the ballroom tonight. I'll be the one emitting waves of *love*," she dramatically declared, laughing at herself. She blew me a kiss and danced her way out the door.

I grinned with the lingering, sweet spell of her aura. Even a second sip of the tea didn't sour my mood. But Lenka did. She marched in on the tail of Pia's exit. I braced myself for an hour of callous remarks and sneers. However, none of her usual irritation was evident. I relaxed somewhat and tested her emotions for her changed mood and the triumphant way she held her head on her matchstick neck. Without a word, Lenka lifted me to my feet. At a clap of her hands, my other attending maids entered, each bearing a box tied with silver ribbon.

"What's all this?" I asked warily.

"New robes." Lenka's nostrils flared with pride. "Commissioned by His Imperial Majesty, Our Lord Emperor himself."

My shoulders fell with understanding. Tonight Lenka would have her glory by me. I would look the part, once and for all, of the grand sovereign Auraseer.

✦◦❧✿❧◦✦

Three hours before the ball began, my maids returned, and the copper tub was brought inside my bedroom. My skin tingled at the remembrance of whom I had last seen using it. The maids gave me the careful attention of a bride on her wedding day. All the cleansing, dressing, primping, and perfuming was done with a slowness that set my teeth on edge. Beyond the walls of my rooms, I felt flurries of panic at the last-minute preparations. The fact that six maids were deemed necessary to wait on me when they could be used elsewhere made me feel ridiculous. I thought of the widows living in rags in the border towns of Riaznin, scraping meals together for children who would only grow up to be soldiers, without a choice in the matter. All the while, my face was powdered, my nails trimmed, my lips stained red.

The emperor's gift was suited to me in that the robes bore no fur trimmings. According to Lenka, Valko even insisted I wear no corset, which, for the first time, made me want one. He must have known my waist was never laced tight in bindings. His hand had been on my waist often enough. A corset would have provided another barrier beneath my white satin gown.

But did I really expect him to make another pass at me tonight when he was so desperate to finalize his arranged marriage? He would be a fool to try.

I ran a hand across the bodice of my dress and skimmed the bones of my ribs beneath it. Even though Valko had ample reason to leave me alone, I wasn't comforted. I didn't trust myself to deny him, even if he didn't make an obvious move. I hadn't forgotten the first time we kissed. *I* had initiated that.

As Lenka continued to clothe me, I tried to bolster my courage. Anton once said I'd fared remarkably at resisting his brother. I could fare remarkably again. I could resist my own desires, as well.

My next article of beautification was a tall headdress of embroidered silk stretched over a flat crown standing six inches off my head and dangling with ropes of pearls that brushed my shoulders. Perhaps the emperor thought the pearls would be safe for me, that an oyster didn't die when it was robbed of its jewel.

He was wrong.

And there were more on the gown itself.

Seed pearls were sewn into swirling patterns across my robes, and when the two front panels parted as I walked, a sash of crimson gossamer could be seen circling my waist.

Unlike touching the potent blood of the deceased dowager empress, the pearls only bore a dull sting. Still, I felt an echo of the oysters' ghostlike misery. I exhaled, but their auras remained trapped inside my breast. I should be thankful. They would keep me grounded tonight, focused on one type of energy instead of the myriad bound to come.

A large but limited number of nobles dined regularly at the palace. I had grown used to their presence, but tonight would be different. Tonight, both the first and second class of court ranks would be in attendance. I'd heard Councilor Ilyin say that would be nearly seven hundred people.

I fretted over their numbers while Lenka and her maids wrapped long locks of my hair around a heated iron until they fell in soft curls. That my hair should be unbound was another of Valko's requests. By the time my maids were finished with me, I felt like nothing more than the emperor's doll.

I stared in my gold-framed looking glass. I could have seen more of myself in the full-length mirror of the ballet room, but I kept that place secret. Besides, I had no desire to see any farther than the sparkling rubies at my throat—seven, to match those in the emperor's crown.

"May I go now?" I asked, eager to escape the maids' prodding hands. The three hours they had spent in my rooms felt like ten.

As her eyes swept over me, Lenka beamed like I was Izolda reborn. "Of course. Your guard is waiting to escort you."

I followed her to the door, but no one was outside. Lenka's shriveled lips pinched together. She craned her neck down the corridor. "Yuri!" she hissed.

The guard who had captured Pia's heart stood conversing at Anton's open door. He startled, jerking his gaze in our direction. Anton's door thudded shut.

Lenka clapped her bony hands at him. "Get down here, you idle boy!"

Yuri had the sort of ruddy skin that was always in a constant flush. Now it crept to his jawline and ears. He jogged down the hallway and bobbed nervously on his feet upon reaching us. "My apologies." He gave me a little bow—the first time he ever had. I hoped he wouldn't do it again. Things had always been informal between us.

With a farewell to my maids and one last bit of fussing from Lenka over some excess powder on my chin, Yuri and I set off down the long corridor and began our descent down two twirling flights of stairs. The strained repression in his aura made it difficult to breathe, let alone speak. I wanted to ask why he'd been conversing with the prince, but I kept my lips sealed. Yuri attended to more people in the palace than myself, including the emperor, so why not Anton? Still, I couldn't brush my curiosity aside. The young guard seemed to have been infected with the prince's air of mystery just by lingering too long at his door.

"You look very nice tonight," he said at length.

"Thank you," I replied, and glanced askance at him. It wasn't that I didn't think him sincere, but I sensed he was trying to distract me from something. Was he in on Anton's scheme, whatever the prince meant to have happen tonight, specifically *midnight* on Morva's Eve? The thought sent a ripple of anger through my chest. Why had Anton confided in one of his attendants, but never me?

After the ice broke between us, Yuri kept up a babble of

one-sided conversation—the increased number of guards out-side the palace; his first impressions of Floquart de Bonpré, whom he saw arrive with his entourage of Estens; whether Pia had mentioned if she'd be serving in the ballroom or shut away in the kitchens. His nervous prattle continued until we reached the orchestra's door to the ballroom, a more covert entrance than the great double doors, where the hundreds of guests must be lined up and ready for the grand procession.

My empty stomach fluttered with their eagerness. I hoped that would be the worst I'd experience from their auras tonight, though I doubted I would be so lucky.

"You *will* see Pia," I said before Yuri took his leave of me. "She has a surprise in store." I smiled, and unable to resist myself, added, "Though I doubt it will happen at *midnight*."

A jolt of shock ran up my legs. My stomach cramped with anxiety—and something darker I couldn't name.

Perhaps it was cruel, but I couldn't help testing Yuri. And feeling what he did confirmed what I'd suspected—he *was* in league with Anton. Whatever they'd planned months ago was still transpiring, despite the grand ball. Perhaps Yuri was even the mysterious companion Anton had spoken with that night outside the stables.

I curtsied a farewell before the stunned guard could think to bow, and left him and his troubled aura as I entered the ball-room. My duty may be to the emperor tonight, but I was also determined to discover what Anton was hiding from me.

CHAPTER SEVENTEEN

THE BALLROOM WAS ABLAZE WITH CANDLELIGHT. CHANDE-liers hung from the ceiling, and candelabras lined the windowsills and the mingling tables that edged the vast room. Beyond them, tall lamps rested in even intervals along the walls. The colors of Riaznin—red and gold—were strung together in silk bunting adorning the banquet tables and curtain valances and every available space.

The grandest use of Riaznin's colors surrounded the emperor. Red velvet cloaked his dais like a luxurious carpet, and the fabric also made its way into his kaftan and the upholstery of his high-backed throne. The gold of his crown, his buttons, and his sash, which fell diagonally across his chest, broke up the blinding abundance of crimson. The last glimmer of gold was displayed on a low, satin-cushioned stool situated on the right side of the throne, like it belonged to a favorite pet. Dread knotted in my stomach. Somehow I knew the stool was for me.

Valko's mouth stretched wide when he saw me approaching. "Welcome, Sonya," he said, using my first name since no one but ourselves was in the room. The guests were still waiting to be admitted. I rubbed my hands against my skirt and wished to brush off my anxiety. How much longer until the people entered?

Curtsying deeply, I bided my time before I had to sit at Valko's side. "My Lord Emperor."

"The robes flatter you well," he said as his gaze traveled over me. "You look remarkably fine this evening."

"Thank you," I replied, hoping to sound unaffected, but my blood pulsed faster and a flush of heat swept my cheeks. *Stop it*, I commanded myself. *I don't want Valko's attention. I won't respond to it.*

"Come take your place." He gestured to the stool as if it represented the highest honor in Riaznin.

I struggled to focus on the deathly aura of the pearls. I struggled to focus on anything but Valko and *his* aura. Because once it became entangled with my own, I might come undone. Stepping onto the dais, I awkwardly lowered myself at his side. My shoulder touched his hand on the armrest, and that was enough. A warm tenderness settled beneath my breastbone, and with it a touch of sadness and regret. It made me turn to the emperor as if pulled by hidden strings.

"Would that you were the king's niece in Estengarde," he said softly.

I blinked. My heart quickened at his fervent tone. Is this

who he would be if he had been raised a country boy, and not the heir of an empire? This gentle, thoughtful boy was one I would not waste my energy resisting.

"It's tradition that I dance with every first-class-ranking lady." Valko swallowed like he was actually nervous, and from the way I twisted my fingers in my lap, I knew he was. "But I must confess I would rather hold you in my arms."

I cast my gaze to the ballroom doors, where the nobles would be entering at any moment. "Is it the custom for the sovereign Auraseer to dance?"

"It is now." He set his hand on mine, and heat prickled up my neck. "Dance with me tonight, Sonya. Promise."

My palms itched. I felt jittery all over. Did these sensations belong to the emperor or were they mine? "What about the emissary?" I asked. "Will your favor to me upset him?"

Valko waved a hand, as if he could so easily dismiss my worry. "I'll make some excuse to appease him."

I tilted my head. "Forgive me, My Lord, but I don't understand. You've worked so hard to prepare for this ball—for this marriage. You *do* want it, don't you?"

As he considered me, his smile slipped away, his zealousness of the past two days returning. "I do need this alliance, Sonya. It is imperative. I intend to be a great emperor, like my father before me. The duty of our dynasty is to spread our people's culture and religion and way of life as far across the world as possible." He spoke like I was a councilor who needed convincing. "Riaznin's future depends on our growth.

We must expand before we are trampled upon. I *need* Shengli."
He jabbed a finger on his leg, as if it were a map of countries.
"And I need the strength of Estengarde so I can rival the force
of the Shenglin army."

Valko's adamant passion flowed through me. My qualms
over his plans for invasion, which I'd so vehemently shared with
Anton, seemed a faraway concern. Still, I couldn't grasp why the
emperor would gamble with that "necessary" future because of
me. "If it would risk the alliance," I asked him carefully, "then
why do you ask me to dance?"

His gaze wandered back and forth between my eyes. His
mood shifted as he tentatively touched a lock of the hair I'd
worn down at his request. "Because I want you nearby," he said,
then gave a small shake of his head, like that wasn't quite the
right answer and he also needed to explain it to himself. "So
much of my reign is uncertain, and you make me feel safe."
His brow furrowed. "No, it's more than that—you know every
feeling that makes up who I am, and you accept it." He bit at
his lip. "You are the only thing getting me through this evening,
Sonya."

A sweet pain flowered in my heart. I yearned to comfort
him, to stroke his cheek and whisper all would be well.

He brought my knuckles to his lips. "Say you will dance
with me."

The red and gold of the room seemed to blur in my periphery as my focus on Valko intensified. I felt nothing but the
heady blend of our auras. "I will, My Lord."

He leaned nearer, and just as my eyes were beginning to close in anticipation of his kiss, the ballroom doors opened. The master of ceremonies entered. Valko pulled back, hurriedly let go of my hand, and sat up taller on his throne. In a flash, he became the dignified emperor with his head held erect and his gaze forward and stoic. With his sudden grandeur swelling in my breast, I corrected my posture and sought to look just as important on my little stool.

The royal orchestra filed in on the opposite side of the ballroom, taking their seats and tuning their instruments. A moment later, the conductor took up his baton, and the strains of the grand polonaise resonated through the air. My chest tightened. This was happening. They were coming. All seven hundred guests.

The master of ceremonies beat his staff twice upon the marble floor, and my heart pounded in trepidation. I reached for the pearls of my headdress and prayed for their sting to distract me from the wave of oncoming auras.

"I hope the reversed order of arrival will be easier for you," Valko murmured without breaking his gaze from the great doors where the first of the guests filed in at the master of ceremonies' heralding.

I frowned, my mind fuzzy as I tried to think past my anxiety. "How do you mean?"

"Per the custom of the grand procession, I would have arrived last, and you with me as my guardian. But if we had done so, this room would already be teeming with people. You would have to contend with their collected auras at once. Now you can acclimate to each of them one at a time."

I stole a surprised glance at him. "Do you mean to tell me you arranged it this way . . . for *me*?" A tingling sensation spread through my chest. I'd thought Valko had wanted to appear the gracious host by reserving the last entrance for the emissary.

He gave a subtle nod. "This occasion will bring together my greatest supporters and worst accusers—a veritable recipe for danger. Is it not in my best interest to ensure my sovereign Auraseer isn't overly tested before the evening has begun?"

I shifted on my stool, a little abashed for feeling self-important when his reasoning came down to politics. "Yes, of course, Your Majesty."

A smile teased the corner of his mouth, making him seem all the more young and handsome. "That is what I told my councilors, anyway. In truth, Sonya, I only wish to make you as comfortable as possible."

Valko's gaze finally detached from the approaching nobles and slid to mine, warm with affection. The tingling in my chest returned and spread lightness through my limbs and fingers and toes.

I returned the emperor's smile, then sucked in a sharp breath as the master of ceremonies beat his staff once again and announced more guests.

Past the great doors came the arch-marshal, the civil servants, the military officers in their regimentals, the diplomats from Shengli and Abdara with their small assembly of noble foreigners, the bearers of Riaznian court ranks, the dukes and duchesses, counts and countesses, barons and baronesses.

As Valko had promised, their gradual entrance was far easier to bear. But that didn't make my task simple. I had to gather all my wits about me and summon my full strength. Inhaling and exhaling, I reminded myself of the work I'd done with Pia to prepare for this challenge. I called up everything I'd learned.

I first studied the allegiance of the Riaznian nobles by the red and gold of their sweeping gowns and tailored kaftans. Their dress was another decree from the emperor. As for the beard decree, I caught the grumbling auras of some men with little nicks along their jaws and throats, the evidence of shaving with unpracticed hands.

I felt more than that.

Now that my hyperfocus on the emperor had subsided, a wash of new emotions and sensations tumbled into me with sheer force.

My pulse slowed as an elderly baron leaned upon his cane. It raced as a maiden twirled and showed off her dress to a young lord. I flinched when two dukes exchanged bitter glances. My stomach cramped when a lady put a hand on her waist, likely shrunk by diuretic tea. Awe and scorn mingled with my pent-up breath as the nobles stared aghast at me, observing where I sat on the dais, a place of honor that had never been reserved for a sovereign Auraseer.

As, one by one, the nobles approached the emperor's dais

to bow and be acknowledged, I fought to contain the impulses begging for release inside me.

"Everything is hanging by a thread tonight," Valko said in a low voice meant for only me to hear. "You must let me know how the foreign diplomats receive the Esten emissary, and how my nobles receive *him*. Here in the palace we may smile at one another, but do not forget there are wars on all borders of Riaznin."

"I will not fail you, My Lord." I sounded as calm and collected as the master of ceremonies when he heralded each guest, but the pressure inside me bubbled to the surface like an overflowing kettle. The dowager empress's murderer was likely in this very room.

My hands, clutching the pearls, began to tremble. How could I do this? How could I control myself *and* guard the emperor? I swallowed hard and looked out among the finely dressed people, much greater in number than the peasants had been at the convent's gates.

We are far from the border wars, I reminded myself. *These guests are largely in good humor. They're not a violent, single-minded mob. I have nothing serious to fear.*

As I tried coaxing reason into my brain, I realized I was tugging the black ribbon around my wrist, the pearls of my headdress forgotten. At the thought of the convent, my imagination went wild. The Auraseers seemed to circle me like wraiths. *Something is very wrong with you,* I recalled Nadia's accusation. *You were the ruin of me,* Yuliya would say if she had life to move her lips. The dead peasant man joined them as they swarmed me, his skin blistered and charred from being burned to death at my hands.

A small whimper escaped me as I stared at the mass of guests in the ballroom, the scores of palace servants behind them at the walls, the guards stationed near every window, every exit. I felt them all.

After a lull of arriving guests, the master of ceremonies abruptly rapped his staff again. I startled to find I'd been rocking back and forth and pulling my hair. "His Imperial Highness, Prince Anton Ozerov."

My head jerked to the ballroom's entrance. Awash in candlelight, Anton stood, his kaftan black and gold and perfectly cut to his body. His emotions were shrouded, his brows drawn low in concentration. Somehow the sternness only made him look more handsome.

A warmth cascaded through my body and settled my nerves. I wasn't the only lady in the room admiring the prince, but the reaction radiating inside me was assuredly my own.

That inexplicable certainty, that grasp on my aura, pushed back the others fighting for space within me. The ghosts of my past also fled, shying away from the luminous feeling swirling through my breast. My ribs expanded. I took a deep and sustaining breath.

"Has my brother caught your attention, Sovereign Auraseer?" the emperor said as the last of the House of Dyonovich paid their respects and strolled away from the dais. Valko wore a light smile for me, but his jealousy scraped against my bones.

I strove to appear natural and shrugged one shoulder. "Only in that the prince is wearing gold with black, rather than gold with red like the other nobles."

"Mmm." Valko's eyes darted from me to Anton, and the bone-scraping sensation dulled to a scratch. "He always insists on making a spectacle of himself."

"Indeed, My Lord," I replied, even though I regarded Anton's rebellious nature as far more subtle than that. The emperor had no idea what the prince was really up to this Morva's Eve. Then again, neither did I.

I allowed myself only one more glance at Anton, who never returned my gaze, then turned to face the orchestra. I concentrated on their music and forced my mind away from the prince. The diversion worked, and the scratch of Valko's suspicion abated entirely.

A moment after the prince was heralded, the murmur of guests in the ballroom silenced. Their energy rose in a crescendo of intrigue—and a note of disdain. They had anticipated who was to come next. "His High Nobility, Monsieur Floquart de Bonpré," the master of ceremonies announced. Anton stepped away from the double doors, not bothering to approach the dais as custom dictated, and in the place he vacated stood the emissary.

The fashion in Estengarde must have been monochromatic elegance, for the gentleman wore only pale hues of gray: his silk waistcoat; his ballooned breeches, gathered at the knee;

the hose on his legs; and his cunning heeled shoes, complete with satin bows. Lace dripped from his collar and the cuffs of his sleeves. And his hair, fastened at the nape of his neck, was flocked with an abundance of white powder.

The emissary advanced down the aisle of parted nobles, his entourage of similarly dressed Estens behind him, until he reached the foot of the emperor's dais. There, he bowed with a flourish, his hand somersaulting through the air.

The emperor stood and grinned. "Monsieur de Bonpré." Valko's horribly affected Esten accent made me bite down a smile. "Welcome to Torchev, the heart of Riaznin."

Floquart glanced about the room as if it summed up the city. I remembered my amazement when I'd first set eyes on the great hall. It was nothing like the emissary's expressionless gaze upon the ballroom, an equally dazzling space. Perhaps everything was a blur, and he needed a monocle. "Very charming," he said, his voice jarringly low in register. I'd expected the high pitch of a bell for how daintily he dressed. But beneath his fussy exterior, I noted his broad shoulders, bulging calves, and large, vein-ridden hands. His aura, above all, demanded respect. I sensed even Valko shared my intimidation, despite the emperor's puffed-out chest.

"Please be seated," he said to Floquart. "You must be weary from your journey." Valko motioned to a pair of servants, who brought forth a silver chair and set it on the vacant side of the throne. I clasped my fingers in my lap, sat up higher on my stool, and tried not to feel spurned.

A wave of disgruntlement echoed from within the Riaznian nobles. Valko had broken protocol twice tonight—first by allowing me on the dais, and second by inviting a foreigner to accompany us.

The emperor was oblivious to everyone's prejudice, and I carefully let their auras slide off to the fringes of mine. There I kept them in painstaking balance as I endeavored to hold on to all of the skill I had practiced over the past few weeks.

After the emissary was seated, Valko motioned to a servant, who brought forth two goblets on a silver tray. Giving one to Floquart, the emperor took the other in his own hand. As he raised it before the assembly, the orchestra's grand polonaise came to an abrupt halt. Glancing about the ballroom, I noticed the majority of the guests had procured a cup in anticipation of the emperor's toast. I turned around for a servant to bring me a glass, but their trays were empty.

"Welcome, lords and ladies of Riaznin, friends from within our borders, as well as friends from beyond!" Valko's voice bounced off the marble floors. "I will not bore you with a long and arduous speech," he assured them with a smile. "I know the reason you have come tonight. To celebrate! So drink with me and let the dancing begin!"

The people cheered in unison and tossed back their aqua vitae, sending a jolt of energy up my spine. At the snap of the conductor's baton, the musicians' bows crossed their strings to the tune of a cheerful Esten waltz. My palms flared with a zing of panic. Without thinking, I'd promised the emperor a dance, though I'd never learned more than the skirt-swaying undulations of the Romska. Leaning forward on my stool, I studied the couples as they revolved and revolved and tried to memorize the rhythm of their feet, the position of their hands.

Valko, who had returned to sit on his throne, made a slight movement. I tensed, expecting him to rise again, this time to guide me to the dance floor, but he only shifted closer to Floquart. As they engaged in a private conversation, I slouched with disappointment. How quickly the emperor had disregarded me. I tried to shrug off my frustration. It was just as well. His attentions would be dangerous with so many people watching. Besides, I had more important things to concentrate on.

Turning my attention back to the room of nobles, I studied them, felt their heightened arousal at the occasion of holding someone close in the name of a dance. I cast my awareness deeper for what might be lurking beneath their obvious emotions. I needed to be sure they didn't bear any danger to the emperor. Fingering the pearls, I willed their sting to keep me grounded as I searched the ballroom for the foreign diplomats.

My gut clenched when I saw them. As Valko had suspected, they were not pleased. Their gazes riveted to the dais where they observed the emperor, deep in conversation with the emissary. Certainly the foreigners had drawn conclusions as to the nature of Valko's plotting with Estengarde.

I focused in on the diplomats and absorbed every detail of their body language, every twitch of their eyes—anything visual that would help me tune myself to their auras. The surest way to ascertain their feelings would be by using touch, but I didn't think Valko would appreciate me wandering around groping his guests tonight. And so I resigned myself to intently survey the foreigners, until their frustration formed a hard knot in my stomach. Nevertheless, I was able to loosen it after a few moments' concentration. It seemed safe then to assume that the diplomats' upset with the emperor, while enraged, was not lethal.

Relaxing somewhat, I cast my gaze about the room for Anton, first scanning the perimeter where people weren't dancing. The prince was sensible. If he must attend a ball, he would use his time wisely. He'd discuss the concerns of his province with any noble who might have the means to lend him aid. Perhaps his scheme for Morva's Eve was nothing more than that.

In my search for the prince, I found Pia at one of the banquet tables. She gave me her promised wink as she refilled a large bowl of aqua vitae. Had she found a moment alone with Yuri? I waited for her to catch my eye again so I could nod him out to her. He stood at attention on the opposite side of the ballroom. But my maid's gaze was downcast as she mopped up a spill from the table. A nobleman moved in front of her and blocked her from view. Taking a silver cup, the man dipped it into the bowl of spirits. The candlelight glinted off of his amethyst ring. I sucked in my breath. The ring circled his smallest finger.

Could he be the same man who had passed the letter to Anton on our travels? The man with the letter about Morva's Eve?

As if he sensed I wished to see him better, the man turned around. He looked to be in his midthirties, with a lean but muscular physique and a great mop of wavy hair. All in all, he had the appearance of a brown-petaled flower. I would have passed him off as being gentle in nature if not for his pensive gaze. He took a sip of his drink, his eyes roaming over the couples spinning to the music, until they landed on a specific person.

When I saw who it was, my stomach plummeted to the soles of my satin slippers. Anton was dancing. *Anton*, who took no time for social pleasantries. Aloof, solemn, and pragmatic Anton had his hand on a lady's waist, her outstretched hand in his. I took in her shining red hair, her rosy complexion, and—above all—her grace as she glided across the marble floor.

Something dark and bitter coalesced inside me. Heat flashed through my veins. Who was this woman that the prince should dance with her and never bat an eye at me unless I barged into his room?

I gritted my teeth and pulled a smug smile to my lips. Anton could dance with as many ladies as it pleased him. Did he think that would distract me from finding out what he was truly up to? If so, he was wrong, for I'd discovered something he meant to keep from me: the nobleman with the silver cup *was* in league with him, as well as Yuri. The nobleman's ring and the way he'd sought Anton out from the crowd were too suspicious, and I was desperate enough to call anything evidence now.

I laced my fingers together, though every nerve in me begged me to launch myself from the dais and confront Anton.

I needed to keep my cool. If I left the emperor's side, Valko's gaze would only follow me. I didn't want him suspecting anything until I'd discovered what this was about. As maddening as the situation was, I had to wait and keep watch on Anton, Yuri, and the nobleman. With enough patience, I would learn more. Midnight would come. If Anton thought he could protect me from all the palace politics, he was wrong. I wasn't the naive girl he took me to be, the simpleton he fleetingly tried to rescue from distress. Why couldn't he be the hero to me in public? Why always behind closed doors?

The emissary laughed at something Valko said, and I glanced sidelong at the emperor, wishing to hear the end of the joke. He muttered it to Floquart, however, not bothering to share it with me. The anger I'd already felt at Anton multiplied as yet another Ozerov brother chose to pretend I didn't exist. I knew it was ridiculous that I should feel so jilted, but I couldn't help it. I was Sovereign Auraseer, but I was also a girl who had spent the day being beautified, albeit against my will, a girl who had made very few friends in her life, and now, like any other girl in this ballroom, I wanted to be *seen*. Admired. Talked to. Danced with—as I'd been promised I would be. Instead, though I sat on the dais in a position of esteem beside the emperor, I was trapped here in a cage of my loneliness while all the other guests were at liberty to do as they pleased.

My wretchedness and resentment, like yeast beneath a sprinkling of sugar, began to grow and fester. I wanted to burn out of myself all of the desires and dreams other girls had.

When had I begun thinking I was entitled like them? I was an Auraseer. I had no rights, no freedom. Besides, I didn't deserve happiness. If the Romska were wrong and the gods were real, I would one day find myself in the deepest pit of the underworld for all the wrongs I'd committed. I deserved that punishment. I was darkness personified.

My eyes grew heavy, and my heart beat a slow and tormenting rhythm. My gaze fell to the blue tracery of veins on the emperor's wrist, where it lay on the arm of his throne. I imagined the sharp edge of a blade pressed there, like the knives Yuliya would use to cut herself. Her flowing blood would match the color of Valko's velvet sleeve and the carpet beneath his feet.

The waltz ended, and my dark thoughts broke apart. I gave a shaky exhale. I wanted to scrub at my eyes to chase away the images of death and blood, and with them my harrowing guilt. Did I need to torture myself *during* the ball? Couldn't that wait until afterward when I could be alone with the statue of Feya?

Seeking the nearest method to distract myself *from* myself, I slid closer to Valko, to the command of his aura, and latched on to it as I listened in on his conversation with Floquart de Bonpré.

"When Madame Valois is escorted into Torchev," Valko said, "it will be magnificent." He brandished his hand in the air, painting a picture. "She'll ride in a carriage with ten perfectly matched horses. Four companies of Riaznian cavalry will accompany her, as well as all the high noble lords. Her path will be paved with roses, and the gates to the palace will open with the heralding of a thousand silver bells."

My astonishment at the emperor's words was the distraction I'd been hoping for. Was his marriage to Delphine agreed upon, then—and so soon? The council had arranged to convene with both the emperor and emissary tomorrow afternoon. I'd expected the terms of the union to be bargained upon then, not tonight.

"Delphine dotes on that kind of attention," Floquart said, his knees crossed over each other in the Esten fashion. He leaned on the armrest with one elbow and motioned for a servant to fan his face. "Though I will share with you her preference for white horses spotted like a leopard. Do you breed such horses here?"

Valko angled himself to match Floquart's artful posture. "But of course." Deceit bled from his aura and made my pulse race. He had no idea how to procure such horses. They were native to Estengarde, and I sensed Floquart knew it.

"The Romska trade those horses every summer at Orelchelm," I said, feeling the need to back Valko, as if a kind gesture could erase all my sins.

Floquart's brows darted up. I realized too late I'd surely broken a rule of etiquette by trespassing upon their conversation. He squinted one eye at me, and my cheeks burned with a rush of self-consciousness. I hoped it didn't belong to Valko, that he wasn't ashamed I'd spoken. If so, he would have heated words with me later—maybe more. My back still twinged with pain from the violence of his last kiss.

The emperor craned his head around to look at me. My gaze flickered to the tendons on his neck, taut like Nadia's had been when I'd locked her in the east wing of the convent. Had part of me wanted Nadia to die? How often had I imagined strangling her myself and smirked at the thought of her open-eyed, dead stare. Yuliya and I had *laughed* as we'd joked about it. I should have known those secret and murderous thoughts would build until I dared one day to do something reckless about them. I just didn't realize how many lives that would cost me.

I flinched when Floquart spoke. "What does a young Auraseer know of the gypsies?" he asked. "Didn't you spend your life in the convent at Ormina?"

My heart hammered as I tried to shake away another flood of horrible thoughts. I refused to look at Valko, for fear he would see the guilt in my countenance. It took me a moment to remember what we were talking about: I had told the emissary where the Romska traded spotted horses. "My brother has a fascination for horses," I replied. "He wrote letters." A lie. I had an older brother, but he had died when the Abdarans raided my hometown of Bovallen five years ago. Or so the Romska had told me. I couldn't remember my brother's face, either.

The emissary studied me a moment. His gaze dropped to where my shoulder pressed against the emperor's throne. He turned a scrutinizing look on Valko, as if amazed he tolerated my close proximity. Perhaps Valko shouldn't, not with someone like me.

Again, that self-consciousness, that shame and darkness,

churned in my belly. I locked my jaw and struggled to prevent another wave of destructive thoughts.

At length, Floquart pursed his lips and fluffed the lace spilling out from the hem of his sleeve. "I trust your laws are severe in regard to the gypsies," he remarked to the emperor. "They're a loathsome people, always begging, always on the move. A plague to civilization. Why, Estengarde put quite a number to death a few years ago when their tribes multiplied beyond reason."

I stared at him in horror. Bile rose in my throat, and my dismal remembrances were forgotten. "How inconvenient for you," I bit out.

Oblivious to my anger, the emissary sighed and shook his head. "Indeed, it was inconvenient."

I dug my fingernails into my palms, sensing his false and barren compassion.

"But to maintain order, a kingdom—an empire, I dare say," he added to Valko, "the monarchy must be prepared to wrestle with such decisions and make the choice for the greater good, whether that means thinning the gypsies . . . or even abolishing harlotry." He wrinkled his nose at me. "It is widely known our Esten ladies prize fidelity in a partner above all else."

I recoiled, both confused and affronted. Was he insinuating I was a harlot? What roles did the Auraseers in Estengarde play that I wasn't aware of?

I was a breath away from telling him what I thought of his greater good, his butchered ideals, and his disrespect to me, when Valko abruptly stood. "Shall I show you our treasury, Monsieur de Bonpré?"

Floquart blinked, but recovered quickly from his surprise. I didn't hide mine. What was the emperor doing? Wouldn't he defend me? "Thank you," the emissary said as he rose and gave his coattails a straightening flick.

I pulled myself to my feet, my body rigid, already dreading the hour I was to spend with them. It was all I could do not to scratch out the emissary's eyes.

"Sonya, you stay behind." Valko's voice was firm, as was his grip on my arm when I tried to advance. Floquart's gaze riveted to where to the emperor and I touched.

"But—" I said, eyes flashing at the emissary, "I am your protector."

"Then protect me from *here*." Valko gritted his teeth. He spun away and descended the dais. Floquart tossed me a grim smile as he fell in tow.

I crossed my arms and watched the emissary leave, all the while struggling to contain my boiling fury. *Condoner of slaughter. Callous fop.* All manner of silent curses filled me until I was fit to burst. Why was Valko angry with *me* for being insulted? His pretty speech before the ball had made me feel revered. Why hadn't he stood up for me when Floquart essentially called me a whore?

As Valko and the emissary retreated through the great doors of the ballroom, the orchestra went silent and the nobles faced the emperor and bowed. Several Esten and Riaznian guards followed behind the two men. I paced back and forth. At least the emperor would have some level of protection. Not that I cared. Perhaps it was better this way. For all the tortuous thoughts I was having, some time away from Valko might be best.

When the last of Floquart's entourage swept away, my gaze fell upon a young Esten girl, close to my age. She wasn't dressed in the pale silks of her fellow countrymen. Instead, she wore a simple black dress that did nothing to complement her sallow complexion. Her dreary countenance and sunken eyes were just as distressing. In her favor, however, she had a lovely shade of auburn hair, which helped me see how pretty she would be if she smiled or showed some spark of vitality.

No matter how I focused in on her, I couldn't latch on to the weak pulse of her aura and guess at why she had traveled with the emissary. But as she shuffled to the ballroom's threshold to exit through it, she suddenly halted and turned to look me directly in the eye. The hair on my arms shot up. The girl's aura strengthened and reflected my own curiosity. The ultra-aware energy she emitted was deeply familiar. It prodded around inside me like an animal testing a new cage.

That's when I recognized her for what she was—the like of which I hadn't seen or felt since I gave Dasha and Kira a final glance of farewell at the convent in Ormina.

Another Auraseer.

CHAPTER EIGHTEEN

I GASPED AS THE ESTEN GIRL WALKED OUT OF SIGHT. MY MIND whirred as I tried to absorb what I'd just discovered.

Auraseers were scarce. As girls who suffered the full range of feelings from others, we were drawn to each other, almost as if we shared the same blood. That compelling connection made me hope I'd find more than one friend at the convent. But even among them, I was too strange, too unusual. I touched my black ribbon. Too dark-hearted.

I stepped to the edge of the dais and yearned to follow the Esten girl, but my shoulders fell when I realized I couldn't. She had left to attend Floquart and Valko in the treasury, and the emperor had said I was not welcome. With a heavy sigh, I returned to my stool with all the grace of a toad landing on a mushroom.

As the music and dancing resumed, I fought to remember my duty as sovereign Auraseer. It might help the time pass more quickly until the Esten girl returned. I had so many questions for her. She was in the service of Floquart de Bonpré—a nobleman, but not royalty. Was it true, then, that Auraseers in her country didn't belong to the crown? Were they really sold like slaves to the highest bidder? I gave a dismal laugh. So much for Estengarde's praised culture. And what about Floquart's offhand remark about harlotry? Was the Esten girl also abused in that regard? I shuddered to think of it.

My eyes found Anton—dancing, yet again. This time with a raven-haired lady, Riaznian, though her amber eyes lifted in the corners like the Shenglin. What did the prince think of the way the Esten Auraseers were treated? Our lot in Riaznin was bad enough. *You couldn't have attained freedom no matter what you went through,* the prince had once told me. He'd spoken like the empire was as unjust as I knew it to be. And that unjustness had led to my daunting and obligatory role as sovereign Auraseer.

Once again, I tried to focus on my responsibility tonight. Whether or not it was compulsory didn't matter. If I failed in my duties, Dasha and Kira would be forced to take them up in my stead.

Resolved to do my best, I lowered my guard to the guests in the ballroom as I tried to ascertain what they were feeling. Once my defenses were down, their auras leapt at me like cats waiting to pounce. I gave a little jolt, and my hand flew to my pearls. The sting helped me draw back some of my barriers, and with the remaining gap I left open, I first studied the foreign diplomats. With Valko absent, I dared to leave the confines of the dais and walk through the midst of the people.

The Shenglin whispered among themselves, their distress palpable but not as strong as before. As for the Abdarans, they mingled near a bowl of aqua vitae. An alluring Abdaran lady sipped from a cup, working around the veil concealing her nose and mouth. When I reached for her emotions or those of her party, my mind felt fuzzy. Perhaps they had drunk away their frustrations with our empire.

After I'd checked the diplomats, I drifted off to other parts of the room to observe the Riaznian nobles. They were also slightly numbed with the detached sensation of too much drink. Once I felt satisfied their auras were safe, as far as the emperor was concerned, my eyes, of their own accord, found their way back to Anton.

Dance after dance, I watched him, my ribs squeezing tight as I compared myself to every other female in the ballroom. *All* of them had basked in the prince's attention. Perhaps that was an exaggeration. But at least nine ladies and counting had taken a turn twirling in Anton's arms. Those nine felt like a thousand. Never once did he stop to converse with the amethyst-ringed man or even Yuri. Never once did his gaze turn toward me, not even with the emperor absent. His eyes simmered only for the ladies before him.

Their jewel-toned dresses collided in my vision. Their auras combined and ganged up on me until they formed a blend of perfection I could never attain. They knew the art of teasing a smile from the prince's lips. How to keep up a stream of lively banter. How to lean forward in such a way that made his hand spread farther across their backs.

I could no longer endure it.

When the orchestra reached a crescendo at the end of a minuet, I strode across the ballroom just as the girl Anton danced with—surely younger than myself—curtsied in parting. The moment she walked away, I asked the prince, "Would you care to dance?" My words were a tumbled, undignified mess, and a few surrounding ladies tittered at my forwardness. But I lifted my chin and owned my request.

Anton's jaw contracted. He smoothed the end of his kaftan and finally looked at me, though only at my nose, a trick he'd mastered as we'd journeyed together in the troika—surely another method to keep me at a distance. "Auraseers do not dance, Sonya. Not in Torchev."

"They do now. The emperor himself made me promise one."

The prince's nostrils flared ever so slightly. My stomach tightened like I'd just swallowed rancid milk. I hoped to the gods I felt what he did, that I'd inflicted on him the jealousy he'd been inflicting on me. "Then you should save your strength," he said, and turned to walk away, his manner casual. He nodded at a few lords conversing nearby.

I rushed forward and kept pace beside him. He wouldn't evade me so easily. The auras of the ladies who had flirted with him met my bloodstream. They amplified my own desire and escalated my boldness to new heights. "I have strength enough for two dances," I declared, catching up the length of my robes so I wouldn't trip. In truth, my strength was waning. Even standing made my heart beat faster, my breath come quicker. Vaguely, I realized these were complications of dehydration brought on by diuretic tea. No matter. I clung to the women's auras and strove to bolster myself. I could eat something later. I wasn't finished with Anton.

"I am glad you are feeling well." He served himself a cup of aqua vitae. "I, on the other hand, am quite fatigued."

I balled my hands. It wasn't midnight. He wouldn't retire from these rooms. Not yet. Perhaps he wouldn't even leave when the time came. His secret business could be enacted here.

I resisted the urge to hang on him like a beggar. All I wanted was one dance. More than that, I felt desperate for one, desperate that the prince take this chance to prove to me—in the presence of everyone else—that I was a good enough person to be in his association. If he would dance with me, maybe I could hope for something more between us. Or better yet, drive the darkness from my soul.

Anton took a long drink and watched the dancing resume, his lips pressed together in a firm line.

"He's gone," I said, referring to the emperor.

A beat later, Anton replied, "I know."

I folded my arms. "The nobles can see we're conversing, even if you don't look at me. Though I'm sure no one can hear our words above the music, not from this corner, if that's what you're worried about."

Anton sighed and drew his brows together. Something

sharp lodged in my chest near the region of my heart. "Sonya, what do you want from me?" He kept his eyes averted.

I shifted on my feet. What *did* I want? What was this fragile thing between us? Did it only exist when the palace was asleep and we were closed away from the world? Was it only in my imaginings that Anton cared for me in some small way—some way that would still exist if he didn't feel the need to protect me from his brother?

"I want a dance," I said.

"No, you don't. You want more than a dance, more from me than what you understand. I *know* you. You're reflecting something that is not your own. Let it go."

My mouth fell open as hurt and anger suppressed my breath. More powerful was the cold and lonely part of me wanting to warm at the hidden meaning in his words. But he kept pushing me away. "I'm not a mirror, Anton. And I don't break like glass. I'm capable of my own feelings. You told me as much. The difference between you and me is I don't hide my emotions. The part of me that's *me* has a chance to shine through."

"Emotions alone can't tell you the whole truth of who a person is," he replied defensively.

"Well, they're all I have to go by," I quipped. "And you hide *more* than your emotions; you hide your potential for greatness. You would discover it if you embraced who you are." When he didn't respond, I lowered my voice, despite my surety no one could hear us. "You could be greater than any man in this empire."

He set his cup down hard. The remaining liquid sloshed out. "Hush, Sonya!" he rasped. "Leave me be."

My eyes burned with the prick of frustrated tears. I was only trying to make him see how *I* saw him. I whirled to leave, to return to my stump of a stool, when Anton brushed past me and asked another lady to dance, even though the quadrille was halfway over. Steam practically rose off my skin. Through the haze of my jealousy, I formed a mad idea. Resolved, I wove through the ballroom and searched for someone. Not just anyone, a man with an amethyst ring. I found him in a corner, laughing with two young noblemen.

I curtsied deeply and offered the required salutation: "Your High Nobleness."

His eyes rounded. "Sovereign Auraseer." The men behind him exchanged glances. Something like panic fluttered in my belly. Did I make them that nervous? Were they *all* anxious, or just the amethyst-ringed man?

"Are you acquainted with His Imperial Highness, Prince Anton?" I asked.

The butterfly inside me beat harder. The man shot a look at the crowd, no doubt at the prince, though I didn't turn to see. "Every nobleman has an association with him," he answered with a smile, though it didn't reach his eyes.

"Well"—I batted my lashes—"the prince and I have a little wager. He's dared me to see if I'm brave enough to take my pick of the barons and ask the most handsome to dance." I'd taken a wild guess at the man's title. Based on his fine attire and demeanor, he seemed higher in ranking than the other noble-men at court.

The man chuckled, and the butterfly's wings beat slower. My flattery had hit its mark. "Is that so?" He took in the length of me. "Well, I'm afraid I cannot consent."

My brows launched up. Was I seriously being rejected again?

"Oh, come, Nicolai." One of the young men slapped him on the shoulder.

"Nicolai?" I asked. The image of Anton's unfinished letter blazed across my mind. "Nicolai Rostav?"

He shrugged. "The very same."

"Let me guess. Are you denying me a dance because you're a count and not a baron?"

His grin broadened. "I'm afraid you've found me out." Step-ping closer, he added, "Though if Anton might bend the rules, I'd be happy to help you win your wager."

I put my hands in the air, palms up. "I'm afraid he won't. If you know the prince, you'll understand what a purist he is to his principles. I shall have to find some other, unassuming man."

The nobles behind Count Rostav looked hopeful. I gave them a demure smile and glided away, returning to the dais.

I wouldn't ask anyone else to dance. I'd shocked the ladies of the court enough for one night. Besides, at just the drop of his name, Nicolai had given me another piece to the puzzle of Anton. The more evidence I gained, the sooner the prince would relent to sharing his plans, the sooner he'd permit me into his ring of trust. That was better than turning circles with him to the sweetest melody. Or so I kept telling myself.

When I reached my stool and whirled around to face the room, there at the far end of the dance floor was what I'd been longing to catch all evening—Anton's attention, planted firmly on me.

He was not pleased.

CHAPTER NINETEEN

GOOD, I THOUGHT, AND MET THE PRINCE'S GAZE HEAD-ON. *Let him wriggle in his discomfort.* I hoped he had seen me speak with Nicolai, that he knew I was up to something and hadn't forgotten the snatch of the letter I'd read so many months ago.

I lifted my chin and looked away from him first, finding some measure of power in that. Petty or not, it felt wonderful.

I sat on my stool with my back straight, my Auraseer's robes spread at my feet like a fan. A dark sensation twisted inside me, like a serpent writhed in my gut. I exhaled and struggled to release it, but it only coiled tighter. My gaze flickered to Anton. Was this him? I'd been so fixated on his aura. But I'd never sensed something this disturbing within it before.

The music fell silent. The nobles faced the doors of the ballroom in expectation. Valko and Floquart reentered. They'd been gone such a long time, it led me to wonder how vast

Riaznin's treasury was, how much wealth we hoarded in the palace while so many went without.

As the guards filed in behind them, I saw Yuri a pace back from the rest. A few moments after him came Pia, her head lowered as she hurried to the nearest banquet table. She peeked up at me, her cheeks dimpling as she suppressed a smile. With the healthy flush of color on her skin, she was practically glowing. It appeared she'd stolen a dance, after all. At least one of us had.

I scanned the procession for the Esten Auraseer, but the girl with sunken eyes and auburn hair was nowhere to be seen.

The bitter feeling in me grew stronger, thicker like black tar. As the emperor drew nearer, it oozed into my mind, across my heart. The self-loathing I'd felt before Valko had left to the treasury came back with full vengeance. My thoughts reverted to Yuliya's blood, Nadia's death, the peasant man's burning. The darkness spread inside me.

There were more ways a person could die. Suffocation. Smothering.

What would it feel like to hold a pillow over someone's mouth? Who would let me close enough so I could try?

Would the emperor?

I slowly twirled a lock of hair as I watched him through murky vision, as if the blackness had bled across my eyes. I could knock on Valko's door tonight, let him kiss me, let him do more, and while he slept in my arms, I could snuff the last breath from his lungs.

He smiled warmly at me from across the ballroom. His gaze held triumph. No doubt, the private meeting with Floquart had been successful—so successful the emperor had forgiven my indiscretions. I could already imagine his hot fingers on my skin. What would it feel like to break them?

The nobles fell into bows as the emperor's procession carved across the dance floor. I restrained my curtsy until he was so near I could no longer afford to be indifferent. Now wasn't the time to betray my dark intentions. He'd know them soon enough.

I rose from my curtsy and grinned up at him through my lashes, the taste of his promised death like sugar on my tongue.

Some niggling speck of reason flitted through my mind. When had the emperor wronged me to such a degree that I should feel so violent?

With a nod to the conductor and a slight motion to a servant, Valko recommenced the music and summoned a goblet of aqua vitae for the emissary. Floquart's large hand encircled the cup. His cunning mouth took delicate sips.

The serpent in me slithered as I considered the emissary. Riaznin would benefit from a union to Estengarde. The wars at our borders would cease—at least to the west. The Esten army would fortify ours. Valko could invade Shengli with such strength, whether or not that was wise.

But what did Estengarde stand to gain by allying with *us*? Where we were surrounded by three countries, they had the sea on all sides except one—their northeastern front with the

Bayac Mountains, a natural fortress. The border wars that devastated us did little damage to them or their numbers.

The serpent inside me slid under my ribs and squeezed my lungs.

While it was true Riaznin was less fortified, we were, however, wealthy—even if that wealth did little to assist our people or give us the united culture of which the Estens were so proud. They were rich enough without us, but if I knew one thing about greed, it was that its appetite was endless.

Floquart's eyes peered over his goblet as he drank again, this time to take in the expanse of the room. His gaze held more admiration than the first glimpse of his arrival. Whatever he saw in our treasury had tipped the scales. He may think us unrefined, but we were still gold in his pockets.

The serpent coiled up toward my heart.

Valko grinned broadly. "I am ready to dance!" he announced to anyone within earshot. Turning to Floquart, he added, "I do hope you'll take the opportunity to become acquainted with our Riaznian beauties. And I shall do the same so you may have proof for Madame Valois that her intended is as nimble on his feet as he is in his promise to lavish every luxury on her."

Floquart nodded, his eyes trapped on mine, anticipating Valko's next move. But the emperor wisely chose someone else—Countess Dyomin of the first-class-ranking nobles. As he led her out on the dance floor, the emissary's shoulders relaxed. Still, there was a motive I had yet to discover in the man. It seemed the utmost importance I do it now.

But try as I might over the next few waltzes, minuets, and Valko's rotating dance partners, I couldn't find proof that the darkness I felt originated with Floquart. Every time my jaw clenched, my knees locked, or my nerves flared, he merely seemed bored. His eyebrows didn't so much as twitch when horrid images surfaced in my mind.

Perhaps, with my shameful history and weakening barriers against my viler self, I needed to accept that the likeliest source of the darkness was me.

At the end of a contredanse, Valko left his partner and came to my side. He took my hand and brushed it over with his thumb. His touch burned like a kiss. Something shivered in my chest and unfurled like a flower, but threatened to wither in the darkness still holding me captive.

"Are you ready to redeem your promise, Sovereign Auraseer?" he said. No . . . he *asked* me. Like a gentleman would, no demand in his voice. *He asked me.* Like I'd asked Anton. The flower inside me raised its head.

The niggling reason in my mind grew stronger. Floquart was watching us, lip curled and eyes narrowed. Some instinct warned I shouldn't dance with the emperor now; I should focus on my duties. But I couldn't. I couldn't deny Valko like Anton had denied me.

I curtsied, my hand still resting in his. "I am ready, My Lord Emperor." Despite the swarming darkness, despite my suspicious thoughts of Floquart, I wanted this dance. I wanted, for a moment, to be just a girl.

Valko kissed my hand, which made Floquart's eye spasm, and then he guided me deep into the nest of dancing nobles. They pulled back a little to give us a wider berth, but the air still felt too dense to breathe. Taking hold of my waist and raising my hand in the air, the emperor and I assumed the position of the waltz. My legs trembled, whether from my self-imposed starvation or the probing and judgmental auras fighting for purchase within me, I didn't know.

"I don't want to embarrass you, My Lord," I said, already stumbling on my feet. "But I was never taught to dance." *Not like this.*

He grinned as if my confession were the most becoming thing in the world. "Relax in my arms, Sonya, and I will carry you." I did as he said, and like magic, we spun in a graceful circle. An amazed bubble of laughter tumbled out of me. I felt as elegant as a princess the more I fell in step with Valko's confident lead. As we revolved and revolved, he gazed steadfastly upon me. His gray eyes fairly glowed from the abundant candlelight.

How kind he is. How patient.

No. The darker half of me obliterated my pleasant thoughts. *He thinks I am weak, and he likes it. He likes being stronger than me.*

We twirled around and around. I fought a dizzying rush, not only from the dance but the prying emotions of the nobles and their needling curiosity at seeing the sovereign Auraseer dance—and with the emperor. I battled their energy and tried to push them away, and then the writhing darkness did it for me. Like a billowing cloud of smoke, it overcame them. And as it dissipated, their auras were replaced in my mind with images of poison, sharpened knives, the knot of a noose, pooling blood.

Think, Sonya, think. The darkness couldn't wholly be me.

I looked past the swirl of jewel-tone dresses to Floquart. He leaned on one elbow in the careless Esten way that wasn't careless at all. His eyes were fast on me. I was a threat to him, though I didn't know why.

Valko glided me around once more and pulled my gaze until it fell on Anton, who conversed with the most pompously dressed woman in the room. One bell tolled the quarter hour. Fifteen minutes until midnight. I imagined the prince's boot tapping with impatience.

The emperor and I circled near Count Nicolai Rostav and his noblemen friends. The count's lips were only slightly curved, as if his smile had faltered when he heard the bell. His panic reared up and beat again like a trapped butterfly inside my chest.

I searched for Yuri as I spun three more revolutions, but the guard was gone—as well as Pia. Had they sneaked another moment away together? Would Yuri leave her in time to join Anton, or did each man in the prince's league intend to act his part alone?

Once more, I wondered where the Esten Auraseer was. Perhaps she had slipped back inside the ballroom through the orchestra door. But I couldn't find her among the group of

Estens gathered near the dais or with the servants on the outer edges of the room.

Valko and I spun again. My knees buckled at the sight of a new man. He wore an ill-fitting kaftan of brown silk, surely not his own. And, unlike the Riaznian nobles, this man sported a trimmed beard despite the emperor's decree. Feliks was here. Feliks, the commoner. The man from the city. The man Anton had passed the reins of his troika to upon our arrival—and his secret letter.

How had Feliks gained entrance to the ball?

"Are you all right?" Valko asked, catching me upright again.

"Yes." My breathless voice, however, revealed I was not. "But I suppose I'm not as clever a student at dancing as I'd hoped to be. Even with a master for a teacher."

He held me closer and twirled me around with more tenderness, more vigor. Nicolai's panic, which had stuck inside me, grew stronger. Nausea gripped my stomach—my own ailment for not eating all day.

It took me a moment to locate Feliks again. He'd moved closer to the doors. His piercing blue eyes surveyed the ballroom, especially the quadrants containing Anton and Nicolai. At last, with a flex of his fists, he turned on his heel and abruptly left.

At that moment, Nicolai yawned. He gave a short bow to his friends, ambled around the edge of the room, and exited after Feliks.

It was happening. Whatever plan they were enacting, it was happening right now. And they were doing it together. Yuri had already left; he'd never reentered after disappearing a second time with Pia.

My heart thrummed with anticipation. I looked past Valko's shoulder to Anton. I tensed as I waited for him to follow the others. In brief flickers, I watched him as I spun in the waltz, finding careful moments to glance away from the emperor. A long minute passed in which the prince continued conversing with the pompous lady.

Leave, I silently pleaded with Anton as I revolved again. I needed to be right about this. I needed Anton to realize how clever I was and think me capable of joining his league. I *would* join him, that I knew. His cause had to be noble. I would believe nothing less of him. Perhaps it could be the means of giving him the glory his birthright could not.

When I thought I might burst, when I entertained a mad-dening thought of grabbing the prince's hand and yanking him from the room myself, he finished speaking to the woman. In another three flashes of my vision, their conversation ended naturally. She gave the last word, curtsied, and initiated the farewell. After Anton parted from the woman, I studied him through a new series of stolen glances. He stopped at a banquet table, took a sip of aqua vitae—adding to the illusion he was in no rush at all. And then—at last—he walked out of the room.

My mouth went dry. My legs shook violently. The dizzying

turns of the waltz seized me. I dug my hand into Valko's shoulder. I would not faint. Not now.

"I was wrong, My Lord," I said, fighting for breath. "I'm not all right. I'm afraid I'm not accustomed to the demands of this dance." In truth, I was as ill as I needed him to believe, though I couldn't determine if the mounting sickness came of starvation, my own anxiety, someone else's energy, or if it was part of the darkness I strove to hold at bay.

Valko brought us to an immediate halt, which only made my head spin worse. "Do you need something to drink?"

"No, no, only some air." Worried he might follow, I added, "I have a tonic—in my room."

"I'll send a servant."

"No, the solitude will do me good. The weight of so many auras is difficult to endure. A little distance and a moment's peace will make my recovery all the speedier." How quickly the words came to my tongue, despite my light-headedness. "I'll return soon, My Lord." I curtsied and dashed out of the ballroom before he could talk me into staying. Surely I was the only Riaznian to ever abandon him without his dismissal, but if I didn't go now, I would lose Anton's trail.

Outside the doors were a handful of guards. The rest were within. The spacious lobby beyond was empty and dim with only a few lit candle stands. I studied the many branching corridors and cursed Anton for being so fast.

"Did you see which way the prince went?" I asked the guards. "The emperor wishes a word with him." It was a stupid lie; my faint head was getting the better of me. Valko would send a servant to fetch Anton, not his sovereign Auraseer. But at the moment I couldn't think of a better excuse.

If the guards thought me strange, they didn't show it. Neither could I sense it from their auras, though mine was too clouded to judge them properly. The darkness inside me seemed to pulse with its own heartbeat. It grew more and more urgent with every passing moment.

A Riaznian guard furrowed his black brows in concentration. "That way?" He pointed to the right.

"No," his neighbor replied. "It was Count Rostav who went that way."

They went in separate directions?

One of the Esten guards, blond-haired with droopy green eyes, chuckled under his breath at the Riaznians. "Do you know where the prince went?" I asked him.

"Oui." He smiled crookedly.

I gritted my teeth with impatience. "Will you tell me?"

He swept a gaze over my body that made me feel naked. From his penetrating eyes to Floquart's pointed comments, it was clear Auraseers in Estengarde held no respect whatsoever. *"Le dauphin négligé* took that corridor." He nodded to the one farthest left.

I didn't bolt straightaway. The guard's name for Anton made my feet stick to the floor. *"Le dauphin négligé,"* I repeated. "What does that mean?"

He licked his lips, his grin catching the other corner of his mouth. "The neglected crown prince," he answered past his thick accent.

I frowned. "Neglected?"

The guard nodded. "So we called him in my village."

"And where is that?"

"Montpanon. At the eastern base of the Bayacs."

Nothing was adding up. So why was my stomach tightening like I was about to be kicked? "Are you telling me the prince lived in Estengarde?"

"That's a matter of debate." He leaned on one leg. "I would say yes. The Riaznian farmers would say no. There *is* a reason we fight." He shrugged like it was an unavoidable fact of his life.

"And you *knew* he was the prince?" I asked, still bracing myself, still confused. What was the point of Anton being raised in secrecy if an entire Esten village knew about him?

"No," he admitted. "Not until the prince left and his brother was crowned. But I will say our *king* knew of him. We were commanded that Trusochelm Manor was never to be touched in our wars. We avoided it like a river snakes around a rock."

Understanding took seed inside me. *Dauphin. Crown prince.* "The king thought he was protecting the future emperor," I said, voicing my revelation. Perhaps the king thought he could make peace with Izia's successor. But then Valko took the throne and Anton remained the neglected prince. The Estens hadn't given him a happy name.

"I suppose your king wasn't too pleased Anton's brother

lived," I baited the guard. It would have injured the king's pride to realize he was thwarted after all the protection he'd offered.

"Who can say?" The guard jutted out his lower lip in the quintessential Esten shrug. "I can only tell you that after the prince left, we raided Trusochelm—and we weren't reprimanded for it."

I took a step back as the blow crashed into me, an icy gale tearing through the wrong season. The force of it chilled me with misgiving and made my gut fold in cramps.

I turned the guard's words over in my mind. Why had they provoked such an ominous feeling? If the Esten king hadn't protected Anton, he would be dead. Was the darkness inside me casting everything in a sinister shadow, when in reality there was nothing amiss? Or was Anton's life still somehow in danger?

I became aware of every guard in the lobby, their perplexed eyes locked upon me, the all-too-inquisitive Auraseer.

"Thank you," I muttered to the Esten guard and walked briskly to the far left corridor. Once I was out of sight, I broke into a run. My weakened legs threatened to snap like bird bones, and my breath came thinly, but on and on I fled.

Everything I'd just learned spun around in my mind, along with the mystery of where Anton had gone. He was the most notable of his party. Surely, he took a detouring, less obvious route to where his men were meeting—if they *were* meeting at all. I slid to a halt upon approaching an intersecting corridor to the right. Down that direction and up a flight of stairs was the council chamber. I couldn't imagine Anton going there. But past the stairs were more branching hallways, and beyond them a library—a place no one would be lingering on the night of a ball.

With no better plan, I took the corridor to the right. As I sprang forward, my headdress fell to the floor. I snatched it up, not bothering to fasten it on again, and kept running. The pearl ropes stung my palms. I felt the faint song of their mother oysters' deaths, their agony at being ripped open for the jewel in the cradle of their shells.

What torture had the dowager empress also suffered when she was torn from her young children? What had those little boys endured when they were severed from their parents to be raised in hiding?

How had that estrangement altered them?

And what of the Esten king? When Floquart journeyed home, what report would he give of the Riaznian emperor, who in the king's eyes should have been Anton?

The blow struck my gut again, this time with piercing directness. I stopped short as dizziness assaulted me.

Floquart.

The king's mouthpiece. The man who came here so readily at Valko's request, despite all our conflict with Estengarde.

I'd felt the emissary's greed. He wanted to share in our wealth. He knew his *king* would. But which brother would that king wish to forge an alliance with? And which brother could be done away with by some cunning means?

The lurking serpent inside me took form, its fangs seeking blood. I put my hand on the wall for support.

Floquart was behind the darkness I was feeling—maybe even some of his men.

Before the night was through, the Esten emissary meant to have Valko murdered.

CHAPTER TWENTY

ON INSTINCT, I SPUN AROUND AND RAN IN THE OPPOSITE direction—back to Valko. I gave myself horrible names. *Slow-witted. Blind. Incompetent.* I'd left the emperor with Floquart—twice. I prayed the emissary hadn't already taken his opportunity and poisoned Valko while they were together in the treasury. He could be dying this very moment, and there would be nothing I could do to save him.

I've failed in my duty. I'm going to be executed. They'll bury me beside Izolda. Dasha and Kira will be next. They'll fail and die, as well. I'll have more blood on my hands.

I stopped again, realizing where I was. Backtracking the way I'd come would be a slower route to the ballroom. I was closer to the main corridor leading there by continuing on in the direction I'd been going. I kneaded a stitch of pain in my side, turned around once more, and forced my legs onward.

My vision flecked with stars. I tried to breathe deeper past the pounding of my heart. Looming ahead were two marble pillars, which marked the crossroad with the spacious main corridor. I slowed when the pillars' shadows touched me, partly because I was on the verge of fainting, but mostly because my mind seized on Anton as I considered "the neglected crown prince" in a whole new light.

What if, together with his other followers, Anton was also in league with Floquart? What if collectively they'd planned Valko's assassination and the alliance to Estengarde? Anton wouldn't have told me, of course. Beyond any distrust, he knew I couldn't betray Valko. If the assassination failed and I'd known about it and hadn't warned the emperor, I would be executed, though now I'd surely be killed anyway for sensing the danger too late.

I reached one of the pillars and leaned against it with my shoulder. My chest rose and fell. I stared ahead, past the main corridor, to the path leading to the library.

Would Anton really kill his brother—or allow him to be killed?

When I'd told Anton he should be emperor, did I think he could achieve it without Valko's death? Had I only encouraged him in a plot he'd devised months ago?

I'd accused the prince of not having the stamina to attain his potential for greatness. Without so many words, I'd called him a coward.

In truth, *I* was the coward. And that was a name I was willing to own if it meant Valko lived.

I set my jaw and inhaled a great breath of air. I would return to the ballroom. I would warn the emperor. As it turned out, I was not prepared for the cost of greatness.

I rounded the corner past the pillar and prepared to run. But as I launched myself, I collided with someone rushing toward me. My headdress was knocked from my hands and slid down the main corridor, the pearl ropes skittering along the marble. I moved to retrieve it, but a girl caught my arm.

"Sovereign Auraseer?" she said. Her r's rolled in a heavy accent.

I snapped my gaze to her—the Esten Auraseer. "What are you doing?" I blinked as panic flashed through my veins. It might have been hers. In the darkness, I saw the whites of her eyes. She hadn't removed her trembling grip from my arm.

Through our heightened connection, I confirmed my earlier instinct—she *had* been abused by Floquart de Bonpré, and in more ways than I cared to imagine. I felt a hint of his foul aura inside her, as if it was imprisoned there and she'd forgotten how to let it go.

"*Ne lui fais pas confiance!*" she pleaded.

"Pardon?"

She leaned nearer. "Do not trust him!"

My deep sense of misgiving amplified. "Who?"

"Sonya?" a man called, a stone's throw away down the main corridor.

The Esten Auraseer flinched and darted into the darkness behind me. "Wait!" I hissed, but it was no use. She had disappeared, as well as her frightened aura.

Footsteps approached. "Is that you?" the man called again. This time I recognized his voice, felt his signature energy.

"Valko?" It was the first time I'd addressed him by name. I didn't apologize. I was too relieved to see him.

He came forward into the light of a glowing candle sconce. In his hands was my headdress. "Did you drop this?"

I nodded. "I—I tripped and it fell off." I didn't wish to implicate the Esten Auraseer since she clearly hadn't wanted the emperor to see her.

Valko accepted my poor explanation without question. He seemed to have something of more importance on his mind. He guided me around the corner from where I'd emerged and placed my headdress on a table set between two doors. As he turned back to me, his aura shifted in intensity and made my nerve ends tingle. "I was worried about you," he said, his gaze searching my face. "Are you feeling better?"

I shook my head. I didn't know where to begin. I was still rattled from my mysterious encounter with the Esten Auraseer. Had she meant to warn me of Floquart? Or was she more practiced than I was and sensed the danger emitted from Anton? Did it matter? Both men were likely co-conspirators.

I tried again to speak again, to form the words to condemn the prince, but they caught in my throat. I had no real proof of his betrayal, and my suspicions alone might be enough to have him harmed. Perhaps worse. I couldn't send Anton to his death just as surely as I couldn't send Valko to his.

The emperor came so close our noses brushed. I released a quivering breath. He studied me. "You feel it too, don't you, Sonya?"

"What?"

"*This*," he replied. "The deep bond between us." His fingers trailed up my wrists to my shoulders and slipped along the silk of my sleeve. My head spun as my chest expanded with a surge of overruling rapture.

"I feel it," I whispered. How could I not? His aura was so powerful, and, starved as I was, I felt so weak. Weak against my own attraction to him. I tipped my head back and leaned closer. I shivered with anticipation of the press of his lips. I bared my teeth and prepared to bite.

I gasped and pulled back, shocked with myself, at the darkness still reigning inside me. I fought to quell it and collect my thoughts. Valko was in danger. I had to warn him. But I didn't need to mention Anton. I could simply caution him about Floquart.

"What is it?" Valko stroked my face like a child's. He was so patient with me, so tender. But why? Why on the night he'd committed to marrying another?

"We can't do this." I batted his hand away. "Floquart—"

"Is that what this is all about?" He laughed. "Are you worried about the emissary?"

"You're in peril, My Lord."

"Floquart knows I do not love Delphine. I've never even met her. Love is not a factor in a royal marriage. Monarchs must look elsewhere for that." He came at me again, so quickly I couldn't deny him. Our lips met. His kiss stoked a fire in my belly. The scalding was so sweet, it took me several long moments to break away.

"Please, listen," I said. Then, hearing footsteps coming from the ballroom, I took Valko's hand and pulled him deeper down the narrow corridor. I stopped where the hallway broadened in a circular area surrounded by four doors—perhaps servants' apartments. "I feel a darkness inside me."

He grinned. "This isn't darkness, Sonya." He grazed my lips with a brief but tantalizing kiss. "This is abandonment. Of everything that seeks to repress us. This is *life*, to fully know each other. It is glory." His zeal for what he believed we were equaled his passion for expanding his empire. "Together we share acceptance and understanding—both of us born into power and with great destinies. Those things are uniquely difficult to endure."

I frowned and shook my head in amazement at him. Did he really think I'd been born with a beautiful gift? That I was taken from my parents to live in a whitewashed convent by the sea? He didn't know anything about my life of hiding with the Romska, that they had to rope me to trees until I'd stop screaming from the pain of all their auras inside me. He didn't know my parents were killed when it was discovered they had a "blessed child" they'd given away before the empire could take her. He had no idea how hard-pressed my life had been.

Valko didn't understand me, but on the other hand, did I

truly understand him? How did it feel to live a lie for so long, to pretend you were someone else because the person you really were had been declared dead? When his mother came to visit, did she tell him of Anton, that his brother lived and thought himself heir? How many years of bitterness could that breed in a person? And after all that time, only to return to the palace and be met with suspicion, rumored by some to be an imposter?

We didn't have as many things in common as Valko thought, but we had enough. And it made me feel true pity.

I let him kiss me again. I *would* tell him of Floquart, but for the moment I could not cause him more suffering. We were safely tucked away from anyone seeking to do him harm. For the moment, and after such a life, he could taste a form of beauty that had nothing to do with wealth and power. And I could surrender myself to the exalted way he made me feel.

Our kisses deepened. His breath came in rasps. He held both sides of my face like I might vanish if he slackened his grip. Candles flickered in sconces along the wall and cast us in a pool of light. The darkness swirled inside me, but I kept it at bay by offering more of myself to the emperor.

"Be my mistress, Sonya," he said. "Share my life with me. I may give my hand to another, but my heart will be yours."

My skin prickled with warmth. A lightness flowed through my limbs. I felt weightless, buoyant.

Mistress. The word took on new meaning. It sounded like an honored title.

After all my years of hiding, after my parents sacrificed

their lives to give me freedom, was this what I was to become? Burning beneath my breast, I felt the tender flame of Valko's adoration. Could it be my parents were wrong? Was it such a very bad thing to be owned by the empire?

"Say yes," Valko prodded, as if this were a secret proposal and he had asked me to elope.

The loveliness of the life the emperor painted for us began to warp like a water-damaged canvas. Harder questions began circling my mind.

What had prompted Valko to care for me in the first place? Did his affections begin because he saw Anton's interest in me first—or, more accurately, my interest in the prince? Would the emperor have fallen for me without the rivalry of his brother?

And what about Valko's Esten bride? Would she give us peace and accept our relationship?

I stared into the emperor's achingly beautiful gray eyes and realized what he wished for us could never be. "I believe you're wrong about the Estens, My Lord." I had traveled near the border enough times to understand the frame of their culture, and I didn't see how I could be Valko's mistress while he was married to Delphine. "They require fidelity in marriage, whether or not there is love . . . and, I daresay, whether or not the match is royal."

Someone gave a sardonic laugh. Valko and I whipped around to find Floquart in the corridor shadows. His posture indicated he'd been listening for a long time. I tensed and searched for his dark aura within me. Would he now seize his moment to kill the emperor? Would he kill me, too?

"Your Auraseer is very insightful." He stepped forward into the candlelight. It caught the planes of his face at an odd angle, making him appear gaunt, no longer the prim gentleman his clothes dictated him to be. "But, I suppose, that is her occupation."

Valko smoothed his hair in a rush. I'd done a fine job of disheveling it. "Monsieur de Bonpré, this isn't what it seems."

"No, I believe it is far more." He wrinkled his nose in distaste at me. "I'll be taking my leave in the morning."

The emperor's astonishment struck my chest and made my ribs contract, as if my bones welded together. "You misunderstand," he said. "I am devoted to Delphine, to a union with Estengarde."

Something in Floquart snapped. "Delphine is my goddaughter!"

I blinked. Had Valko known this?

At the emissary's heated exclamation, a clamor sounded from a nearby room, as if a chair scraped the floor.

"She was not raised in gentility to be defiled by you!" he went on. "Your Riaznin may be grander in wealth, but your savage ways"—he sneered, darting his gaze between us—"are deplorable. I'd hoped at least the monarch of this empire to be above such shameful relations, but I was wrong. We will not stoop to align ourselves with *whoredom*." His eyes settled on me, ripe with derision. "Your kind," he spat, "is sold in my country. And if the nobles find your talent unworthy of a bid, you take to the gutters where your filthy breed can scavenge upon any lowlife who will toss you a coin for your virtue. Often enough, you give it away for no money at all. Such is the quality of the Auraseers you Riaznians so prize."

My mouth fell open at his brazenness. The emissary's endearment to his goddaughter must have fueled his contempt, but that didn't excuse his blatant hatred of me. His insults tumbled inside my chest as if caught in a whirlwind. I couldn't contain the fury. I became the storm.

"Don't treat me as if you are my better!" I lashed out at him. "Don't pretend you are not above reproach yourself. I've seen the Auraseer in your company and sensed the telltale signs of the abuse she has suffered at your hands." I was sure now that she'd meant to warn me of him. "How dare you speak to the emperor about defilement when you have absolutely no respect for humanity!"

Floquart's face mottled to purple. A vein spasmed at his temple. I met his enraged expression without batting an eye, justified in all my accusations. Surely Valko shared in my vindication. I looked at the man who'd just rained affection on me, promised me a life of adoration . . . but that man was gone. I felt it in the absence of warmth in my breast. In the ice crusting over my heart.

As if he hadn't heard a word I'd just spoken, Valko said to Floquart, "You are right."

My eyes flew wide. At the worst, I'd expected the emperor's silence, not his *agreement* with the emissary. Did he want Estengarde so badly he would suffer his pride—and my dishonor—after such a vicious attack? "I will end this here." He jutted out his chin. "She will not tempt me again."

My lungs constricted and made it difficult to breathe. I felt like he'd just struck me.

Floquart's lip curled with hostility. He leaned forward nearer the emperor, his brows peaking at a severe angle. "I will not be satisfied unless *she* leaves"—his eyes threw daggers at me—"and you relinquish the position of sovereign Auraseer."

Valko blanched. "Relinquish?" His squared shoulders drooped as some of the ice in his aura melted. "You understand she is my guard—my most important guard—not a mere fortune-teller."

"You have enough guards in Torchev to stop the border wars. They are sufficient to defend one man."

"Come, now, Floquart, you are taking this too far. Perhaps you are still tired from your journey. Why don't you get some rest, and we can come to another agreement in the morning?"

"We cannot. This is my offer. If you are serious about your marriage proposal, the decision is simple."

Valko stood as still as a statue. His brows drew so low they nearly touched his eyes. Everything twisted inside me—the emperor's wrestling indecision and pride, Floquart's stubbornness, and buried beneath them both, the glimmer of my own feelings.

I should want this. I should want Valko to give me up. My life wouldn't balance on the curve of a saber. The empire would no longer cage its Auraseers. Dasha and Kira could have a chance at a normal life.

So if I should want my freedom, what was this silent prayer behind my pressed lips, the plea that Valko would keep me in the palace? Did it have to do with Anton? If I left, I would certainly never see him again. Or was this about Valko? Did I wish to stay in order to comprehend how deeply his feelings ran for me? They were authentic enough when I sensed them in his aura, but they were also fleeting. I could not forget how little he noticed me in the days preparing for the emissary's arrival and how he never came to my defense when Floquart accused me of harlotry.

If I left the palace, where would I go?

Valko drew in a long breath, while I held mine. His hand curled, then flexed. "I need her," he said, and something like shame spooled inside me—inside *him*. "She stays."

I exhaled with disbelief.

Floquart arched a thin brow. His eyes slitted like a cat's. "Then this is my farewell." He adjusted his cuff links. "I will be gone by first light, along with any hope you ever had of an alliance." With the fierceness of a lion, he marched away, his coattails flapping.

Valko paced back and forth. He yanked his hair at the scalp as he watched the emissary go. I remembered the emperor's finger on the map tracing the river of Shengli, his manic attention to detail in preparing to receive the Estens. I thought of the end of the border wars at the base of the Bayac Mountains. He'd given all of them up. I couldn't understand why.

Apparently, neither could he.

Once Floquart was out of sight, Valko slammed his hand against the wall. It echoed oddly from within the closed room behind him. "Dammit, Sonya!"

I flinched. His aura shifted so quickly I could scarcely prepare myself.

"Do you see what you've done?" He hit the wall again. This time something sounded from the room with such distinctness it couldn't possibly be an echo.

I stood erect, determined not to cower before him. "Nothing I said to the emissary was unwarranted."

Valko laughed and rubbed his eyes with his palms. "The *mere act* of you speaking to him was offensive. Have you no idea of your station?"

His rebuke burned inside me like acid. I tensed my body to ward off shaking. "*You* chose me over Estengarde! This isn't my fault."

"No?" he shouted. "Am I to blame?" The door behind him opened a crack, though I couldn't see within. The darkness, which had been my constant companion all evening, seemed to swirl out from the crack in thick waves. "You glide into my life with your intensity, with that wildness you keep restrained. Yet when I taste it, it is so intoxicating I don't know whether to nip at you or devour you whole!"

My jaw muscles locked. He blamed his desire on my reckless passion? Did he remember the truth of me was so devastating it killed all but three people at the convent? "You would do well to keep your distance."

His nostrils flared. He prowled around me like a panther. "You're right. You're a demon in a girl's body! You've been sent here to destroy me, haven't you?"

"You tell me." By the gods, I couldn't hold my savage tongue any more than he could. "From the looks of it, I seem to be succeeding."

He grabbed me by the shoulders and threw me against the wall. My head followed like the lashing of a whip. Through my blackening vision, my gaze wavered to the slitted door. I could have called out for help, but a rush of boldness overtook me. I turned back to the emperor and gave him a vixen's smile.

"It's not too late to do away with you, you know?" Valko's thumbs slid along my collarbone until they probed the base of my neck. He pinched my airway and sent blood throbbing through my head.

I drew in a ragged breath. Deep inside me someone screamed, someone pleaded for something I no longer had ears to hear. I cared more for the ultimate suffering the emperor tempted me with, my final amends to the Auraseers at the convent. To Yuliya. Perhaps death was what I had wanted all along. The necessary sacrifice for redemption. I set my jaw. "Do it, Valko. End my suffering."

The door opened wider on silent hinges. Anton emerged on the threshold. The shadowy figures of other people in the room stood far behind him. In the prince's hand was a dagger.

Valko still thought we were alone. With his back to his brother, his lips stretched over his teeth. His hands clawed up to my face. "You are mine!" He shook me. "No one commands you to leave me. Not Floquart. Most certainly not you." In another abrupt mood change, he yanked me forward until my mouth crashed on his.

The darkness overtook me completely. Had it sourced from me all along? I kissed him back, fangs and forked tongue like the serpent I was. Nothing resembling love or tenderness emitted from either of us.

When Valko's lips traveled to my neck, my gaze fell on Anton. I saw him dimly, like peering at someone past a sheet of rain. His aura couldn't reach me, not in the state I was in, but his eyes held everything I couldn't feel. Sorrow. Pain. Not the pain Valko infected me with—the pain I welcomed—but a lonely variety. A mourning pain, like I was lost, and there was nothing he could do to recover me.

Was I lost? Was I the mirror I'd pledged I wasn't? Did I only reflect the madness of the world?

My hands trembled as I fought to raise them. I set them on Valko's chest. I pushed him away. I wasn't lost. "Stop."

His eyes narrowed, his face flushed with passion. "You can't have it both ways, Sonya. Not anymore. You can't be the doe *and* the demon. I know you now."

My teeth rattled as I struggled against his emotions. "You don't know me at all."

"Don't tell me what I know!" He slammed me back again.

I winced where the wall connected with the lump at the back of my skull. Anton's dagger lifted. The blade caught the candle-light. I shook my head infinitesimally. I couldn't let him get involved. Valko would have his brother executed if the prince tried and failed to kill him. And even if Anton aimed true, I wasn't sure I could allow the emperor to die. Not even now. "You will respect me!" Valko shouted.

Find a space within yourself and cling to it.

This was that space—the small part of me that pulled away from the emperor, that defied him. He grabbed my wrists, one after the other, and pinned them against the wall. My head pulsed from being hit twice. My belly rumbled from starvation. My legs shook, ready to give way.

The space in me wasn't great enough. Not against him.

A sob racked through my labored breathing, the weak fight in me to hold myself together. I needed emotional release. Every Auraseer had a form. Yuliya's blood. Kira's tears. Dasha's hair. Nadia had the bite from staining her skin. Izolda, no doubt, welcomed the sting of splinters beneath her nails. Every release had one thing in common: pain.

My heartbeat thrashed through my ears as I fought to chan-nel myself into a tiny space of control. Tremors racked my body in resistance, but I forced my suffering to intensify. I focused on every part of me that hurt. I needed pain to ground me for now, and in desperation, I sought it. I clung to it.

The throbbing ache of my bruised head. Valko's iron grip on my wrists. The cramped knots in my starved stomach. The fire lining my throat from being half strangled.

I whimpered. I didn't want to feel more. I didn't know if this was helping at all. Pain would give me emotional distance from Valko, but it wouldn't free me from his physical abuse.

"Do you respect yourself?" I asked the emperor in a fragile, broken voice. I faltered between succumbing to the beast in him and my inward chanting of *I'm not enough. Nothing's enough.*

Valko's mouth hovered near mine. His aura growled with hunger, with the dominion he sought to prove over me. "Of course I do."

My breath came in short gasps. My heart hammered. "You were once a child like me, torn from your parents, from everything you knew. Abandoned when you needed love. You still need it." His eyes rose from my lips to meet my beseeching gaze. "But not like this," I said. "This isn't love."

I'd said the wrong thing. One of his hands released mine, only to rear back, preparing to strike me. Anton's grip flexed on his dagger. He was close enough to reach us by one leaping bound. *No.* I couldn't let him kill his brother. I couldn't let him suffer the damnation of murder I knew only too well.

"What would the boy you once were think of you now, in this very moment?"

A spasm ran through Valko's brow. His raised hand froze, but he didn't lower it.

"You have lost much tonight," I rushed on. "Estengarde. Shengli. You let them go because of me, and you question it. But if the only reason you saved me"—*if I could call this saved*—"was so I could tell you, you *don't need* to stretch from sea to sea to achieve greatness, *you* are enough—*Riaznin* is enough—then that would be well worth the price."

I sensed my words pricking his defenses, but his rage still boiled beneath his skin. If I didn't take care, his mood would snap again and Anton's dagger would fly.

I needed to do something more—not seek my own emotional release, but seek the emperor's. If the space within me wasn't large enough to push him away, perhaps it was large enough to pull him in. If I let myself become one with his aura, could I do more? Could I inhabit his limbs, his heart, his mind? Could I finally persuade him?

Valko's breath was hot. His knee dug into my leg and forced me flush against the wall. "You can't tell me what I need."

By some miracle, I felt the sudden shift in his emotion the moment before his hand came smarting down. I dove for that space inside myself, and I thrust it open. Valko permeated my aura, every quality that composed who I was—my gifts of character, the energy of my spirit, the defining fibers of my body. The serpent slithered away. It didn't belong to the emperor. He had his own brand of darkness.

Like medicine, I sent myself back to him, back through the flowing channel between us. I felt Sestra Mirna's long-suffering care for Yuliya in the infirmary. The hands of the Romska when they stroked my hair and tried to soothe my mad spells away. Tosya's smile that helped me know my life wasn't as bad as it often seemed.

My head didn't whip to the side because Valko never struck me. His hand halted near my cheek. He swallowed, his chin quavering. "They think me incapable," he abruptly confessed.

In my periphery, I saw Anton's eyes widen. Had his brother truly admitted to weakness? "Who?" I asked gently.

"My councilors . . . Anton." Valko gave a sorry laugh. "The populace of my empire." His hand fell to his side, and he released my arms from the wall. "They think I died as a child, and they're now ruled by an imposter. Don't you see?" His eyes glistened with tears. "I have to show them my power, that I'm even mightier than my father." His voice cracked. He sounded anything but mighty.

Holding his aura with my empathy, I replied, "I know what it is to feel incapable. I understand you." I ignored my still-burning wrists and took his hand, cupping it in both of my own. "Let me be your balm, Valko. That is better than your mistress." I kissed his hand, hoping to show him the sweetness of some other kind of companionship. "Let me be your seer. Let me reveal what you can become."

He looked at me like I'd transformed into a living beacon. All his remaining pride shattered. He crumpled in my arms and wept like a boy. I felt the release of his emotions, like everything he had ever suffered culminated in this moment. Despite the monster he had been tonight, my heart broke for him. I cradled his head and let his sorrow escape through me.

As I met Anton's gaze, Valko's tears fell from my eyes. The prince sheathed his dagger. He no longer stared at me like I was lost. Because I wasn't, I had found myself. And that finding had more implications than either of us could understand at that moment.

I didn't sever my connection to Valko, but beyond it I sensed Anton's aura. Within it, I confirmed that the embers in the prince's gaze reflected hope.

A shiver ran up my spine. I didn't know if I could bear such hope. The weight of it fell heavier than the burden of the emperor's mourning. With such hope, I could one day forgive myself, wash the blood from Feya's statue clean.

As Anton stepped silently back and closed the door, I still felt his faith in me like a mantle I could never remove. I shut my eyes and more tears slipped down my cheeks. I hid my face against Valko and from the dream of a purer form of redemption.

CHAPTER TWENTY-ONE

LATER THAT NIGHT I TOOK A CANDLE AND WALKED PAST THE red door, the lavender door, and set my key to the lock of the evergreen door. The train of my nightgown swept a path through the dusty floorboards, a path I recarved every evening before I went to sleep in the bed of the tapestry room.

My legs were a bit steadier than earlier. Pia had brought me a pastry and a cup of blessedly nondiuretic tea. She seemed keen to talk about her dance with Yuri, but I made for a poor listener. Keeping Valko in check had stripped me of all my energy. The emperor and I had never returned to the ballroom. After he'd wept in my arms, he pressed a platonic kiss on my hand and walked me to my rooms before retiring to his own— alone—no mistress in tow. I'd touched two hands to my head, then my heart, giving the goddess Feya my thanks for escaping that role. She was gradually becoming more to me than the chalice of Yuliya's death.

A flicker of energy awakened inside me as I turned the lock of the evergreen door, as I came even closer to Anton's room. I searched myself for any lingering darkness, any murderous thoughts. I felt none, only a mingling of anticipation and hope. I opened the door.

At the same time, from across the tapestry room, the midnight-blue door opened. Anton stood at the threshold, backlit by the glow of candles spilling out from his bedchamber. He had removed his kaftan, but otherwise was dressed in the shirt and trousers he'd worn to the ball. His hair was beautifully soft, fallen to his cheekbones in a way that reminded me of how the wind had moved through it when he'd driven the troika.

"You didn't knock." Unlike the teasing cleverness of a court lady, I blurted it out, then wanted to kick myself for doing so, in case he thought he was unwelcome. I couldn't think straight. I was too distracted by the feeling in my aura. Not dark. Most definitely not dark.

"Forgive me." Anton's gaze briefly lowered to my nightdress, as if realizing the impropriety with which we always seemed to meet. But it wasn't enough to keep him away. He took another step into the tapestry room. "I need to know if you're all right."

I gripped my candle with both hands. I couldn't divert my eyes from his, not when they held mine so fervently.

"Now you look at me," I said, attempting to lift my voice with a laugh, but my words rang with the disappointment I'd felt at the ball.

Anton moved even closer, tentatively, like he was approaching a wounded animal. "How is your head?"

I shrugged a shoulder. I didn't wish to reveal that it throbbed whenever I moved too quickly. When Lenka had earlier undressed me, I'd had to hold the frame of the box bed for balance.

My breath caught as the prince's hand moved under mine to raise my candle to my face. His skin was warm, his pressure gentle but unyielding. He studied my eyes for several moments, examining me like a physician. It took all my willpower not to drop my gaze to his lips. What was the matter with me? Hadn't I kissed enough Ozerov men for the night?

Finally satisfied that my eyes were working properly, Anton reached for my head, then paused. "May I?"

My heart was a symphony of percussion, but I nodded. His hands carefully turned my head and skimmed over the sore lump. "Are you dizzy at all?" he asked.

"No." *Yes.* I couldn't be sure if my light-headedness came from my injury or Anton's touch, his nearness. With my head twisted to the side, all I needed to do was lean into him and my cheek would rest against his shoulder. I forced myself back a smidgen and rotated to meet his gaze. At the movement, his hands slid around to hold my face. We stared at each other. How aptly I'd once called his eyes a simmered-butter brown. "I'm all right," I said, but my knees rattled.

He caught me as I swayed, and did more—he lifted me in his arms and carried me back through the evergreen door, the lavender door, and the red door to my chambers. When I saw the box bed, the lovely spell I'd fallen under dissipated.

"I don't sleep here," I confessed. "Not since the night you told me I could stay in the tapestry room."

He regarded me, first with a subtly arched brow of surprise, and then his aura warmed with a glow of pleasure and radiated through my limbs and up to my face. Without a word, he turned around and carried me back through the red door, the lavender door, the evergreen door.

"This is ridiculous," I protested, sure I was blushing. "I'm able to walk."

"Hush, Sonya." He drew back the covers and laid me down on my side, mindful of the lump on my head. Despite my declaration of strength, I weakly lolled onto the pillows. In truth, I couldn't be sure if I was all right, if this was the culmination of my injury, too little food, and sheer exhaustion, or too much prince of Riaznin for my own well-being. "You've had a long night," Anton said.

I noted how he kept every touch minimal and essential, even while he'd carried me and tucked the covers across my lap. How I wished he would lie beside me and let me drift to sleep cocooned in his warmth. I'd given Valko all the comfort I had to offer. Now I needed it from someone else.

"I'm not as simple as you think I am," I said.

He froze in the act of standing up from my bed. "Pardon?"

"I didn't forget about Morva's Eve. And I know who you met with tonight. Count Rostav. Feliks. Yuri. Were you in Pia's room? Did Yuri steal her key, or did she allow all of you entrance?"

The prince contemplated me, then set my candle on the bedside table. The soft light cast a reddish hue to the stubble on his chin. "Pia wasn't involved."

"But you don't deny it was her room?"

He sighed and avoided my question by saying, "I don't think you're simple, Sonya." With a humorless laugh, he dragged his hand through his hair. "Don't you see what precautions I take around you? It's because you . . . well, you're complicated."

I frowned, my finger trailing along the weave of my blanket. What did he mean by that? I wished to the gods I could sense where his aura differentiated from my own. Was any of my attraction to him reciprocal? Is that what he meant when he said, *You're reflecting something that is not your own?* Did he think his feelings for me were one-sided, or did he have no feelings for me at all? I supposed it didn't matter. Even if he did bear any desire for me, he would never act on it. I knew that much about the reserved prince. If he would never give me a dance, he would never give me a kiss. Why would he when every time he turned around, I was caught up in some mad embrace with his brother? "You think I'm weak," I said.

Anton leaned closer. A spark of anger creased his brow. "Why would you say that?"

"You always discover me in Valko's clutches. You see, again and again, what he does to me, what I allow him to do. You said he would make mincemeat of me." I shook my head, wanting to bury myself in my covers. "You were right."

"Stop!" Something deeper than anger emanated from him

now, something I couldn't name, but riveted me to his gaze. "Please don't tell me what I think or what I feel about you." With a growl of frustration, he added, "Don't you see yourself at all? Do you know what you did tonight?"

"I made the emperor lose his alliance with Estengarde."

"Riaznin doesn't need Estengarde. And that wasn't your doing."

"I nearly committed to becoming the emperor's mistress."

"But you didn't."

I shrugged. "I evaded him for the time being."

"You evaded him when he was in such a rage as I'd never before seen. You evaded him when your life was in danger. When I was ready to kill my brother myself, *you* evaded him. *You* did that, Sonya." Anton's hands fisted into the mattress at my side. "Explain to me how you did that."

"I . . ." My heart thundered. I couldn't make sense of all the mixed signals the prince gave me. He looked upset, but the heat behind his anger was *supportive*, not derogatory. Nothing like the kisses Valko lavished upon me after slamming my head into the wall. "I opened myself to him," I admitted. "Completely. I found a . . . *connection*, and I used it to persuade him to relent."

Anton nodded. Behind his eyes was a millstone grinding a thousand thoughts together. "Could you do it again?"

I thought of the desperation it took to bring me that far, the weight of the emperor's emotions when they fully overtook me, the relief when I'd curbed him, when I'd saved my own life, when I'd saved *his* from the threat of his brother. "I'm not certain."

Anton gripped me by the shoulders. It wasn't the first time an Ozerov had me pinned tonight, but unlike earlier, I felt anything but trapped. "You listen to me, Sonya. You are not weak. You're the strongest person I know. So very few are willing to stand up to Valko—and they don't have to wrestle with the intoxication of his aura like you do. Your strength is genuine. It is priceless. And I'm willing to wager the fate of Riaznin that you can prove your strength again."

I blinked, feeling the mantle of his hope settle over me with a power I could feast on, though it was terrifying. "What do you mean?" What was he asking me to do?

"I believe you're more than an ordinary Auraseer. You're *meant* for something more."

I searched Anton's emotions, so tangled in my own. *"What?"* The word came out as a desperate plea. I yearned to know the secret, what it was I could become. I longed to be something other than the bringer of death and pain to all those I loved.

A grin touched his lips. "I have something for you."

Perplexed, I watched him rise and go through the door to his room and then return with a book. As he moved nearer, it caught the candlelight. It was the book with the pale-blue binding. The book he'd turned over the last time I'd glimpsed it so I couldn't see the title. But now he placed it in my hands as if he was passing over a treasure. I glanced at the cover: *Lament of the Gods,* by Tosya Pashkov.

"Tosya?" I asked in bewilderment. "Tosya of the Romska?" Tosya, who was like a brother to me?

"Tosya the poet." Anton nodded, confirming they were one and the same.

"You know him?" I asked as he walked back to his room. I couldn't put my lanky, freethinking friend and the somber prince together in the same space. And when had Tosya started writing poetry? As far as I knew, he'd only composed songs.

"Read the book, Sonya." Anton retreated farther. "And do not let a soul find you with it."

I set it down and clenched my jaw in annoyance. "You still haven't told me what you were doing tonight."

"Read."

"I felt a darkness. Were you aware that someone plotted to kill the emperor?"

Anton halted at his door. A fragment of surprise cut past the shared aura between us, followed by a grim acceptance that made me exhale with him. He nodded slowly. "Assassination isn't the solution. We'll make them see that."

"We?"

"Read. The. Book."

A spark of candlelight twinkled in his eye as he closed the door. I was left, once again, with too many questions and not enough answers.

I thumbed the edge of Tosya's book with a sigh, then brought it closer and cracked the spine.

CHAPTER TWENTY-TWO

RIAZNIN WAS A BIRD IN TOSYA'S BOOK, A WHITE-WINGED dove. The gods formed her and promised her a sky broad enough to fly in, a land vast enough that her children would never go hungry. No matter which siblings came first or second, no matter which ones were lovelier, or which were male or female, each was blessed to share the bounty of the land in equality.

Hear my song, O my children.
Stretch your wings. Embrace your birthright.

"Are you finished yet?" Anton asked the following night, peeking his head into the tapestry room. Granted, this time he preceded it with a light knock.

I rolled my eyes. Of course I wasn't finished. The volume wasn't thick, but the reading was dense. I'd never studied much poetry before. Ironic, since Tosya had been my reading teacher.

Closing the book around a finger to mark my spot, I said, "Tosya was in a caravan I traveled with every spring. He was like family to me. He would sing me songs and read me stories. He knew how to make me laugh when I thought I'd never laugh again."

I saw him in my mind's eye. Tosya had a stretched look from his brows to his chin, the opposite of Valko's slightly smashed appearance. In fact, everything about Tosya was long—his nose, his fingers, his legs. His aura was just as lengthy, so open there was space for me to crawl inside and escape the world for a time.

"How do you know him?" I asked Anton. Tosya was intelligent, but as poor as any Romska boy. How would he ever have had the means or connections to write a book of poetry and have it published unless he had a benefactor? Could that have been Anton? How would Tosya's path have even crossed with that of a prince?

"You weren't the only one Tosya graced with his friendship," Anton said with a smile.

I thought of Montpanon, the village close to Trusochelm Manor where the prince had been raised. The Romska camped nearby at the eastern front of the Bayac Mountains when they tracked herds of wild horses. "When did you meet?" I asked Anton. "How?"

"Good night, Sonya. Keep reading." The midnight-blue door closed. I groaned and threw a pillow after it. Then, once more, I opened the book.

Valko kept to his rooms for five days. He didn't emerge to see Floquart and his entourage of foreigners leave, and I doubted the emissary would have allowed it. I pitied the Esten Auraseer who must accompany Floquart and regretted my missed opportunity to somehow free her from her abuser. At the very least I had a respite from mine, for the emperor also abandoned his council meetings and dinners with the nobles. As for the servants in the palace, after the frenzy of preparing for the ball, they fell back into their quieter routines. My muscles eased with their relaxed auras. In the city, a few small celebrations were held in honor of the fertility goddess, Morva, highly neglected by the nobles, who were too weary from dancing and sick from head-splitting goblets of aqua vitae.

In the healing quiet of those days, I wrote a letter to Sestra Mirna, asking after Dasha and Kira; I allowed Lenka the pains-taking task of trimming my thick hair; and I let Pia sneak me midday snacks and tell me at length about Yuri's eyes and his promise to marry her. His parents were warming to the idea of having a serving maid as a daughter-in-law. "Just wait until they discover I'm well educated, too," she'd said brightly. To that I'd smiled. "Are you saying you'd like to tackle arithmetic next?" I'd shrugged with a dramatic sigh. "There I cannot help you." She'd laughed and read me the last page of the Armless Maiden story, her words slow and labored, but filled with wonder as she reached the climactic moment where the maiden mystically grew back her limbs to save her baby from a well.

My favorite parts of each day were the stolen hours when I crept into the tapestry room to do my own reading. Curled up on the bed, I'd pore over Tosya's book of poetry.

The throne is the land to seat the mighty.
The mighty isn't one, but many.

On the fifth night, my candle—one of many I'd replaced since Anton gave me the book—was a nub of wax. Its flame sputtered on its last bursts of light. The prince knocked and opened the door.

I sat up. "I'm not finished yet!"

He closed the door before my pillow could hit him in the head. Giving a little laugh, I plunked back down, but the movement stirred the air and my candle snuffed out. I sighed and shut the book for the night. More for tomorrow. With any luck, Valko would remain in his rooms.

He didn't. Lenka came bright and early the next morning with her clapping hands and announced the emperor required my presence. He meant to take me on a stroll through the palace gardens. A pit of dread formed in my stomach. How freeing it had been to escape Valko's attentions for a time. The bruise on the back of my head had almost healed.

I met the emperor in the lobby outside the great hall. He wore somber colors—a dark, olive-green cape over a gray shirt and breeches. Lenka hadn't divined his mood, for I was wearing a dress of pale yellow with a lavender jacket that conformed to my waist and fell to the first ruffle of my skirt. I felt ridiculous and longed for the simple clothes of the convent Auraseers and unrestricted styles of the Romska. But if I'd hoped to camouflage myself into the emperor's flower beds, Lenka had served me well.

I settled my gaze on the bridge of Valko's nose—Anton's trick to distance himself from me—and swallowed as I curtsied. The emperor's bridled temper made me at once suspicious, and I felt a bit shy in his presence, remembering how helpless and broken he'd been in my arms. I couldn't predict how he'd act around me now, if he'd seek to prove his superiority or let the incident bolster his trust in me. His aura was remarkably reserved. I allowed myself an easy breath for the moment, but kept my muscles tense.

"Shall we?" He offered his arm. I saw no alternative but to take it.

Two liveried servants opened the doors leading to the rear gardens of the palace. Birdsong filled the air as I inhaled the scent of green things after such a long winter. Tulips and daffodils grew in clever bunches amid the sculpted hedges and blossoming trees. Pavers in the manicured lawns created a labyrinth of private walkways. I closed my eyes and felt the sun on my face. I already lamented when I'd have to return back inside.

As I opened my eyes, I caught Valko's wistful smile. I hoped it was an omen of a nonviolent morning. "You look at home here," he said.

"I feel at home," I replied, thinking of the growing things of the earth and the home among them that the Romska had taught me was mine. But perhaps it was the wrong thing to say, for the emperor moved closer to my side. My heart pounded, and I resisted the urge to flinch. Instead, I kept my hands close to my body to discourage him from touching me.

We walked along a curving row of flagstones, a retinue of guards several paces behind us. Butterflies danced in our path, adding to the illusion that this was a beautiful moment we were sharing, when all I felt was the strain of pretending I could ever feel normal and truly adored by the emperor again. My tongue seemed glued to the roof of my mouth. I didn't know how to relax without first understanding what Valko wanted from me. I prayed this wasn't another attempt at securing me as his mistress.

We crossed a bridge over a stream—one of many trickling waterways springing off the Azanel River that ran through Torchev. The stream fed into a pond, nestled in the shade of an outdoor pavilion. Its marble columns and terraced steps gave it the appearance of a small temple. Valko motioned for me to sit beside him on a bench, while the guards waited outside the pavilion.

I clasped my hands in my lap and watched fish turn lazy circles in the pond. The sun rose higher in the sky. At length, the emperor spoke.

"I've been thinking about what you told me, Sonya."

"Oh?" He must have been referring to the night of the ball, when I'd told him many things. *I'm not a good person. You don't know me. This isn't love.*

His next words sounded practiced. They came at more cost, with more humility. "You promised to show me what I could become." He examined his hands. "You said I was enough."

"You are." Had he really listened to me? Did he truly believe Riaznin didn't need to expand from sea to sea?

"The emissary said something that struck me: we have enough military in Torchev to stop the border wars with Estengarde."

I considered Valko. The same could be said of many needs in the empire. While we feasted to excess and danced under the gold-domed shelter of the palace, so many outside our walls were starving and in need of more support. So many were taxed while the nobles were exempt. The common people were the spine of Riaznin, yet they were drafted into fighting our wars, paying too much of their own wages, crops, and furs to the empire, and receiving far too little in return. "I believe that's true, My Lord. We have the means to spare."

"And if we had *more* means . . . think what we could do then."

The enthusiasm that had been broadening my chest and filling me with hope was swiftly punctured by doubt. "I'm not sure I follow."

"What did I need Estengarde for?" he prodded.

The hole of doubt opened wider. "To conquer Shengli. But you agreed Riaznin was enough."

"We are!" Valko stood and walked about the pavilion. "If we have the strength to stop the border wars in the west"— he talked quickly with animated hands—"why not send that strength to the east where our military can gather the necessary forces to triumph over those barbarians?"

I cringed, remembering how Floquart had called *us* savages. How conveniently each country thought themselves more civilized than their neighbors. "With all due respect, My Lord, I would hardly call a people with a superior knowledge of medicine and astrology barbaric, not to mention their unsurpassed skill in the art of warfare. The Shenglin have their own culture, their own supreme god. I don't think peace will come by uniting with them."

"This isn't about peace! It's about claiming what is duly ours. *Our* gods created this world. This blessed land wasn't divided a millennium ago. The jade and timber-rich forests should be used to honor the gods who created them. The Shenglin owe us centuries of servitude to amend for their abominations. If we conquer them, they will till our land, mine our ore, and build great strongholds like Torchev across Riaznin."

Valko picked up a handful of pebbles and tossed them, one by one, across the far reaches of the pond. "I see the day, Sonya, that Riaznin's strength will multiply until it is enough to forge the Bayac Mountains and defeat Estengarde, as well.

I understand now." He whirled to face me, his eyes bright and alive. "This is why my bloodline brought me to the throne. This is why I was born first. Can you imagine the great honor it will bring the gods to see the world as one empire kneeling at their altars? With one emperor to usher in all that glory?"

Bile infested my stomach. It scraped up my throat. Lines of Tosya's poetry kept coming at me and trampled Valko's vision with one far more beautiful. "What if the gods see all of us as brothers?" Brothers didn't seek glory through inequality, by rising up in the world off the backs of slaves. I knew well enough what life offered when you didn't have a choice. "What if the gods wished for each of us to choose our own path?" Like the Romska who were content to live without religion, or Yuliya, whose devoutness to Feya brought her solace, or even the Shenglin, who worshipped not the seven gods of Riaznin but one all-powerful creator.

"Yes, yes, exactly!" Valko pulled me to my feet. "One family under the same gods."

I shook my head. "How can there be lesser or greater within a family?"

"There must be, or else chaos would reign. The wiser must govern, and the infants must be carried and shown the way— the right way."

And who were the infants in this structure of his? The Shenglin? The Estens? The peasant Riaznians, no doubt. What about me? "Is that what I am to you? An infant?"

Valko's confusion swept through my aura. I could almost

hear him thinking, *Why doesn't she understand?* "You are my sovereign Auraseer. I depend on you."

"As a master depends on a serf to reap the harvest," I quipped.

His brow furrowed. "Does it matter? We will eat the fruit together."

"But *you* will profit from the excess." The emperor had claimed to need me, but I would never stand on equal footing with him.

He regarded me a moment. "I think I know why you are angry." He threw his last pebble in the pond. "I can't marry you, Sonya."

My eyes flew wide. "I wasn't speaking of marriage." As if I had any wish to mingle my *common* bloodline with his.

"You've made it clear you have no desire to be my mistress."

I clamped my mouth shut at that. He was right.

"I'm afraid I can't raise your status here any higher than that."

I suppressed an eye roll. Of course he thought becoming his illegitimate lover would be greater than my current occupation.

"We care for each other, however . . . don't we?" he asked.

In truth, I wasn't sure how much *care* bled through his infatuation. In the same regard, how many of my feelings for him were my own and not an echo of his—or my concern for the people of the empire not a reflection of his passion for expanding it? As he waited for some kind of answer, I replied, "Yes." I *did* care for the broken child in him, the child who had never asked to be emperor.

"It's enough for me that you are my balm, my seer, as you said." He kissed my hand, and his aura blazed to life again. "Dear Sonya." He softly grinned. "You've already done so much for me. You were right. You showed me who I am, and look what is happening. Look what I see!" He spread his hands wide to show the expanse of the pond, as if it represented the world—*his* world, *his* all-encompassing empire.

He began pacing again. He threw more rocks and prattled on and on, faster and faster. He spoke of what we could do with the riches of Shengli, how we could lower the age of the draft to increase our armies, how we could build greater navies, greater strongholds. His manic nature made my skin crawl as if I were covered with a thousand insects.

He's becoming a monster. And he thanks me for it.

I kept my lips sealed. I dared not say more because he didn't listen. Everything I spoke he twisted, until it fit his corrupt vision of glory.

And so I sat and bided my time. I didn't pretend to share so much as a spark of his enthusiasm, for I had none. It wouldn't have mattered if I did. Valko was so caught up in himself and his ramblings of a greater empire that he no longer sought out my encouragement—or whatever his reason was for desiring my company today. He hadn't even apologized for hurting me the night of the ball.

I hadn't realized until now that I'd clung to a small shred

of hope that he might be sorry, that he might revert back to the charming boy whose touch had so often made my blood quicken.

I would never waste my hope on him again.

I knocked on the midnight-blue door that night. Anton opened it. "Your brother is mad," I said.

He nodded, his eyes lowering to the volume of Tosya's poetry in my arms. "Did you finish the book?"

> *And the gods weep to see the children of the dove in a*
> *   closed nest.*
> *And they rend their holy robes that the birds will never*
> *   see the skies.*

"Yes."

> *Break apart the thatch, O children.*
> *Unfurl your downy wings.*

"Come in."

CHAPTER TWENTY-THREE

ANTON DREW TWO CHAIRS NEAR HIS TILED FURNACE. SPRING-time in Riaznin was lovely enough during the daytime, but the cold still bit at night. I traced the gilded lettering of Tosya's book while the prince tended to a copper samovar, which whistled with uncanny timing. He poured two servings for us in glasses lodged inside pewter casings, not delicate Shenglin porcelain like the emperor used. The aroma of briar tea filled the air.

"Jam?" Anton asked. I nodded and watched him spoon something of the rose leaf variety into my glass. In his own, he tipped a dash of rum. Perhaps he needed something to settle his nerves—perhaps some of the anxiety dancing through my veins belonged to him. This was going to be a night of answers. I felt it. My mind whirred with what they might be.

He set the tea glasses on a small mahogany table between our chairs. The wood matched the other varnished furnish-ings in the room and complemented the earthy colors of the upholstery, bedding, and curtains. Several candles were lit. Again, I wondered if he'd anticipated my visit, if he knew, somehow, enough time had passed for me to finish the book and be ready for him.

My gaze drifted over his clothing—a loose shirt tucked into breeches and tall black boots. The only time I'd caught him wearing less was the night he'd just finished bathing. I began to wonder if he slept wearing those boots. I twirled the soft ends of corded belting on my night robe. Perhaps he slept wearing nothing at all.

Blood warmed my cheeks and I took a sip of tea, but the hot liquid only made my blush bond to my skin. The wood crackled behind the grate of the furnace. It was altogether too stifling in here.

"Are you all right?" Anton brought his glass to his mouth. The tea made his lips glisten.

I stood and looked away. "Yes," I answered a little breathlessly, then shook my head. "That is, no. Valko—I mean, His Imperial Majesty—was quite impossible today."

Anton stilled. "What has he done to you?"

Fire raced up my spine at the prince's altered mood. I eyed him. He must be imagining the worst—me swept up in another violent fit of his brother's passion. "Nothing like that, I assure you. He was gentlemanly enough."

Anton's scowl told me he doubted it.

I smoothed my robe. "The night of the ball I was able to comfort Valko in the loss of his alliance. When he stayed locked in his rooms these past days, I thought . . ." I shrugged, real-izing how mistaken I'd been. "I thought it was over . . . that he'd humbled himself and seen the error of his ways."

The prince looked down and thumbed the rim of his glass. "But my brother's thirst for power emerged stronger than ever?"

I nodded and launched into a recap of the entire morning: Valko's plans to utilize the Torchev military, lower the draft age to include mere boys, and then march against Shengli—all to plunder our neighbor and enslave its citizens, who more likely had the might to conquer the whole of Riaznin.

Anton seemed disturbed, but not surprised. "And you think your efforts to persuade him were not sufficient?"

"I thought they were the night of the ball, but I was wrong. And what I said today never reached his ears."

He inhaled a long breath. "You may be right."

I folded my arms, feeling cold now. Disappointment iced over my limbs with the fear that Anton had lost his confidence in any positive influence I could have upon his brother. But it was the truth. Nothing could be done to rein in the emperor, and I wasn't sure I could endure a life in his shadow while I watched my homeland canker in ruination.

"One thing can be certain, however," the prince said. "You do have the power, when you truly wish it, to persuade him. I've seen it. It isn't enough to control him long-term, but we don't need that. We simply need him tempered for one critical, well-timed moment."

I shifted on my feet as caution and excitement—even

hope—fluttered inside me. "What do you have in mind?"

He took a deep drink and placed his glass on the table. "Sit down."

I lowered myself into the chair, my hands tucked beneath my thighs until I forced them onto my lap in a show of confidence. This was it. I was on the cusp of receiving the answers I'd been waiting for. Anton needed to see I was ready to hear them.

"What did you think of Tosya's book?" he began.

My gaze fell on the volume beside the tea glasses. "Tosya is brilliant."

"How so?"

"The way he clears the fog away." As Anton leaned closer, I tried to elaborate. "The people subject themselves to harsh rule and unrelenting taxation because they've been conditioned to believe the gods sanctioned one man to lord over them, as well as those of noble birth. But Tosya takes the faith of the people and turns it in their favor. He portrays the gods as loving of *all* of Riaznin's children equally. Gods who mourn that we cannot see ourselves the way they do."

"And this you gleaned after reading one book?"

"I'd had some of these thoughts, but Tosya distilled them for me."

"What do you think the common people would do if they felt as you did?"

I considered the prince. "They would likely demand new rights."

"What rights would you give them?"

This was beginning to feel like a test. Somehow that didn't bother me. I was too zealous about the subject. "Equal privileges and punishments among the nobles and peasants. Equal taxation. The freedom to choose how to lead one's own life, so long as it doesn't infringe on someone else's liberty to do the same."

Anton rested his elbows on his knees. "What about the right to self-govern?"

My lips parted. For a long moment I couldn't say anything. The breeze rattled the windowpanes. "I'm not sure I understand."

"Shouldn't equality mean the people have a right to collaborate on who rules them? If they can vote, they have a voice. They could even choose to campaign for leadership."

An ache flowered in my temple. I rubbed it, hoping to also wipe away my confusion. "But *you* should lead—as emperor. The people would follow you. They wouldn't need to cast a vote about it."

Anton tilted his head. "What if I did lead? What if I even granted the people the rights you spoke of? Could I ensure that my eldest son would uphold the new law when his time came to rule? What about *his* son?"

"You can't *give* the government to the people!" I rose to my feet and stepped away from him. "Commoners and nobles drawing up laws together? Working side by side to enforce them? It's preposterous! Unheard of!" Is this what he and his friends had been plotting all this time? What part did he expect me to play in it? I'd hoped the prince somehow meant to usurp his brother. But *this*? This was an impossible scheme of madness.

Anton stood and planted himself in my path. "Why is it such a radical idea? Why should one man decide the fate of so many? How could he understand them all? He would need your abilities, but to feel the auras of hundreds of thousands of people would drive a person insane. Ruling them *without* that insight is enough to do so. Look at Valko."

I rubbed the pain in my temple and twisted away from the prince. He took my arm and pulled me back. "Talk to me, Sonya."

I shook my head, panic overwhelming me. "You won't listen! You and your brother both have your wild visions, and neither one of you will listen to me."

"I will. I'm listening now. Tell me why this won't work."

I swallowed as I remembered the fury of all the auras in Ormina, the mob of starving peasants rallying against the convent gates. "I've felt what the wrath of injustice does to a people," I said. "And when they learn how deeply they've been wronged, and then are given the reins of such power—such shared dominion . . . Anton, it will be a massacre! They'll seek to destroy everyone who has ever oppressed them." I placed a hand to my stomach, imagining what that kind of energy would do to me—to those I loved. "I don't see how this can come about peaceably. Change on that scale will mean war—among *ourselves*. Can you really condone that when one great man"—I looked at him beseechingly—"could carefully *nudge* them in a better direction? Perhaps in a century we would be prepared for a 'people's government.'"

Anton smiled—actually smiled—after all I'd just told him. "Would it surprise you to know I share your same concerns?" he asked. "Do you realize I'm a pacifist? Sonya, I don't wish death on anyone in order to bring about this revolution, not even my brother. And you are right that too much change, too fast, would result in chaos. I daresay the noble lords aren't, at present, willing to let the serfs earn their portion of the land. But if every man and woman, rich or poor, had a voice—a representative—surely we could bridge to equality over time. One thing, however, is certain: we can't postpone this new government. If we leave the empire in Valko's hands, there may be no Riaznin left to unite. He will bring war in his fixation to expand. He'll have us slaughtered by the tens of thousands until no one is exempt from his draft, and his dream of glory is nothing more than a wasteland covered with bones and ash."

"And what of *your* dream?" I asked tentatively. "You were bred as an emperor, as well as your brother. Have you truly no desire to sit on the throne?"

The prince sighed and rubbed the back of his neck. "That was what I thought my life would be . . . for far too long." His face was confined in a strange spot of shadow in the candlelit room.

I moved in closer, trying to see his eyes. "What changed your mind?"

He scuffed his boot on the floor. "Valko lived . . . I swallowed my pride." His brow twitched. "It tasted far more bitter than I anticipated." With a sharp inhale, he lifted his chin to meet my gaze. "I met Tosya. He lingered around the woods of my estate every summer when his caravan rolled through. He didn't treat me as his better; he treated me as a friend." Anton lowered his eyes briefly. "A friend was a luxury I'd never had." He scuffed the floor again, then straightened and ran a hand through his hair.

"Tosya asked if I could lend him books from the manor library," the prince went on. "He pieced together quite an education by studying them over the years. I sponsored him at university and later printed his book, though nobody but he and myself knows that." A glint of pride, sweet and noble, caused my heart to swell. "More people than you realize have read that book, Sonya." Anton smiled, leaning closer in his earnestness. "And they have spread the most important phrase to those who haven't read it: *The mighty isn't one, but many.*" The candlelight now burned in the prince's eyes. "There is a revolution already brewing, Sonya. I don't desire to be emperor anymore. I desire to be a part of the uprising."

I felt Anton's goodness in my soul, just as certain as the breath of *rightness* that filled me when I'd read Tosya's words. But fierce insecurity also swept through me, nearly knocking me to the ground. *He can never care for me as much as he cares for this cause. Nothing will ever be as important to him.* "I am Sovereign Auraseer," I said, striving to remember my duty, though unlike Anton's devotion to self-government, mine stemmed from compulsion, not choice. "Is that why you haven't shared your vision with me until now? Because it is treasonous? You know that I'm required to tell Valko of any threats to his crown."

I couldn't fathom doing so, but I needed to know that Anton understood what was at stake by confiding in me. If I were caught with the knowledge of what I'd learned tonight, it would cost me my neck and require Dasha or Kira to take up my stead.

"I trust you," he replied.

"This isn't about trust! You haven't trusted me for months! You *need* me now." I crossed my arms and scrutinized him. "You only gave me that book after you saw me with the emperor the night of the ball," I added, as if I'd caught him guilty of a great crime. "Something has changed, and you need me now."

"You're right," he answered unapologetically. "I do. I care too much about your welfare to endanger you otherwise."

Something fluctuated between our auras. He composed himself so quickly, however, that I dismissed it as my own restless gut. The revelations of the evening were taking their toll on my body.

"But you're wrong that this isn't also about trust," Anton continued. "That night, you proved to me you had the mettle to stand up against Valko, that your strength of will would always find a way to shine through. I also understood you had no wish to unite yourself with him."

"I gave him compassion," I said, feeling slightly ashamed.

"Because it was a tool of resistance—a remarkable tool! One I'd never considered."

I turned my head away to study the intricately painted tiles of his furnace. My heart drummed in my chest. Some part of me always knew how dangerous the prince's secrets were, yet I'd been relentless about digging them out. And now that I knew them, they might cost me my life. As I turned to meet his gaze, his eyes warmed with belief in me. I asked, "What is it you want me to do?"

He took both of my hands. He squeezed them. "Persuade Valko to give up the government."

My brows shot upward. My mouth went paper dry. I wanted to laugh. I tried to, but Anton's aura, rooted inside me, was sober, as if none of the rum in his tea had met his bloodstream. "Abdicate? That's not . . . How could I possibly . . . ? You've lost your mind!"

"You're the key, Sonya. With you, this revolution can succeed without bloodshed."

I found myself yanking away from him, but he kept his grip on my hands. "You're spectacularly wrong about me!"

"You have a power over my brother I've never seen the like of. He gave up Estengarde for you."

"I didn't ask him to do that! That had nothing to do with my ability. I stopped Valko from *kissing* me—from hurting me. That's pitiful next to what you're talking about. He won't relinquish the throne of his empire because I whisper comforting words in his ear!"

Anton's conviction didn't falter. "It was no small thing for him to let you go that night, not after what he lost because he couldn't bear losing you. He wants you, so very, very badly. He could charm a snail from its shell, and yet you keep him in check. Do you know how many women he's seduced?"

I thought of Pia succumbing to the emperor's kiss—*Pia*, who was devoted to Yuri. "Valko only wants me because I pull back. I'm a game to him."

"It doesn't matter the reason, whether it has to do with you or with me."

My heart gave a funny little jump. "What do you mean, with *you*?"

He shut his eyes, as if catching himself. A cascade of warmth flooded into me, distracting me from the magnitude of Anton's request. It shivered across my skin and awakened me with sensation. The prince opened his eyes to look at our joined hands. His own softened over mine. "Valko lusts for power," he said carefully. "I believe his desire for you equals his desire for Riaznin." His gaze lifted and roamed over my face.

He hadn't answered my question, not directly, but at the moment I didn't care. The way he was staring at my lips made me feel beautiful, priceless, wanted. I inhaled a shaky breath and tried to steel myself back to what we were talking about. I couldn't think of a thing to say except that I could never accomplish what he was asking of me.

"My failure in this will mean my death, and the death of everyone I care about." *Kira, Dasha.* They wouldn't last long here. *You.* I searched Anton's eyes. This impossible plan also put his life at stake. Valko would discover his involvement, I was sure of it. I couldn't bear the thought of bringing him any harm.

"Why didn't you dance with me at the ball?" The words tumbled out of my mouth of their own volition.

His gaze flashed up to mine, his aura echoing my own surprise with myself. "It's late," he said. "We can talk more tomorrow night." He let go of my hands, but I caught his back.

"Why?"

"Dancing with you would have been inappropriate," he said matter-of-factly and looked away.

I angled closer and tried to force him to look at me. "It was more than that."

He set his jaw. "It would have upset Valko, and I knew he would take out his anger on you as a result."

"He wasn't there."

"There were eyes and ears enough for him."

I supposed I could understand that, but—"There is no one with us now."

Anton frowned and his brows hitched together. His aggravation warred with the warm feeling still sliding beneath my skin. Cocking a sardonic half smile, which looked false on him, he said, "Are you asking me to a midnight waltz?"

"Don't make light of me. I'm not a child."

His smile dropped. "No. You're an *Auraseer*." His tone was so accusatory, I knew I'd discovered the meat of the matter.

"You don't trust my feelings?" *For you*, I wanted to add, but I was too swollen with hurt.

His hands in mine went stiff. "I'm trying to protect you."

"From *yourself*?"

He lowered his gaze to the floor. "From any emotions that don't belong to you. You suffer enough as it is."

I let go of his hands. Frustrated tears welled in my eyes. I wanted to break something. Find a mirror and shatter it to prove it wasn't me and wouldn't make me bleed. As difficult as it was for the prince, he'd just admitted that he cared about me—and not in the brotherly way I'd always tricked myself into believing, but the achingly beautiful way that made me want to fold myself into him.

I didn't. I backed away, my tears spilling over. "Suffer?" I bit out. "This"—I gestured to the space between us—"this is suffering."

"Sonya." He gave me a pleading look.

"You don't trust me!" I wiped at my cheek. "You don't even believe I'm strong enough to have my own feelings. How can you even *think* to ask me to betray the emperor, to risk my life?" I looked up at the ceiling and tried to see past it to the gods. Perhaps they could make me understand him. "How is it you believe I don't care for Valko in that way, yet you somehow also believe I don't truly care for you?" I paced the room and shook my head. *Care* wasn't the right word, but I couldn't think beyond the betrayal I felt to find a better one.

Anton dug a hand through his hair. His eyes were wide and lost. "I respect your freedom," he tried to explain. "I want you, above all, to be free."

"You think I'm the helpless girl you brought back from the convent. Maybe you're right!" I laughed and threw up my hands. "Maybe I still am. In that case, you've made a grave mistake by confiding in me. How do you know I'm truly committed to your cause? I could be feeling *your* steadfastness to these ideals, *your* loyalty. Is that enough for me to see this through?"

He sighed, his sadness pulling at my own. "Not all of my concern for you goes both ways, Sonya. You know I believe in you."

I stopped pacing. "No, I don't. Not truly, not fully. And *everything* should go both ways, even when it comes to Valko. You speak of respecting freedom, but what of his? What liberty is he given if I force his choice, assuming I'm miraculously able to do so?"

Anton spoke slowly and struggled for words. "Revolution always comes at a cost. As far as I can see, this is the least detrimental price we can pay."

I rubbed at my face and tried to wash away the emotions overwhelming me. An unattainable task. Too many things fought for space in my mind. A trade of freedom for freedom— at too much risk, too much pressure. And all this asked by a prince who, in the end, didn't have faith in something as simple as my feelings for him.

"You're right." I tugged the panels of my robe together. "It's late. I should go." I moved to the midnight-blue door.

"Sonya . . ." Anton's voice rang with misery.

I left without saying good night. Once alone in the tapestry room, I lay on the bed and watched the moonlight shift across the woven forests and meadows on my walls, but felt none of their beauty bring me peace.

How many times had I pushed aside my feelings for the prince? Even Pia could sense them without my gift for reading aura. *I* was the one who had been blind, always seeing myself below Anton, unworthy of his regard, only noticed when I needed protection. The truth was, I'd fallen for him long ago on a snowy journey to the palace, before ever meeting his brother. And if deep in my heart I believed I wasn't Anton's reflection, despite how many times I'd berated *him* for not believing the same, I knew the one thing the prince couldn't trust about me, the final wedge and wonderful truth between us.

He'd fallen for me, too.

CHAPTER TWENTY-FOUR

THE NEXT DAY VALKO HELD A COUNCIL MEETING. TO MY surprise, Count Rostav was in attendance, as well as Anton. I took my usual seat between the royal brothers, while the count sat across from us. His great mop of hair made his head appear larger than the heads of the councilors seated beside him.

I shifted uncomfortably. A disconcerting energy had formed between Anton and me since last night. For once, I was just as studiously avoiding his gaze as he was avoiding mine. I had an equally difficult time looking at the emperor. My treasonous conversation with the prince was enough to condemn me, even if I never acted upon it.

Fortunately, Valko was so impassioned that he seemed oblivious to my awkwardness. He delved at once into his detailed plan to conquer Shengli. It was met, at first, with grumbles and wary glances from his councilors, but slowly, over the course of the afternoon, they became intoxicated with his vision for a grander Riaznin. Valko had even commissioned an artist to draw out a map without a border separating us from our neighboring country.

Upon the map, the existing townships in the cold and barren stretches of east Riaznin were illustrated with the additions of luxurious, onion-domed buildings, fortified city walls, and irrigation channels from the rivers of Shengli, which fed us new and green farmlands. Surrounding them were noble estates and bunches of little blotted figures representing Shenglin serfs, numbers scrawled above their heads ranging from the hundreds to the thousands. Closer to Torchev were towering convents and universities, centers for study of all kinds—religion, art, mathematics, philosophy. There was something here to appeal to anyone.

"Councilor Ilyin," Valko said, grinning at the aged man across the table, "isn't your eldest grandson a budding physician? Does he have to contend with the nobles' archaic abhorrence to medicine? Some still believe drinking a glass of aqua vitae with a peeled clove of garlic will cure any ailment." He chuckled with a shake of his head. Leaning forward, his eyes sparked with zeal. "What if every city had a medical lodging where, for a fair price, someone could receive the unparalleled care of an educated doctor? Wouldn't that trump sweating out one's maladies in the local hothouse?"

Councilor Ilyin's lips pursed. His gaze returned to the map.

"And what of you, General Lazar?" The emperor looked to the sharp-cheeked man seated two chairs from Count Rostav.

"You have often lamented the state of our navy and said we could better defend ourselves against Estengarde by utilizing the Artagnon Sea. How many times have you told me we should bypass the Bayac Mountains altogether to settle our quarrels with the Estens?"

General Lazar grunted. "Too many to count, My Lord."

The emperor nodded with sympathy as he accepted the general's censuring tone. "We have never been able to afford a resplendent navy, not with the expense of maintaining an army massive enough to fortify the sheer breadth of our nation." Lifting his brows, Valko held up a finger. "But if we conquer Shengli, our resources will double, our empire will flourish with more wealth and prosperity. Then we can reinforce our navy—build it up to unrivaled size and daunting strength. Don't you see?" Valko smiled. "We could do better than merely defend ourselves against Estengarde. We could *conquer* it from the seas. And you, General Lazar, would captain the undertaking!"

The general scratched the back of his neck, all traces of his disgruntlement gone as he stared at the rendering of a conjoined Riaznin and Shengli. In his mind, he must be erasing the dotted border between our empire and Estengarde, as well—that and pinning another silver badge on his regimentals.

He wasn't the only one evaluating Valko's proposal in a new light. Every councilor's gaze traveled over the map with growing hunger.

Soon no one had any qualms about lowering the draft age or partitioning a large percentage of our Torchev military to bolster our forces for the Shengli invasion. No one but Anton. His words last night rang through my mind: *Revolution always comes at a cost.*

Valko's dream of Riaznin was the emperor's own kind of revolution, but his came at the expense of war. The earth would soak up the blood of millions, no matter which country prevailed in battle.

Anton's hands were folded together on the table in a picture of calm reasoning, but his knuckles were white and his aura white-hot. "Assuming Riaznin could rise up to be the marvel of the last millennium by actually defeating the Shenglin," he said to Valko, his voice cool and even, revealing only the finest grain of contempt, "what is in this for the woman who loses her husband and her sons for this shining empire you have shown us? What is in it for those who fight and come out victorious, but have no rights? The nobility need not fear. They are exempt from military service, so they will flourish and build up their estates." He waved a hand over the map. "They will attend your universities and dine in your great hall, while those who *sacrifice* for you"—his voice rose and lanced through his mask of complacency—"will continue to do so through taxes your nobles aren't required to pay. Those who give the most for their empire's glory will remain in ignorance because they'll have no means to educate themselves."

The emperor, who had been in the midst of pointing out a new road he could pave from Torchev to Gensi, paused to level a narrowed gaze on his brother that turned my bones to ice.

"The people are already divided," Valko said. "They will always be divided. We need a thriving noble class to set an example."

"Of what?" Anton shrugged. "Something they can never attain, neither by bloodline nor by wealth?"

Valko didn't reply. His coldness invaded my aura and threatened to frost my breath.

Anton looked to Count Rostav. "Wouldn't you agree, Nicolai?"

The count blanched and shifted in his seat. His eyes darted to the other councilors before landing on Valko. Nicolai swallowed and cleared his throat. "I appear to be the exception. My title came by my father's merits in his service to the empire, not by his wealth or ancestry."

They were fine enough words, fine enough logic, but they contradicted the shame pulsing off the count in waves. He wouldn't return Anton's disappointed stare, but he shot me a guilt-ridden glance. He knew I must feel him out for the coward he was.

"There!" Valko grinned at the count. "You see, Anton? The system isn't flawed. Those who are truly superior will always rise to the top." My blood warmed as the chill abated, but I didn't feel relief. I knew, in the end, I could never do enough "rising" for Valko. I had no wish to marry the emperor, but it bothered me greatly that he would never see me as an equal, despite his professions of admiration.

"In fact," Valko continued, "that is why I've invited Nicolai today. His father was a champion in the Five Years' War. I was a child at the time, but I know my history well. Count Rostav the First rose in the ranks to become a lieutenant-general. Many believe his actions changed the tide of battle and gave us the winning edge over the 'undefeatable' Shenglin. If you remember, brother"—Valko cast a haughty glance at Anton—"Riaznin proved to be a marvel then as we drove out our intruders and reestablished our border." The emperor sat down in his chair, his aura greedy as he focused on the count. It scraped the lining of my stomach with pangs of endless appetite. "Perhaps he shared with you some of his tactics," he said to Nicolai.

Everyone turned to the count, who paled a shade further. Two seats beside him, General Lazar flared his nostrils and my skin prickled with gooseflesh. No doubt the general didn't appreciate someone else giving the emperor advice in his stead, for that was surely what Valko had implied Nicolai should do— assist him in battle strategy.

The count proceeded to mumble a rushed account of the Five Years' War and his father's victorious moments, surely nothing Valko didn't already know himself. It was clear Nicolai was holding back. I felt it in his aura, the heightened sense of confinement and anxiety within him, like the world was shrinking in from all sides until we balanced on the pinnacle of a mountaintop. One slip in the wrong direction would be fatal.

Strangely, Valko wasn't frustrated by the count's lack of forthcomingness. In fact, the opposite was true. A smug grin tickled the corner of the emperor's lips every time he shot a glance at Anton. The prince remained silent for the rest of the meeting, his brows drawn tight as he regarded the count, a member of his trusted circle.

I contemplated Nicolai. What part was he playing in Anton's revolution? I hadn't thought to ask the prince last night about the count's involvement—or Yuri's or Feliks's. I'd been too concerned that Anton was devising a people's revolution at all. And now he'd asked *me* to participate, *me* to perform the most critical and impossible task of convincing the emperor to abdicate his throne. I hadn't told Anton I would—or even that I could, for that matter—but did he still expect it of me?

I tested the energy between us and gave the prince a long look, one he didn't return. He couldn't. Not here. As for my daring, I only hoped the emperor would interpret my motive as my incredulous opinion of his brother.

In truth, I wasn't daring at all, nor did I think Anton's concerns for the future of Riaznin far-fetched. Perhaps I surpassed Nicolai in cowardice. Like him, I also hadn't defended the prince this afternoon. Is that what Anton wanted me to do? Use my ability to slowly curb the emperor's fixation on Shengli and his indifference to those meant to be sacrificed for his vision of grandeur? Was I to do this here, publicly, in front of the emperor's councilors? I could scarcely conceive of controlling Valko, let alone manipulating the emotions of everyone present.

When the meeting was over and I was dismissed, I walked back to my rooms and opened the casements to let in some much-needed fresh air. As the conflicting auras from the council chamber left my body and I returned solely to my own thoughts and feelings, my shame lifted somewhat. I remembered my other reasons for not committing to Anton: his lack of complete faith in me and my qualms at the prospect of stripping Valko of *his* freedom.

In the bare solace of my bedchamber, I pulled Tosya's book of poetry out from beneath the mattress of the box bed and read several passages. When I still felt undecided about helping Anton, I knelt before the windowsill as if at the foot of an altar. Yuliya's statue of Feya, goddess of Auraseers, looked down at me from the simple wooden planes of her face. I didn't touch the blood spatter. I prayed with a devoutness that was foreign to me. I had been raised by the Romska to believe a common energy bound all souls together, not any deities. Still, I prayed. All I had known was energy—aura—and I needed something more to guide me now.

I tried to quiet my mind and prayed until the sun went down, but no answers reached my heart. I was still undecided.

Someone knocked on my outer door. The noise startled me to my feet. Lenka would come any time now, but she always entered without invitation. I crossed through my antechamber and paused in front of the door. Curiosity and anticipation tingled through my skin and brought a smile to my face. Only one person could make me feel happiness so easily. I turned the latch. "Hello, Pia."

"Hello." She gave a mischievous grin. In her arms, she

balanced a tray laden with bread, cheese, and a steaming bowl of soup garnished with spring herbs.

I arched a brow. This was more than her usual evening snack. "Did the kitchen staff not tell you we had dinner served in the council room?"

Her smile broadened and she giggled. "Who says this is for you?" She glided inside and set the tray on my tea table. "I'm always hungry when there's something *salacious* going on."

I shut the door. "What are you talking about?"

She sat and patted the spot to her right. I joined her, distrusting the sly giddiness dancing along my nerves. Her anticipation exceeded what normally accompanied her usual snatches of gossip.

She dug into her apron pocket and procured a letter. The sealing wax was flat with no embossment. She waved it in front of me and waggled her eyebrows.

"Is it from Yuri?" I asked. I couldn't think of what else would cause her to act like this.

Her smile revealed all her teeth. "It's from Prince Anton."

My heart lurched at his name. Then it fell. "He wrote to you?"

"No, you oaf!" She smacked my arm with the letter. "He wrote to *you*, and he asked me to deliver his missive."

My heart reared up, pounding so hard it sent a rush of blood to my cheeks. "Oh." *Why?* Why would Anton send me a letter when he could simply knock on the door to the tapestry room in an hour? I took the folded parchment and held it in my lap, my finger idly bending one corner.

Pia waited all of three seconds, then exhaled with impatience. "Oh, read it now!" She bounced in her seat.

"Did he say what it contained?"

"No," she admitted. "But, it's the *prince*. Sonya, he wrote you a *secret* message! Don't you think that's romantic?"

Before last night, her question would have triggered an eye roll. But now her rosy vision of Anton and me was one I hoped for, too. What would Pia think if she knew the prince had seen me more times than I'd like to count in nothing but my nightdress? Unfortunately, the truth would disappoint her. Anton would never act on his feelings for me, nor would he ever trust in my feelings for him.

"I'm sure this letter has nothing to do with romance, Pia."

"Prove it to me." She grabbed my wrist. "*Please?* Nothing exciting has happened all day."

"Wasn't last week's ball enough excitement to tide you over?" I asked. She'd told me how Yuri had given her quite the passionate kiss after their stolen dance together. I couldn't help but wonder if it finally outmatched the one Valko had given her months ago.

"Yes, well, now Yuri is gone for a fortnight on some recruitment errand for the emperor."

I turned the letter over and wondered if Valko had already sent men throughout the empire to announce the lowered draft age. The council had approved the directive. Anton and Nicolai were outnumbered.

Pia touched my knee. "You don't have to read it aloud. Just tell me if I'm right and it *is* romantic. I have no shame in living through you until Yuri gets back." She grinned.

I shook my head at her. "That soldier needs to marry you quickly. You're going to torture me every day until he does."

She giggled. Despite myself, I laughed along with her. "Just read it!" she said.

"Fine." I groaned a sigh. "But you're going to be wrong."

I rose and moved a few steps away so she wouldn't peer over my shoulder. I broke the seal, unfolded the paper, and pressed a free hand to my stomach to settle my nerves.

> *Meet me an hour after midnight at the kitchen door*
> *facing the stables.*
> *Wear a simple dress.*

That was it. No salutation with my name or signature of his. There was little to go by, but knowing Anton, this was a critical errand if it involved endangering me. Surely I would be punished if I were discovered fleeing the palace, even though this outing must be brief since he didn't ask me to bring anything more than what I had on. Only I couldn't wear *this*. Lenka would come soon and change me into my nightgown. Anton knew that. He knew my clothes weren't stored in my bedroom.

That's why he had sent Pia with the letter, I realized, so I would find a way to keep my dress and evade Lenka. But I couldn't think of an excuse that would fall below her suspicion. Besides, the fabric of my dress was a rich brocade. Not exactly discreet.

Pia, however, was someone I could trust with at least part of this plan. Anton had trusted her to the extent he gave her this letter. Yuri had, as well, in that he used her room as a meeting place for Anton's league of revolutionaries. The prince had said Pia was uninvolved beyond that. She wasn't a part of his inner circle, and I could see why. She was too scattered with light emotion and free with gossip to trust implicitly. Still, she was my true friend, and the only ally I could secure tonight.

"Well?" Her large eyes were round and beautiful.

I folded the letter. "No one can know what I'm about to tell you."

She nodded and inched forward in her seat. "I understand."

I bit my lip, preparing for her to draw the wrong conclusions. "It seems I'm going somewhere for the night, though I imagine I'll be back before dawn."

Pia's mouth dropped open.

"And I need your help," I went on in a rush. "I need a plain dress."

She sprang up from the couch and threw her arms around me. "Oh, Sonya! I'm so happy for you! Didn't I tell you it would be romantic?"

It occurred to me that was the only cover I could give her—one she was already willing to believe. And so, feeling like a fool, I let her excitement ripple up my throat into a noise I hoped came off as happy. To my ears it sounded like a squealing pig. "You did!" I replied.

Lenka entered the room with her always-horrible timing. I hid the letter at my side and broke apart from Pia, who darted for the door and wished me good night, forgetting her tray in her hurry. When Lenka's back was turned, Pia winked at me, then exited. Her giggles rang through the hallway.

Lenka pinched her brows and sucked in her bony cheeks. "What's come over her?"

I backed closer to my furnace. "Oh, she's always like that." With a little flick of my hand, I tossed the letter behind the grate.

My maid's gaze followed the movement, but she couldn't have seen what I'd done.

I turned around and offered her the laces of my dress. "I'm so glad you've come. I'm exhausted." *Overdoing it*, I chided myself.

Lenka didn't say a word, not then, nor during the rest of our nighttime routine. Her aura was no longer irritable—it was closed. She must have learned how to conceal her feelings after all her years of serving Izolda, just as Anton had an ability to when he focused hard enough. I wasted a moment trying to pry Lenka's aura open, but it was no use. As her wiry fingers jostled me out of my gown and brushed and braided my hair, I wondered what in Feya's name I was thinking in so readily agreeing to sneak out with Anton. I didn't even know what he meant to do, and now I'd gotten Pia involved and likely raised the suspicion of my head maid.

I may not have committed to helping the prince with his revolution, but he still held me in a measure of his power. Or perhaps I held him in a measure of mine. Perhaps this secret night together was a way for him to prove his full confidence in me. I only hoped it was worth the risk for everyone involved.

CHAPTER TWENTY-FIVE

Apparently, the only key to my wardrobe was in Lenka's possession. Pia could see no way to fetch it from her, so she brought me one of her spare uniforms.

"I can't go dressed like a maid," I said.

"Dressing like a maid will get you to the kitchens unnoticed. I have something else for you there."

She helped clothe me and we walked together, our chins tucked low as we made our way down the servants' stairs. Once we reached the kitchens, Pia glanced around to make sure we were alone and ushered me inside a pantry so large it made the convent's ample food stores seem pitiful. Behind a barrel of pickled cabbage, she pulled out a dark-blue sarafan. The bell-shaped peasant dress would be perfect. "This is also mine, but I think it will do." She grinned. "I chose the color to help you blend in with the night."

"You're having far too much fun with this."

That drew a laugh from her, not the hardest thing to do. "True." She helped me change again and wrapped a bright, floral scarf over my head.

"And what does this blend with?" I smirked.

"Nothing." The apples of her cheeks lifted. "But it will hide your hair and bring out the hazel of your eyes. A good trade, in my opinion."

I relented to wearing the scarf. I couldn't deny the part of me that wanted to look pretty for Anton. And since I couldn't fill out Pia's dress at the chest and hips, I needed all the help I could get. Her shoes didn't fit, so I settled on wearing my night slippers and hoped they'd go unnoticed under the long hem of my skirt.

We left Pia's uniform in the pantry so I could change back into it later, assuming Anton would return me before Cook and her staff began their early hours of preparations. Then Pia guided me to the specific kitchen door the prince had indicated. "Don't do anything I wouldn't do," she whispered.

"That leaves nothing."

She giggled and gave me one last hug. "Have fun. I want to hear all about it tomorrow!"

"Of course."

Oh, the lies I'd have to spin!

Pia dashed off on tiptoes, and I was left leaning against the door and wringing my hands in the dark. The air was spiced with soap and blood from the butcher's tables. The auras of dead beasts drifted around my nostrils. I resolved to touch nothing.

Having arrived early, I waited a quarter hour with jittery and restless legs. Finally Anton came. I pressed back into the shadows until I was sure his silhouette belonged to him. The span and angle of his shoulders were a good clue, but it was the profile of his handsome, aristocratic nose that gave him away. A part of me wanted to remain hidden and admire him from afar for several more minutes. Recognizing how deeply I cared for him was a gift. Even if he didn't trust my feelings, I did. That surety had taken me long enough to discover over the past few months, and now I wouldn't deny it.

I stepped into a shaft of moonlight from a nearby window. "I'm here."

The prince moved close to me. I caught his scent of musk and pine as his eyes traveled over what I was wearing. In his arms, he held a bundle of clothing. "You came," he said, a thread of amazement in his voice.

"Did you doubt I would?"

"I only dared to hope. I know how dangerous this is for you."

"What exactly are we doing?"

Something creaked. Anton dropped the bundle. It landed on the floor with a quiet thud. At the same time, he grabbed me and thrust us both into the shadows by the door.

Another creak sounded, this time from a farther distance. The padding of footsteps emerged, then grew softer like some- one was walking away. When the sound completely faded, I became aware of Anton's arms wrapped protectively around me. My fingers clutched his shirt at the chest.

As one, we slowly looked at each other. My vision had done enough adjusting to the dark to make out the heavy-lidded set to his eyes. His heart thumped against my hand, and his aura bathed me with heat.

"Did anyone follow you here?" he asked, his deep voice making a true whisper impossible.

"No." Pia didn't count. She had come *with* me, not after. But perhaps she'd stayed waiting and watching, hoping she'd see something scandalous. I wouldn't put it past her.

He nodded. "Good." But he didn't release me.

My fingers curled against him. His gaze fell to my mouth. I had the overpowering urge to kiss him, but I pulled back before I ever leaned in. At my first twinge of resistance, Anton let me go.

We moved a foot apart, a healthier space that granted me my breath. He rubbed the back of his neck and bent to retrieve what he'd dropped.

We kept stealing awkward glances at each other. My lips tingled with the absence of our almost kiss. But if I *had* kissed Anton, he would have only accused me of mirroring his desire. "Shall we go now?" I asked, turning slightly away.

"What gave you the idea we are leaving?"

My head snapped back to him. I blinked twice. "Well, the dress you made sure I wear." I shifted on my feet. "The door by the stables . . ." A sinking feeling of disappointment made my shoulders droop. "We *are* leaving, aren't we?"

He chuckled. By the gods, was he actually teasing me?

"Yes, we're leaving." He cocked his head. "You're an anxious one for a bit of freedom, aren't you?"

I rolled my eyes. "I think you know that much about me." Was I actually bantering with the stoic prince? "And since you're a revolutionary," I added with a grin, "you really can't talk."

Immediately, a sober demeanor overcame him. "Shhh." He touched my lips, and my heart surged, beating faster. "Not here." I nodded, and he pulled his hand away.

"I brought us cloaks." He divided the bundle in his arms and gave me half. I draped the roughspun around my shoulders and pulled the hood up over my headscarf. So much for drawing out my hazel eyes. The prince donned his own cloak. "Ready?"

I followed him out the door to the stables and expected him to fetch Raina. I felt a little foolish when he came out with a tawny draft horse. Of course he would choose a less noticeable breed. Perhaps Pia wasn't the only one with a romantic dream of what this night would hold. I needed to pull myself back to reality. I still didn't know where we were going or what we were up to. Neither did I ask Anton as he saddled the horse and muffled its hooves with strips of cloth. As we readied to leave the palace grounds, my stomach fluttered and every part of me felt wide awake. I could scarcely keep from bouncing on my toes. The mystery of our destination only made our escape more thrilling.

We didn't yet ride the horse. We walked alongside it as Anton sneaked us to a small gate at the side of the palace walls, not the main entrance at the southern front. He muttered something to the guards and handed over a purse. Apparently the prince schemed with more soldiers than just Yuri.

The gate opened and we slipped outside. My chest expanded, and I drank in the air that already tasted so much cooler and clean. I felt lighter on my feet the farther we progressed down a dim road enclosed by arching cherry tree branches. Their white blossoms dotted above us like stars. In our everyday clothes, I imagined we were peasant lovers stealing away in the night. If only the common life was such a sweet dream in Riaznin.

After turning into the third alleyway, Anton felt it safe for us to ride the horse. He lifted me onto the saddle and mounted behind me. His hands slid around my waist to take the reins, and I smiled as his heightened aura made my nerves sing. He could tease me all he wanted about my itching for freedom, but his eagerness was just as palpable.

As he nudged the horse along at a steady trot, we rode away from the noble quarter of the city to the fringes where commoners still roamed the streets in the dead of night. At the sight of them—the feel of them—my elation snuffed out. I hadn't expected to encounter any stray auras tonight. I'd hoped Anton and I would be alone in whatever errand he'd fashioned for us.

The commoners' Torchev dialect rang out harsh and lazy as they laughed over shared crocks of spirits or hollered at ladies sauntering across brothel balconies with pushed-up curves that nearly spilled out from their bodices.

All of their auras mixed inside me, dark and jovial and rebellious . . . yet also sad. Exhausted after a long and hard day and now seeking release. I leaned against Anton, not wanting to taste them too deeply. His arms moved in closer at my sides, as if he understood my difficulty.

"We're almost there." His rumbled attempt to whisper breathed warmth against my ear.

A burst of raucous laughter split the air. I flinched, but it wasn't directed at us. Five or six young people were playing some sort of game with rocks on the road. They clapped one of their comrades on the shoulder. The boy must have won. He was gangly but round-faced, probably no older than fourteen. His friend shoved coins into his pockets and tossed him toward the brothel doors. He grinned, but his foreboding drummed inside me. I closed my eyes, feeling at once sick and disgusted and sorry for the boy, a reflection of his own emotions. Trying to purge myself of his energy without losing the contents of my stomach, I turned my head into Anton's chest and inhaled his pine scent like a lifeline.

"Just another moment, Sonya," he promised.

I nodded. The auras of the peasants were harder for me to resist acting upon than those of the nobles in the palace. The city people were brasher, more open. And while the nobles weren't any less decent at heart, they were more skillful at masking their feelings to survive the game of politics they played.

True to Anton's word, he led us back around the brothel to an even narrower alleyway, thankfully empty of people. At its end, we passed through the gate of a small lodging. The prince helped me off the horse and tied him to a lone tree in the yard.

Taking my hand, he led me to a door of patched-together wood. He rapped three times.

A middle-aged woman with frizzy hair and a red bulbous nose appeared on the threshold. She grunted. "He said you would be coming"—her small eyes looked the prince over before scrutinizing me—"but not another tart. We have enough of you around here."

I would have been offended, but the woman's aura radiated more fear than revulsion. I hoped Anton was right about no one recognizing us.

He broadened his chest. "Don't insult her," he said to the woman, and clutched my hand tighter. "She is respectable. I assure you he will want to see her once he knows she is here."

Who were they were speaking about? *Who* would want to see me?

The woman pursed her lips. "If he says no, the girl leaves. No more words about it."

"Agreed."

The woman grunted again and spared me another glance before moving back to let us in. We entered a cramped lobby with peeling paint. A rack strung with shabby coats and shawls was the only decoration. The woman left us and hobbled up a flight of rickety stairs. She seemed to have an ailment in her leg.

"What is this place?" I asked Anton.

"A house for boarders, often fugitives or those seeking somewhere to stay when they travel to the city and don't wish the authorities to know." He let go of my hand and drew back his hood, unlacing his cloak and hanging it on the rack.

I did the same and adjusted my headscarf. "Why does the woman risk the occupation?"

"Her name is Ruta, and she is desperate"—he sighed—"like anyone dwelling in this quarter. She has no family and must make a life for herself the only way she can."

I looked over my slumlike surroundings, more grateful for my own lot in the empire. "Who does Ruta think you are?" They seemed to know each other.

"A university friend of 'the gypsy,' as she calls him just to try to provoke him."

Gypsy? My heart pounded faster. "Anton, who are we here to see?"

"You must call me Gavril."

"Gavril, then," I said impatiently, *"who* is here?"

The stairs creaked. A young man stood on the landing and held a candle. He wore a vest and flowing peasant shirt with the sleeves rolled back to expose his long arms. His legs were also long, stuffed into trousers and worn leather shoes. In fact, everything about him was long, even his endearing face. I gasped, my mouth stretching into a wide smile. *Tosya?*

CHAPTER TWENTY-SIX

Tosya took one step down the stairs, and his gaze narrowed. Did he truly not recognize me? I had seen him every spring for eight years, though the last one we'd shared together was a full two years ago. Tosya had been my family among the Romska, the closest person I had to a brother. I pulled the scarf off my head. The motion brought my blond braid over the front of my shoulder. His eyes popped wide. His lips parted as if to say my name.

Anton put a hand on my back. "Misha," he said, addressing Tosya by a false name, "you remember Klara, don't you?"

Tosya blinked, quickly catching on. "Yes, yes, of course." He turned to Ruta, who had carefully watched his reaction. "It's all right. This girl is, uh, Gavril's . . ."

Tosya and Anton spoke over each together, finishing my introduction.

"Cousin."

"Wife."

I jerked my head up to Anton.

Even in the dull light, I saw color sweep his cheeks. He cleared his throat. "We're married now. I married my cousin."

Tosya's brows lifted as he suppressed a grin. "You have my congratulations."

Anton gave him a warning look.

"Very well." Ruta frowned. "But I don't want any trouble. Go to the parlor and keep your voices low. I won't have you waking the other guests." As Tosya descended the stairs, Ruta tugged her shawl closer. "There's a tray of bread and jam in the kitchen, and a bottle of kvass in the cupboard."

"We'll be fine," Tosya assured her. "Get some sleep."

She grumbled, muttering to herself as she hobbled back to where her upstairs room must have been.

"I think she likes you," I whispered when I was sure she was gone.

"I'm a favorite with all the ladies." Tosya preened himself by smoothing his vest.

I laughed, and he hopped off the last step and swooped me up in his arms. He kissed my cheek and set me down. "Did you get shorter?"

"No." I smacked his chest. "You got taller."

"That's what my friends keep telling me, but I have this theory that everything in the world keeps shrinking but myself."

"Hmm. I think your education gave you an ego."

"A necessary requirement of a poet. That, and a wide range of insecurities."

I laughed again and shook my head as I breathed in all of him. He carried the scent of the forest mulch and campfires surrounding the Romska wagons. His aura was equally familiar—light on the surface, but beautifully deep and awe-inspiring beneath, like the sea under the shallows where the sunlight reaches. "It's so good to see you."

"And you." His humor simmered to something more sincere for a moment. Then he clapped Anton's arm. "I can't believe you went off and got married without telling me!"

The prince's eyes lifted to the ceiling. "Don't start. I had to say something since you were tripping all over your words. You're better with a quill, you know."

Tosya scowled at him and threw me a teasing smile. "Your husband is frank to a fault."

Anton groaned. "Shall we move to the parlor?"

"And domineering," I added.

Anton brushed past us, muttering, "Maybe it was a mistake bringing you two together."

Tosya and I giggled like naughty children and fell in tow behind him.

The parlor was at the back, down a narrow hallway and adjacent to the kitchen. Everything in the lodging was a little off-kilter, from the slanting floors to the crooked windowsills and doorframes. But with Tosya at my side, the place was starting to grow on me.

We sat around a small, circular table, probably meant for a game of cards. Our three pairs of knees kept colliding—Anton's because he sat closer to me, and Tosya's due to the length of his legs.

Tosya set his candle on the table and leaned forward, his chin propped on a knuckled hand. "I never imagined I'd see the two of you under the same roof. How is it you know each other?"

Anton glanced back to the hallway. In a quiet voice, he answered, "She is the sovereign Auraseer."

Tosya turned large eyes on me, which swiftly softened. "Oh, Sonya . . . I didn't know. I'm so sorry."

I swallowed and fought to resist his pity. "It isn't so bad." When he didn't reply but only stared at me, his aura tightening my throat, I added, "At least I have Anton." I'd chosen my words poorly. I'd made it sound like I owned him or belonged to him or that we were somehow *more* . . . more than what we were.

Anton's leg settled against mine beneath the table and made the complicated energy entwining us pulse with more intensity. I felt Tosya's piqued curiosity, as if he wondered, all joking aside, what the prince and I really meant to each other. If he'd asked us directly, I wasn't sure we could have answered.

Tosya sighed and templed his fingers at his mouth as he gazed at me. "We were so good at hiding you." I knew he meant my days with his caravan and countless others. "I thought we could hide you forever. Now to see you *found* . . . like *this* . . ."

He shook his head. "What a life for you."

His words brought back memories. Once I had grown older and a little more cautious with my ability, I should have been safe from the authorities. Though discretion was never my talent, I would have escaped notice had the bounty hunters not tracked me from the time I was fifteen, when my parents were executed for withholding their gifted child from the empire. And at the end of last spring, when Tosya must have been at university, the bounty hunters had finally succeeded in finding me. My arms had been covered in bruises from their brutal grip as they'd dragged me away.

Rubbing his brow, Tosya turned to Anton. "Did you bring her here so I could hide her again? I would gladly do it. You know I would." My chest constricted with his guilt. Why did he blame himself for what had happened to me? Even if he had been with the Romska caravan that spring, it wouldn't have changed the outcome. The bounty hunter, Bartek, once he'd discovered my whereabouts, held five Romska children hostage, with me as their ransom. Tosya wouldn't have let them die; he would have made the same choice their families had.

Anton remained silent, giving me a chance to answer Tosya's proposal. I considered my friend. Leaving Torchev behind was a wonderful temptation. But then Kira and Dasha seemed to ghost through the room, two little girls huddled in the folds of Sestra Mirna's skirts as they watched me leave on one of the hardest days of their lives. They were now the children I had to save, their fates dependent on me.

"I wish I could see the Romska again," I admitted. "But my days of hiding are over."

Tosya nodded and watched me sadly. "How do you bear it? Serving the emperor? Being walled inside the palace with so many people?"

He must still see me as the haunted girl I was at fifteen, the girl troubled by the fresh wound of her parents' death, a reality that woke me screaming from my sleep. Somehow Tosya had been able to coax smiles out of me, even an occasional laugh. He'd distract me with stories and quiet musings. And now I had read his book of poetry. *The mighty isn't one, but many.* Words Anton told me were sweeping across Riaznin. I didn't want Tosya to think me weak. "I've grown stronger," I answered him.

"She's truly incredible," Anton added, the energy between us burgeoning with pride.

Tosya's curiosity bubbled again. He turned calculating eyes on his friend. "Have you shown her your birthmark?"

Anton's aura jolted. He pulled his leg away from mine. "Is anyone hungry? Ruta mentioned bread and jam."

"Have you?" Tosya asked, unrelenting.

"What birthmark?" I spun to Anton. "What is he talking about?"

Neither man answered. Anton couldn't bear the weight of Tosya's stare for long. He stood and walked back to the kitchen.

"What birthmark?" I asked Tosya again, this time lower so Anton wouldn't hear.

"It's nothing. I only thought he might have . . ." He idly

rubbed a spot on his inner forearm, his gaze drifting back to the prince. "It's nothing."

Clearly it wasn't nothing. My skin tingled with the remembrance of when Anton had drawn back my sleeve and examined my arm in the very same spot.

Unable to restrain myself, I pushed up from my chair and followed Anton to the kitchen. I'd spent enough months in the dark, as far as his secrets were concerned. I thought they'd all come to light, but I was wrong. And the prince was, too, if he thought he could keep something else from me.

Anton stood by the slab of the kitchen table. He diligently avoided my gaze as he unwrapped a loaf of bread from its cloth.

"Give me your hand," I said.

He removed the lid off the crock of jam.

"Anton."

"Let this go, Sonya."

Ignoring him, I took his right hand and revolved it, then slid back his sleeve. He sighed. There on his inner forearm, just where I knew it would be, was the birthmark Tosya had mentioned. It was pinkish brown, no larger than my fingernail, and reminded me of the head of a lynx in profile: snarled mouth and pointed ears, slightly longer than an average cat's. I brushed my thumb across it and Anton's skin pebbled, his muscles tight as balalaika strings.

"What has this to do with me?" I asked.

"It doesn't. That's the point."

"Then why did you look at my arm that night?"

His frown deepened. "I don't know."

"Why won't you tell me? Don't you trust me?"

He closed his eyes. My question of trust hammered on the wedge dividing us. "This isn't important." His eyes slitted open, but he kept his gaze trapped on the leaning floor planks. "It has nothing to do with the revolution. It's only some nonsense Tosya's teasing me about."

"He wasn't teasing."

"Sonya . . ." Anton gave me a miserable look.

"Please?" I softened my grip on his arm, trying to show him it was safe to open up to me.

He inhaled a long breath and stalled another moment before he finally gave in. "When I had to leave Trusochelm Manor," he said slowly, haltingly, "when Valko required me in Torchev and under his watchful eye—I was torn about it. I'd learned to accept my fate, but rumors of my brother's unforgiving rule had already spread across the countryside. I wasn't sure if I could endure being with him . . . witnessing Riaznin crumble under his reign."

As I listened, I wondered what all of this had to do with a birthmark, but I dared not interrupt for fear Anton wouldn't finish his story.

"It was the end of another summer, and Tosya was on leave from his university studies. He took it upon himself to cheer me up. We got drunk and"—Anton shrugged like he couldn't believe he was admitting this—"Tosya took me to an old Romska woman to have my fortune read. I suppose he thought it would bring me some comfort."

The prince stopped there, scuffing the toe of his boot on the floor.

"What did she tell you?" I asked.

Scuff, scuff. He glanced down to the parlor and sighed again. "That I would live to see the dawn of a new Riaznin, that the words of my Romska friend would part the clouds for the sunrise."

I contemplated Anton. It wasn't like him to heed a fortune-teller. He was familiar enough with the Romska to know there was nothing mystic about their ramblings. They only did what they had to do to bring food to their families, like all the common people. But I could see why Anton believed the old woman—she showed him what he most wanted to have.

"What else did she say?" He was still dancing around the heart of his unease.

Scuff, scuff, scuff.

I moved my hands down from his birthmark and wrapped them around his fingers. "Anton?" I whispered.

His eyes lifted to mine and captured the glow of moonlight past the grime of the kitchen window. His aura made my chest ache. "She told me I would meet a girl who would change my life forever. Our two souls were fitted for each other."

The pain in my chest expanded and rose to my throat. I thought I understood him. "And she would bear a mark like yours?"

A mark I didn't have.

"Yes."

I nodded slowly.

"I told you it was nonsense." He grinned, but it didn't sit right on his face.

"Was the old woman an Auraseer?" Not that my kind had the gift of foretelling the future. As far as I knew, no one did, but at least an Auraseer could sense what the prince hoped for and know if what she foretold rang true. Though most people in their desperation were fairly easy to read, even by those without my ability.

"I don't know . . . she was different. Sometimes I wonder what magic encircles all of us, what we could do if we were sensitive enough to unearth it. Look at you, your connection with the dead. There's been no Auraseer like you before."

He was trying to console me, I realized. Distract me from the disillusionment of his confession—that he, despite all his wiser judgment, believed in the fortune he was given.

I had to stop troubling him to reveal his secrets. I wished I could give him back this one.

His large hand, cradled in both my own, felt heavy. I let it go. "I believe we decide our own fate," I said, unfailingly stubborn, as always. It was better than letting my heart break. "No one has the right to dictate who we are or what we can become. I thought that's what you believed, too, what you were fighting for."

"I do." He managed to shake his head, cross his arms, and shrug at the same time, altogether not knowing what to do with himself. "I am."

At some point Tosya had moved closer. He stood with his shoulder pressed against the crooked wall of the kitchen. With an affectionate smile, he said to us, "Come back to the table. The night is waxing late, and much as I'm delighted to see you, Sonya, I doubt Anton's purpose in bringing you here was to reunite two long-lost friends."

The prince cleared his throat and pulled down his sleeve. His shame thickened my throat as he quietly brushed past me and moved back to the parlor. He left the food tray forgotten. Numbly, I covered the bread and crock of jam.

Tosya approached me.

I traced a hairline fracture on the lid. "Why does he push me away? Why does he find any *trifling excuse* to shut me out? Why won't he just confess he doesn't believe I'm good enough for him?"

"Of course you are good enough, Sonya. It has nothing to do with that."

I met Tosya's deep-brown eyes. It was such a comfort to see him, this boy who'd been like a brother, to remember who I was when he had known me, the feeling of fragile self-worth he'd fostered within me. But Tosya had no idea of what I'd done since I left the Romska, no idea the convent's burning was because of my willful recklessness. The black ribbon at my wrist itched.

I shouldn't chide Anton for his secrets. Mine were so dark I hoped he would never uncover them.

Tosya put his hands in his pockets. "Anton once treated me the same way he treats you. Being abandoned at such a young age . . . it had a profound effect on him. It's difficult for him to place his trust in anyone."

"I was also separated from my parents."

"Yes, well, as he said, you are truly incredible. Don't judge him too harshly for grieving differently than you. Be patient with him."

I looked past Tosya's dim figure to Anton, several feet away. He sat, head lowered, hands clasped together on the parlor table, as if steeling himself for another long council meeting. "I don't think any amount of patience can outlast his resolve. When it comes to me, the prince is determined to remain distant."

Tosya rubbed my arm. "Perhaps that's because he needs you more than anyone and doesn't know who he would be if that need in him was gone. He's only ever learned to *fight*, to be without everyone he's ever cared for, to guard his emotions from others."

"Until he met you."

"Yes," Tosya relented. "But through me he's found another reason to keep fighting. That is what binds us in the end. I was content with the Romska, writing my songs and secret stashes of poetry, until Anton saw something within me larger than myself—something in my words that could give people hope. And I'm assuming he's seen something bigger within you, as well, and you're now a part of this fight."

I nodded, though I'd never quite committed to the role the prince had laid out for me.

Tosya leaned closer and whispered with a chuckle, "It's terrifying, though, isn't it?"

I looked at him in surprise. Tosya may have inadvertently launched a revolution, but he was still the same unassuming Romska boy who had been my friend for years.

"I try to let Anton and the others do all the talking and political maneuvering," he confessed. "My poetry has said all I want to say." With a wink, he added, "Now I'm just the pretty face of the cause."

I lifted a brow. "One who will be executed if he's ever discovered by the authorities."

"Always the first to sour the mood, Sonya."

That drew a small laugh from me.

"Come on." He draped his long arm around my shoulder and guided me back to the parlor. "Let's go pretend we're as qualified for this revolution as the prince believes we are. With any luck, we'll start believing it ourselves."

Tosya's humor could only briefly lift my spirits. It might have been terribly selfish of me, considering we were talking about war and the future of the empire, but all I could think of was that no amount of luck would make a lynx-shaped birthmark materialize on my arm.

CHAPTER TWENTY-SEVEN

"Feliks is still pressuring me to overthrow Valko and claim myself as emperor," Anton said as he scratched the growing stubble on his chin.

He and Tosya had spent the last half hour catching up on all the latest happenings. The situation was dangerous for my Romska friend. He'd been accused of high treason, the empire's bounty hunters and soldiers were searching for him, and any copies of his book were to be burned if discovered. He spent most of his days in hiding and had taken a great risk in coming to Torchev to meet with Anton. Tosya was supposed to have convened with the prince and his revolutionaries on Morva's Eve, but when the night before the modest holiday had turned into a grand ball in honor of Floquart de Bonpré, Anton instructed Tosya to stay away.

Their thus-far-quiet rebellion was coming to a head, the wrath of the people transforming into its own beast. Something violent was on the brink of happening. Anton feared the spark might be ignited when the people learned of the lowered draft age. "Feliks believes it will be easier to transition the government to the people if I first take it myself," the prince said.

"Why *don't* you do it that way?" I asked, seeing the merits of Feliks's reasoning. I'd learned that the man with the piercing blue eyes was also Anton's representative of the people. Every large city or group of villages in Riaznin had a similar leader in the plot of the revolution. They held secret meetings, shared their dreams of freedom, and reported back to Feliks, who also headed up the circle in Torchev.

"Then you'll have the backing of the nobles," I added. "At least for a time." Many would support Anton as emperor; many believed Valko was only the changeling prince. "In that case, Count Rostav would be a stronger ally." While Feliks represented the people, I'd discovered Nicolai was assigned to the nobles, only a tiny fraction of whom were being slowly conditioned to the infant steps of equality. "He would have more time to persuade other nobles to your cause and grant the peasants and serfs more rights."

Tosya leaned forward, arms folded on the table. A nearly empty tumbler of kvass rested beside him. "Is Nicolai holding steadfast?"

I remembered the count's disturbing neutrality in our last council meeting. Anton hadn't forgotten it, either. "He is faltering, the more perilous this becomes." The prince sighed. "My vision for this revolution is peaceable, and Nicolai has clung to that. He isn't the warrior his father was, and in truth, I'm not confident he can remain loyal to our cause. It's all happening too fast, and if we can't persuade the people to be more patient, blood will spill, and too much of it."

"Which is why Feliks's idea isn't a bad one," I said, circling back to the version of the revolution where Anton took the throne first before carefully giving the people their rights.

The prince frowned as he studied me. Dark rings had surfaced beneath his eyes. "You know why I won't rule over my brother. Because he *is* my brother. And by order of birth, the throne is his."

"Yet you seek to take it away from him, regardless. By direct manipulation. Through *me*. Which is worse?" The challenge between us coiled hot in our auras. It broke apart at Tosya's exclamation.

"You wish Sonya to force Valko to abdicate?" His brows lifted with incredulity. "How?"

We hadn't gotten to this part—Anton's pivotal, impossible plan. "Sonya can do more than sense emotion," the prince replied. "She can alter it in someone else."

"Once!" I said in exasperation. "I was only able to do it one time!"

Tosya stared at me like a stranger. "Truly? And when did you acquire that gift?"

"When Valko tried to kill her," Anton replied flatly.

Tosya's brows raised another notch. "Ah," he said, his gaze drifting between us, all too keen on everything left unspoken. "I see."

I felt blood rush up my neck into my cheeks. Here, in this run-down boardinghouse, I felt far away from the palace, far away from Valko and the spell of charisma and attraction he'd cast over me, the link of mutual understanding he'd claimed we shared. It was hard to believe how conflicted I had been, how torn I'd felt between my desire for him and his brother.

"You've had an interesting few months at the palace, haven't you, Sonya?" Tosya asked. Despite himself, he grinned. His perplexed and light emotion sent a tickle under my arms.

"Don't tease her," Anton said. "It isn't funny."

That only gave his friend permission to laugh. "You're right. It isn't." Tosya tried to compose his features, but his humor only rose and flitted across my skin. "It kind of is." He snorted, his eyes watering. "Just a little."

I sucked in my cheeks and struggled not to laugh with him and let his aura overtake me. Anton's frown deepened "What's the matter with the two of you?"

"It's him." I pointed at Tosya, lips quivering.

"Stop it," Anton commanded his friend.

Tosya chortled harder. I smacked his shoulder, and he buried his face in his hands. His palms pressed against his eyes and his entire body trembled with laughter. "I'm sorry! Truly, I am. It's late and I can only handle so much surprise in one evening." He pulled his hands away, his face red with merriment.

"Thus far I've learned the two of you are not only *acquainted*"—his emphasis on that word designated it as a euphemism for something far more complicated—"but also that the young girl I once knew, who once rolled in the mud with the pigs when she had a sudden urge to cool off, is now the sovereign Auraseer, and that her entanglement in our revolution means she must 'alter the emperor's emotions' to the extent that he willfully and joyfully hands over the throne."

"You see?" I said to Anton. "Even he thinks it's ridiculous!"

The prince's jaw twitched. He leveled a firm stare on his friend. "You haven't seen her do it."

Tosya shrugged. "Granted." He tossed back the dregs of his kvass and strangely gained sobriety in doing so. "So let's see her do it now."

I blinked at him. "Are you serious?"

"Yes. Maybe that's why you were such a charmer with the wild horses in your youth. Could you bend their emotions, too?"

My mouth opened and shut a few times while I considered him. "If I did, I had no idea what I was doing," I finally answered.

Tosya cocked a half smile. "Come on, then. Show me something. Make me get up and do a jig."

"This is absurd!" Anton snapped. "She doesn't do parlor tricks."

"But we're in a parlor."

"Tosya."

"Couldn't resist."

"I've had enough! This isn't a joke!" Anton's voice was severe. "Sonya *has* this gift. She's suffered enough to discover it; she doesn't have to suffer more to prove herself to you."

"Very well, Anton." Tosya held up his hands. "If you say Sonya has this power, I'll believe you because I *trust* you, and I trust her. But please tell me you're aware of all the danger you're putting her in." He turned to me, all of his humor gone. "And please tell me *you* were aware of the danger before you committed yourself, because when I penned all those lofty words, I never dreamed they would put anyone in peril."

"I haven't committed yet." My hands slid under my thighs.

"And she isn't cornered," Anton added defensively. "I've given her the choice." His nostrils flared as he lowered his gaze. "Though the life she is forced to live is already stripped of any freedom."

Swirling the ghost of kvass in his tumbler, Tosya eyed Anton. "This is why you brought her here tonight: you want *me* to persuade her."

Anton didn't deny it. He exhaled and met Tosya's accusatory stare. Their auras fought inside me and caused my stomach to cramp. I felt like I was back in the council chamber, sitting between the prince and his brother, not the prince and his closest friend.

"Well, I won't do it." Tosya crossed his arms. "Sonya is right. Whether she manipulates Valko or you defraud and usurp him, neither method is less ugly. The emperor *must* be overcome for this revolution to succeed. He must be hurt. You cannot prevent that. With great change always comes some destruction of the old. *'His throne will be timber to build new cities. His palace gold for bread,'"* he quoted from his book. "You need to remember that. You need to accept it."

I watched Anton's haggard and beautiful eyes, and despite the fact that he'd dragged me out here in the middle of the night to have a poet convince me of my part in the revolution, I wanted to kiss his cheek and lay his head against my breast.

All this debate, this worry eating away at him, filtered down to how deeply he respected humankind. He wanted liberty and equality for all of us. He didn't want anyone to suffer—not even his brother. Anton *loved* Valko, I realized. Maybe not the man he was now, but the boy he had once been, the man he could have become—that he still had a hope of becoming. That was why Anton wanted me to bend the emperor's emotions, because perhaps Valko stood a better chance at redeeming himself after abdicating than he would if Anton usurped him. The prince didn't wish to tear from his brother the barest part of his identity—that he was Emperor Izia's eldest son, whether or not he continued to rule Riaznin.

"I'll do it," I said. When both men turned to me, their auras radiated amazement. I took a steadying breath. "At least I'll try." The task seemed as formidable as ever.

"Sonya." Tosya set down his tumbler. "We planned this revolution without you, and it's going to happen regardless of your involvement. Your parents never wanted this for you."

"They never wanted me to be free?" I managed a grin.

"They *always* wanted your freedom, but not at the expense of your life."

"That's what life is—a massive choice." I sat up straighter, trying to reach some of Tosya's height. "One day you, like me, won't be able to hide any longer. The authorities will find you, and you will have to face the consequences of everything you wrote in that wonderful book. I've read it, Tosya, and I'm so proud of you. I fear for you, as well. But I would never wish to take away the choice you made by writing those words. That was your part in this, your stand for what you believe is right. Now I must take mine."

He smiled sadly at me. "I suppose I always knew I couldn't comfort you forever. You would travel to another caravan and face your nightmares alone."

Beneath the table, Anton found my hand. His skin was warm as he laced our fingers together. His aura burned with gratitude and something deeper, something far more powerful.

"I'm not alone," I said.

❦

Anton and I rode the tawny draft horse back to the palace. We'd left soon after I'd declared myself a fully fledged revolutionary. The dark sky was graying, growing closer to dawn. Soon the kitchen staff would arise to bake bread and pluck feathers from the fowl that would grace the emperor's tables.

Thankfully, even in this unsettling quarter of the city, the streets were finally empty. I let my eyes fall closed and trusted Anton would hold me upright.

A little while later, when the prince must have thought I was sleeping, I felt the warm press of his lips on my head.

CHAPTER TWENTY-EIGHT

THE NEXT MORNING, AFTER THE SNATCH OF SLEEP I'D GOTTEN in the tapestry room, I crept back through the doors to my own chambers. I'd left Pia's clothes and her pretty floral scarf in a folded pile in the corner of my room. I knew, like clockwork, she would arrive a quarter hour before Lenka—perhaps even a few minutes earlier since she must be eager to hear about my "romantic getaway." I nudged my tired brain and tried to dream up some scintillating lies.

But Pia never came.

I chewed at my lip and looked at the table where she'd set her tray of food last night. We'd never eaten in our hurried plan to sneak me out of the palace. But now the tray was gone. Tosya's book of poetry was also missing. I'd left it near the statue of Feya during my prayers and forgotten to hide it, though I checked beneath the mattress of the box bed to be sure. I also rummaged through the stacks of Pia's reading lesson books against the far wall, but it was no use. The volume of poetry was nowhere to be seen.

I flexed my hands. My nerves crawled with unease. What if Pia had taken the book last night? She could have noticed it when she came back for her tray and thought it might contain a love sonnet—the sonnet I'd encouraged her to practice for Yuri.

What if Pia had been discovered with something treasonous?

The clock on my wall chimed the hour. I hid Pia's clothes in the bedsheets I always rumpled so it appeared I'd slept there. My gut was a cavern of anxiety by the time Lenka opened the door.

She glided in, my other attending maids behind her like a row of ducklings. I stood in the center of my antechamber, my arms crossed as I felt Lenka's smug aura. Her skin looked particularly gaunt and stretched today over her jutting bones.

"I haven't eaten yet," I declared, noting my headdress and Auraseer's robes in the arms of my other maids. What special occasion merited such finery?

The corners of Lenka's mouth pulled slightly upward. "This is a wise day for fasting," she replied, dismissing my words. "It will help you focus. The emperor's welfare is in your hands."

"The emperor's welfare is *always* in my hands."

"Yes, but today he will be surrounded by more than nobles. He is opening the palace to admit the public."

"A reception for the people?" I asked, unsure if I'd understood her correctly. When she nodded, I raised my brows. These receptions had once been a monthly tradition at the palace, an opportunity for the people to lay gifts at the emperor's feet or beseech him with their requests. But in all my days as sovereign Auraseer, Valko had never held one. Rumor persisted that he'd only done so twice during his reign. Today's reception surely had to do with his scheming for Shengli. He wanted to appear benevolent so the people would accept the lowered draft age with grace.

"I don't wish to fast," I said. "Could you please send Pia up with a tray?"

Lenka angled away from me and brushed a lock of hair back into her tight bun. "I'm afraid Pia is indisposed."

My cavern of anxiety widened to a crater. "What do you mean?"

Lenka shrugged, but I still sensed that smugness about her. "I'm sure we'll learn soon enough." With that vague and unsettling explanation, she clapped her hands. Two servants entered with the traveling tub that seemed to rotate between my room, Anton's, and surely other high-ranking staff. A flock of attendants followed with steaming buckets of water and reminded me of my first day in the palace.

"Come," Lenka said. "We haven't much time before the emperor requires you."

✳◠◡◠✳

The tables in the great hall had been removed. The only remaining furniture rested on the dais: Valko's magnificent throne and my small stool. Guards flanked the perimeter of the room, tripling the amount that had served the night of the ball. Yuri wasn't among them, still off on his recruitment errand for the empire.

Nobles milled about and left a wide berth around the center aisle for the forthcoming people. The commoners stood in line outside the closed doors. I'd passed them when I'd entered. Their auras wove a web of resentment, desperation, and curiosity within me. I kept a hand on my headdress's dangling pearls, but the sting brought little relief.

It was harder to meet Valko's eyes now that I'd made a pact against him. As I rose from my curtsy, he stared down at me from the height of his throne. "My Lord Emperor," I said in greeting.

"Sonya." His gaze softened, and he extended a jeweled hand to my stool. I lighted up the dais and took my seat.

The double doors to the great hall opened. The nobles quieted. Valko's chest puffed beneath his brocaded kaftan.

The common people filed in, some with wide eyes as they took in the spectacular domed ceiling. Others trembled the nearer they advanced to Valko. But most wore grim looks of determination, their hands fisted, their faces set in stone.

Some were farmers who shared detailed reports of crop failure, despite the rains and melting snow. The soil was cursed, they said, and they pleaded with the emperor to petition the gods for relief from the famine. Others wanted more than Valko's "royal channel to the heavens." They came meeting their monarch in the finest clothes they owned—threadbare and patched—and asked him, while observing firsthand the extravagance of his stronghold, if he would share in his plenty until the earth yielded up her fruits again.

Valko had similar responses for all them. "Be of comfort. The time of prosperity is at hand." Or "Hold fast. The gods have spoken and declared Riaznin will flourish."

He meant every word. I felt his surety fill my breast. But I pushed out every breath of empathy for him. His means of restoring the empire were heartless. My role was to reveal a better way—a way that no longer required his leadership. More than that, I was to make him believe it.

My gaze wandered over the nobles as I searched for Anton. I yearned to speak with him, to concoct some sort of plan for approaching the enormous task before me. He must have some ideas for slowly breaking his brother down. At least, I hoped he did.

But the prince wasn't here. I slouched a little on my stool, then chastised myself for being disappointed. It wasn't as if we could have a treasonous conversion here, anyway. Or even a flirtatious one.

After the farmers, other people came with more grievances: quarrels with their neighbors, pleas for fortifying the villages around Torchev that didn't have securing walls like our city. One thin-shouldered woman complained that the Azanel River was making her children sick. Refuse was dumped in the river, and she lived downstream of it. She wanted the sewer outlets diverted, or at least funds to dig a proper well.

Valko held a placid smile as he listened to her, but my fingernails dug into my legs with his grating impatience. He wouldn't be able to brush her off as easily as he did the farmers. "I shall discuss the matter with my council," he said at last. "It is my desire that *all* have clean water." He lifted his gaze to the continuous stream of peasants while extending his ringed hand to the woman. With reluctance, she kissed it. As she left, Valko motioned for Councilor Ilyin to step forward. "Please see that this matter is addressed at our next meeting," he said loud enough for everyone to hear.

The graying councilor bowed. "If I may, My Lord Emperor," he said quietly, "the woman's request is one of many in the city. If you wish to recruit a younger, *healthy* army, you would do well to clean the water supply."

Valko frowned and tilted his head at the old man. "Councilor Ilyin, did I never abandon the beard law? By the gods, you should grow yours back." He reclined against his throne and muttered, "I suppose something must be done about the water. We'll discuss it later." He waved him away.

There was a lull in the receiving line as Councilor Ilyin ambled back to the others, his hand on his smooth cheek. As the next peasant waited for the signal to advance, Valko sighed and turned to me, the seven rubies on his crown twinkling. "Such is the tedious lot of an emperor," he said from his comfortable chair. I didn't comment. The peasants had waited in line for hours before they were even admitted into the palace. "I'm itching to go over battle strategy with General Lazar," he went on, "but I saw the wisdom in receiving the people today."

He smiled and bent a fraction closer. I tensed, wondering if he'd dare to touch me with his public watching. His gaze dropped to my clenched hands, before lifting back to study my eyes. After a beat, he said, "I'm glad you are here, Sonya. Anything is easier with you by my side."

The emperor's soothed aura sent a wash of warmth across my shoulders. His well-timed sincerity weighed me with guilt. I felt the swirl of conflicting emotions that plagued me the night of the ball. I *did* know that I helped him. He'd opened up to me and shared who he was when at his weakest. That humbling experience had forged our relationship to a deeper level. But he would never change. I had to remember that. While his fondness for me might intensify, his fundamental qualities of greed and lust for power would remain ingrained. They were the very things I needed to alter if I wanted the revolution to succeed. My stomach folded into knots. I had no idea how I would go about achieving what I'd promised.

Perhaps I should try to test Valko now, see if he could be persuaded to feel any genuine concern for these people. As I scanned the peasants for the perfect candidate to invoke the emperor's compassion, my gaze fell on the next person in line— an elderly man leaning on a crutch. If Valko couldn't pity him, I didn't know whom he could.

As the man prepared to hobble forward, I also readied myself. I dug into Valko's aura and felt his restlessness where it made my knees bounce, his trapped energy as it sped my heartbeat. I struggled to empathize with the emperor. He had spent so much time designing his grand plans for Riaznin. This reception must seem so minuscule in comparison to his larger, more important campaigns.

As I had on the night of the ball, I tried to open myself up to Valko, to connect on a level of pure understanding. Only then could I twist his feelings and encourage his regard for the old peasant man—who was now approaching. But the link between the emperor and me only half flickered, like a flame on a candlewick too short to sustain it.

The problem was my false empathy.

I cringed with the old man's pain as he winced with each advancing step. Who would help him if I couldn't?

Behind him, a commotion rose up as someone shoved his way to the front of the line. The people stumbled aside to reveal a brawny, ginger-haired man, his beard worn in two braids and studded with painted beads. A wave of revulsion flooded me, made no easier when the man's abrasive aura scraped mine.

Valko observed my strained expression. "Are you all right?"

I shook my head. "That is the bounty hunter who brought me to the convent. His name is Bartek."

"Ah." The emperor's gaze searched my face. "So your parents did not report you to the empire of their own accord?"

I lengthened my neck, taking some measure of pride in their decision, even though it had cost them their lives. "They did not."

A pulse of anger shot through me and made my muscles

contract. Valko must have finally pieced together something he hadn't fully realized until now: unlike so many Auraseers at the convent, it was never my desire to be owned by the empire, or to end up here by his side.

His fingers curled around the armrests of his throne. With a stiff set to his jaw, he turned his attention to the bounty hunter, whom the peasants were bottlenecking back. "Let him forward," Valko commanded.

The crowd fell away, all but the elderly man, whom the bounty hunter knocked aside with his shoulder. The man buckled to his knees, and his crutch skidded across the parquet floor. A peasant woman came forward to assist him and shot livid glances at Bartek.

"Your Imperial Majesty." The bounty hunter bent at his paunchy waist. When he rose, our eyes met. A flash of recognition curved his lip. "I have come seeking a reward."

Misgiving spooled around my lungs. Had he found another Auraseer? If so, why would he bring her here and not to the convent?

"Who is it you have captured?" Valko asked. "By all appearances, you are alone."

"I have come regarding the treasonous revolutionary."

Tosya? My lungs compressed tighter. My pinched-off air spotted my vision.

"Which revolutionary do you speak of?" Valko's anger sent fire through my veins. "Many such fools have a price on their heads."

Bartek jutted out his chin and adjusted the traveling bag slung around his shoulder. "Yuri Sergeev."

I blinked. Tosya was safe. But—"Yuri is wanted?" My voice faltered. "I thought . . ." Had Yuri used his recruitment errand as an opportunity to conduct business for Anton? "What has he done?" I asked.

Valko regarded me. "Do you know that unfortunate soldier?"

I nodded in a daze. "He has been my escort on many occasions." When the emperor's brow arched, I felt the depth of my precarious position. As sovereign Auraseer, it was my job to detect any kind of threat or danger to the emperor, and I'd just admitted that I'd been with—on more than one occasion—a man wanted for treason. "I swear to you, My Lord, I never felt anything suspicious about him."

That wasn't true. I'd found out Yuri was in league with Anton before the prince ever admitted to it. Then there was the snaking darkness I'd sensed the night of the ball. Could that have belonged to Yuri? Anton said some of his men were growing impatient for Valko's reign to end. "What has he done?" I asked again, and hoped the question would deflect my failure to act in this matter.

Valko cast a bored look at Bartek, who stood on the balls of his booted feet, ready for permission to address the emperor once more. "We have first accounts of Yuri working with the wanted traitor Tosya Pashkov," Valko answered.

I swallowed and scanned the room again. Where was

Anton? Would he come to defend Yuri?

The emperor sighed. In it, I felt his tedium at having to reprimand one of his soldiers, just as tiresome as helping the woman with her well. The only silver lining was that the emperor didn't seem to appreciate how real and far-reaching this revolution was growing. Nevertheless, my heart ached for Pia. There was only one punishment in Riaznin for treason—death. She would lose the man she loved.

"Bring forth the soldier," Valko said. "You will have your reward."

Behind Bartek's oily grin, I felt his twinge of discomfort. "Yes . . . about that. Yuri is still at large."

Valko's brow furrowed. "You said this bounty regarded him."

"It does. You see, I've captured *another* person—not a known fugitive, but I'm confident you will reward me, Your Imperial Majesty, once you learn she is just as treasonous as her lover."

My face prickled as my blood drained away. "Whom do you mean?" I asked him. The aura of the nobles in the room blazed with censure at me, but I didn't care that I'd spoken out of turn. My heart seized in my chest. Bartek couldn't be implying what I thought.

He put two fingers to his mouth and released a shrill whistle. The nobles jerked back. Some covered their ears. Behind the long line of peasants, someone whimpered as she was roughly ushered inside. I tamped down my awareness, too afraid to let myself sense her aura just yet.

Feya, don't let it be Pia. Let Yuri be a scoundrel and have another lover. Only don't let her be my friend.

Two brutish men, traveling companions of Bartek, dragged a young woman forward. Her head hung, her brown hair masking her eyes. Bartek yanked her up by the chin. Her hair parted around a heart-shaped face. My body turned to ice.

Pia.

A purpling bruise marred her left cheek. Fear overwhelmed her aura and made my hands tremble, my throat thicken. A tear slid down her cheek and stung my eyes.

"What have you done to her?" I gasped, rising to my feet.

When I made a move to descend the dais, Valko commanded, "Sit down, Sovereign Auraseer."

I whirled on him. "But it's *Pia*. You know her." He had singled her out months ago and tried to seduce her. "She's harmless, and she needs our help. That man"—I pointed at Bartek—"cannot be trusted!"

The bounty hunter's braids swung as he let go of Pia. She collapsed and a small cry escaped her. "Rumor spread that this girl went missing this morning," Bartek said coolly, as if he hadn't heard me at all. "I caught her outside the city walls." He grunted a laugh. "She didn't even think to travel off the road."

The emperor's gaze swept over Pia without emotion as he spoke to Bartek. "You're very bold to presume I'll pay a bounty for someone I've never found guilty."

Heart pounding, I moved closer to Valko's side. *He is handling this well. He will see she is innocent.*

"I did not *first* think her guilty," Bartek admitted. "I sought this girl out as a means of tracking Yuri. She revealed nothing as to his whereabouts, but she did confess to aiding his friends in the palace. They used her room for secret meetings."

My pulse thundered in my ears. This couldn't be happening. Pia . . . accused of treason? And by a bounty hunter, of all people? I took in my friend's skirt, bloody at the knee. The way she held her arm at a funny angle. No doubt Bartek used torture to glean his information.

Valko's aura darkened another shade. His boredom transformed into something ugly. "Whom did she aid?" He positioned himself on the edge of his throne. Not knowing what else to do, I set my hand on the emperor's arm below the shoulder and hoped to distract him with a calming touch. But he shrugged me away, his aura bristling with the sting of needlelike lances. "Did she give you any names?" he prompted Bartek again.

"She insists Yuri never told her."

My shoulders sagged with relief. For one terrible moment I thought the bounty hunter might say *Anton*. Thank the gods Yuri never shared with Pia any more of his revolutionary scheming. I inhaled a deep breath and lifted my voice to the bounty hunter. "I do not see why this maid is guilty of anything. For all she knew, she was granting her room so Yuri's friends could play a game of cards."

Some of the nobles scoffed in disdain at me. Once again, I'd broken custom by speaking in the emperor's place. I didn't care—not about them or any foolish rules of etiquette. What was happening to Pia was wrong. I couldn't stand idly by.

"Sonya." Valko's voice held an edge of warning.

"This man is foul!" I replied defensively. "I know his methods, and he must be in desperate need of coin to stoop so low that he would torture a maid for false information."

"Quiet!" Valko said past gritted teeth.

"But that maid is—"

"*Quiet!*" His voice rang into the dome above us. Everyone fell silent—the murmur of the nobles, the rustle of weary peasants. They all startled at the man who held dominion over them, the man who should be holding dominion over *me*. "I forbid you to speak another word! You are my *Auraseer*. Your duty is to warn when *I* am in danger, not when someone else is!"

I recoiled and jerked my head away, then balled my hands. Awaiting Valko's verdict, I turned pensive eyes on Pia. Her head was bowed, her cut-up mouth moving in a rapid, silent prayer. As her desperation compounded my own, I could no longer endure my inaction, despite Valko's fury with me. I fell to my knees at his feet. "Please, My Lord, let her go. She has done nothing wrong."

He looked down his nose at me. "Get up, Sonya," he hissed. "If you were anyone else, I would have you publically lashed for your insubordination."

"I don't care if I suffer." I took his hand and pressed a kiss to it, trying to do anything I could think of to reach his mercy. "Just believe that she is innocent."

Roughly exhaling, Valko rolled back his shoulders and

cast his gaze to Pia. I tried to unearth any compassion buried beneath his apathy. What did he feel when he looked at her? Did he even remember they'd shared a secret kiss? Did he have any pity at all?

With my hands over his, I tried to use my ability to persuade him. I labored to place in him all the love I had for Pia, her sweetness and laughter, her bright smile and the heart she gave so freely.

The emperor's deliberation continued as he tapped a finger on his armrest. Each beat suspended in time.

One, two, three, four.

"Take her to the dungeons," Valko commanded his attending guards.

I shut my eyes. His words fired like a cannon ball to my chest.

"No!" Pia wept harder.

I spun around, watching in horror as two guards apprehended her. Her bloodshot eyes rounded like a deer's in the moment an arrow pierced its hide.

I revolved to Valko. "Please! She is—"

He backhanded me.

I released a gasp of amazement and blinked in pain as I touched my smarting cheek. Had the emperor really struck me in public?

His nostrils flared as he fought to compose himself. Adjusting the sleeves of his kaftan, Valko addressed Bartek. "I will give you one hundred rubles. However, from this time forward, you will let the law dictate whom you are permitted to seize into custody."

The bounty hunter prostrated himself in a low bow, the picture of humility now that money was guaranteed him. "I thank you for your generosity, Your Imperial Majesty."

"You are dismissed."

Bartek bowed again and tossed me a smirk without bothering to glance at the broken girl he left in bonds. He sauntered out the way he came.

As the palace guards dragged Pia away, she whirled to give me one last pleading look.

My heart ached past endurance. I stumbled off the dais and rushed toward her.

A group of guards emerged in my path. I tried to push past them, but they formed an impenetrable barrier. Beyond their shoulders, I watched helplessly as my friend was taken from the room, her cries descending into sobs of despair.

CHAPTER TWENTY-NINE

ONCE VALKO DISMISSED ME, I RACED BACK TO MY CHAMBERS and hurried through the doors—red, lavender, evergreen, and midnight blue—but Anton wasn't in his room. I couldn't wait for him. Something had to be done. Hurrying back the way I came, I hefted the box bed into place on its casters just before Lenka entered my antechamber. Her aura still reeked of arrogance. She'd played a part in this. I knew it.

"Did you report Pia missing?" I asked before she had a chance to speak. She drew nearer and reached for the laces at the back of my dress. I shifted away. "Did you?"

She lengthened her wiry neck. "That girl is beneath you. I don't understand why you concern yourself with her."

"She is my *friend*." Something Lenka most certainly was not. "And now she is in the dungeons, thanks to you."

My head maid's lips pursed with a sunburst of wrinkles. "Pia had a simple duty to perform in the palace, but she grew too self-important. She thought she could fritter away her time with you and come and go as she pleased. It's time she learned her place. I merely told the guards she had gone without permission." Lenka shrugged a bony shoulder. "It isn't my fault she is facing the consequences of being a traitor."

"She isn't a traitor!" I pressed the heel of my hand to my temple, where a deep ache pounded through my skull. "It's you who doesn't know your place. Pia doesn't answer to you. You had no business interfering!"

"*You* are my occupation," Lenka retaliated. "Pia put you in danger. But I didn't report you, did I?"

I studied her, the sly bending of her aura. "You knew I left last night."

She clasped her hands in front of her apron. "Your note never reached the coals to burn."

Everything came back to me. The way her eyes flickered to the furnace after I'd tossed Anton's letter behind the grate. She'd never seen Pia give me the message, but she must have discerned her involvement when I later wore her clothes. That noise Anton and I heard in the kitchens had been Lenka.

I frowned at her. "Why did you protect me?"

"Because you are *Sovereign Auraseer*, blessed by the gods and born to serve the holy emperor. You are young, but you can be molded. You can be great like Izolda."

I shook my head in bewilderment. "Do you think Izolda idealized this life?" Grabbing her arm, I ushered her back to the box bed. "Look inside. Those are the marks the *blessed* gift left on her soul!"

Lenka didn't peer within. She must have known what was there. "Izolda never complained of her lot. She understood the honor of sacrificing for a noble cause."

I wanted to rattle my maid until some sense knocked into her brain. Pride was at the core of her. It always had been. "You think if I rise, you rise with me. If only you could see everyone on equal footing."

"Such talk is revolutionary," she spat, as if that word was enough to clap her in irons.

"It shouldn't be."

Her lips formed a hard line. She wouldn't speak to me anymore—not about this. She reached once again for the laces on my dress, and once again I angled away. "I will not change into my nightgown," I declared.

Lenka arched a brow. "Do you intend to sleep in this?"

"I intend to speak with the emperor." *And I won't cross his threshold unless I'm fully clothed.*

She huffed a sardonic laugh. "You really think he will receive you?"

Oh, my poor, miserable maid. *She* was the simpleton. She claimed to see so much, but she missed everything. "He *will* receive me," I said.

Despite how I'd publicly defied Valko today, I knew he would forgive me, just as he had after I lost him the Estengarde alliance. His forgiveness would permit me into his rooms, and there we would frankly speak of Pia without an audience to amplify the emperor's pride. I would save my friend. I had to.

Guards were stationed outside Valko's door. He hadn't sent them away because he hadn't plotted my coming. For once, I initiated a meeting with him. The guards didn't admit me, but neither did they turn me away. One of them, a man with long hair tied at the back of his neck, went inside to petition the emperor. I paced, not wanting to squander any time when I was sure he would let me in. He did.

Humid air greeted me. Steam rose from the bathing pool, but its warmth never reached my bones. Sprigs of rosemary and juniper needles floated on the surface and gave off a heady aroma. Valko sat on a mound of velvet cushions, wearing nothing more than a silk robe, no trousers or nightshirt beneath. His wet hair lay in dark waves, and droplets of water clung to his chest where his robe parted in a V. I recollected how I'd also barged in on Anton when he was fresh from his bath, but how I felt in this moment could not compare to then. Anger scraped me like a hot knife. Valko had wrongly imprisoned my friend. He might have prevented me from helping her in the great hall, but he would not prevent me now.

"I wish to discuss Pia Lisova," I began, and descended the steps into the receiving area. I forced myself to curtsy.

The emperor's eyes roamed over my dress as he evaluated my first line of defense against him. Unfortunately, it wasn't enough. His gaze lingered at the swell of my breasts and hips, and dark desire flowered in his aura. My brows hitched together. His altered mood deeply disconcerted me. Wasn't he upset at all? Did he remember that he'd hit me, or was that sort of violence commonplace to him now? Did it go hand in hand with his passion?

In Valko's lap was an open book. He snapped it shut. I drew in my breath, my heart racing when I saw its pale-blue binding. Was he the one who had taken it from my bedroom?

"This is what's causing all the upheaval in my empire," he said, ignoring my request as he held up the volume.

I couldn't tear my gaze away from it. Would I be sent to the dungeons now, too?

"This is what I have to contend with," he added, "the words of a *poet*—and a common one at that. A mere gypsy!" He sighed and rubbed his face. "Floquart was right about their breed."

My jaw locked as I bit down on a defensive remark. Now wasn't the time to persuade him to see the Romska in a kinder light, not when I might also be accused of treason and must plead for my friend who'd been accused of the same.

I waited for his condemning words, but when Valko didn't say more about the book, I released a trembling breath and tried to push my anxiety aside. "I don't know if you're aware, My Lord," I continued to implore him, "but Pia is my serving maid. I'm well acquainted with her, and I can assure you she has no sinister motives against you. Her aura is as sweet and innocent as a child's."

Valko tilted his head at me. There was something he was

concealing. It snaked fog around the edges of my mind. "Come, Sonya." He patted a cushion beside him.

I twisted my fingers together, but did as he commanded. I needed to appear humble if I wanted his mercy.

"I understand your frustration," he said. "You're angry with me for admonishing you in public."

"That it isn't why I came here."

He lifted his brows like he didn't believe me. "I'm sorry if I've given you the wrong impression." He took my hand and brought my knuckles to his lips. His aura teased me with a chill of pleasure. I smothered it. He wouldn't get far with his game of seduction. He brought my hand down and rested it against his thigh. "Perhaps my indulgence in you has given you the idea that you can be my mouthpiece." He grinned gently, like he was explaining something to a little girl. "Even my wedded empress would not have that privilege, dear Sonya. My affection for you doesn't change the order of our relationship. At court, you are my guardian, nothing more. But here . . ." His hand swept the hair from my face. "Here I welcome your boldness." He leaned in closer to my mouth.

I froze with revulsion. I would never let him kiss me again. But as his currant-tea breath drifted nearer, and the tease of his aura nudged mine, another tactic presented itself. If I gave him what he wanted, would he soften and relent to my plea? Then again, if I truly had the ability to curb the emperor's emotions, I didn't need to surrender to his advances. I needed to test my skill. My friend's life might depend on it.

"Wait." I pulled back and stalled him with what I hoped was a demure smile. "Not yet." *Not ever*, I silently promised myself.

"You're not still angry with me, are you?" His thumb brushed the center of my lower lip.

I wanted to laugh. My friend in chains? My neck sore with whiplash from being struck in the face? "I'm not angry," I replied, and knew he had no gift to feel my deception. With my own, I clawed deeper into his aura and sought his puppet strings. All I felt was his voracious yearning. My head grew dizzy as I fought to resist him. "But I do wish to talk with you."

The night of the ball I'd manipulated his emotions by first letting them swallow me whole. But if I did that now, I might lose myself to his lust. I needed to distract him first and find a safer pathway to his aura.

He groaned softly at my hesitancy, but maintained a smile for the gratification I'd hinted was to come. "Then talk to me." His fingers traced the neckline of my dress. "Quickly."

Grasping at straws, I picked up Tosya's volume of poetry. It might serve as a convenient way to stoke his feelings in a different direction. "Tell me more about this." By Valko's actions thus far and his amorous mood, I felt safe in assuming he hadn't found me guilty of possessing the book. I didn't even know if this was my copy.

At the sight of it, the emperor's mouth contorted like he'd tasted something sour. "It's nothing more than the ramblings of a madman in verse. Sheer blasphemy. I can't understand why anyone heeds it." A flint strike of anger lit inside him. Good. I was familiar with anger. I clung to it. My hands shook with his flickering rage. I compounded it. I thought of Pia bruised and weeping behind the bars of a cell.

"But I take it people *are* giving it heed," I replied. My trembling fingernail slid into the groove of the title's embossed lettering. "Or else you would not be so upset." Deeper and deeper I burrowed into his aura in my desperate search for the means to overpower him.

Valko eyed me with a chuckle. "Am I so easy for you to read?"

I made myself smile back at him. "Sometimes."

He shifted nearer. "What I would give to see you so transparently."

His double meaning didn't escape me. A rush of his heated desire swept through my body. Just as I wavered with it, my muscles clenched in resistance. But should I fight his unwarranted lust? I needed to harmonize myself with his feelings. As his aura curled with longing, my heart tripped over itself. I redoubled my efforts to bring him back to his anger—an emotion I wouldn't struggle to push away.

"Is this Yuri's copy of the book?" I asked, and examined it closer. "Was it found in his room? Perhaps that's how suspicion was raised about him working with that poet, Tosya Pashkov."

Now that I'd baited Valko again, I combed through his aura for another spark of resentment. I found it when a dull pain in my jaw surfaced, as if I'd spent the night grinding my teeth. I bit down hard, and the pain intensified. *Stay angry*, I silently commanded him. If he did, I might find the synthesis between us and use it to bend his will to free Pia.

"I don't need to worry anymore about that soldier." Valko took a long breath of overconfidence.

Alarm coursed through me. His emotions were already shifting. I quickly inhaled his sudden pride and fought to trap it in my chest.

"He will come to me," the emperor declared.

"Oh?" I worked to understand him, but panic gripped me. I felt closer to finding a deep connection with him, but it kept faltering, like I was trying to light a match in the wind. I had to work harder. I couldn't lose ground now. I focused on my fierce desire to rescue Pia and frantically tried to produce thoughts that might give me empathy for Valko.

How intolerable it must be to know a guard who had been trusted and privileged to attend him—the grand ruler of all Riaznin—and even bunk right beside his room, had also betrayed him in order to follow after a lowly poet. An example should be made of Yuri in front of the common people before their insufferable ideas of entitlement got out of hand.

"Why will Yuri come to you?" I asked and tried to weed inside myself for an opening to grant Valko full purchase of me. I needed to manifest the nearly impossible feat of perfect understanding with him in order to grasp my hidden power of curbing his emotions.

He stroked the shell of my ear. "You have much to learn about men, Sonya. We like to be gallant. It's hard to watch a lady in distress. And gallantry swiftly turns to vengeance." He nuzzled closer. "Vengeance is a powerful tool—powerful and dangerous. But I needn't fear, for I have you. When Yuri returns, you will warn me."

I wasn't sure I was following. "You think he will attempt to rescue Pia?" I strove to tamp down my hope and stay aligned with my forced empathy.

"Not rescue. Yuri will come back for revenge."

Everything around me seemed to slow. The flicker of the candles. The rustling curtains at the windows. I shrank back. My heart pounded. All my efforts for persuading the emperor scattered like ashes. "Valko, what have you done?"

He broadened his shoulders. "Nothing any monarch would blink an eye at. I've simply executed a person guilty of treason."

I stared at him. His words cut off all my sensation. I had no lungs to breathe, no pulse at my throat, no blood pumping past my absent heart. The world itself stopped moving, stopped revolving, stopped existing. There was nothing but an inconceivable truth. "Pia is dead?"

Valko was unable to hold my gaze. "Yes."

"But . . . that isn't possible. I saw her today. She . . . she was only just imprisoned and . . ." I couldn't think clearly. An avalanche of thoughts crowded my mind, but only left me in a stupor. How could Pia be gone? Had I really said the word *dead* aloud? That couldn't be right. I hadn't had time to free her. I was going to. I'd been trying. I . . .

My gaze fixed upon the pattern of an embroidered pillow until it seared spots into my vision. My ears rang with the silence of the room. The emperor wasn't looking at me. Why? He always looked at me.

Pia.

The truth gutted me again.

Pia is dead.

A painful whimper tore from my throat. I choked it back with my stubbornness. I refused to accept Pia's fate, refused to acknowledge the absence of her aura, the missing glow I felt when she was in the palace, that faint surge in my blood that was present when blood flowed through her veins. And yet how easy it was to believe Valko would have her killed.

A horrified breath purged from my chest. Another tumbled after it. They quickly escalated into dry sobs. Each heartbeat struck my rib cage like an iron mallet. I shook my head again and again, unable to contain my tormenting emotions. I was nothing but pain now, nothing but feeling.

"She was innocent," I whispered, my tongue tasting of bile.

"She was *guilty*, Sonya." Valko finally met my eyes. "After her arrest, we had her belongings searched." He pointed to the volume of poetry in my hand. "That was found in *her* room, not Yuri's."

A wave of coldness flooded over me. The book slipped through my fingers and thudded to the ground. My hand flew to my mouth as a violent cramp of nausea made my shoulders rack.

This was *my* fault. She found that book because I'd forgotten to hole it away.

Pia was dead because of me.

"You've made the worst of mistakes," I said. Tremors of shock chased through my body. "Pia could barely read. I was . . . I was teaching her . . ." Past my wild panic and grief, I knew I had to protect myself from blame. For Dasha, for Kira. For Anton and his dream of liberating Riaznin. "Yuri must have left the book in her safekeeping, knowing she wouldn't understand what it was." I dug my hands through my hair as the horror of her death crashed over me again, a wave that wouldn't recede. "How could you have done this, Valko?"

He reached for me as if to offer comfort, but I wrenched away in disgust. "Did you truly think your *kisses* and your *twisted affection* could make me forget her? She was my friend!" I shouted, holding back none of my rage and sorrow. "She was nearly your lover!"

His eyes flew wide at my outburst. "She was a *maid*."

"Do you hear yourself?" My eyes stung with bitter tears. "I am also your servant. Does my life mean so little to you?"

"Sonya." He set his hand on my leg.

"Don't touch me!" I stood abruptly. My shins knocked the edge of the low table, and I hissed out in pain. Valko reached for me again, but I jerked back and limped around the pillows of his receiving area.

"Sonya, calm down." He rose to his feet. "You're acting irrational."

"Irrational?" I whirled on him. "Is it irrational to mourn a friend? Is it irrational to feel fury and agony?" My voice burned.

"You've always wanted my abandoned emotions. Now you have them. This is *me*, Valko!" I shouted. "I am every black feeling! I *cause* them! I cause every dark thing to happen!"

I caused Pia's death.

Rage blinded me. Rage at Valko. At myself. Unable to contain it, I stumbled up the stairs to his lobby and raced for the door.

"Sonya!" Valko called.

I flung the door open and slammed it behind me. I sobbed and fled down the corridor. My hand groped the wall for support as my vision blurred and tilted. At last, I found Anton's door—his outer door, not his covert, midnight-blue one. I pounded on it, making no effort to be quiet.

The prince answered. His brows peaked with surprise. I shouldered past him. "What are you doing?" he asked. "The guards can see you."

"I don't care." I choked on my words.

He shut the door and observed me more carefully. "What is it? What has happened?"

My grief consumed me. I trembled with my fury.

"Sonya, talk to me." Terror was written across Anton's face. "What has he done to you?"

"He's a monster! I hate him! Give me a knife, and I will kill him myself!"

"Shhh." He extended a hand toward me.

"Don't!" Anton's touch would only heighten his aura within me, and I couldn't endure anyone else's emotions right now.

He pulled back. "All right."

I yanked at my hair. A torrent of tears released from my eyes. "She's dead because of me!"

"Who is dead?"

"Pia." The word came out in a whimper. A beautiful name. Melodic and pure. Light as air, bright as morning.

"What?" The prince's energy flashed cold. He paced in a circle around me and rubbed his hand across his face. "I learned she was imprisoned, but . . . Valko executed her so quickly?"

I nodded. "She was dragged like a dog through the people's reception. I tried to defend her." I wiped under my nose and cried harder. "Valko wouldn't listen to me! He's *capricious* and *willful* and *impossible*." I slammed a fist on my chest. "I have no power over him!"

Anton swallowed and blinked hard. "That isn't true."

"Stop!" I held up my hands to ward his words away. "I don't deserve your faith. I've done nothing to merit it."

"Sonya, please. Just breathe." He hovered around me, unsure how to bring me any comfort when I wouldn't allow him to touch me.

I wept with abandon and crumpled to my knees. "I destroy everyone I love. I killed Yuliya, too. I only wanted to help the starving peasants." My fingers shook near my mouth, as if trying to trap back my darkest confession, but Anton needed to see me for what I truly was. "They hated me. They would have stopped me. I locked them in because I hated them, too."

The prince crouched beside me. "Whom did you lock in,

Sonya?" he asked gently. "What are you talking about?"

"The Auraseers." I sobbed and rocked back and forth. "And there were others. The sestras asleep in their beds. Basil—the old caretaker at the convent. *He* didn't hate me. He was kind to all of us."

Anton listened patiently, as if sensing I had more to tell. Revealing my dark past to Valko had been so much easier in comparison to sharing it now. How aptly that marked the difference between my feelings for both brothers. Losing the prince's good opinion would surely break my heart.

I tried to capture Anton's ardent expression of tenderness, because after I confided the rest of my story, he would never care for me again.

"I never helped the peasants." I tugged the black ribbon around my wrist until my fingers went numb. "The wolves chased them away. Except for one man. He suffered from madness. I brought him inside the convent and . . ." I shook my head. "There was accident. I started a fire." Shuddering a breath, I released the worst of my confession. "The convent burned because of me! The Auraseers were trapped inside their rooms. So many people died!" My shoulders curled into my chest with my weeping. I wanted to bury myself, to hide away from what I had done. "Yuliya was already ill. She died because she felt their suffering too keenly. I may as well have held her knife."

The prince's eyes were as pained as I felt. The ache in his aura rent at my heart. "Why didn't you tell me?" he asked.

I shrugged as tears streamed down my face. "You made me feel special—honorable." I could scarcely speak past my sobbing. "It was a nice lie to believe."

"It isn't a lie."

I gasped with incredulity. How did he maintain his faith in me—especially after everything I'd just told him? "Don't you see?" My cries hardened with frustration. "I can never become anyone's savior. I'm nothing but a curse! I brought death to my parents. I endangered the Romska. The sestras in the convent *feared* my unnatural ability, and they were right to. All I am is darkness!"

Anton shifted closer so I wouldn't look away from him. "I want you to listen to me, and I want you to listen carefully. You are *not* a curse." His brows lifted in earnestness. "You are a *gift*," he said softly. "You are *my* gift. A savior to me."

I raised my gaze to him. Tears clung to my lashes.

His brown eyes were a well of sympathy, stronger than any Auraseer's. "Let me hold you, Sonya."

I tensed, and my throat constricted. How long had I accused him of withholding himself when I was just as guilty of doing the same? But now that he knew the truth of me, could I really believe he still held me in regard? Could I allow him to try?

I managed a small nod.

That was all the permission he needed.

Within a moment, Anton's warm arms surrounded me. His chin tucked over my head. At once my chest expanded and made room for the breadth of his compassion. He held my sorrow in his own, my suffering in his suffering. He held understanding.

"I'm sorry about your friend." He smoothed back my hair. "I know she meant a great deal to you." I sobbed into his chest. "I'm sorry you lost Yuliya, and your parents. I'm sorry for the tragedy at the convent, and that you never had a home, that you had to come here."

He didn't bolster me up with more talk of my ability—of seeing my duty through to the end and my commitment to the cause of freedom. He just let me be sad. And for that I felt overwhelming gratitude.

His hand steadily rubbed my back. "Shhh, shhh," he murmured, and in his voice I didn't hear an admonishment to be silent, but instead the rushing of mountain water, the ebb and flow of the ocean tide. He spoke comfort like a language I'd once learned as a child but had long since forgotten.

Gently scooting us across the floor, he guided me to the corner where his bed met the wall, and then opened his arms again. I crawled right back inside them. Pulling my hair over one shoulder, he coaxed me to turn around and lean against him. As he combed his fingers through my hair, he hummed a lullaby in a low and soothing voice. My sobs came softer as I listened to the haunting and peaceful melody. I rested my head on Anton's shoulder and laced my fingers through his.

I cried for what seemed like hours, and when I realized I had stopped altogether, I felt ashamed and tried to muster up more tears. But it was useless. I was spent like a wrung rag.

Despite the tragedy of the day, I didn't wish for this moment between us to break. Anton was my solace, our auras knitted so intricately together I couldn't tell where mine began and his ended.

I tilted my head up to see his face. The shadowy rings were back beneath his eyes. This was the second night I'd deprived him of much-needed sleep.

"Thank you," I said quietly.

He stopped humming, and a grin touched his lips. He kissed the top of my head. With his voice thick and drowsy, he replied, "You're welcome."

I shifted around to take in all of him. His hands moved to settle on my waist. The candles burned low, but I still noticed the smoothness of his chin. My hands cupped his face, and my thumbs skimmed his jawline. "Let me guess, you heard the beard law is no longer in effect. So, naturally, you shaved."

His eyes were half-lidded as he smiled. "You've found me out."

"You're an unabashed rebel, Prince Anton."

"Truer words were never spoken."

His haggard drowsiness and humored expression made him appear all the more devastatingly handsome to me. His aura never felt so relaxed and open and welcoming. I gently kissed him.

I kissed him.

I drew back and searched his face for his reaction. He looked as stunned as I was. "Sonya." His voice was a soft warning. I heard what he meant: *I want this. I don't want this.*

His face still rested in my cupped hands. Heart pounding, I leaned closer. He smelled of pine and juniper and spring water. I breathed in all of him and savored every wondrous feeling in my aura. Very deliberately, very carefully, and with exceeding tenderness, I kissed him again.

His hands on my waist turned to stone, but as my mouth slowly explored his, his grip yielded and slid down to the curve of my hip. His mouth found rhythm with mine, and soon we matched cadence, two birds soaring on the same current of air.

He exhaled and pulled me closer. His hands traveled up the sides of my bodice and back around to weave through my hair. My heart opened. The stitches that bound my grief tore free. I'd wanted this for so long. Within him, I felt the same sweet sense of release. Our auras entwined in a beautiful dance and affirmed the rightness of our union. I parted my lips and tasted him deeper. He was the mist in an evergreen forest, the reeds sighing into a river. My fingers curled around the nape of his neck. His warmth radiated sunlight through my body.

That effortless feeling, like floating on water, heated to something just as wonderful, but more turbulent. Our kisses pressed harder. Our hands roamed faster. My chest tightened as my breath became difficult to find. Even when I drew back to inhale, the feeling didn't abate. It intensified until I recognized it as a seizing of panic. Anton grabbed my arms and pushed me away.

"I can't . . ." His face was flushed with a light sheen of per-spiration. "We can't do this."

My head spun. Every nerve under my skin longed to stay connected to him. It took me a moment to understand the panic was *his*. "Why?"

He worked to steady his breathing. "It's late . . . and you've had a horrible night. Now isn't the time to . . ." He sighed, and his eyes drooped at the corners. "You're broken right now, Sonya. I don't want to press my advantage."

"You're not," I said. He slid up straighter against the wall and put a small measure of distance between us. It felt like an insurmountable gash in the earth. "This isn't you, Anton. You're not forcing me to feel this way. *I* need you—especially now. *I* want us to be together." Why couldn't he feel what was inside me, what was my own? "I want *you*," I said, and reached for his hand.

He pulled back and raked his fingers through his hair. "Please." His voice was pained. My gaze drifted to his sleeve, fallen back to his elbow to reveal his lynx-shaped birthmark. I wished I could blot it out, retract the words of the Romska fortune-teller, find the little boy in the prince and tell him his mother still loved him, even though she had to let him go. I'd felt the dowager empress's devotion in her very blood. Why couldn't it erase all his heartache? Why couldn't I?

I moved closer, as close as Anton would allow me. "Do you remember that strength inside me you asked me to find and hold on to? Well, I've found it." I smiled, trying to show him what it felt like. "It's what makes me most grounded and sure and resilient. It's my feelings for *you*, Anton. I don't doubt them. They give me hope, like I've done one good and smart thing in this world by setting my heart on you."

As he gazed back at me, his brows drew together in anguish. I felt him wanting to believe in my words, but he didn't know how.

"You've lost just as much as I have," I said. "You're just as broken. I'm not the only one who needs comforting."

I yearned to touch him, but I didn't dare. He sat so rigidly and withdrawn into himself. As I watched him, a pang of loneliness and sorrow lodged in my breast. I couldn't lose him now, not when I felt with the fullness of my aura that we were meant for each other.

I memorized every plane, curve, and slant of his achingly beautiful face, like I had long ago in the troika. I found the small mole near his eye, the delicate sculpt of his upper lip. And more wonders came to surface. A little freckle along his jaw. A tiny scar above his right cheek. The slightest unevenness of his aristocratic nose. Somehow it felt like I might never see him again, like through the small separation of our bodies, he was already slipping through my fingers like sand.

"You said I was your savior," I said, "but you won't let me save you, not truly."

He shrugged in misery. "I don't know how to be saved."

I tucked my knees to my chest as my heart sank. We were at the same impasse as ever, divided by his inability to trust my feelings for him. And perhaps there was more, something deeper Anton didn't trust about himself.

The light of the candle nearest us wavered as the wick sagged into the last of the melting wax. When at length it sputtered out, I rose and slowly brushed the dust from my dress. "Thank you for tonight," I said. "I don't know what I would have done without you." My insides twisted with guilt and regret. They weren't mine.

"Wait." Anton stood. He blew out a shaky breath. "Stay."

I frowned with uncertainty.

He advanced a step. "I promise I won't kiss you again."

I sighed. "I *want* you to kiss me."

"Stay."

I crossed my arms and kept my distance. I wasn't sure if I had it in me to keep falling for him when he couldn't commit to fully opening his heart.

"You let me hold you," he said, "even when it was difficult." A foreign emotion of timidity seeded within him. "I'd like to allow you the same." He winced like he wasn't expressing himself correctly. "That is, I'm asking you." His shoulders wilted. "I'm *trying*, Sonya. This is the best I can do."

I bit my lip.

He searched my eyes. "Stay."

A breeze pressed against the windowpanes. The gilded walls of the palace creaked. My flimsy barrier against the prince came undone. I walked away, but not to the midnight-blue door. I climbed into his bed. A sliver of moonlight angled across the blankets from a crack in the window curtains. He took a long breath and followed me. We sat opposite each other, me with my legs curled at my side, him with one knee propped up. Then we moved nearer, as if this was the most delicate dance of all, as if we hadn't already spent the greater part of the night in each other's embrace. Somehow this was different. This was him relenting to me. It felt fragile, like a painted porcelain egg.

I lay back on the pillow and held out my open hand. He eased himself down and settled his head in the crook of my neck. I slid one arm beneath him, the other on top, and pressed my lips to his brow. His body sank lower in the mattress. His hair brushed my cheek and smelled of soap and evergreens. I smoothed it back as he'd smoothed mine.

It wasn't long before Anton's chest rose and fell beside mine in the pattern of peaceful dreaming. Two silent tears tracked down my cheeks, my last thoughts of the night for Pia, and then my eyes drifted closed, my head drooping against the softness of Anton's hair.

CHAPTER THIRTY

SOMETHING WHITE AND PIERCING AWAKENED ME. A RAY OF
sunlight sliced through the crack in the curtains like a dagger. I
cringed and turned my face so the beam moved out of my eye.
Then I caught sight of Anton and remembered with amazement
that I had slept beside him. Our positions had shifted in the
night. His head lay across my stomach, his mouth open in deep
slumber as his arms draped along my sides. One of mine was
bent above my head on the pillow, while my free hand was burrowed in his hair. He appeared younger, more vulnerable, more
beautiful now that his cares had slipped away in the realm of
sleep. I wanted to stay with him like this forever.

With a sigh of blissful contentment, I cast my gaze back to
the window curtains. Then I frowned, blinking at the shaft of
light as I studied it closer. It wasn't hazy with the gray of dawn;
it was cut with bright lines. I gasped and nudged Anton. "Wake
up!"

He lifted his head and peered up at me with one eye, his chin resting over my dress at the navel. "Sonya?" he said, as if still dreaming.

"I'm supposed to be back in my bedchamber!" I hissed. In all the nights I'd spent in the tapestry room, I'd never once slept so soundly that I hadn't awoken before Pia came.

Pia.

An ache emerged in my throat, but I swallowed it down. I couldn't lose myself to tears again. "I have to go," I said. "Lenka will be looking for me." Why had I come to Anton's room last night? My selfishness put him in danger, too.

A sharp rapping came on his outer door. The prince and I jolted upright. I scrambled for the other side of the bed, aiming for the tapestry room, but the hinges of the outer door squeaked and the handle turned as it prepared to open.

My jaw hung. I couldn't think. I would never make it out of here in time.

Anton's reflexes were faster. None too gently, he tossed me across the bed to plunk down on the opposite side of the floor. I landed squarely on my rump, and a little yelp escaped me.

The door creaked open. "Good morning, brother."

Valko. I ducked lower. My nerves flashed cold. Beneath the bed, I watched his polished black boots approach Anton's bare feet and clip along the floorboards from across the room.

The prince cleared his throat. "Good morning"—the boots halted—"Your Imperial Majesty."

The emperor's boots came three steps nearer. My breath

thinned as they swept close to the bed. "It's been a busy two days," Valko remarked casually. "The people's reception went well, I daresay. There was that unfortunate matter about the serving maid"—he slightly rocked back on his heels, then revolved and put a little more space between himself and Anton—"but what's done is done. It was necessary."

I narrowed my gaze on the gleam of black leather. Why had the emperor come? Was this usual for him to barge in on Anton and ramble about tedious matters of the empire? Never mind that they regarded the death of my dearest friend.

The tendons contracted at the back of Anton's ankles. "And what is the news of today? Is it cumbersome, as well?"

My stomach knotted from their auras. Their voices were light, but cords of tension strung between them, thicker than ever.

"On the contrary," Valko replied, "the gods are smiling on me. Only yesterday I raised the bounty threefold on refugees from the law, and already I've received word that one man has been captured." He chuckled. "Seems people can't resist their share of a bounty hunter's purse, especially when all that is required is the whispering of a criminal's whereabouts."

"Indeed," Anton replied stiffly. "Am I to presume then that Yuri has been apprehended?"

"No, no. Someone far more valuable." The heels of the boots snapped together, side by side. "That infamous gypsy poet."

All my breath rushed out of me. Anton's toes clenched white against the floor. "Tosya?" After a strained moment of silence, the prince walked past Valko, no doubt so his brother wouldn't see the look of horror etched across his face. "Tosya . . . Pashkov, isn't it?" Anton tried to sound disinterested, but I heard the tremor in his voice, mirroring the tremor inside him. My entire body quivered with it. He knew as well as I did that Tosya's fate was sealed. If Pia had been executed for mere association with a traitor, there was no question the supposed instigator of the revolution would not be spared.

"The very same," Valko answered.

Anton's feet turned slightly toward the emperor. "And is he here now? Imprisoned?"

"I've seen him myself. An odd fellow. Rather too tall to be hunched over a writing table."

The prince twisted around to fully face his brother. "If I may, My Lord, I would caution you not to execute him straightaway. He has won the favor of many countrymen, and they will demand a fair trial. You wouldn't want any riots, not when you are seeking to boost your popularity in light of the lowered draft age."

I silently praised Anton for his quick logic. The only card he had left to play was delaying Tosya's execution for as long as possible. Perhaps, with a little more time, we could find a means of helping our friend escape.

The emperor shifted, leaning his weight into his left boot. "Tosya *will* be tried," he said at length. "Publicly," he added, "so all those intoxicated by his words will discover him for the defamer and blasphemer he is."

"Good thinking. I agree that is the best recourse," Anton replied, masterfully turning the conversation so the trial seemed to be the emperor's idea in the first place.

"I will speak to my councilors." The black boots clipped back to the door, first with deliberation, then they slowed, hesitating. The emperor spun around to the prince. "You haven't seen Sonya this morning?"

I pressed my body flat to the floor. The jealousy in his aura tasted bitter on my tongue. Was this the real reason Valko had come, to see if I was here?

"No, I haven't." Anton didn't miss a beat. He lazily padded toward the furnace where he kept his samovar. "Perhaps she went on a stroll through the gardens."

"Yes . . . perhaps."

I cringed and waited for Valko to say more—that he knew I hadn't returned to my rooms last night, nor was I there at daybreak. But when he didn't pursue the subject any further, I presumed Lenka had covered for me, once again.

The emperor opened the door. "If you do see her, tell her I've left her a gift in her antechamber. A peace offering. She'll know why."

"As you wish."

The black boots left. The door thumped shut. I closed my eyes and rested them on the backs of my hands, allowing myself to breathe. Valko hadn't discovered me. Still, I dared not move. What if he burst in again?

Anton seemed to share the same concern. A long minute

passed before I heard the floorboards creak under his quiet footsteps. The door opened and shut again. "It's all right, Sonya. He's gone."

I lifted myself up on shaking legs and gripped one of his bedposts for balance. My gown was a rumpled mess.

Anton barely looked at me. He rushed to a small drawer in his dresser. "I'm assuming you don't have your key." He withdrew an identical copy and crossed to the midnight-blue door. "I have to leave at once." He opened it. "You should return to your rooms."

I stood frozen behind the bed. "Where are you going?"

"I need to speak with Nicolai and Feliks—together if I can arrange it."

"About Tosya?"

"Yes."

My heart sagged with unbearable weight. The world seemed to be crumbling at its foundations.

Anton strode back, took my arm, and ushered me to the door. He wasn't being harsh by any means, but time was of the essence and I was only slowing him down. Unless—"Can I come with you? I could wear a disguise."

"No . . . I can't . . ." His jaw ticked. He wouldn't meet my gaze, but his voice came tenderly. "I can't risk losing you, too."

Disappointment flooded me, but I didn't argue. My place was here at the emperor's side, my duty to both the empire and my pact to the revolution. "I'll return to him," I promised, knowing it had to be done. "I'll try to persuade him to free Tosya." At least I'd have a fighting chance. Tosya, unlike Pia, was alive—for the time being.

"Please be careful," Anton said.

"And you, as well."

He finally locked gazes with me. In his eyes, I saw every-thing that had transpired between us last night. In his aura, I felt the ghost of our last kiss. I longed to kiss him again, to find some means to bring him comfort, to let him know all would turn out right, even if I didn't believe it myself.

I leaned forward on my toes, but he anticipated me. "I must go." The door shut between us. I blinked, staring at the swirl of painted stars.

⁂

A vase of blue hyacinths sat waiting on the table in my ante-chamber. Beside them was a small, varnished box. A ribbon wrapped around it, tied together with embossment wax and the emperor's royal seal—a V beneath a crown with seven rubies. I broke it and lifted the lid. Inside, on a bed of velvet, was a large sapphire surrounded by diamonds. It hung from a diamond-linked chain. The cut of the sapphire was oval. The facets winked at me in the sunlight from my window.

I closed the box and pushed it to the far end of the table. Did Valko think I could be bought? That a gem could replace a dear friend? The scent of the hyacinths burned my nostrils. I paced away. My hands flexed. My anger brimmed. The necklace was worth enough to feed a family for a year. It could repair Ruta's boardinghouse and give the Romska children more time to play in the fields rather than beg for copper coins in the cities.

I dropped down on a chair at my writing table and tried to wash away my disgust. There would be no giving away Valko's gift. I'd have to accept it if I wanted to restore myself to good terms with him. As insufferable as that was, it was nothing next to becoming one with his aura, persuading him to release Tosya, and, while he was at it, give over his throne.

I scrubbed at my eyes. Fatigue turned my bones to lead, but I gritted my teeth. I wouldn't give in to desperation and self-pity. My task might be monumental, but my gift—my curse—was the only means I had of making a difference in this world.

CHAPTER THIRTY-ONE

THE DAY PASSED WITH MADDENING SLOWNESS. MY NEW
serving maid showed up before Lenka did. She seemed kind
and able enough, but my chest felt hollow, my body cold, as I
compared her to Pia. Her freckled skin to Pia's golden olive.
Her thin frame where Pia was voluptuous. Her lack of a ready
smile. She left with a curtsy, and I picked at the supper tray
she'd brought, but found everything tasteless. Lenka arrived
shortly afterward. She must have been informed of my magical
reappearance.

I didn't answer her inquiries about where I'd been last
night. After my refusal, we didn't mince words. I instructed her
to make me presentable to the emperor, and she performed the
task with signature skill and dressed me in a pale-silver gown.

I learned the emperor was in a long meeting with his councilors. I would have had to spend the day with them if he'd
known I'd returned.

I descended a twirling staircase and made my way to the council chamber. The sapphire burned like ice against my throat where the necklace encircled it like a collar. I wasn't eager to see the emperor's gratified expression when he saw me wearing it.

As I reached the second level, I halted, clenching the banister as panic gripped my aura. At the same moment, Anton entered the palace through the grand lobby below. He looked up. His chest expanded when he saw me, but his anxiety still had me on edge. Servants milled about him and attended to their chores. He tipped his head to the left, a subtle motion, but I understood.

His dusk-blue cape flapped behind him as he strode down the corridor toward the great hall. Composing myself, I descended another flight of stairs and caught his trail. I tried to keep my pace casual but also fast enough so I wouldn't lose sight of his broad shoulders. Anton paused up ahead to remove his gloves and cast his gaze about for any onlookers. A moment later, he slipped in through the doors of the ballroom.

My heart pounded faster. Anton's dread roiled in my gut. I quickened my step, and with a glance over my shoulder, I entered after him and shut the doors. "Did you meet with your men?" I asked. "What has happened? Your aura is making me ill." I pressed a hand to my nauseated stomach.

Heavy curtains were drawn over the windows. Only a weak glow of sunlight rimmed their edges. It was enough for me to see the fuzzy contours of the room—empty of furniture, the great chandeliers wrapped in cloth to keep away the dust, the throne on the dais abandoned, everything a haunting echo of its grandeur on Morva's Eve.

Anton pulled me flush to the wall with the double doors so we weren't in plain sight should someone enter. His gaze fell briefly to my sapphire necklace. I touched it self-consciously. It felt like iron fetters clamped around my throat. He shook his head, paced back a moment, then cursed, throwing his gloves on the floor. My hand had moved to undo the clasp, when I froze at his outburst. "Feliks is a bloodthirsty fool! He'll ruin everything we've worked for."

I let go of the necklace and pictured the man I'd seen only twice. I'd always felt unsettled by him, but I'd attributed it to his shockingly blue eyes or his mysterious involvement with the prince—the letter about Morva's Eve that Anton had discreetly given him, or the way Feliks had exited the ballroom first when the bell tolled twelve times. "What has he done?"

Beside us, one of the doors opened. I gasped and receded against the wall.

"Hello?" a man asked quietly. In the dim light, I made out his generous mop of hair.

"Behind you, Nicolai," Anton said.

The man whirled around. He was, indeed, Count Rostav. He turned a distrusting gaze on me. "What is she doing here?"

"Sonya is a part of this now. You know that."

"The emperor is looking for her." Nicolai rubbed a hand over his face in frustration. "By now he must also be eager for my return. I had to leave a *council meeting* to come here," he added, making it sound like the ultimate cause for offense. "I drummed up some excuse about urgent business." He laughed weakly. "I'm sure the emperor wondered what could be more important than convening with him."

Anton frowned. "Why did he request you a second time in council?"

"His damned insistence that I lend my expertise in plotting the Shengli invasion." Nicolai threw up his hands. "I don't know the first thing about battle strategy! My father was the soldier, not I." As he talked faster, my nerves jangled and a strange sense of foreboding scuttled up my spine. "It leads me to wonder if the emperor is keeping me close because he's suspicious."

"Valko is suspicious of everyone." Anton shrugged, as if that were the least of our concerns. "Why not use his reliance on you to our advantage? If the revolt fails, you have a better chance than his councilors or I do to persuade him to postpone his attack. That will buy us more time should we need to regroup."

Nicolai laughed again, this time with despair. "Persuade him? How can he be persuaded in anything?"

There I could sympathize with him.

"You're speaking as if we're doomed to fail," Nicolai went on. "Are we?" When the prince didn't answer fast enough, the count raked a hand through his hair and cast his gaze about the room. "Why are we meeting *here*—under the emperor's very nose, of all places?" He sighed. "Please tell me this is necessary."

"I wouldn't endanger you otherwise," Anton said. "You will

need to call up your courage, Nicolai. Our situation has become dire."

"*Become* dire? Isn't it already? Tosya in prison and Yuri with a bounty on his head. I'm next, I know I am."

Anton's jaw contracted. His patience was unraveling. Between his irritation and Nicolai's escalating panic, I wanted to crawl out of my skin. "We are *all* in danger," I snapped. "We all have something to lose."

The count scoffed at me. "You are an Auraseer of the empire—and, I'm told, an orphan. You have nothing to lose but your own life."

I recoiled at his words. He didn't know anything about me. I'd already lost Pia. I was responsible for the fates of Dasha and Kira. And Anton . . . My throat tightened at the thought of what losing him might do to me.

"Take a care with your tongue!" Anton lashed out at Nicolai. My knees buckled at his anger. "This isn't a twisted contest of martyrs."

"I have a *wife* and a *child!*" the count retaliated. His flood of emotions made my nose sting.

My mind flashed back to the cottage where the prince and I had stopped on our journey to Torchev. Past the cottage door, I'd seen two pairs of hands. One, amethyst-ringed, belonged to Nicolai, who'd passed Anton the letter. The other was smaller, a woman's, and weathered from work. I'd known the two of them didn't belong to the same class. Had that woman been Nicolai's wife?

"Our marriage is secret," the count said, his eyes turning to me, as if he wished me to understand why he felt so desperate. "We live apart. My family . . . the nobles . . . they would never accept her. I thought this revolution would bring me a chance at that—at helping everyone see one another in a similar regard."

Thought, I caught him say. *Thought*. As in the past. As in he no longer believed it.

I contemplated him, his fine clothes, perfectly groomed mustache, and the amethyst ring—perhaps a family heirloom. No doubt he had a good heart: he'd married for love, joined the revolution, played a role in trying to sway other nobles to the notion of equality. But how much of Nicolai's good heart was really in it? I hadn't forgotten how eager he was at the prospect of dancing with me at the ball—strange for a devoutly married man. And he didn't attempt to back Anton at their last council meeting. I feared how long he would be able to lend his support at all.

Despite everything he'd said, I suspected the root of his fear was cowardice, his unwillingness to risk his own life above his consideration for anyone else's.

"I'm sorry for your difficult circumstances," I replied. "The good aspect of your secret marriage, however, is that if you *are* compromised, your wife and child won't be endangered by association. My friend Pia didn't have that same luxury." I managed a thin smile. As an Auraseer, I often had no trouble finding empathy for another. Perhaps I was becoming heartless because I could find none for Nicolai. "So, you see, you and I are equal, after all. Our own lives are what we fundamentally risk."

He blinked at me. His shame made my insides clench.

"Now"—I faced Anton—"I believe we are ready to hear why you have summoned us."

The prince gave me a look of gratitude. His energy was still deeply troubled, but I felt him holding himself together to show a brave face for Nicolai, and perhaps even me. With a steadying breath, he said, "Feliks no longer supports me in a peaceable revolution. He was with Tosya at his arrest. Since then, Feliks has rallied his web of followers to spread word that the 'Voice of Freedom' is to be silenced by execution—and at the emperor's hands."

"But there will be a trial," I interjected. "Did you tell him that?"

"He doesn't care about a trial. I don't believe he even cares if Tosya dies. The people will have no reserve in taking up arms against my brother after an execution." Anton shook his head. "I didn't realize how perilous things had become. I enlisted Feliks to spread Tosya's *philosophy*, but he has done more—he has stoked the people's desperation into *hate*. They are coiled now, their forces gathered and ready to strike. All they needed was a catalyst. The lowered draft age didn't help, but Tosya's imprisonment—that was the fatal blow."

Nicolai's aura lost all its color. It leeched me of my spirit and left only the pale ash of dread. "Speak plainly, Anton," the count said. "What does this mean for us?" *For me*, he might have asked. "What is happening?"

Anton's broad shoulders expanded, as if fortifying himself against the weight of every soul in Riaznin. "The revolution has gone public. They are coming."

"The *people* are coming?" Nicolai gasped. "They will march on the palace?"

"Tomorrow at noonday," the prince added grimly.

Nicolai laughed, though it didn't bring a smile to his face. "They'll never stand a chance!" He steepled his fingers at the bridge of his nose, then dragged them across his face. "The emperor has a *walled fortress* here, countless guards with fire-arms. It will be slaughter! We will surely be compromised."

"Nicolai, I need you now. Do not falter." Anton gripped his friend's arms. "What is done cannot be undone. We must hold together. . . ."

The prince's words seemed to fade until I was deaf to them. The only sound was the thundering of my heart. I envisioned the mob of peasants at the convent's gates—the mob I'd become one with in their single-minded fury. Surely the revolutionaries approaching tomorrow would be far more numerous, far more impassioned. How would I restrain myself from doing some-thing violent along with them?

A warm hand touched my back. "Are you all right, Sonya?" Anton murmured.

I sharply inhaled as I fought to collect myself and scatter the waking nightmare from my mind. "Yes."

His hand slid up to my shoulder and squeezed it before he turned to Nicolai. "How many nobles will stand with us?"

The count gasped with amazement. "*You* intend to fight with them?"

I whirled on Anton, my eyes round, my dread giving way to surprise. *Would* he fight? I didn't believe it possible.

"We still have hope of preventing bloodshed," the prince replied. "If Valko abdicates, no lives will be lost." His gaze riveted to mine, and I swallowed, knowing what he saw in me. *I was the hope he spoke of, the last means of attaining his dream for freedom *and* peace.*

The count watched us, but I didn't sense Anton's faith spread to him. Nicolai only reflected my own lack of confidence. There could be no drawn-out persuasion with the emperor now. I had one day to make Valko see that the fate of the people was better entrusted in their own hands, when they were anything but trustworthy right now. And I had to do it before they marched here and made my task even more impossible.

"If everything goes as planned," Anton continued, "the emperor will call off the battle and give the government to the people. But I want *all* people represented. I need to know how many nobles are on our side. We can't risk a civil war."

"There aren't many." Nicolai gave a shrug of apology. "There hasn't been enough time to convince them—and this wasn't what I promised. They agreed to stand in support of *some* rights for the peasants and serfs, not to be stripped of their own lands and titles, which will surely happen if the people take the government so quickly. It will be *chaos*, Anton. There has to be a better way. If this is what we have to offer the nobility, I'm afraid you will be standing alone."

The prince crossed his arms and gave the count a long look. "And what about you, Nicolai. Will you stand by me if no one else does?"

The amethyst on the count's finger trembled. "I . . . of course I will."

Anton's eyes narrowed. He moved forward, closing in on his friend. "No matter what happens, no harm is to come to Sonya, do you understand?"

The prince's foreboding stabbed my chest. What did he mean? How could Nicolai harm me?

Coming nose to nose with the count, Anton said, "At all costs, she must remain uncompromised. If not, you will find my retribution swift. I am not above violence if the cause is truly justified." An image surged through my mind: Anton holding a dagger, ready to strike Valko when he threatened me on the night of the ball. "I have many allies who would be eager to assist me," he added. "Am I clear?"

I didn't know if Anton was bluffing about his many allies, but Nicolai shifted back a step. His ring quivered harder as if he was sick with the palsy. "Yes."

"Then we should return to the council meeting, though we mustn't draw suspicion by doing so together. Nicolai, you enter first. Sonya, you join him after a few minutes. When I feel it is safe to arrive, I will come last."

"Very well," Nicolai said, as if the order of appearance in the council chamber was the only decent plan we'd concocted.

He bowed and wasted no time in exiting the room.

I stared at the door he shut and tried to make sense of what had just happened. "Why did you threaten him like that?" I turned on Anton. "That's not like you—you, who believes everyone should be free to make their choice without coercion."

He didn't answer, only took me by the elbow and hurried me to the nearest window.

"What are you doing?" I asked. My pulse raced with his sudden anxiety. I frowned at the window frame stretching from the floor to an arched point near the ceiling. The curtains rustled as he planted me in front of them. Why had he brought me here?

"It doesn't matter what happens to me," Anton said, "but you must live." His aura was fierce and blazed along my spine. "Without you, all is lost."

My brow creased. "Well, you must live, too." I didn't understand what had come over him. "You're not leaving, are you?" My legs went weak at the thought.

"I will stay with you as long as possible."

Why did he make it sound like there would be a time we must inevitably part? "If it comes to it, you *will* fight," I said. A command, not a question. "If you mean to tell me by all of this you won't even raise up arms to defend yourself, then I will." He wasn't the only one with a penchant for protectiveness. "I will take your saber and be your shield."

He grinned at me sadly. The dust in the glow from the window gilded the edges of his face, as it had on that day in the council meeting. Somehow it made him look holy and already distant, despite how close we stood together. "You will be wonderful," he said, and I knew he meant something else entirely. "You were born to do this."

I placed my hand on his chest. "Anton . . ."

At my touch, he stiffened and a look of heavy resolve fell upon him. "Though you were not born to be with me." He stepped back and created more space between us.

My hand dropped, my fingers curling with hurt. "I thought you believed in equality. Why am I not good enough for you?"

"Sonya . . ." His brows hitched up in pain. "Have I ever made you feel that way? Equality is an *ideal* but rarely the truth. In all respects, you are my better."

My heart swelled with love for him. I blinked back tears. Why did this feel like an ending, like the glass of the window would shatter with the first volley of musket fire?

This couldn't be the end. I wouldn't allow it to be, not unless he truly understood my feelings for him.

A commotion rose from behind the doors to the ballroom. Boots clapped the marble and echoed louder—nearer—like the rolling of thunder. "In here!" someone shouted.

Anton cursed. "Nicolai," he spat under his breath.

My eyes flew wide. "The count betrayed you?" I asked in disbelief. "And you *knew* he would." To save his own neck, Nicolai must have revealed Anton's part in the revolution, regardless of his word to stay true to the prince.

The muffled sound of sabers being drawn split the air. An

onslaught of Imperial Guard was coming.

Anton shoved me behind the curtains. "Promise you won't make a sound."

I stumbled into the recessed window and squinted against the harsh sunlight outside. My heart pounded. "No!" I turned and wrestled with him past the heavy cloth. "You can't leave me like this. I won't stand idly by while they take you away!"

"Listen to me!" Anton slid in past the curtains and held me still. "I have done my part. I need you free to do yours."

"But—"

"Hide and live and reach my brother. If you care for me at all, Sonya, do as I say." His face was stark in the light. Dark shadows plagued his eyes from fatigue, but his irises were golden, regal as a monarch's, the king he would always be to me.

The raucous noise of the guards reached a crescendo. My throat thickened with emotion. I couldn't draw forth any sound, so I nodded my promise, my heart ripping in two.

And then his beautiful face was gone, just as the great doors groaned on their hinges. I pressed back into the glass.

"Seize him!" someone commanded. With a start, I recognized the voice as Valko's. His familiar aura met mine like poison.

Boots shuffled with the rattle of chains as the guards clapped the prince in irons. Anton didn't groan or make a sound of struggle. I wanted to scream, to burst out and fight the men, even though I had no weapon. Instead, I squeezed my lips together and fought to keep my labored breathing silent.

"Take him to the dungeons." Valko's words were emotionless

now that Anton was captured, as if arresting his own brother was nothing of importance. But I knew differently. I felt the triumphant smile in his aura. "He can make his bed on the muck of his favorite gypsy traitor."

Chains clanked and boots clipped the marble floor as they guards went to leave, no more thunder in their movements, only the sad patter of an abating storm. I sensed their reluctance to lock away the prince of the empire alongside their resolve in their duty.

"Keep an eye out for the sovereign Auraseer," Valko called after them.

I tensed at his words.

"She had no involvement in this!" Anton's anger scorched my skin.

Valko ignited. His voice was no longer cool and apathetic. It flamed with rage. "Not warning me of the threat of a traitorous prince is all the involvement she needs to be sentenced to death!"

A shock of cold seized my body. *Would Valko really kill me?* I trembled as Anton's chains clashed and scraped in his struggle to break free. "You bastard!" he shouted.

"No, brother," Valko replied, his voice so arrogant I could almost see the sneer on his face. "Unfortunately for you, I didn't die. I was never the changeling prince."

The ruckus of jangling irons and angry curses grew dimmer as Anton was dragged away. I scarcely dared breathe. If I did, I would scream.

How could I help Anton now? How could I save him? How could I save anyone?

Valko's energy lingered in the room. I felt the horrible weight of the sapphire around my neck. My fingers curled like frozen claws against the windowpanes. I fought the urge to rake my nails down the glass. *Go away*, I silently pleaded. I couldn't face Valko now. I had no chance of persuading him when all I felt was my own harrowing fury and despair.

At last, the emperor's haughty footfall receded as he swaggered out of the room, and the latch on the door clanged shut.

All of the oxygen rushed out of my lungs. My tears fell. My body slid to the floor. I burrowed into the window, my cheek pressed against the panes. The heat of the sun melded into my bones, but brought me no warmth.

Outside, a man with a flop of dark hair and sloping shoulders exited the palace. He took the long walk from the porch to the gate in quick strides.

"Coward!" I cried in a strangled whisper, and smacked the glass with my fist. I held no empathy for him, only hatred.

I forced myself to stay hidden until I felt no trace of Valko's aura. Then I fled the ballroom and ran down the main corridor, across the amber lobby, up the twirling flight of stairs, and into my chambers. Shoving my box bed aside, I raced through the red door, the lavender door, and crumpled on the dusty planks of the nursery room.

I sobbed and shook and screamed until my throat burned dry. The painted eyes of the rocking horse and nesting dolls watched me with disinterest. I picked up the largest doll and prepared to hurl it across the room, when a rush of frenzied curiosity urged me to be silent.

I listened. Moments later, I heard the muted sounds of a door burst open, furniture knock about, and thuds hit the floor. The emperor's guards must be raiding Anton's chambers, only two rooms away.

My heart pounded as I clutched my hair at the scalp. How much longer could I hide? How was this serving anyone I still cared about? Because I hadn't acted fast enough, Pia had died. When I went to plead for her life, Valko had already executed her. Now Anton and Tosya were next.

From the moment I had agreed to take part in this revolution, I knew I would have to confront Valko and use my ability to persuade him. I had hoped when the time came I'd be courageous, like the plaintively beautiful Armless Maiden. She looked down at me from the flaking mural of Riaznian fairy tales. Pia had finally read me her entire story; it took her seven long nights to stumble through the words.

As I imagined my friend's sweet voice again, I recalled my favorite part of the tale. In her moment of trial, the maiden wasn't brave, she was terrified. Her baby had fallen into a well, and to save him she needed to reach inside. Having no arms below the elbows, she despaired, knowing the task was impossible. But when an old man asked her to apply fortitude and faith, she did. She stopped seeing herself as the victim of her past and started believing in a future where she was whole again. Her arms grew back until her hands were restored and she was able to reach her son.

My situation was just as dire. I couldn't have dreamed of worse circumstances in which to try to bend the emperor's emotions—not when I was wanted for arrest, Anton and Tosya were imprisoned, and the people were coming to storm the palace.

I shook my head and rocked back and forth. There was too much pressure, too many ways my attempts could go wrong. Too many people who would die if I failed.

I looked up to the Armless Maiden. Her face was heart-shaped like Pia's.

Try, Sonya.

Reach.

I remembered the lovely depths of my friend's eyes, the sun in her aura.

I had to do this for her.

Still trembling, I rose to my feet and wiped the tears from my eyes. I brushed the nursery room's dust from my dress and walked through the evergreen door, the midnight-blue door, and when I met the surprised looks of the guards in Anton's chamber, I said with as much strength as I could muster, "I believe the emperor is looking for me."

CHAPTER THIRTY-TWO

As the guards ushered me into Valko's chambers—their grips tight as vises, despite my willingness to come—my gaze riveted to the emperor across the room. He stood in the open doorway of his balcony. Sheer curtains wisped around him. The breeze played through his hair and made him appear gentle and handsome. Adding to the effect were his bare feet jutting out from the base of his trousers, and his loose, untucked shirt. He leaned against the doorframe, his gaze lost on the city. Something in his aura was also lost, also forsaken.

The largest guard shoved me in the back and prodded me forward. I blinked as pain smarted between my shoulder blades. It was enough to return my focus to the task at hand.

I studied the emperor with new eyes, and my muscles tightened and locked around my bones. A wave of revulsion swept the length of me. I had no desire to sense Valko's sorrow or grant him pity. He had killed Pia and arrested Tosya and Anton.

He was callous. Heartless. I wouldn't believe he could be anything more than cruel.

But of course that's exactly what I needed to feel—that it was possible he was genuinely suffering and miserable, and that he had reason to be. Only then could I find any point of connection with him. I needed pure empathy to use my gift to persuade him to abdicate. Without that grafting branch of compassion, I had no hope of overpowering him.

"We have brought the sovereign Auraseer, Your Imperial Majesty," the largest guard announced, and prostrated in a bow without easing his grip on my arm. His pride transferred through the sleeve of my dress and my skin, but I pushed it away. Pride was not an emotion that would help me.

Upon hearing his guard's declaration, Valko's gaze snapped around. His eyes brightened with longing, as if he couldn't believe I stood before him. My heartbeat quickened and relief surged through my breast. I frowned with astonishment. Was it possible he still cared for me?

The warmth in his eyes only lasted a moment before it rapidly hardened to ice. My shoulders fell, and fear wrenched through my stomach. His affection for me must be shattered, and I'd been counting on it to use against him.

"Leave us," Valko told the guards.

My throat ran dry as I tried to swallow. I already dreaded being alone with him. The large guard holding me scowled with confusion at the emperor. He surely expected him to send me straightaway to the dungeons. But I knew Valko. He would privately rebuke me first. His obsessive nature required nothing less. I would be lucky if I survived his wrath to even make it to the dungeons.

"Go!" he barked at the guards.

Reluctantly, they bowed and retreated, then shut the door behind them.

I blinked at the emperor and inhaled a shaky breath. I didn't know what to do now that we were alone together. I shouldn't break protocol by speaking to him first, not when I sought to appear penitent. Rooted by the door, I waited for Valko to approach or permit me to advance. He did neither. He only watched me silently from the other side of the room.

As his coldness slowly subsided, heated rage began to twist and coil inside him. It churned a pit of dark and molten energy, building pressure to erupt. My nerve endings flared with it. My muscles spasmed and cramped. I fought not to panic as I imagined all the ways he could torture me.

"Come forward, Sonya," he said at length, his voice strangely calm.

Heart pounding, I made my way toward his magnificent bed. I had to skirt around it to reach the balcony doors where he waited. Such a large bed could only make a person feel minuscule and inconsequential. I clung to that pitying thought and scrambled to summon more like it—anything that would help me feel the tiniest sliver of empathy toward the person who had destroyed my friends.

Valko was justified in his anger for me. Beneath it, there was surely hurt. I was someone he'd held in his closest confidence, given up alliances for, showered with praise and affection, even though I ranked far below him. Why would I betray him after all we'd shared together? Why had I protected his brother? Why side with Anton of all people—*Anton*, his utmost rival, the brother so many would choose over him to be ruler?

I curtsied once I reached Valko, but try as I might, the words *My Lord Emperor* stuck in my throat. My teeth ground together with my own anger, my own reasons for feeling betrayed. All the times Valko had professed his admiration only to bruise me later. His small kindnesses followed by stark reminders of my inferior place in his life.

"Sonya," he said with that same false calmness as he unhitched himself from the doorframe and moved closer. His fingers skimmed the sapphire at my neck.

Every cell in my body screamed to recoil from him, but I held statuesque. His touch would be useful to me. It would heighten my awareness, help me understand what he was feeling.

"Your eyes are red," he observed coolly. "Has it been such a terrible day?"

My brows lifted. What was he playing at? He knew I must be suffering after Pia's death and Anton's arrest. "Has the day been terrible for you?" I asked, and kept my voice soft and high, so as not to antagonize him. "I felt your grief when I first entered."

He grinned, and his gaze explored my face. "Such a clever

Auraseer." As his fingers stroked my collarbone, I sensed his rage recede to a secret chamber of his aura, where he kept it within careful reach.

My perplexity over his mood change made my heart race with trepidation. Where was his retribution? How could he tease me with a provocative touch when he'd been so monstrous?

The only recourse I could think of was to play along with him—pretend my life wasn't forfeit, as he'd told Anton it was. On the off chance this wasn't a game and the emperor *could* grant me mercy, I might connect with that measure of compassion in him and use it to build a bridge between us. I could widen it to benevolence for *all* people and persuade him to relinquish the throne.

"Your grief is warranted," I replied, and labored once again to show him my understanding—and find it for myself. "It must be a great blow to learn the only person left in your family may have plotted against you."

Valko's smile fell away. His hand withdrew from my collarbone. "There is no 'may have,' Sonya. Anton *did* plot against me."

"Oh." I feigned shock and sympathy. "The people will take this news hard, especially since that poet, Tosya, is already in prison. You must be worried the commoners will revolt." I touched his arm, and his resentment amplified. I let it eat its way through my gut. He felt so abandoned within. All his life he was molded to be emperor. That destiny required his separation from his family, the taking of another boy's life to protect his identity . . . And now, after all that sacrifice, the people of

Valko's hard-earned empire were uniting against him. "My duty compels me to warn you, My Lord, that the commoners are most unhappy."

His jaw muscle spasmed as he turned back to stare at the city. From here, it shone crystalline in the fading sunlight. The Azanel River sparkled unpolluted. The height of the nobles' dwellings blocked the view of grime and poverty in the other Torchev, the half the emperor didn't want to see.

I gently stroked his arm. "Perhaps, if you understood the reason why they are—"

I flinched, cutting myself off a second before he did as I felt the scorch of his sudden rage.

"I don't wish to speak about the people!" He whirled on me with blazing eyes. "Your warnings do not serve me if they come too late!" Pressing nearer, he asked, "What did you suspect about my *brother* these past months? When did you plan to warn me about *him*?"

My hands balled into shaking fists as I fought not to let his fury overwhelm me. But then why fight it? I should abandon myself to it. "I've never sensed any hatred in Anton for you!" I lashed back, letting his fire stoke in my belly. "What could I warn you about if the prince never wished you any harm? He is not a violent person!" My body trembled with rage.

Valko smirked and laughed a little as he tilted his head. In an instant, his scornful mood slid away, beneath its trapdoor. In its place emerged a twisted curiosity. "You seem to know Anton well," he mused.

Again, I was baffled by his shift in emotion. I sensed his threads of manipulation wrapping around me, but not his motive.

"I am familiar with the prince's aura," I confessed, my anger quelling when his did, my voice lowering to match his volume. "It is my job as your protector to understand all those closest to Your Majesty."

He arched a sardonic brow, but his gray eyes were flat with no amusement. "Then you could not be blind to Anton's feelings for you."

I winced as a flicker of his rage singed me.

"I believe he loves *you*," I retaliated, turning Valko's accusation back on him.

He barked out a laugh. "*Love* me? He's never stopped scheming for my throne!"

Startled by another scorch of anger, I retreated a step. The mounting betrayals of the past days were taking their toll—Valko was so unstable right now, so unhinged. I feared he was losing his grip on his sanity.

"Acting as the benefactor of a rogue gypsy," he spat as he paced about, "is just another one of Anton's tactics to turn the people's allegiance." The emperor's words came faster as a manic temper seized him and made me claw at my wrists. "He's already won the favor of the nobles. They would rather him rule than me. I can see that. I'm not a fool, Sonya." He tapped his head like a madman.

It was impossible to grasp his aura, to bond with it. It was too slippery and scattered by erratic anxiety and hysteria. "As he is someone sharing your anointed blood," I countered, "I only thought you would give the prince a fair trial."

Valko's eyes crinkled at the corners, but they were nothing like merry. He stopped his pacing and drifted nearer, so close his dangerous aura lifted the hairs on my arm. "I'm not a fool, Sonya," he said again in a whisper. "Has my brother won your favor, too?" He traced a finger from my temple to my chin, then up to my lips. "Have you given yourself to him, when you've denied me?"

A dark sense of foreboding descended upon us. I stared into Valko's eyes and realized with distinct clarity what had upset him most of all, what had provoked him beyond any other betrayal—he believed I had fallen in love with Anton. And he was right.

My heartbeat grew heavy with dread. I should have never turned myself in to the guards, never have come here. I should have tried my luck in persuading the jail master to release Anton and Tosya. There was no hope in overpowering Valko now, not when all his energy was bent on punishing me for the worst of crimes. I had struck the nerve of his greatest insecurity—that his brother was loved more than he was. And now Valko would do everything in his power to make me suffer for it.

"What's wrong?" The emperor's finger still hovered about my lip. "Have I hit upon the truth?"

I shook my head. I wouldn't admit to my feelings for Anton. Surely that would mean the prince's swift execution. "It's just— you're frightening me, Valko. Your aura—"

"Yes." He lowered himself to eye level, leering closer. "What about my aura, Sonya? Can't I feel anything passionately? Must I always be restrained as emperor? You see what I do daily to prove myself to my empire, to my councilors, to everyone who pretends to support me at court. What must I do to prove myself to you? I've given you wealth." He lifted the sapphire necklace and pulled me inward by the collar so our noses brushed. "Position." His lips pressed against my cheek near the corner of my mouth. "I've given up Estengarde for you." He kissed my other cheek, and I bit it on the inside to keep from whimpering in terror. "I'm not sure I'm ready to kill you, Sonya." His mouth traveled to my ear and wetted it with warmth. "I still have faith you can learn to submit to me in all ways."

I gasped for air against his suffocating desire. It flowered within him—within me. A sickly fragrance that made my nose burn.

"Your defiance is irresistible, Sonya, and that dark well of passion inside you is what allures me most." Valko swept my hair behind my shoulder and traced the length of my neck with his fingernail. "I will not share you with my brother. You belong to me. You are an Auraseer of Riaznin, born with a gift for one purpose only—to serve your anointed emperor. When at last you fully abandon yourself to your emotions, I will be the one to taste it."

I closed my eyes. This time I could not bite back my whimper. Was giving myself over to total abandon the last option remaining to me? Was baring all my darkness what was required to become one with Valko's aura—to reach that point of empathy where he could inhabit all of me and I could inhabit all of him?

How could I endure it?

"Do you want marriage, Sonya?" he asked. His kisses traveled from one side of my neck to the other above the collar of my necklace, as if trying to sear it to my skin. "Is that why you hold back? The ancient law of Riaznin states an emperor can have three wives. Perhaps after I wed someone of high birth, I can condescend to marry you."

I shuddered as revulsion soured my gut. The more Valko touched me, the more self-loathing I felt. He didn't want to commit himself to me, but he did, and not out of anything mirroring love.

"Until then"—he slid my dress from my shoulder and grazed my skin with his teeth—"there is room for you in my bed."

I wrestled away, no longer able to bear his monstrosity. "Please . . ."

"Please, what?" He straightened, his mood blackening again. "Don't you understand? It doesn't matter if you are my Auraseer or my mistress—the truth is, you are mine."

I shifted backward. "Then as your Auraseer I must beg leave of you. I must have my rest if there is to be a trial for both a prince and a poet." I turned to bolt for the door.

He caught my arm and clucked his tongue. "There will be no trial—for either of them." His voice grew cold and menacing as he leaned to my ear and whispered, "They will be executed at first light."

My mouth parted in horror. My heart collided with my rib cage. I couldn't find my breath. I had to leave—now. Find my way to the dungeons. Find a way to free Anton and Tosya.

"Tonight you will not leave me." Valko's grip tightened like manacles. "Tonight, you stay."

I gasped, a weak and terrible pleading sound as he pulled me closer, taking his time, knowing he could, knowing I was no match for his strength. Tears pooled in my eyes. So many times I had evaded him. But now with the sun lost under the horizon and the night gathering its forces in the sky, with his body silhouetted by the remnants of dying light, I knew I'd reached the breaking point of my war against him—the war I had waged since I first set foot in the palace—to keep my own integrity. To hold sacred that space within myself that was my last fragment of honor, of liberty. The space that was mine to share, and not anyone else's to take. And now he would strip it from me until all his lies of esteem and high regard would be exposed for the pitiful truth they were. I wasn't his beloved. In his eyes, I was lower than the ground he trod on. And he would relentlessly trample me into nothing. Until there was no Sonya remaining. Only a possession. Another forgotten treasure he held under lock and key.

As his mouth neared mine, as tears streaked my face, an

orange glow framed his hair, different from the dwindling sunset red. It almost looked like . . . *fire.* I glanced past him to the city, to the wide avenue that cut its long path to the palace. There, in the distance, was a band—no, a battalion—of people. My heart surged with hope. They were mere specks from here, but they were coming. The orange glow must be their torchlight.

"Valko," I said as I pointed to the city, to his night of reckoning. The people were meant to come tomorrow, but they were already on their way, as if they somehow knew tomorrow would be too late.

The emperor's eyes flew wide. He dropped my hand and rushed to his balcony wall. "They wouldn't dare," he breathed.

I backed slowly to the door of his chambers. My fingers clutched the latch when he noticed me. His gaze narrowed. "What are you doing?"

I pulled my gown back over my shoulder. "As your Auraseer, it is my duty to warn you your life is now in grave danger." I opened the door. "However, it is *not* my duty to fight for you, and it will *never* be my duty to lie with you. I bid you farewell. You will soon discover how much the gods value your life."

His face hardened to stone. "If you leave me, Sonya, you will live to regret it."

"Perhaps." I drew up taller. "But I *will* live. I cannot say the same for you." I whirled around and raced down the corridor.

"Sonya!" Valko bellowed. "Guards, seize her!"

I panted, my lungs already burning. Of course he would

send his guards after me, and not to reinforce his regiments outside. I knew I'd damned myself by being so bold, but I couldn't help it. The people gave me strength—the same daring people whom Anton feared coming and Nicolai didn't believe stood a chance against the emperor's forces—I believed in them. I felt their courageous energy steel inside me. And I no longer cared if they slit Valko's throat in order to throw down his reign.

I grabbed the banister of the twirling staircase and hurtled downward. I tripped over the hem of my dress, barely able to stay on my feet. The guards' sabers rang out from their sheaths. At least they hadn't fired their muskets. They must know Valko wanted me alive.

I stumbled onto the landing of the second floor and stole a backward glance. Ten or so guards were on my trail. They would soon be upon me. "Let me alone!" I shouted with a ragged breath as I descended the last staircase. "Don't you know where the danger lies?" I pointed to the great doors of the palace.

I sensed their panic and understood their compulsion to serve their emperor. I had once felt the same. But there came a time when obedience needed to be broken.

"The people are coming," I said, "and they will bring this government to an end!" I stared at them beseechingly and willed the guards to feel the might of the revolutionaries. With all my conviction, I shouted, "If you want to live, now is your last chance to join them!"

Their expressions of determination went blank. They shuffled to a halt and looked to the great doors. Surprised I had stalled them, I didn't waste my opportunity. I fled down the remaining stairs.

Once my slippers clapped the lobby floor and I turned my focus to finding the dungeons, my spell over the guards broke. Their boots picked up speed, and they rumbled like a storm down the marble staircase.

I darted for the corridor in the opposite direction of the great hall and ballroom. When the guards reached the lobby, half bolted for the great doors, their curiosity propelling them outside. The others stayed fast after me.

I pressed onward at a relentless pace. The entrance to the dungeons had to be this way. Perhaps the auras of desperate prisoners would lead me there.

The storm of guards came louder. They were gaining on me. I lengthened my stride and ran faster. My legs trembled. My throat burned raw. My vision flashed with white. Auras danced inside my breast. The righteous indignation of the people. The shock of the servants. The dogged tenacity of the guards.

With my waning physical strength, I kept their energy at bay and forced my purpose to take precedence. *Anton*. I had to free *Anton*.

A dark, unlit corridor loomed to the left. I took it on a whim. I could very well be headed in the wrong direction, but I was running out of options.

This part of the palace was built haphazardly—added onto over time as the laws became stricter and the prisoners multiplied. Corridors branched in a mazelike fashion as they blurred before my eyes. I reached out for any new auras emanating from the dungeons, but my racing pulse was too much a distraction.

A shadowy figure flickered to my right. I spun around. It was a man. Bearded, but young. Somehow familiar. Close-set eyes. A wide nose. And—my nerves surged with panic—wearing a soldier's uniform.

"Sonya?" he asked.

The thunder of the Imperial Guard pounded behind me. Any moment now and they would turn the corner. I took a desperate chance and whispered, "Help!"

The man grabbed my hand and tossed me behind him. "Hide," he rasped. I did my best and flattened myself behind the jutted edge of an uneven, patched-together wall.

The man sprang into the hallway where the guards had just emerged. "There!" he shouted. "She ran that way, past the door to the wine cellar! I think she's headed outside."

The guards advanced without pausing. The word of their comrade had been enough. I waited a few moments and prayed they wouldn't backtrack for me. When I felt assured I was safe and made ready to peel off the wall, the bearded guard flashed in front of me, the barrel of a flintlock pistol aimed at my chest.

"I'm sorry, Sonya," the man said, "but I need you."

I blinked at him, this time with recognition. His new beard had disguised him. It covered his jaw and lips with matted blond hair. "Yuri?" I asked in amazement.

CHAPTER THIRTY-THREE

I STARED AT THE SOLDIER. HE WAS BACK, ALIVE. PIA'S YURI. A member of Anton's league, not captured. Still loyal. Or maybe not. I glanced at the pistol. "How is it you are here?" I asked. "The emperor has a bounty on your head."

"I still have friends at the palace." He looked around, his thumb jittery on the pistol hammer. Apparently not enough friends to make him feel safe. "We must hurry. You're a favorite of the emperor's. I need you to arrange for me a private audience with him."

A flare of panic seized me at the thought of returning to Valko, but it dwindled as I took in Yuri's red-rimmed eyes, his aura crazed and violent and broken. "You know about Pia," I said in realization, my shoulders falling as his nostrils flared with emotion and a vein engorged on his brow. "Oh, Yuri, I'm so sorry."

His voice wavered. "Please tell me you pleaded for her life."

"I did. I was too late."

"Then this can also be your vengeance. If you truly loved Pia, you will help me." He swallowed with determination and planted the pistol barrel on my breastbone.

I sucked in a sharp breath from the cool bite of metal. "It appears I don't have a choice."

"See it how you will." He shrugged. "Let's go."

"This isn't necessary," I said, desperate for some means to persuade him. I was losing time to free Anton. "Do you know the peasants are marching?"

"The emperor will die at my hands, and no one else's."

My racing heartbeat slowed as I contemplated Yuri and considered a new strategy. "If I promise to help you, I'll need a favor first."

"What?" he growled.

"You said you have friends here. Guards. Are any loyal to you in the dungeons?"

His jaw ticked. "Some. Why?"

"Tosya isn't the only one imprisoned. Anton is in the dungeons, as well. Valko plans to have them both executed in the morning."

Yuri's brows pinched together, then he shook his head. "It doesn't matter. When Valko dies and the people storm the palace, they will be freed, anyway."

"I need him." I gripped Yuri's arm, then flinched as the pistol bit harder into my skin. "I can't chance anything going awry until he is released." When Yuri didn't budge, I added, "This *revolution* needs him. They need a leader. After all Anton has done, doesn't he deserve to stand alongside his people?"

"I can't." Yuri dropped his gaze. "We have to find Valko now."

"Please . . ." How could I reach him? "He is to me what Pia was to you. Please . . . help me."

Yuri's pistol hand shook harder. I felt our shared love for Pia intensify his struggle.

Tentatively, I touched his arm. He made a muffled noise of pain. "She would want you to help me," I said, and I believed it wholeheartedly.

He cursed and lowered the gun, raking his hands through his hair. "Very well, Sonya. But quickly."

The entrance to the dungeons wasn't far away. As Yuri opened the door, he exposed a winding stone staircase. The cloying stench of refuse and rotting flesh assaulted me. I held my sleeve over my nose and rushed down as quietly as possible.

When we reached the dungeons' floor, Yuri grabbed my arm. "Stay here until I return," he whispered before he strode off through a stone archway where the light of the sconced torches couldn't reach him.

I tucked away into a corner. The walls dripped with condensation. A rat skittered across the stones. How much longer did we have before the peasants stormed the palace, before the chaos of raging battle came?

When I thought I might scream from impatience, Yuri

finally returned. "The gods are with us." He grinned. "The jail master is sleeping, and one of the guards stationed at Anton's cell is my friend. He's willing to distract his partner, pinch the keys, and give you five minutes to do your business."

I exhaled with amazement. Perhaps the gods *were* real and lending their assistance. "That's wonderful."

Yuri's grin slipped. "He *is* my friend, but he still wants some kind of payment for taking such a risk." His gaze dropped to my sapphire necklace.

"Yes, of course." I unclasped it and handed it over without a second thought.

He tucked it into his pocket. "Ready, then?"

I nodded. My heart beat wildly at the thought of seeing Anton—of freeing him.

"Keep close behind me. Be light on your toes. When I hide, you hide. Understand?" Only then did I notice Yuri had holstered his pistol and now held a gleaming knife. A smarter weapon, I realized. Gunfire would draw the attention of every guard in the dungeons, but one could stab a man silently. A hand at the mouth would even muffle his death cry. My stomach turned as I imagined it—imagined Yuri capable of such a thing. Even now his dark, unbalanced aura made me twitch and dig my nails into my palms.

We advanced into the dungeons. The corridors seemed a reflection of the mazelike hallways above as they twisted and branched without order. The torchlight was minimal, the sconces spread apart with long patches of blackness between them. Rodents' tails occasionally slithered at my ankles, but I swallowed my fright and made myself keep walking. I awaited the moment Anton's steadfast aura would take hold within me.

"We're close." Yuri's beard scratched my ear as he turned around and whispered. "Wait here while I signal my friend."

I leaned against the mildewing wall and counted my heartbeats, preparing for another unendurable wait. The growing panic of the residents in the palace started to infiltrate me. Their awareness of the danger and the coming people's army chafed my skin with icy terror. *I want the peasants to come*, I reasoned with myself, and fought to push the other conflicting emotions away.

"Sonya." Yuri's hoarse voice bounced off the stones. "*Now.* We must hurry. Five minutes." I startled as I felt him at my side. I hadn't seen him coming in the darkness. He passed over a heavy ring of keys. "This way." He set his hand on the small of my back and guided me forward.

We rounded a corner into a pool of torchlight. The stench of the dungeons increased tenfold. A long gallery of cells loomed in the distance. The quiet misery of countless prisoners gripped me and surpassed the terror of the upstairs servants and nobles. The prisoners' auras held the expected hunger, pain, and affliction—but their energy was weak and without hope. Their collective despondency made me want to lie down and sleep in the rotting straw that littered the floor. It spilled out past the iron bars from what must have been their pitiful beds and refuse heaps. The dreary feeling made me never want to wake up.

What was the use? Who would save me?

A burly guard kept watch and walked away from us down the gallery of cells. When he turned on his heel to pace in our direction, Yuri hurried me to a heavy oak door. Unlocked. We crept inside. The helpless auras of the prisoners abated to the extent that I was able to widen my eyes and take in my new surroundings.

The room was split in two, the middle divided by a wall of bars. This place seemed to be a separate, solitary prison for the more dangerous criminals of the empire. My side of the room held two torch sconces and nothing more. The side beyond held two weary friends, who after all their years of plotting a glorious revolution had been led to this miserable fate.

Tosya sat in the far left corner on a bed of fresh straw. It hadn't mildewed yet, as he'd only arrived last night. The intervening time seemed enough to sober him more than I'd ever seen. He had his knees bent to his chest and twirled a piece of straw between his fingers like it was the most precious thing in the world. Like it was the last thing he would ever look upon.

Anton rested against the middle of the wall, his ankles crossed over each other, his aura strangely at peace. He didn't seem to fear for his life—perhaps due to his confidence in me. Until this moment, he probably thought I was with Valko as the emperor crawled like a subservient dog at my feet. He must have imagined I'd succeeded in the hellish task he'd given me. I hesitated to disturb his calm surety, even for the promise of rescue.

But then Anton saw me. His eyes lifted to roam over my face with wonder. He knew me well enough to see what I couldn't hide. I *hadn't* overcome Valko; he'd nearly overcome me. I hadn't persuaded the emperor to abdicate.

"Sonya." He sat up from the wall.

The empathy in his gaze undid me. All of the fear and helplessness I'd felt with Valko as he'd tried to force me into submission came back to me now. I'd suppressed it as I fled to Anton like the needle of a compass to north. "I'm sorry," I said and hovered near the door. "Valko tried to . . . I couldn't . . ." A sob caught in my throat. "I'm so sorry, Anton."

A look of sadness crossed his face. Perhaps he was disappointed. Perhaps he simply felt my pain—as if he, for the moment, were the Auraseer. He rose up on his feet with difficulty—had the guards wounded him in their struggle to bring him here?—and came to the barrier between us, to its bolted door. He reached past the bars, and I rushed to him, feeling the warmth of his arms enfold me, despite the cold iron at my chest.

"What are you doing here?" he asked, and pressed a kiss on my head.

I blinked back my emotions and fought to awaken myself from the spell of his tenderness. "We've come to free you." I pulled away. My hands trembled as I flipped through the keys for a size to match the lock. "Yuri knows one of the guards," I explained.

Tosya stood and glanced past me. "Yuri? Is that you?"

The soldier came to my side. "Apparently a beard makes me invisible. I should have grown one long ago, but Pia . . ." His voice hitched. He cleared his throat and took the ring of keys. "Let me. Our time is running short."

As he tried key after key, I looked to Anton and Tosya, my spirits lifting. "The peasants did not wait until tomorrow. They're marching on the palace as we speak." When Anton's face fell, I said reassuringly, "This is *good*. The emperor planned to have you both executed in the morning."

The prince stepped back and rubbed a hand across his jaw. Tosya quietly studied him, as if he knew what he was thinking. "This *isn't* good," Anton replied. "Our lives aren't worth the deaths of so many. And make no mistake, the casualties will be enormous—no matter which side wins."

I stared at him in bewilderment. "They're coming whether you like it or not, and I won't leave you here if the palace burns. Now is your chance to fight for the dream you've given these people!"

"I *have* been fighting, Sonya. For years. But not like this. Not with gunpowder and sabers. If that is the dream I gave, I want no part of it."

"Will you not even defend yourself?" His obstinate idealism made me want to reach through the bars and shake him.

"Hush, you two!" Yuri struggled with another key. "You'll alert the guards and—" His words fell silent as he put all his strength into turning the lock. His fingers went white. His veins bulged at the temple. But it was no use. "Damn!" He hit the barred door. The noise rang through the chamber with greater volume than that of my or Anton's voice. "None of these fit."

I gaped at him. "Well, then go and tell your friend he fetched the wrong set."

"This is the only set, the only ring! Don't you understand? The jail master doesn't have the key."

The weak fabric of hope holding me together threatened to rend at the seams. "Then we must find it."

"If he doesn't have it, no one in the dungeons does." Yuri paced away and kicked up the straw. He left the last key jammed in the lock.

"Valko has it," Anton said, looking at all of us with grim acceptance. "He must. It makes perfect sense. He's sought to have me imprisoned for ages. Now that he's succeeded, he won't trust anyone one else with the means of releasing me. He's too suspicious of his own people—too worried, in the end, of their shifting loyalty to him."

My stomach hardened into stone with the heavy weight of dread. "I must return to the emperor."

"No, Sonya," Anton said resolutely. "I won't ask that of you." Tosya kept his lips sealed and lowered his eyes, entrusting his fate to his friend.

"I must. I won't leave you here! What if the revolution doesn't succeed?"

"It's going to succeed." Yuri broadened his chest. "And you needn't worry about the emperor. Just grant me access, and I will finish him. I won't fail this time."

Despite the desperation of the moment, the urgency, and the blood rushing through my veins, I felt a darkness in Yuri. And I recognized it—its snakelike writhing in my gut. I'd also felt it the night of the ball, when I was sure someone meant to kill Valko. But Yuri never tried to kill him then—never *failed* at that time—only plotted. What failure, then, was he referring to? Suddenly understanding dawned on me, as crystal clear as the goblet Yuri must have tainted. "You killed the dowager empress," I gasped.

Yuri's mouth fell open. His eyes flew wide, darting to Anton. "What are you speaking of?"

"You tried to kill the emperor before, by poison," I said. "You evaded Izolda by using Pia." The mystery unfolded before me like a row of painted murals. "The sovereign Auraseer would have never detected an unknowing girl's involvement. You wouldn't have told Pia, of course. She was too pure to ever consider being your accomplice. But it would have been simple enough—perhaps something laced in the herbs of the emperor's tea. You could have dropped it in while kissing Pia in the kitchens. Of course, you would have made sure to be far away when it was administered, so Izolda wouldn't sniff you out. But you still failed. The empress consumed what was meant for her son."

"This is absurd!" Yuri shifted backward. His neck and ears flushed red.

"She was with me," Anton said, more to himself than anyone else. "My mother had taken up the custom of bidding me good night to make up for all the times she couldn't. After she spoke with me, she went to see Valko. I was on the verge of sleep when I heard shouts to summon a physician. I ran into Valko's room and . . . I was with him when our mother drew her last breath." The tendons of his throat contracted as his eyes flashed to Yuri. "Tell me you didn't do this."

The soldier's beard trembled near his mouth. His aura almost buckled me over with grief and madness. "The revolution was at a standstill," he said, his confession pouring out of him. "Nicolai was scarcely persuading any nobles, and you denied Feliks his desire to gather the peasants for a public revolt. Meanwhile, the empire grew stronger, more oppressive . . ." He shook his head in misery. "I found out from another guard that Valko forced himself on Pia," Yuri finally admitted, as if that were the root of his justification.

I blinked. Had Yuri known all this time what Pia had labored to conceal from him? The truth made my heart ache for my friend.

"I was incensed!" Yuri said, and gave Anton a pleading look. "I wasn't thinking clearly. But I swear to you, I never meant to harm your mother."

The prince's brows were unflinching. "You didn't harm her, you *killed* her."

Yuri dropped his chin. His wretchedness was palpable as he lowered his gaze. "Forgive me," he whimpered.

Anton's diamond-hard aura locked my knees and straightened my spine. "You are to leave this palace, leave Torchev," he commanded. "I don't ever want to see you again. And you will *not* lay a finger on my brother."

"But . . ." Yuri's eyes rounded. "He killed Pia. He's killed *thousands*. He deserves to die."

"Valko will face trial, and his fate will be determined by the voice of the people, not you."

A wave of hurt crashed over Yuri. He flared his nostrils. "You are not my superior. *You* taught me that. You cannot order me in anything. I will have my way with Valko, and you won't be at liberty to stop me." He grabbed my arm and yanked me to the wooden door.

"Let her go!" Anton rattled the bars.

Yuri whirled on him. "We all have a price to pay for this revolution. You taught me that, as well. This is hers."

The wooden door flew open on its hinges—but not by Yuri's hand. A bleary-eyed hulk of a man burst inside. His gaze riveted on the ring of keys dangling from the prison cell's lock. Yuri reached for his knife, but the man—no doubt, the jail master—already had his dagger unsheathed. With one clean swipe, he dragged it across Yuri's throat. I cried out as my captor crumpled over. His knife tumbled across the floor until it clanged against the iron bars.

My body seized with terror. My pulse flooded my ears. I spun to face the jail master. He would show me no mercy. His entrails would be ripped from his body if Anton and Tosya escaped under his watch.

The jail master advanced on me. His dagger dripped with

blood. I had no weapon. Yuri's knife was out of reach. Still, it was my only hope. I turned to dive for it, but it was gone.

A fleshy thud punched the air. The jail master gave a harsh, stunned grunt. I drew in a shocked breath and clutched my stomach, momentarily feeling his pain. Eyes bulging, the man careened over as his life drained out of him. I shuddered and looked about me, trying to make sense of what had happened.

Anton—the pacifist prince—was on his knees, one hand grasping an iron bar while the other jutted past it, fresh from flinging Yuri's knife.

Tosya's expression of amazement surely reflected my own.

"Anton," I gasped, marveling that I was alive and, moreover, that he had actually killed someone to save me.

"You must go." His face was ashen at what he had done. "Others will soon be coming."

I knelt before him on the other side of the bars. I wrapped my fingers around his shaking hands. "I won't leave you."

A dull roar filled the air. Dust fell from the mortar of the stone-lined ceiling. Anton swallowed and looked from me to Tosya, who glanced upward. "It has begun."

I regarded both of them, knowing they were trapped here while I was free, that they were willing to die for this mad dream—a dream neither one of them had wanted to end in violence. The least I could do was honor them by trying once more to end Valko's reign peacefully. I would be risking my life, but it had always been at risk . . . from the moment I'd committed myself to the revolution, and even before, when I was brought to the palace in forced servitude. In truth, my life was compromised when I was born an Auraseer. This was my opportunity to break the chains. Or die trying.

"Do you really believe he deserves to live?" I asked.

Anton knew whom I meant. "No," he admitted. "But I see in him every day what I could have become if the throne hadn't been taken from me. If I were in his place, I'd like to think I would have a chance at redemption."

I nodded slowly. "Then I will go to him one last time."

He held steady to my hand, and his gaze searched through me. "Are you certain? Is this *your* choice, Sonya? I don't want my desires to ever persuade you in anything."

There was so little difference now between his aura and my own. We both knew what we must do. "Trust me," I said, and laced my fingers through his. "And trust what is in my heart. My feelings for you are here when I am alone, when you are miles from the palace. I keep you with me. I choose to. You are the most impossibly stubborn person I have ever met. You are also the most honorable, the most caring. I love every part of you."

A tremor ran across his brow as I said the word *love*. Even now, I felt him guarding himself from me.

"Our souls are fitted for each other, not because an old Romska woman foretold it, but because we *choose* them to be."

The prince's chest rose and fell. The indomitable barrier around his heart, at last, came crashing down.

"This feeling inside me is *mine*," I said. "I am blessed to know you share it."

Behind him, Tosya softly smiled and turned away, granting us the only measure of privacy he could. Anton reached past the bars to cup my face. Every time he'd beheld me in the past, his eyes had carried a measure of pain. And now that pain transformed into the ache of luminous joy, only dimmed because this might be our last moment together.

I would not waste it.

Tears blurred my vision. "I love you, Anton."

He pulled me close, as close as the bars would allow. The space between them was just large enough for him to kiss me. And he did.

He gave me every breath of his aura. It filled my body with light, with strength, with a beauty I had never known. It couldn't cleanse away everything I had suffered, every dark mistake I had made, every loss. Nor could mine erase his, all his loneliness, all the betrayals of those he had trusted. But our union was a haven from it all, a place for healing and hope. It felt like home. A home neither one of us had been able to depend on until now.

When he drew away, it wasn't with any regret for the vulnerability he'd just allowed himself. His light still reflected within me and sang through my veins. "Please go now, while you can," he said, kissing me briefly one last time.

I nodded and stood with more iron in my bones, more resolve to do what had to be done—and, for the first time, with unequivocal determination. I removed the jail master's cloak and Yuri's cape and draped them over their bodies to give them what honor I could and what peace I could offer Anton and Tosya, who must share this room with them awhile longer. I already sensed the guilt eating away at the prince for having had to kill a man.

Teeth gritted, I slid the knife out from the jail master's belly and retrieved the dagger from his hand. I took Yuri's pistol from his holster and tossed the weapons into a bed of straw past the bars. "Swear to me you will defend yourselves, if necessary."

"We will," Tosya answered for both of them. "Be careful, Sonya." His aura held me with brotherly affection.

I nodded and stepped over the dead bodies, my heart clenching for Pia's lost soldier. At the threshold of the open door, I turned my gaze once more to Tosya and Anton. "I will come back."

CHAPTER THIRTY-FOUR

I STUMBLED THROUGH THE MAZE OF THE DUNGEONS. ABOVE the stone ceiling, more muffled pops of musket fire rang out. Distant shouts came as a growing roar, like I was nearing a massive waterfall. My heart pounded faster, harder. The auras of the peasant army rushed inside my breast and gave me fierce courage. I hurtled onward through the darkness.

Boom!

A huge blast echoed through the corridor and shook the ground and the very foundations of the palace. I crashed to my knees. The ceiling split apart with fissures. Chunks of stone rained down around me. I cried out as the panic of the servants, guards, and nobles burned like acid on my skin. My hand flew to the wall and groped for support as cramps of nausea racked my body.

The shaking stopped, but terror still seized me. It seized

everyone. I pressed my fists to the sides of my head and rocked back and forth.

I couldn't do this. I couldn't bear the auras of both the oncoming revolutionaries *and* those fighting in defense of the palace. I couldn't bear *any* of them.

After a brief lull, the shots fired again. The peasants took up their battle cries.

I fought to breathe, to stop all my limbs from trembling. I wanted to run back to Anton and burrow into his protective warmth. I pictured him in his jail cell, his ankles crossed over each other, his energy calm and assured. His faith in me gave him that confidence. I wanted to be the person he believed in, to see myself as he did. He always trusted that I had inner strength. Once on a snowy troika ride, he'd taught me how to prevent my loss of control. But the power he gave me over the onslaught of city dwellers was more than the distraction of his handsome face. It was an intangible power, rooted in something far more beautiful, which gathered its forces when the prince and I joined in unity.

I found that power now, past my sheer anxiety and racing fear. Deep within my aura, Anton's radiant light and love still burned brightly. I let his presence fill me, combine with mine, and ground me with self-command.

Setting my jaw, I took a long breath. I got back on my feet.

As I clung to Anton's aura, the myriad surrounding me abated until I was able to move and think of my own volition— until I was certain my feelings were my own. Rushing forward,

I puzzled my way through the dungeons' maze and finally reached the stone stairwell. I ascended to the main floor of the palace, traced my way back through the corridors, but skidded to a halt in the grand lobby. My mouth fell open in shock.

The amber floors were blasted apart in sections and littered with broken glass. Gunfire continued to pour inside and ricocheted off the walls, blowing bits off the marble statues. Servants screamed and ducked for cover, while others abruptly joined the revolutionaries and battled the guards with shards of glass and half-demolished beams.

Moonlight and torch fire flickered in through the shattered windows. Beyond them, I saw the peasants had yet to penetrate the gates of the palace. But they raged a war through its bars, never ceasing their volley of musket fire and screams for justice, for liberty. For the freeing of Tosya Pashkov. For the head of the emperor. The guards shot them down, but more rose up where their comrades had fallen, a ceaseless wave of fury.

The people's auras were stronger now and attacked my thrown-up barrier with their own war of demanding emotions and sensations. Gritting my teeth, I breathed in slowly through my nose. I filled my lungs with air. I focused on the inner workings of my body, on my aura and Anton's. And I stayed single-minded to *my* purpose, *my* mission—and not anyone else's.

I crouched low with my arms wrapped protectively over my head and struggled to keep moving forward. I scrambled up the nearest flight of stairs and passed guards stationed on the steps, their muskets behind the ramparts of the banister, as if it were the crenellation of an ancient castle. They paid little attention to me. Either they didn't know who I was and that I was wanted, or they no longer cared.

The muscles in my legs burned as I reached the third floor of the palace and leaned against a wall to catch my breath. Valko's rooms stared at me from the end of the dragon's tongue, the red carpet rolling out from his door.

My heart drummed. I set one foot in front of the other to inevitably close the distance to him. As I passed the door to my chambers, I pictured the statue of Feya on my windowsill. I touched two fingers to my forehead, then my heart, and prayed for the goddess to be with me—for Yuliya to lend me her calm peace from Paradise.

I remembered my friend's bravery in the face of death, the feeling she had finally reached past her pain and terror. I'd only tasted that courage the first time I'd touched the blood spatter on Feya. From then on in my self-torture, I'd let go before the comfort could come. I allowed it to fill me now. It was always there, hidden inside me.

I prayed for Yuliya's forgiveness, for the mercy of all those who had died because of me. The Auraseers of the convent. Pia. Yuri. Even the jail master. Each person had been dealt a harsh lot in this life. Each person tried their best to come out alive. I *wanted* them alive.

Anton was right. The world had seen enough death. I had the chance to stop any more from happening. At least on this day. At least in Torchev.

More than twenty guards surrounded the emperor's door. Unlike below, here the soldiers recognized me and had me bound in their arms before I advanced any nearer.

I allowed them. They would not kill me. They would bring me faster to the person I must see. He stood where I'd left him, at the doorway to his balcony. Only this time he was dressed in his finest kaftan, his red sash tied diagonally from shoulder to waist, his saber hanging at his side, his ceremonial crown upon his brow. If he were to go down, he wouldn't go down like a beggar. He would show his power until the very end.

With his hands clasped behind his back, Valko stared at the rampant battle below, watching from a safe distance where no musket could aim true. His only acknowledgment of my arrival was a slight turn of his head as the guards ushered me into the room and his nod for them to depart.

I exhaled and approached him, reaching for his aura like the tentacles of a sea monster closing in on her prey. My fingertips tingled, my brow spasmed as I strove to cast my awareness wide enough to sense Valko, but not the raging throngs of people outside.

"Tell me what I'm feeling," he said when I was three feet behind him.

I halted. What game was he playing at now? "Pride," I began tentatively, "in your entitled position as emperor." His energy puffed out my chest. "Anger at those who question your supremacy." I balled my fists. "Betrayal from those you had trusted." My rib cage compressed against my heart.

He turned to face me. "Is that all? A common child could divine those things."

I came nearer, close enough to touch him if I wanted. My legs trembled as I remembered all the times he had hurt me, how readily he'd executed Pia, how unflinchingly he planned to kill his own brother. Despite that, I had to find empathy for him. A pure connection between us was necessary if I hoped to overpower his aura. I had to bind myself to him no matter how vicious he became.

"Your chest constricts as you fight for air," I continued, and drew in a sharp breath. "Tension pulls your shoulder blades together." Pain knotted my back as I stood before him. "Deep within you, the very fibers of your body seem to be shrinking, losing their place to hold you together." The domed ceiling stretched to a towering height above me and made me feel small and alone. "The hateful curses of the peasants burn in your ears." I winced at their cries, then clutched my stomach. "A terrible hollowness is overcoming you, like your insides have been gutted and laid bare. Pressure closes around you from all sides. It makes your head ache and your muscles cramp for space. It's as though everyone is gathering to demand more greatness of you, yet greatness is all you've ever labored to deliver, and now you feel you have nothing more to give."

Valko's jaw muscle quavered, and his brows hitched together. His armor chipped away, and the pitiful boy in him emerged.

"The truth is you've always had room within you to be

wonderful," I said, offering an affectionate smile for the man he could have become. "Your capability for warmth and tenderness. Your determined mind, fit to help so many people." I shook my head in mourning. My chest fell as the flickering hope of that version of Valko vanished, eclipsed by the blackening reality of who he truly was. "Instead, you've chosen to destroy others in the quest to conceal your insecurities, to put the changeling prince you're identified with once and forever to rest—as surely as your father attempted when he ordered an innocent boy to be murdered in your place."

Valko's eyes flashed with indignation. His aura mounted to unleash his full wrath.

"Your heart is shriveling," I continued before he had the chance to speak. I grafted onto his anger. Attaining true understanding demanded I share the beast in him, as well. What was more, I had to become beastly. "You slaughter innocent people like they're dispensable pawns at your chessboard." My pulse hammered at my boldness. Fear seeped through my pores. I knew how much I was provoking him, but to abandon all restraint, I couldn't hold back the worst of his traits—the worst of me.

"You care more for prestige and the possession of your throne than the lives of the hundreds of thousands of your people." My voice rose in volume as I flung the truth at him, every word more spiteful, more impassioned with his escalating rage. "You rip young sons from their mothers, forgetting how you were torn from yours. And when you do remember, you are glad." My mouth curled with a savage smile. "They will know your pain, you tell yourself, and they will die as soldiers for Riaznin feeling it."

I rolled back my shoulders. Valko's haughty self-importance flooded the length of me. "You mean to spread your reign far and wide upon this land until it scales the mountains of Estengarde and crosses the forests of Shengli, until the world is under your heel and you can grind it to dust. Then the people will believe you are great. They will lift their faces from the muck of the earth and worship you."

Valko's lips pressed into a thin line. His eyes went from flint to fire. A thousand dark emotions teemed in a seething undercurrent beneath his faltering mask of indifference. "Is that all, Sovereign Auraseer?" he asked.

"It is," I bit back, fully aligned with his pent-up fury. "And you were right—even a child could have divined it."

His hand flew out to strike me. I raised an arm to protect myself, but the force of his blow made my head lash to the side. White stars popped in my vision. My forged bond to him severed.

"You forgot to mention my aura regarding *you*." His hot breath stung my eyes.

I straightened and met his gaze squarely, despite the pain bursting in my head, the fear swarming inside me that crowded my chest for breath. I refused to give power to the emperor's favorite trick for belittling me. "Utter disappointment," I answered him. "Hatred. Made worse by shame because you thought you loved me."

Valko inhaled with approval, then moved to an ebony lacquered dresser opposite his bed. He opened a small drawer. From within, two metal objects gleamed in the candlelight: a brass key and a thin dagger with a carved bone hilt. He removed the latter.

"Do you know how my father died?" He turned the dagger over in his hand, his rage tamped to a silent storm of darkness brewing inside him.

My heart was in my throat. I couldn't tear my gaze away from the deadly point of the blade. "The black fever," I replied, recalling what every Riaznian knew.

Valko ambled back to me. "In actuality, my father survived the illness." He spoke like a tutor giving a history lesson, as if gunfire wasn't railing on our ears from the massacre below. How many guards were already dead? How many peasants? "However," he continued, "it left him disfigured, his face covered in pox scars and one of his legs amputated at the thigh. No one but his physicians and my family knows this, of course, but I see no qualms in telling you. Not now, anyway. Open your hand," he commanded me.

The screams outside grew louder, filled more with terror than scornful curses. I swallowed and darted my eyes to the balcony as I struggled to keep the people's auras blocked.

"Don't worry about them," Valko said. "My guards have things well in hand. It seems no matter the number of peasants, they have a limited supply of ammunition while my men share my plentiful stores."

Panic assaulted me. My defenses against the myriad auras

weakened. But I couldn't let them inside me. Fear locked my muscles at the vivid remembrance of what I became when I gave myself over to the feelings of so many. I'd made a mistake by placing so much faith in the peasants. I'd thought with their multitudes and righteous zeal they would be invincible as a whole. But Valko had spoken accurately. I felt the dire truth of it by the horror clawing its way to my heart, the desperation cutting the air from my lungs with every musket blast.

"Open your hand," Valko repeated.

I hesitated a moment, then cupped it before him with trembling fingers. *Find a common ground with him. Build a bridge between our auras. Truly feel what he is feeling. Then end this. Make him call off the guards.*

"The blade was never washed." Valko lifted a brow. "An emperor's blood, blessed by the gods, becomes something of a relic." He took hold of my wrist. "If you can feel the aura of the dead, perhaps you can tell me the truth of how my father died."

My eyes widened with terror. "No, please—"

He set the blade in my palm. A flood of dark misery ripped a cry from my throat. "He was lost," I gasped. My hand quivered as Valko held it fast. "More lost than you. Alone. More than you can imagine." *Empathy. Connection.* I had to delve deeper within Emperor Izia's aura and discover the linking chain to Valko. "Your father was terrified—of rejection." *His disfigurement would have made him insecure and apprehensive.* "Terrified of losing his dynasty, even if saving it meant separating himself from his only children."

I had no gift for reading Emperor Izia's thoughts, but I filled in the spaces between what his agonizing emotions could tell me and what I knew of Valko's experience. From everything I'd learned about Izia and the upbringing of his children, it wasn't difficult to place the logic behind his suffering.

My skin grew clammy with trepidation. I needed to scratch it, needed to do worse. With a whimper, I watched my palm tremor and bend around the dagger blade. The sharp edges suddenly felt like a pathway of release. My body shook with that longing. Dizziness assaulted me. My heartbeat thundered in my ears. The downward spiral of Izia's desolation threatened to suck me into a mad corner of my mind. How could anyone live in this much pain?

I struggled to open my palm and slightly break the unendurable connection. "Did your father take his own life?" I asked.

Valko's aura seemed to fall. It plunged through the floor of my stomach and sunk its weight into my legs. "Very observant. A child could *not* have divined that."

Behind him, smoke and the wash of orange torchlight blotted out the stars. The screams of the people turned into a chorus of dissonant wails. Their hope siphoned away until their despair combined with all the horror and anguish I felt. Tears burned my eyes.

"The loss of your father was your greatest tragedy," I said, stunned by the revelation, my knees wobbling, the blade like ice in my hand. "You desire to rule like him in majesty, yet never suffer the weakness he succumbed to in mortality. In the end, he cowered from his noble birthright. He died without honor."

Valko's mood abruptly shifted. Revulsion replaced his sadness. He yanked the dagger back, and it cut a red gash across my palm. I cried out. My fingers curled together as blood dripped between them.

"You are wrong!" he said, pointing the dagger heavenward. "My father honored his sanction from the gods!" As the blade arced down toward me, I threw my hands over my head. The dagger point slashed through the sleeve of my dress and bit into my skin.

"Stop!" I hissed in pain, and stumbled backward.

The emperor stepped close. A menacing calm descended upon him. "My father understood that in order for Riaznin to be great, its ruler must be mighty and unblemished, so he struck down the abhorrent lump of clay his body had become because he knew he lived on through *me*—that I would be mighty in his stead, and the blood of our chosen dynasty would continue to flow through my veins."

Valko raised the dagger to my throat. My heart beat violently. I scarcely dared breathe, for even the pulsing at my neck scraped against the blade. "Your father entrusted the future of Riaznin to your strength," I whispered, proving I'd heard him as I grappled to move past my fear. My life depended on giving myself over to Valko's feelings. I had to employ my full energy in finding perfect compassion for him. I needed to identify with the crushing pressure he had lived with under the ever-present shadow of his dead father.

Valko's eyes were pewter gray—hard with determination, yet shining with remorse. "Then you understand why I must strike you down. You are a thorn in my side, Sonya, a plague worse than Black Death. You make me weak, and I cannot abide weakness."

Past his harsh and finite words, I felt his affection still burn within my breast. Although he cared for me, he had no choice but to end my life. I had gotten myself too involved and now people were dying—like they did whenever I released the darkest parts of myself.

"I understand you," I said. Because at last I did. My aura smoothed into a looking glass.

I saw him in me. Myself in him.

My death was the only way to bring about peace. If I lived, I would only cause more destruction. My life held back the good of the empire. The world was in shambles, and it needed a resplendent leader—with no weak link to hinder his reign.

Valko sighed and shook his head sadly. "It's a shame you couldn't make me strong." The tip of the dagger traced a swirl against my collarbone. He leaned in closer. His teeth dragged along my ear. "I shall miss the taste of you."

I understand.

A mournful cry echoed distantly. My brow twitched.

Valko placed the dagger above my heart.

I understand.

Three muskets fired in succession. Pain blossomed across my belly. Had the emperor killed me already?

"Close your eyes, Sonya. I can't bear to have you look at me that way."

I understand.

The blade bit deeper. A trickle of warmth slid between my breasts. Why was I still breathing?

The scent of gunpowder lingered in my nostrils. More far-away cries. Where were they coming from? I could no longer remember what was happening.

The blade at my chest wavered. "Good-bye, love." Valko squeezed my arm where he'd cut me. I sucked in a breath from the pain.

On the brink of my death, something deep, almost buried, but still pulsing within me compelled me to open my eyes. The flickering energy gained strength. It built in illumination and steeled me with courage. At last my mind cleared and I recognized the feeling—Anton's aura living inside me, his rekindled light shattering Valko's dark grasp.

I lifted my gaze to the emperor. I saw no more of my reflection in him, felt no more compassion. "Put the dagger down."

Valko's face contorted with a faint semblance of pity. "It's too late, Sonya."

"No. It isn't." There were people yet alive. I cast my reach out wide for them. Felt each beating heart. Each rise and fall of breath. Each unique energy. I wasn't mistaken about empathy being the key to their salvation, but I'd wasted it on the wrong man. My empathy wasn't meant for one person. It was meant to be given liberally. To all. Regardless of class. Wealth. Position.

I would become one with Riaznin and let the emperor, at last, meet the reckoning of his people.

"You will not kill me because I am your empire." I pointed beyond the marble ledge of his balcony. "Your people's cries are my cries. Their anger is my wrath. Their suffering, my plea for retribution." As soon as I spoke the words, a gate opened inside me. How easy it was to let them in, to let them overcome me. The quiet space within myself I'd labored so long to protect, I tore down of my own volition.

"Their auras fill me. They stretch me beyond capacity." I gasped, shaking. "I feel myself bridge the earth and sink beneath the ground, slipping between the cold bones of the dead. Their auras join us." I opened my hands and welcomed the connection, though it shot ice through my veins. "They cry against you. Against centuries of oppression."

Horror filled Valko's eyes, but he didn't release the dagger from my chest.

"This is your day of judgment. A million voices use my mouth. They will not rest. You do not have enough gunpowder, enough armies, enough endurance to withstand them. They will keep coming. They will crawl over the corpses of their wives and their husbands, their children and their friends, their brothers and sisters, mothers and fathers, and they will hunt you down."

"Stop!" Valko dropped the dagger. It clanged against the tiles. "Do not say another word!" He clapped his hands over his ears.

The haze of the peasants' torchlight cast my dress and skin in a scorching glow. "You do not have glory," I said. "You are tiny. Your blood is mortal, common. Glory is godly, undefiled. And glory joins me with the holy aura of the gods." Tears streamed down my face from the transcendent energy surging through my limbs. "You oppress your brethren in your quest for all power. That is weak. It will always be weak. No man can be all-powerful."

Valko fell to his knees. He wrung his ears and muttered vain prayers.

I stood tall over him. "The gods wish to feed your soul to the fires of hell. You will burn in eternity for the wrongs of every emperor before you because you did nothing to stop the cycle of cruelty and tyranny against your people."

He shook his head as if to ward me away. His incessant prayers grew louder.

"Show them you are only a man," I commanded, and summoned his aura back inside me. It was a pitiful spark next to the powerful inferno within. I pushed my overflowing energy into him so the suffering of his people could no longer be ignored.

As their auras struck him, Valko gasped and buckled at the waist. He writhed in agony and stared up at me with astounded eyes. "Forgive me, forgive me." He clutched at his hair.

"You do not know the meaning of mercy, and you do not have the stomach to do what it takes to redeem yourself."

"I will do anything!"

I looked down at him, so intolerable and wretched. "I want to hear you beg."

"I am begging!" He clung to the skirt of my dress and kissed the silk as he buried his head in its folds. "I implore you"—he rocked on his knees—"tell me what I must do!"

I deliberated a moment longer. "Rise to your feet."

He sniffled, chin quivering as he straightened up.

"Come with me." I led him past the doorway of his balcony, to the ledge outside where every man, woman, and child could see him. Heaps of dead peasants lay in the distance, and more than half of the Imperial Guard had fallen. Still, the lingering soldiers relentlessly fired, the peasants marched forward with their only remaining weapons. Rocks, slings, sharp sticks—anything they could hurl between the gold bars of the gate.

"Remove your crown," I ordered Valko. "Tell the people your reign is over. Riaznin is theirs to rule."

His nose wrinkled in the smoke. His mouth twisted with a grimace. "Never."

"You will, or the spirits of the dead will guide those who live to slit your throat. And when you die, the gods will torture your soul until every memory, every lie of your noble blood burns to ashes."

With a whimper, Valko collapsed to the ground. He hid behind the balcony wall from the people. "I will die, regardless. If I abdicate, they will never allow me to live."

"Then make a trade: your throne for the promise of a trial—the fair judgment you denied so many." *Pia. Tosya. Anton.*

Valko hesitated with indecision. He wrenched into a tight ball of pain, his face blotchy as if he couldn't draw breath. Tendons corded at his neck. Tears streaked to his jawline. Now he knew what it was to have my gift.

"Do it now, or I will kill you myself!" I said. My weapon was no saber or pistol; it was the aura of legions. And for Valko, it was threat enough.

He shuddered against a fresh swell of tears and crawled back to his feet, using the balcony wall to drag himself up. He opened his quivering mouth. His confidence was broken, his voice as thin as parchment. "People of Riaznin," he rasped weakly. The battle didn't cease. No one turned upward. No one noticed him.

I moved closer to his ear. "That is no way to address your countrymen. Do you feel their rage and suffering? They will not listen to the drivel of a weakling. Give them respect and relinquish with grace."

Valko bent his neck and stared down at his hands as they fisted, then uncurled. Swiping under his eyes, he inhaled a steadying breath and lengthened his neck. "People of Riaznin!" he cried. His voice grew in power like an orator's at a great assembly. "Cease your fire! Lay down your weapons! I have heard you!" He withdrew his saber and raised it above his head to gain their attention. Once they quieted, he placed it on the balcony wall in a gesture of truce.

The guards' firearms slowly lowered, but the peasants showed more wariness. They kept their rocks and slings held high. "Release Tosya!" someone shouted.

Valko stole a glance at me, as if hoping that would be all that was required of him. I shook my head. He briefly closed his eyes and swallowed. "I will do more than that!" he continued. "I will abdicate and give you the freedom you desire!"

His claim was met by silence. Somewhere in the distance a baby wailed.

I stepped to the ledge of the balcony. "He has agreed to these terms on the condition you lay down your arms and proceed peaceably." Thinking of Anton and his fervent hope for true justice, I added, "And you must give the emperor fair trial for the crimes of which he is accused."

Valko lifted his chin, but inside he was a mess of uncertainty. "I believe you will find I ruled impartially and to the utmost of my ability!" he told them.

Someone snorted with laughter. Another shouted, "We will judge you, and you will lose your head!"

With shaking hands, the emperor reached up to hold his crown. His brows drew tight, and his jaw muscle flexed.

The populace of Torchev hushed in utter silence. The only sound was the hiss and crackle of their torch fire.

Valko's nostrils flared as he slowly removed his crown from his head and set it beside his saber on the balcony wall. The power was gone in his voice when he replied, "I will take my chances."

The people, the guards—everyone within reach of his declaration—exchanged astonished glances. Then a beautiful cry of victory split the night. The peasants thrust their fists in the air, embracing and dancing, while others crumpled and wept against their dead—the people who had sacrificed so much to win liberty for all of Riaznin. Boys ran back to the deeper reaches of the streets and announced to those who hadn't heard the news, "The mighty isn't one, but many! The monarchy is no more!"

Their auras sang a song of triumph inside me. But I wasn't finished. "Come with me," I said again to Valko, and led him inside his rooms, past his giant bed, the velvet cushions around his receiving table, and the marble pillars to his lobby, until we arrived at his great door. I opened it. Twenty pairs of baffled eyes greeted us. Surely they had heard Valko's decree of abdication.

I turned to the former emperor. "Tell the guards these rooms are your prison. Unless they wish to meet their deaths by the hands of the people—their new masters—they are not to release you under any circumstances."

Valko's gaze was on the floor. "As she says," he mumbled.

He and I retreated back inside his chambers, where I fetched the bone-hilted dagger from the tiles. Valko would not escape this life like his father did. I opened the dresser drawer and retrieved the brass key. Clutching it in my uninjured hand, I walked away and left Valko to his misery.

"Sonya?" he asked when I'd reached the threshold of his rooms. His voice held the fear of a child when his parents must leave his bedroom at night.

Tears leaked from my eyes from the magnitude of all the auras still surging within me. *Almost finished*, I told myself. "Yes?"

Valko's hair was flattened from the absent pressure of his crown. "Don't leave me here alone—you, who understands me so perfectly. You know I cannot suffer it."

How had this boy ever tempted me, ever made me feel inferior? "Then you must learn to suffer, for I am done understanding you."

With ease, I pushed his tiny aura out of mine.

He crumpled to his hands and knees, then curled into himself, his body racking.

I walked out the open door. The guards parted for me. I handed the dagger to one and told another to keep the emperor's saber out of reach.

Valko lifted his head as I spoke with the men who had been his to command only an hour ago. His eyes cut across the room to me with a gaze so sharp it rivaled the blades I'd taken from him. "It is you who will suffer for this, Sonya." His voice simmered with rage.

I didn't acknowledge his warning. I didn't let the edges of his fury so much as nick at my skin. I turned away. Shoulders erect, I strode down the long corridor, the trailing tongue of the dragon that would never ensnare me again.

With the brass key pressed to my breast, I left the corridor without a backward glance.

CHAPTER THIRTY-FIVE

THE DUNGEONS WERE EMPTY OF GUARDS. EVERY ABLE MAN must have been recruited to defend the palace. I opened the heavy oak door leading to the solitary cell, which took all my remaining strength.

Anton and Tosya sprang to their feet and brushed straw from their trousers. Anton's eyes rounded as they swept over my bloody hand and slashed-open sleeve. "Are you all right?" His voice was heavy with concern.

I nodded and straightened my back. But as I came nearer, my legs shook, each step more difficult than the last. I had let all the people's auras go. Now I felt I was nothing but a common girl, exhausted at the end of a very long day.

Nevertheless, from the folds of my skirt, I brandished a shining brass key.

Tosya laughed, his hand covering his mouth.

Anton's body stilled. He smiled softly, his gaze unwavering on mine. "I never doubted you."

Tears threatened to fall again. I held them in check. All I wanted was to feel his arms around me. With trembling hands, I set the key to the lock and turned it over. The tumblers clanged with a beautiful sound. I pulled against the barred door and gave a small cry of frustration when it only opened a hand-breadth. The jail master's dead body blocked its path. I had no muscle to move him. Tosya lowered himself to the ground and pushed the man away with his feet. As soon as the door spread wide, I stepped over the poet's legs and threw myself at Anton. His warmth embraced me, and at last I allowed myself to sob.

I'd never felt more wonderful.

"Shhh." He stroked my hair. "Talk to me. What has happened?"

I steadied my breathing and looked up at him. I wanted to smile, to laugh, but only succeeded in spilling more tears. "You are no longer a prince." His brows drew together. "The emperor has abdicated," I said, answering his silent question. "The people have the government. They have *liberty*, Anton."

He searched my eyes. After a moment, he asked, "Truly?" It was a mark of his profound amazement that his deep and resonant voice achieved a genuine whisper.

I nodded. "There is only one problem."

"What is that?"

"They are still outside the gates." I finally managed a smile. It radiated within me, brighter than the glow of the legion of auras. "I'd like to let them in." I slid my uninjured hand in his. "And I'd like you to come with me."

❦❧

Anton and I emerged from the darkness below, our arms full of gathered food from the kitchen pantries. Past the destruction of the amber lobby, we greeted the night sky. The smoke had lifted. The stars glittered above us, countless as the Riaznians waiting beyond the palace gates.

Tosya remained behind. He felt it his duty to take the jail master's keys and free the other prisoners from the dungeons.

Now, with a retinue of willing servants trailing behind us and carrying baskets laden with breads, cheeses, cured meats, and dried fruits, Anton and I descended the palace steps and wove through the guards. Many had already removed their military coats. As the masses of peasants saw us approach with our offerings, they quieted and helped their injured comrades to their feet. Some shot narrowed glances at the Ozerov prince, but when their gazes fell to our joined hands, a portion of their worry abated. Whispers darted among them.

"It's the girl from the balcony."

"The sovereign Auraseer."

"She was with the emperor when he abdicated."

Anton and I crossed the gravel and came closer. The peasants' wariness heightened, as if they worked to piece together what my role had been in the critical hour of battle—if I was a reluctant supporter of the revolution or genuinely on their side.

"It's all right," I assured them, and halted a few feet away.

"I stand with your former prince. He is the benefactor of Tosya Pashkov and the secret leader of this revolution. He is the bringer of your freedom."

At that moment, Tosya appeared on the palace porch with a bedraggled entourage of prisoners.

"Tosya is a prisoner no more," I added, watching the peasants' eyes rivet to the poet and take fresh courage. "Neither are you the slaves to tyranny." I turned to Tosya and prompted him with a nudge of my brows. If he was truly the face of this revolution, now was the moment to stake his claim.

He gave me a wry look, like he couldn't believe I was making him do this. Drawing a deep breath, he shouted, "The mighty isn't one, but many!"

The people's voices erupted in a triumphant cry. Some echoed back his words, while others chanted his name like another refrain of hope. Tosya gave a little shake of his head and spared me a glance that said he might kill me later.

I bit down a smile and revolved to face the people. Each one of them was beautiful. I breathed in their auras, and I did more, I understood them—the struggle they had waged for so long to cling to their dignity, to the whispering belief that they held enough power to govern themselves.

As they wept and cheered, Anton touched my cheek and gently turned my gaze to his. "Make no mistake, Sonya," he said. "*You* are the bringer of freedom."

His pride and adoration spread warmth through my limbs. Right there, with the world watching—but with a tenderness that made me feel secluded with him—Anton leaned down, and he kissed me.

I didn't go light-headed or weak at the knees. Instead, my body infused with strength. That strength remained as Anton withdrew from my side and called upon a guard to open the lock of the palace gates.

I brushed my thumb once across the black ribbon on my wrist, and then I stepped forward and wrapped my fingers around the golden bars, welded together into a great door, oiled and perfectly balanced on its hinges.

I exhaled, and pulled it open.

ACKNOWLEDGMENTS

Many heartfelt thanks go to:

My husband, Jason, for championing me, knowing this would happen, and being my steadfast Masterpiece Classics buddy. My three children, for their constant support, even if it meant swatting my hands from the keyboard.

My ninja agent, Josh Adams, and Tracey and Sam at Adams Literary, for their fierce belief in me and their stellar work on my behalf.

My editor, Maria Barbo, who deserves an honorary degree in psychology for her deep analysis of my characters and all the awesomeness she's doled out on this novel. My designer, Amy Ryan, production editor, Kathryn Silsand, and everyone at Katherine Tegen Books/HarperCollins, for your hard work, enthusiasm, and love for *Burning Glass*.

My brother, Matt, for taking my kidney—with it, I would have never started writing. My author dad, Larry, for being my first critic years ago (and dealing with the fallout). My mom, Buffie, who doesn't slay vampires but had ten children (and staked none of us) and who is my trusted reader. My uncle, Brian Crouch, who told me at Grandpa John's funeral that I should write a book about an empath.

Sara B. Larson, for referring me to our agent, lifting me up in the dark times (and on occasional high heels), and being my number-one fan and friend. Erin Summerill, for dragging me out of my hermit's lair and making me sit on her couch, eat color-sorted candy, and write.

My critique group: Robin Hall, my first critique partner, and Wymount Bestie, who helped me never give up on writing, especially when I sucked; Ilima K. Todd, my almost-sister, for honesty, laughter, the best emails ever . . . and for *Sweet Land*; and Emily Prusso, who weaves magical words and never forgets what is most important in life.

Emily Rittel-King, for your faith and intuition, and for always knowing when to call and chat about life and writing. Michelle D. Argyle, for your friendship and giving me your old laptop so I had a working computer with which to write *Burning Glass*. Beta-reader extraordinaire, Daisy, who has read all my stories in less than two days.

Jacques Margeret, who wrote a cool firsthand account about Imperial Russia that inspired many things, including the subplot of the changeling prince. Matthew J. Kirby, who helped me discover where to begin my story. Natalie Whipple, who sketched a map of my world in exchange for a grilled cheese sandwich.

Weronika Janczuk, Kayla Olson, Louise Plummer, and Carol Lynch Williams, for believing in me, taking a chance on me, and teaching me the craft.

And you, dear readers, for going on this journey with Sonya. Here's a sprinkling of snow, a commemorative troika ride, and a buttery-brown smolder from Prince Anton.

My last and utmost thanks I give to God. Life is crazy hard and crazy beautiful. I'm glad You've got my back.

✦◅∾◦∾▻✦

DON'T MISS

CRYSTAL
BLADE,

THE THRILLING SECOND INSTALLMENT
OF KATHRYN PURDIE'S
BURNING GLASS TRILOGY.

"STOP, SERGEI, YOU'LL KILL HIM!" A FARAWAY GIRL CRIED.

I whipped around just as a crack of gunpowder split the air. Gasping, I grabbed the folds of my skirt and broke into a run. Then I remembered the hooded girl.

I spun back around and froze. The space where she'd stood between the two trees was empty.

More shouts sprang up in the distance. I took off running again, racing back through the orchard. Another scream. Boys and girls popped out from behind the trees like field mice from their burrows. "What's going on?" a boy with mussed hair and flushed cheeks asked as I flew by.

I shook my head and called backward between gasps of air, "Anton . . . have you seen Prince Anton?"

"He isn't a prince, miss," the boy replied.

His insolence splashed oil on the fire of my panic. I flung

around, eyes sharp and intimidating. "Have. You. Seen. Prince. Anton?"

The boy gave a hard swallow. "No, I haven't."

I dashed away, sprinting faster toward the shouts and crazed, violent energy that was throbbing madly through my body. I tunneled my awareness on the path ahead. If I wanted to help, I couldn't let myself be overcome by anyone else's aura. Last time I'd failed to do that, half of the convent had burned, along with most of my sister Auraseers.

I tore around a tree just as a dark figure converged onto the same path. We nearly collided. For a moment I thought it was the hooded girl come back to haunt me. Then the moonlight caught the slant of Anton's aristocratic nose and the thin sculpt of his upper lip. I threw myself at him, practically wringing him with my embrace.

"Sonya!" His arms squeezed back with equal force. He kissed my head twice.

"Where were you?"

"I couldn't find you."

We spoke over each other.

A third voice shouted above us, "Sergei, no!" Another blast of gunpowder fired. This time from much closer.

Anton and I stilled. I searched the auras within my awareness. "No one's dead," I said at last. "At least not yet."

He released me, and we launched in the direction of the gunshot. "Stay back," he said, voice tight. "This will be dangerous."

I pushed a branch aside from my face. "You have me."

Anton flinched. His shock of fear chased through my limbs. "You're not getting involved."

More shouts rose up. We didn't stop running. Not even as angry auras clawed through my body.

Anton and I emerged from the orchard into a rose garden on its west side. The night brightened without a leafy canopy above us. A large marble fountain rested at its center, pouring water from tiered bowls.

A few couples from the fern flower quest gathered at the edges of the garden, and more trampled in by the moment. Their auras pinched my breath and locked my muscles. They clung to the tree line, observing what was happening with terrible fascination, as one observes a ship sinking when both feet are on the shore.

Two boys, a noble and a peasant, crouched at opposite sides of the fountain, taking cover from each other. The peasant held a musket, the noble a flintlock pistol. A girl huddled beside each boy. One held her hands protectively over her head, while the other, a baron's daughter I recognized, gripped the noble boy's sleeve, crying, "Sergei, please." My nose burned from her tears. Chunks of the fountain had been blasted off, but no blood stained the stones around it.

Anton leaned to the ebony-skinned girl beside us. "What's happening here? Why are these boys armed?"

The girl's eyes widened when she saw who addressed her. "Your Imperial High—" She caught herself mid-bow and bit down on her lip. "Rurik, that peasant boy"—she pointed at him— "insulted Sergei's fiancée, Helene, during the Blind Man's Kiss game this afternoon. It turned into a fight, and the boys planned this duel. But it got out of hand before it even started."

We glanced back to the fountain, about twenty feet away. The noble boy, Sergei, held his pistol tightly drawn, its barrel pointed upward, his thumb on the hammer. He called out to Rurik, his words a muddled slur, "You think you're above us because your filthy lot conquered *one* battle?" His injured pride made me feel both larger and smaller than myself. My head prickled, and my limbs grew slack. He was drunk. "The emperor may have removed his crown, but the nobility still bear our lands and titles. You peasants are nothing without us!"

Rurik burst out with laughter, but his cockiness wasn't genuine. My stomach quivered with his nausea, my brow flashed with perspiration. "It's only a matter of time before your lands are partitioned and your precious titles are stripped away. Let's see how well you like sweating for your bread then, like the rest of us." He scoffed. "You'd blanch at the sight of dirt under your nails."

A blaze of anger swept my body. My hand fisted. The pistol fired. The bystanders gasped. Their panic ricocheted through my chest. My ears rang as I tried to comprehend what had happened. Sergei's pistol smoked, but it still pointed upward. He'd shot into the air.

Rurik couldn't see that from his crouched position on the

other side of the fountain. With a cry of fear and desperation, he sprang to his feet and whirled around to charge the noble, his musket eye level. Sergei scrambled to reload his pistol. Helene screamed and dashed out from her hiding spot and into the cover of the orchard. At the same time a new influx of people flooded the garden.

Anton ran toward Rurik. "Nobody move!" His voice rumbled with authority. "Lay down your weapons!"

Rurik's eyes rounded. "It's the prince!" Frightened, he whirled to face Anton, his pointed musket swinging around with him.

My heart flared with dread. I rushed forward. Everyone's frenzied emotions begged to manifest through my body. But my own feelings rose above them all. "Don't shoot him!"

Rurik recoiled, jerking the musket toward me.

"Lower your gun!" Anton shouted.

With a start, Rurik returned his aim to him.

"No!" My voice cracked.

A spasm sliced through Rurik's brow. The musket barrel shook. Beads of sweat dripped from his hairline. His shoulders slumped as his panicked intent drained out of him. He lowered his arm, and the gun clattered to the ground. I started breathing again. Sergei gave a drunken chuckle from the opposite side of the fountain. Rurik growled and grabbed his musket. Anton was still in his line of fire.

"No, turn away!" My terror slashed through Rurik's aura.

He spun left and blindly shot into the orchard.

The blast echoed in my ears. Hot pain seized me, and I sucked in a cry.

A gurgled whimper rose from a few feet behind me. The baron's daughter stepped out from the trees and held a clenched hand to her upper arm. Rose-red blood spilled through her fingers. Her head nodded incoherently, and she collapsed to her knees.

"Helene!" Sergei dropped his unloaded pistol and ran over to her.

Rurik gaped, stumbling backward. "I—I didn't mean to . . ."

A few heads twitched toward me. I lifted a trembling hand to my throat. My mouth opened, but I couldn't think to speak. I looked to Anton and shook my head wildly. His gaze cut into me, his shock and rage coloring my shame even darker. Tears flowered behind my eyes.

"It was an accident," I told him. My tongue loosened to spill the words. A ripple of murmurs spun around the garden.

I glanced at the others and clapped eyes on Feliks. His hatred made my gut twist. He looked winded, like he'd just arrived on the scene. He paused near the fountain, his cunning eyes sliding from Rurik to Helene to me. My chest caved with anxiety.

Anton had insisted that, for my protection, the extent of my abilities remain a secret. No other Auraseer had manifested the unheard-of gift to manipulate another person's emotions. If the people found out, I wouldn't be trusted. They would surely fear me and threaten my life. Anton never told Feliks what I truly did to make Valko abdicate. And even then, it was only when Valko held a dagger to my throat that I managed to open a channel between us and use it to curb his will.

Anton's mouth formed a hard line as he caught sight of the man who'd betrayed him in the revolution. "Yes, it was an accident," he said to everyone, his voice strong and edged in determination. He strode over to Rurik and took the musket from his stunned hands. "These boys were only try to bully each other with a little gunpowder. You all saw that." Crossing to the other side of the fountain, he collected Sergei's pistol from the ground. "Unfortunately, someone got hurt." And he tossed both weapons into the water, rendering them useless.

My body still throbbed with the echoes of Helene's pain. She moaned where she'd fallen and rolled onto her back. I hurried over to her side where Sergei knelt and ripped open her sleeve to expose the wound. Around the shot, her skin was folded back, raw and bloody.

Tamping down my revulsion, I tore off a length of my slip and began wrapping her arm. Sergei's nostrils flared. I felt his violent burst the moment before he sprang to his feet.

"Anton!" I shouted in warning.

Sergei launched toward Rurik. Anton raced between them and fought to hold Sergei back. While they struggled, another noble boy darted out from the hedges. He bolted for Rurik and clocked him hard in the jaw. Rurik blinked with pain, then growled and struck back, slugging the noble in the gut.

Then the entire garden broke into chaos. Everyone's pain and anger battered through me. I gasped for breath and dragged Helene back a few feet so she wouldn't be trampled, clinging to her aura so the others wouldn't pummel me.

Someone was thrown into the fountain with a loud splash. In front of me, two boys shuffled back and forth in a double headlock. To my right, a girl dug up stones from the ground and prepared to hurl them. Anton was lost in the madness.

I had to do something. Calm everyone's emotions, bend their impulses.

I winced and let their pain overtake me. I opened myself to all the sensations around me.

As I clenched my jaw, bracing myself against the torture, a pair of piercing blue eyes met mine across the dust-choked air of the scuffle. Feliks's aura lit inside me, a dark flame curling with curiosity and challenge.

He wasn't watching the fight; he was watching me.

Caught unaware, I was thrust back into myself, my growing connection to the people broken.

More people spilled into the garden, among them soldiers. They wore the red and gold regimentals of the imperial guard, but with a sash of blue tied over their jackets, denoting them as soldiers of the new regime. They took aim with their muskets.

"Hold your fire!" Anton's voice shouted above the chaos.

At the warning of firearms, the boys and girls drew to a shuffled halt. A few grunts came from those pinned and half beaten on the ground.

Anton staggered forward, raking a hand through his disheveled hair. His wreath crown was missing. "Everyone will leave the palace grounds at once!" he announced resolutely, though his voice came on a labored breath of air. "I suggest on your way out you pass the monument and think a bit harder about those who died to buy you the liberties you so ungratefully abuse."

His gaze found its way to me, and he glanced over my body, as if to assess that I hadn't been hurt. Once he saw I was fine, his anger slammed my heart against my ribcage. My guilt made it pound harder. I'd lost control, used my power in public, almost killed someone.

"Guards, escort everyone off the premises," Anton said. "The Kivratide celebration is officially over."

Don't miss these books by
KATHRYN PURDIE!

Her gift is the empire's curse.

KATHERINE **T**EGEN **B**OOKS
An Imprint of HarperCollins Publishers

www.epicreads.com

JOIN THE

Epic Reads
COMMUNITY

THE ULTIMATE YA DESTINATION

◀ DISCOVER ▶
your next favorite read

◀ MEET ▶
new authors to love

◀ WIN ▶
free books

◀ SHARE ▶
infographics, playlists, quizzes, and more

◀ WATCH ▶
the latest videos